IN A FAR COUNTRY

When they came out of the theatre, they strolled down to
the wharf, sat on a bench, and talked for more than two
hours. When Roy walked Christine home and they stood
outside her apartment door, he said, 'I forgot what rules we
decided on. Am I supposed to kiss you or not?'

'You're not supposed to.'

'Are you supposed to kiss me?'

'We didn't talk about that.' She put her hands on his
shoulders and kissed him on the mouth ...

IN A FAR COUNTRY

Adam Kennedy

A STAR BOOK

published by

the Paperback Division of
W. H. ALLEN & Co. PLC

A Star Book

Published in 1984
by the Paperback Division of
W. H. Allen & Co. PLC
44 Hill Street, London W1X 8LB

First published in the United States of America by
Delacorte Press.
First published in Great Britain by
W. H. Allen & Co., 1983

Printed in Great Britain by
Cox & Wyman Ltd, Reading

ISBN 0 352 31540 7

Happiness is freedom and freedom is courage.

PERICLES

The shivering dread of the free individual
is still the curse of American civilization . . .
the average man doesn't want to be free.
He simply wants to be safe.

H. L. MENCKEN

But as April happened
December's way piled
rock within her, spoke
postponement. As sheep
divided their wool, apples
knew earth and rotted there.

JOHN REUSCHEL

THIS BOOK IS DEDICATED TO LAWRENCE EISLER
AND TO JACK WOLF
AND TO MY COUSIN BRUCE JOHNSON.

BOOK 1

Chapter 1

These words I am writing should have been written by Russell Atha. Surely he was destined to tell this story. No one knew the people involved as he did.

He clearly intended to write about them. I have no doubt about that. For the past several years, whenever we saw each other in New York, or in California, he talked about it endlessly, exploring alternatives, linking events together, eager to push ahead.

But one overcast afternoon, on the South Island of New Zealand, he walked across a wide beach near Greymouth, sliced the veins in both his wrists, and watched his blood pulse out on the sand. When they found him that evening, he was sitting straight up, wedged against a pile of driftwood, his eyes open still, a serene look on his face.

So it came to me. As his friend and literary executor, it all, quite literally, came to me. In file cabinets and cartons tied with twine. Thick folders and envelopes, crammed with notes and ideas. The pieces of the puzzle had all been gathered. They were waiting to be assembled. But Russell cut his wrists instead.

For my part I had no real interest in finishing a book that someone else had begun. On the other hand, I knew that if I didn't take on the job, no one else would. If I didn't do it, it wouldn't be done.

My name is Ben Gingrich. I have been a writer for most of my adult life. My books have been praised and damned.

There have been occasional triumphs, some smaller successes, and one or two failures. The two books which attracted the smallest number of readers were the finest things I have published.

Such contradictions used to disturb me. No longer. As the hide grows thick to protect the child inside, you learn to feign deafness, to listen only to inner voices, to find a personal rhythm of work and stick with it. It takes a combination of courage and foolishness to continue to throw your heart over unfamiliar walls into alien gardens. But it can be done. When it can't be done the work stops.

Many painters, many writers and sculptors, are tortured by the silent places where they work. Not me. I approach a long and difficult project with a special kind of passion. I define myself in silence. Empty rooms and blank paper.

This time, however, it's different. I have never begun a piece of work with the trepidation I feel now. And not just because I'm doing another man's job. The problem is this: I'm forced to deal with a factual story, with living people. New territory for me.

Russell, in his work, was at home everywhere. He wrote novels, film scripts, poetry, and books of criticism. He published two volumes of what could best be described as contemporary history, and his critical biography of W. H. Auden was nominated for the National Book Award.

My work, on the other hand, has been fiction. Novels. That is the form I prefer. There I feel most at home.

Russell's notes made it clear that he intended to do this book in a fictional form. But I cannot forget that Grace Wheatley and her daughter Christine are very much alive, that Roy Lavidge, Annie Singleton, and Fred Deets also are real, breathing people, and that Abe Singleton, before his death in Ulster, was a vital, flesh-and-blood man.

Knowing these facts to be irrefutable, I will refute them. Knowing that the circumstances and people are real, I will simply pretend they are *not* real. Usually I struggle to give fiction the perfume of truth. In this instance I will use the devices of the novel to tell a totally true and remarkable story.

3

Chapter 2

Between 1975 and 1980 Russell came back, time after time, to the same questions. 'Where's the backbone of this story? It has to be Roy Lavidge. I'm sure of that. All the politics and dissent and the Vietnam shit kick it off but the real meat is the human stuff. I don't give a damn about the mechanics of being an exile. I want to deal with the results. What happens later. What the executioner ate for dinner after he beheaded three men.'

Going through his notes, I found those same ideas, that same determination to make the people more important than the events. At first, apparently, he had planned to appear on the page himself, to tell the story through his own eyes.

When I met Grace Wheatley in the summer of 1949, it never occurred to me that someday I would write a novel in which she would be a principal character. Just then it was hard for me to believe that I could write any sort of book at all. But God knows I wanted to. The images of Camus and Stendhal and Flaubert had been bright and electric inside my head since I was sixteen.

Now I am thirty years older. Much of what I set out to do I have done. I am long past those tortured and ecstatic days with Grace. But it's all clear to me still, like a memorized Camus passage.

In 1967, when I met her daughter, Christine, I was astonished to discover how sharp those memory pictures were, how fresh and still-painful those tormented conversations. The guns had been silent for a long time but the wounds still throbbed.

In his next opening try, dated several weeks later, Russell

4

decided, apparently, to set up shop foursquare behind Roy Lavidge.

His mother's family had lived for generations in Volterra, a Tuscany hill town west of Siena, and his father's father had migrated to America from England, Newcastle to be precise, but Roy Lavidge bore little resemblance to either side.

The Agnellis were delicate people with deep-set dark eyes and shining black, dead-straight hair.

The Lavidges, on the other hand, tended toward bigness. They were bulky and tall, most of them soft and awkward-looking, something of west Norway about them. Blondish or light-brown hair, but all of them, without exception, with brown eyes, as far back as anyone could remember.

His mother's first child, Roy, was a full month late in coming, weighed nearly eleven pounds at birth, and had to be taken with instruments.

At first, because he was bald for several months and had an unusually ruddy complexion for an infant, it seemed that he would resemble his father. By the time he was ten months old, however, his hair was dark, brindle brown and curly, unlike that of either parent. And his eyes, biggest surprise of all, were clear and grey-green.

T. J. Lavidge, Roy's father, got very little joy from his son. Something about the child made him uneasy. At the same time he seemed fascinated; he sat watching the little boy for hours as he tumbled and crawled and climbed, and began to run almost before he could walk.

'Look at him,' T. J. said. 'He's like one of those jungle panthers I've seen pictures of. Cat eyes. Never saw any eyes like that before. Sure as hell never saw eyes like that on a Lavidge.'

Six weeks before he died, Russell wrote in his notes, in longhand, his last attempt at an opening chapter.

5

By the time she was nineteen years old, Christine Wheatley had been in love seven times. It made her feel valuable. Gave her a sense of worth, a nice quietness inside herself.

She had been a remarkably pretty child. And a contented one. Her mother had seen to it that she was raised in peaceful surroundings. Although she was sheltered, however, she was never catered to, by either her family or their servants. She was never allowed to assume that money alone could relieve her of her responsibilities toward herself or other people. Her governess, who had raised dozens of other people's children in Edinburgh and London before she came to Lake Forest, told her, 'You have the chance to become a special person. But only if you earn it. Being gifted is just the beginning.'

The pretty child became a dynamic young woman. At fifteen she could pass for eighteen. At twenty she was in her last year at college. Still ... perhaps because she had matured quickly, because good fortune and her own intelligence had kept her out of tight corners, she sensed that she was untried, like a Thoroughbred that has performed magnificently against the clock but has not yet sweated and stumbled and battered its way through the dirt and mud and a shifting wall of other horses to an open line where the running is easy.

She miscalculated, for example, when she told herself, at nineteen, that she'd been in love seven times. She *had* been loved, certainly. Since her eyes first began to see. And she loved in return, no question of it, her family, her friends and the people she grew up with. But *return* is the key word. She *returned* love. She knew almost nothing about *offering* it.

Then one day she learned. Suddenly she chose a new direction, chose an objective, chose a *person*. And from then on no logic, no persuasion, could redirect her or turn her aside.

On the morning of the day he died, Russell made two entries in his journal.

Sitting here this morning, a fine breakfast in my belly, hot coffee on the table beside me, I am fifty-three years old, very old for my age. And at last I see the world as it is. I see myself as I am.

We live on raw meat and entrails, don't we? Violence and despair. We thrive on that diet. It keeps us alert, hearts thumping, teeth on edge, *aware* of ourselves and our victims. Vibrant and raw nerved, keenly in contact with our raw-nerved children and lovers and neighbours. Attuned to terror. Carefully keyed to destruction and pain. Feeding on it, tearing at it with our teeth, slurping and slavering, wolfing it down. Arsenic in the lemonade.

And this, finally, with the notation beside it: 11.45 a.m.

The things that keep people apart or drive them apart are more significant than the things that pull them together. None of us knows who or what we are. Our lives tell us. And we're told conflicting truths all along the way. The frustrations and disappointments and hatreds, misunderstandings, the envies and quarrels and the betrayals and deceptions . . . these, unhappily perhaps, are the armatures of our lives. Stumbling through the mine fields, we come upon, occasionally, the cases of love and friendship, fufillment and sense of achievement that we like to believe are the rewards of living, but in truth . . .

Just here he had inked over and obliterated almost half a page. At the bottom he left these few lines:

We all know how much there is to forgive, how often we sin and are sinned against. We know, too, that the cruellest sins of all are those that are committed in the name of love.

I spent nearly four months with Russell Atha's files and notes. I made extensive notes of my own, detailing as closely as I could all the conversations we'd had about Christine and Grace and Roy, about Fred Deets and Annie and Abe Singleton. At last I put all the material away, sat down at a clean table, and began to work.

Chapter 3

*I*n June of 1969, when she was twenty years old, Christine Wheatley took a job as summer waitress in a restaurant on Martha's Vineyard. Working with her was a girl named Shirley Hostetler. Because of her, Christine met Roy Lavidge.

Shirley was born and raised on Staten Island, in the bay of New York City. Short, square, and compact, with blonde curls and a mouth like a flower bud, she was called Cuba from tenth grade on. It became her name. But at first only one person knew why. All the girls who had stood with her in the showers in gym class and at least five boys who had taken her out since seventh grade knew that she had an unusual pink birthmark on her stomach, just below her navel. But her geometry teacher, Ellis Veach, was the first one to tell her that the mark was shaped exactly the same as the island of Cuba.

She was very fond of Mr Veach; she was proud of their secret life. She understood that there were valid reasons they had to meet in dark, out-of-the-way places. She never failed to show up if she could help it. She would go anywhere, do anything he asked. Whether they had five minutes together in the shadows between two buildings or half an hour in his car, she never complained.

Her only frustration was that she couldn't tell anyone. No one at all. So the fact that she was able to boast about her birthmark, to call it by the name he had taught her, to call *herself* by that name, delighted her. It was the next-best thing to standing up in school assembly and saying, 'Look at me. I'm Cuba Hostetler. And I'm Mr Veach's girl friend.'

During the first week that Christine and Cuba worked together, Cuba told her about her family, Mr Veach, and everything else that had happened to her since age six.

'Mr Veach really put a hex on me,' she said. 'I can see it now. Now that I've had a lot of psych courses and know all about human behaviour. What I mean is he got me into a thing about older men. I was fifteen when I started up with him and he was thirty-four. Since then I've never gone out with a man who was less than forty. And one dude I lived with for over a year was fifty-six years old. So here I am. Twenty-one years old, about to start my senior year in college, and I've never been turned on by anybody my own age. Not till now, at least. But *now* I think all that's beginning to change. There's a guy here on the island, Tom Peddicord his name is, and he works on that construction job just down the street. You talk about a hunk. He is really a hunk. Not too brilliant, I guess. But who cares? I've had enough grey-haired intellectuals to last me a lifetime. Cigarette ashes on their jackets and soft hands like a woman. No good.'

The next day, during their break between lunch and dinner, Cuba walked Christine down to the construction site to meet Peddicord. 'That's him,' she said. 'Up there on the second level with his shirt off. The towhead. Is he something? He's so strong it scares me. You put your arms around him, it's like hugging a tree.'

'Who's that guy with him? The one with curly hair.'

'Roy Lavidge. He and Tom are buddies. You want to meet him?'

'No. I just asked who he was.'

'That's right. I forgot. You're all tied up with some guy at home.'

'That's right,' Christine said.

'Too bad. Roy's not much compared to Tom, but I think he knows what's happening. I'll bet he could get you through the summer just fine. The four of us could have some fun together.'

Christine shook her head. 'Sorry. I'm took.'

A steam whistle on one of the cranes blew then, and Shirley said, 'That's it. They're through for the day.'

Peddicord stepped off the construction lift and came walking toward them, his shirt over one shoulder, claw hammer swinging from a loop on his pants leg, carrying his lunch pail in one hand, his safety helmet in the other.

'Will you look at him?' Shirley said. 'Too much. Howard Roark in the flesh. Did you read *The Fountainhead*?'

'Not since I was twelve. Ayn Rand sucks.'

'Who cares? If you don't like Howard Roark you don't like men. Remember the rape scene, when he breaks into her bedroom? She's all clean and perfumy and he's covered with dirt and sweat. And he pulls her down on the floor and takes her candy away from her, right there on the rug. Doesn't say anything. Just screws her ears off, then gets up and leaves.'

'Is that what you like?'

'No. *He's* what I like,' Cuba said, looking at Peddicord.

After Shirley introduced her to Peddicord, Christine walked with them to the kerb, where his pickup truck was parked. She stood watching the truck drive off down the street, feeling the late afternoon sun on her face. Then a voice behind her said, 'Hope I didn't keep you waiting.'

Turning around, she saw Roy Lavidge standing there, nothing ingratiating about his manner, not smiling, just looking at her. 'I'm on my way to Mario's for a beer. You want to come along?'

She looked at her watch. 'I can't. I'm due at work.'

'Not yet,' he said. 'You've got another forty minutes.'

'Do you know everybody's business?'

'This is a little town. And Cuba has a fast mouth. Your name's Christine Wheatley and you came from someplace outside Chicago and you've been working at Angie Duncan's restaurant for ten days or so.' He eased away. 'If you don't want a beer at least walk me down there.'

She hesitated and he said. 'Lighten up. I'm not looking for action. One thing this island has a lot of is girls. Peddicord has to fight them off with a bicycle chain.'

They walked slowly down the sidewalk that ran through the centre of the village. 'How about you?' she said. 'You carry a bicycle chain too?'

'Don't have to. I'm not a ladies' man. I have too many other things to do.'

'Like what?'

'Different things,' he said. 'Reading comic books. Building model airplanes. Plucking my eyebrows.'

'You don't have to do a whole number on me,' she said. 'I'm not trying to find out the story of your life. I didn't ask *you* to walk to Mario's. You asked me.'

'Okay. We'll shift gears. Why are you working as a waitress?'

'I have another year of college. I need the money.'

'No, you don't. Those blue jeans you're wearing cost fifty bucks. And the wristwatch cost a thousand.'

'Who says so?'

'I do. I notice those things. People who wear Timexes spend a lot of time looking at ads for expensive watches.'

'You're right,' she said, 'it *is* an expensive watch. It was a gift. So were the jeans. I'm a kept woman.'

'Where did *that* come from? I've read that expression in some old books, but I never heard anybody say it.'

'Now you've heard somebody say it.'

He stopped and stood facing her in the street. 'You're really on edge, aren't you? You must get your own way all the time. Look . . . I'll tell you what. You do the talking and I'll just walk along and nod my head. I'm not looking for a firefight.'

She stood looking at a spot somewhere over his left shoulder and didn't say anything. Finally he said, 'Are you gonna walk me to Mario's or are you heading back in the other direction?'

They walked a little way in silence. Then he said, 'Maybe I said something that threw you off. If I did, I'm sorry. I'm really an easygoing guy. I don't eat with my fingers, and I don't get my kicks beating up on women. I don't expect to get married for ten years or so because I won't be able to afford it. And I'm not looking to get laid any more than the next guy.' They stopped on the sidewalk in front of Mario's. 'You sure you won't have a beer?'

'No thanks. I'll take a raincheck.'

'What I was trying to say is, we're both gonna be stuck here on this island for a couple of months. You're not looking for the love of your life and neither am I. So maybe we could kill some time together. Take a walk, go swimming, have a few laughs. We can fool around if you want to. But if you *don't* want to, we can hold hands and pretend we're brother and sister. No skinny-dipping or kissing on the mouth. What do you think?'

She stood there looking at him for a long moment. Then she started to laugh.

'It never fails,' he said. 'When I get serious, somebody starts to laugh. What did I say?'

'Is that what you call "getting serious"?' She was still laughing. 'I've had better offers than that from the kid who comes to deliver the dry cleaning. "We can fool around if you *want* to . . ." '

'That's the point,' he said. 'It wasn't supposed to be an offer.'

'What would you call it?'

'I don't know. If I had to put a label on it, I guess I'd say it was a suggestion.'

'Sort of an offhand suggestion? Is that what you'd say?'

'That's right. Nothing to get excited about. Nothing that requires any long discussions or a note from home. Just a little conversation on the sidewalk. My name's Roy Lavidge. Did I tell you that?'

'Good-bye, Lavidge. You're irresistible but I have to go to work. Meet me when I get off work tomorrow night and I'll take you to the late movie. No fooling around. No kissy-kissy. Brother and sister. Okay?'

'I don't like movies.'

'You'll like this one. I'll buy you buttered popcorn and chocolate ice cream in a paper cup. See you tomorrow.'

She turned and walked away up the street. When she looked back he had already disappeared inside Mario's bar. 'What are you doing?' she said to herself. 'What in the *world* do you think you're doing?'

That night, when she came home from work, she called Fred Deets in Indianapolis. He wasn't at home but his answering service gave her a number where he could be reached.

'Where are you?' she said when he answered.

'Country club. I played nine holes after I finished work. Then I stayed out here for dinner.'

'Are we eating alone?' she said.

'Not a chance. I'm entertaining the club hooker and a tap dancer from Cincinnati. What do you expect? When you go kiting off to Martha's Vineyard for the summer you have to take your chances. How's your waitress job?'

'I like it. Lots of nice people.'

'Big tips?'

'A quarter a head if I'm lucky. This isn't Chicago.'

'You ready to come home?'

'Are you kidding? I just got here. I'm educating myself.'

'Some wife you're gonna be. I'll be home feeding the kids and the dogs and you'll be off someplace in Ecuador looking for a lost city.'

'You got it, Freddie. Right on the nose. How's the shopping centre coming along?'

'Pretty good. We had a break with the weather. All the foundations are in and the steel work's a couple of days ahead of schedule. We're telling the tenants they'll be in business by Thanksgiving. When you coming home?'

'You're in a rut. You already asked me that. I'll be there in September, a week before school starts.'

'How would you like to get married?'

'I'd love it,' she said. 'Soon as I'm out of school.'

'You can be married and still finish school.'

13

'No I can't. They won't let me play soccer if I'm pregnant.'

'Okay, babe. It's your funeral. You'll be sorry when they drag me off to Vietnam and you're checking the papers every day to see if I got blown away.'

'Nobody's gonna blow you away. You're a survivor, Deets. Money in the bank. Fresh, minty breath.'

'That's right.'

'And you're all mine,' she said.

'Don't you forget it.'

'I won't.'

Chapter 4

*T*he next night, Roy picked Christine up at work and they went to see a film. When they came out of the theatre, they strolled down to the wharf, sat on a bench, and talked for more than two hours. When he walked her home and they stood outside her apartment door, he said, 'I forgot what rules we decided on. Am I supposed to kiss you or not?'

'You're not supposed to.'

'Are you supposed to kiss me?'

'We didn't talk about that.' She put her hands on his shoulders and kissed him on the mouth. 'I'm sorry I can't ask you in,' she said. 'Too many roommates.'

'Don't be sorry. It's a long summer. I'll see you tomorrow.'

She lay awake in her bed till after three in the morning, her eyes fixed on a spot of light on the dark ceiling, her mind running free in great concentric circles. At last she got up, put on her robe, went into the kitchen, and warmed up the coffee on the stove. Then she carried the kitchen phone to the table and called her mother in Lake Forest.

'I hope I didn't wake you up.'

'You know me,' her mother said. 'I'm a night bird. You're the one who's up late. If my clock's right, it must be three thirty there.'

'Three twenty-five,' Christine said.

'Are you all right?'

'I don't know.'

'What happened?'

'Man trouble.'

'Are you and Fred on the outs?'

'Not Fred,' Christine said. 'Another man.'

'He must be a fast worker. You've only been there . . .'

'He's not a fast worker at all. I don't even know him very well. I've only been out with him once.'

'When was that?'

'Tonight.'

Her mother laughed softly into the phone. 'Chrissy, my darling, my baby, my dear, you really don't expect me to take this call seriously, do you? God help you when nobody can give you the shivers. But remember, you're not Sally-Sue from the convent. You're a grown-up woman, sweetheart.'

'Not tonight I'm not.'

'What *happened*?' her mother said.

'Nothing happened. That's what I'm trying to say. I just . . . feel like I'm stumbling around in the dark.'

'What's his name?'

'Lavidge. Roy Lavidge. He's from some squeedunk town on the coast of Maine and he's just an ordinary regular-looking guy who's working on construction, trying to put himself through school. He's like somebody who comes to put a new roof on your garage.'

'But you like him.'

'I don't even *know* him. Tonight we went to some dumb movie and we sat and talked for a couple of hours afterward, nothing important. But when he brought me home, I didn't want him to leave. Or if he left I wanted to go with him.'

'Did you?'

'God, no. We've never even *talked* about anything really personal. For all I know he could have three wives and fourteen kids. He might be in bed with somebody right now. I told you, there's nothing sensible or logical to all this. If I didn't know better I'd think I was getting my period, I feel crummy. I feel like a rat.'

'I'm sorry, kid. I wish I knew what to tell you. Do you want to come home?'

'No, I don't. That's Fred's solution to everything, but it's not mine.

'I know this will sound strange to you,' Christine said then. 'But . . . the thing that's been going through my head ever since I got home tonight is you and Russell Atha. I was lying here in bed and I thought, "My God . . . *this* is how *she* felt. *This* is what happened to *her* all those years ago when I was just a baby." Is that right? Is that what's happening to me, Grace?'

'I hope not.'

'What does *that* mean?'

There was a silence at the other end of the phone and she heard her mother lighting a cigarette. Finally, she said, 'I'm sorry. I didn't mean that. I just meant . . . I don't know . . . what I'm trying to say is that I love it when you call me in the middle of the night and say, "Help." If the situation were reversed I'd do the same thing. But I'm afraid I'm better at asking for help than I am at giving it. Especially when you go back twenty years and ask me about Russell. When I remember that time with him, there at the beginning in Avignon and Paris, it sinks me. When I let myself slide back into those few months we had together, it still makes me look for the closest chair to sit down on. It still *hurts*. Does any of this make sense to you? Do you know what I'm trying to say?'

'I'm not sure,' Christine said. 'I think so.'

'It would kill me to see you go through what Russell and I went through. But, on the other hand, outside of having *you*, it's the only really good thing that ever happened to me.'

'I don't want to get hurt,' Christine said.

'Nobody does. But that doesn't mean you won't.'

16

Chapter 5

*A*t Bowdoin, Roy was asked, in a sophomore composition class, to write a short autobiography. His teacher, a man named Pence, a strict grammarian and a scholar of Smollett and Fielding, scribbled the following note in the margin. 'I think you're trying for something but I can't be sure what it is. It comes across like staccato shorthand. Marbles shot out of a cannon. It has no rhythm. No change of pace. By avoiding any trace of emotion you risk sentimentality. Too little emotion in a work can be as sentimental as too much.'

After rewriting the assignment half a dozen times, he eventually earned a decent mark from Dr Pence. But Roy preferred still the first awkward draft he had turned in.

My father's name is Thomas James Lavidge but he was always called T.J. When he met my mother he was a bartender in Provincetown, Massachusetts. He had been married and divorced twice by then. My mother's name was Maria Agnelli. She was an Italian girl who had come to live with her married sister in Boston. She met T.J. when she spent a week in Cape Cod with her sister and brother-in-law.

Four months later my uncle, Joe Medek, and a couple of his Czech friends went back to Provincetown with my mother, who was pregnant, and persuaded T.J. to marry her. After the wedding they moved to Maine, to Round Pond. I was born there, January 21, 1949.

T.J. stayed around, off and on, till I was four years old, mostly because he was scared of Joe Medek. But one day he disappeared. We never saw him again.

By the time T.J. left, my uncle Josef and his wife Agnes had moved from Boston to Portland. Joe was building garages and making good money. So they brought Mother and me down to Portland to live with them.

When I was ten years old, my grandmother in Siena fell and broke her hip. She was alone, so my mother and Agnes went to Italy to take care of her. Agnes came back in two weeks, but my mother stayed because she thought her mother needed her. She started up then with her childhood boyfriend, a man she had known before she came to America. He had been married but his wife had died. So now he wanted to marry my mother. She decided not tell him about T.J. or me. That way they could be married in the church.

She wrote me a long ball-breaking letter saying she had to do it because of my grandmother, because they needed the money and all that. We'd work something out later, she said. And meanwhile, Joe and Agnes, who had no kids of their own, would take care of me. So that's the way it went. Except nothing got worked out later.

I wasn't a great student at the beginning but I got better. I wanted to go to college, so I worked hard to get good grades. And I ran the half mile and the mile relay in high school, hoping I could get good enough to win a free ride at some small college. I got lucky and ended up with a jock scholarship, mostly because I set a state high school record for the 880. Here at Bowdoin I won my event in every meet I entered my freshman year.

I left out the New York part. From the time I was thirteen till the time I was fifteen, Joe took a job with a New York contractor and we lived in a building his cousin managed, between First Avenue and Avenue A on Ninth Street. It was rough there then, 1962 through 1964. I ran with a gang of Polish and Ukrainian kids. We fought a lot with the Puerto Ricans and the blacks and a motorcycle gang from New Jersey that hung out in a storefront building on 11th Street. That's how I got the broken nose and a scar on my chin. And that's when I learned to run.

18

Chapter 6

When she was eighteen years old, in May of 1967, Christine drove her Ferrari convertible to O'Hare Airport, left it there in one of the underground parking spaces her grandmother reserved year round, and took the nine a.m. flight to New York. After she checked in at the Pierre, she called her mother in Lake Forest and said, 'Guess who's in New York.'

'Good for you,' Grace said. 'How's the weather?'

'Perfect. Aren't you going to ask me what I'm doing here?'

'Not a chance. I'm not the warden. I figure if you want to tell me you will.'

'I was going to tell you I came to see Sarah. But I decided it was silly to tell a fib. I'm going to look up Russell Atha.'

Her mother didn't answer. After a moment, Christine said, 'I'm just trying to fill in a blank space in my life. He's been bouncing around in my head since I was five years old. I've seen his picture in the papers and read all his books. I know you loved him and Grandma hated him. Sooner or later I had to see him in the flesh. So now's the time.'

'How do you know he's in New York?'

'Aaron Gold had an item about him in the *Tribune* yesterday. Said he was at a vernissage at the Whitney. I called his publisher as soon as I checked in here. I left my name and asked them to have Mr Atha call me back.'

'What if you don't hear from him?'

'I already did. I'm meeting him for lunch in twenty minutes.'

About four that afternoon, Russell called my apartment. I wasn't there but my wife was. Not Sheila, my crazy first wife, but Amy, my terrific second wife. When he asked if

19

he could invite himself for dinner that night, Amy said sure. 'Meat loaf, mashed potatoes, and peas. If that doesn't sound good to you, bring yourself a pizza.'

He showed up at six thirty. As soon as he had a drink in his hand, he started telling us about Christine. 'You talk about a wipeout experience . . . this girl is an absolute clone of her mother eighteen years ago. The voice and the eyes and the gestures. Everything. And not only does she look great, she's smart as hell. Also she's read every book I've ever written.'

'That did it,' Amy said, 'I think he's in love.'

That night when we were in bed, Amy said, 'It shook him up, didn't it?'

'Yeah, I think so. Grace was one of a kind in his life. When things started to fall apart for them, I used to sit with him in the Coupole or the Kosmos and he'd drink cognac till his arm got tired, but I never saw him drunk. Not then. He was too miserable to get drunk. He was in shock, I guess, as much as I've ever seen anybody in shock. And it lasted for a long time. Why do you think he married Micheline? I'm not saying he didn't love her in some way or other. But mostly he was trying to cure himself of the Grace disease. It didn't work, of course. He knew it right away, but Micheline had to find it out later, a little piece at a time. One child and five years later she said, "Go find Grace and live with her. You'll never be contented till you do." '

'Why didn't he do that?'

'I can't answer that. He's never been married since Micheline, but Grace has been married twice since she divorced Wheatley.'

'But she's not married now,' Amy said. 'So why haven't they gotten together again?'

'Who knows? Scared maybe.'

'Scared of what?'

'I don't know. Maybe the leftovers of what they had are more important to them than trying to have it again.'

'God, you're romantic,' Amy said. 'It's women who are

20

supposed to have their heads in the clouds, but men get my vote every time. They're both *young*, for God's sake. Russell can't be more than forty and she's no older, is she? I can't believe they would just moon around, both of them, for the rest of their lives, when they could be together and have a good time.'

'I didn't say it makes sense. But we don't have all the facts. When he followed her from Paris to Chicago, when the big breakup from Wheatley was taking place, maybe something happened between them, maybe they said things they can't take back. Who knows? But something must have happened. Because she got married again. Right away. And not to Russell.'

'I never understood that.'

'Neither did anybody else. Especially Russell. That's when he tried to drink up all the Rémy Martin in Montparnasse. And six months later he married Micheline.'

'I still think he and Grace should get back together. Now that he's met Christine maybe she'll fix everything up.'

'I wouldn't count on it,' I said. 'I have a hunch the boat sailed.'

Chapter 7

*W*hen she wrote to Fred, who was still at Brown then, and told him about her meeting with Russell, Christine said, 'It made me feel good about myself. I think it's the first really grown-up thing I've ever done.'

Not wanting to tell her grandmother about it, Christine told her anyway; otherwise she knew she'd find it out through her web of sycophants and informers. 'What a childish thing to do,' Margaret said. 'Clever women don't seek out men like Russell Atha. They take pains to avoid them.'

The reaction did not surprise Christine. When she was twelve years old, at a time when Grace was away from Chicago a lot, her grandmother decided, it seemed, that the time was opportune to bend the twig, to dictate once and for all the way the sapling would grow. The resulting lecture, an out-of-date course in young womanhood, ended with a detailed listing of Christine's mother's shortcomings.

'Grace is my only child and I love her fondly. But your mother has some flaws which I pray you have not inherited. Don't misunderstand me. She is a kind and lovely person. But she is not strong, sometimes she is not truthful, and all through her life she has been influenced by the wrong kind of company. It's not uncommon. Many women, men too, enjoy the company of second-rate people.'

'My mother's not like that. I don't like you to say things like that about her.'

'Let me finish,' her grandmother said. She paused, studied the grim-jawed child in front of her, and tried another tack. 'What I was trying to say is that all of us are susceptible. We can all be fooled. As far as I know, your mother has made only one serious mistake in her life. At a tender age, when she was upset and confused and away from home, she trusted the wrong person.'

'You mean Russell Atha?'

Her grandmother nodded her head. 'I realize you know about him. It wasn't something that could ever be kept secret.'

'Grace was in love with him. She was crazy about him. Everybody knew that.'

Margaret smiled an iron smile and said, 'Of course. He was a tremendous influence on her. That's what I'm saying. She was alone there in France, away from me, away from her husband, she'd just had a baby a few months before, and Atha took advantage of her.'

'Why *was* she alone in France? Why was she there in the first place? Why was I born there? Where was Harold Wheatley?'

'You mean your father?'

'I mean Harold Wheatley,' Christine said. 'I don't think of him as my father. Wilson's more of a father than he is.'

'Wilson's a chauffeur. He works for us.'

'Well, he's more of a father than Wheatley. He's weird. He and that skinny wife of his. She's so pale and skinny, she's *transparent*.'

Firmly, Margaret pushed ahead. 'Russell Atha was an *arriviste* of the worst kind. He set about deliberately to break up Grace's marriage, to force her to fall in love with him. It was like hypnosis, the power he had over her. You were just an infant. Do you think your mother would have left you with a governess for days at a time if . . .'

'She *didn't* leave me. I was with her all the time. She told me so. She wouldn't lie about that.'

'I didn't say she lied. I'm saying she was spending a great deal of time with Russell Atha when she should have been with her child, when she should have been at home here with her husband.'

'Why wasn't her husband in France with her?'

'There's a very simple answer to that. . . .' Margaret thought better of her answer and dried up suddenly.

'What's the answer?'

'That's something I think your mother should tell you.'

'Grace didn't know Russell Atha before she went to France, did she? She told me she met him in Avignon.'

'I believe that's true.'

'If Wheatley wasn't there when I was born and she met Atha several months later, then I guess she wasn't living with my father. Is that right?'

'They were man and wife until their marriage ended, Christine.'

'All right. Tell me this. If this man had such an influence on her, if she loved him like she said she did, and if all he was after was her money, then why didn't they get married after she and Wheatley were divorced?'

'He *wanted* to marry her,' Margaret said. 'You can be sure of that. But after she was back here in Lake Forest with her family, she began to see things a little more clearly.'

'You mean she *didn't* want to marry *him*?'

Margaret nodded her head and smiled. 'I mean she decided to change her plans.'

'Then why does she always cry when she reads something about him in the paper or sees him on televison?'

'I didn't know she did.'

'Well, she does,' Christine said.

'I'm sure I don't know the answer to *that*.'

Chapter 8

Margaret Ainslie Jernegan, Christine's grandmother, duenna of the Jernegan sixty-acre compound in Lake Forest and guardian-administrator of the Jernegan corn products fortune, control office in Chicago, plants in Red Wing, Minnesota, Wichita, and Des Moines, was born August 11, 1908, in Yankton, South Dakota.

Her father and mother owned a produce farm five miles outside Yankton and a general store at the crossroads there. She grew up behind the counter of that store, selling eggs and potatoes and canned goods, measuring out rice and sugar in one-pound bags. There is irony, and perhaps inevitability, in the fact that when she first became aware of Russell Atha, Margaret said to Grace, 'Do you really expect me to believe that the only man in the world who can make you happy is a shopkeeper's son from Kentucky?'

Margaret developed, early on, a quantitative sense of values. Accumulate as much as you can. Buy cheap. Sell dear. She also sensed that the kind of assets she craved could not be accumulated by a woman, in South Dakota, in 1925. They had to be acquired, seized, captured. Inside her tender bosom, behind her remarkably attractive face, lurked the impulses of a buccaneer.

By the time she was seventeen, Margaret knew that her salvation would be a man. A particular man. A particularly wealthy and vulnerable man. She had never seen the man she had in mind, but she knew he existed. In Minneapolis or Chicago or Kansas City. She studied the rotogravure pages of any city papers she could lay hands on, carefully inspected the jowled faces, the paunches strung with gold chains, and the jewelled rings on fat fingers. Just such a one, she told herself.

She also memorized the names of the places where these men were often photographed. The Ambassador Hotel, the Meulebach, the Cattlemans Club, and the Haymarket in Minneapolis.

Her father's sister, Evelyn, lived in Minneapolis. Margaret persuaded her father that it would be very good for his business if she were to spend some weeks in Minneapolis taking a course in commercial bookkeeping.

For several weeks she conscientiously attended her classes, mornings and evenings. In the afternoon she rode the streetcars, and familiarized herself with the city, especially the prosperous district around the Haymarket Club.

One morning she left the house earlier than usual, took a streetcar to St Paul, and checked into a small hotel, registering as Margaret Van Arsdall. On her aunt's kitchen table she left a note saying she was going to Chicago for a few days to visit a girl friend she'd met in bookkeeping school. Her family never heard from her or saw her again.

She got a job as a waitress in Hanratty's, a restaurant in downtown St Paul. Taking full advantage of her quick head for figures and her milkmaid figure, she made an immediate impression on her superiors. And the customers.

After a month, however, she went to her employer, a dapper, white-haired man named Gerd Pfrommer, and told him she was sorry but she would have to leave the job. Then she started to cry, sank down in a chair in his office, and sobbed into her handkerchief. Mr Pfrommer, who had three daughters himself, was touched. When he heard the story she told him, he was shocked. Here was a young girl who had left her home in South Dakota because of bad treatment. A careless slattern of a mother, three drunken brothers, and worst of all, a stepfather who punished her cruelly. And although Margaret was reticent to speak of it, Mr Pfrommer suspected there was also a threat of sexual abuse if she went back to that environment. The crisis was acute. 'They've found me. Two of my brothers and my stepfather are on their way to St Paul to take me back home. They know where I've been staying and they know I work here at your restaurant. So I have to leave.'

'Where will you go?'

'I don't know. I'll have to get another room and find another job. And I don't have much money. All the wages I've earned here I sent home to my mother.'

'I know most of the restaurant owners here in the Twin Cities. All I have to do is pick up the phone and you'll have another job. You're a good worker. Anyone would be happy to have you.'

'That's sweet of you, but I don't think I'll be able to take a job in a restaurant. We have relatives in Minneapolis and sooner or later someone would see me. I may have to take a job in somebody's home. Or in a private club or something. Someplace where I can live on the premises and work there and not be so easy to find.'

Two hours later, Margaret was a waitress-in-residence at the Haymarket Club, the most exclusive men's club in Minneapolis, reciprocal privileges with the Cattlemans Club in Kansas City and the Commonwealth in Chicago, frequent host to out-of-town gentlemen when they travelled north to inspect their properties, to buy and sell, or simply to carouse in a city other than their own.

In 1925, the year Margaret started to work at the Haymarket, the wealthy families of the Midwest were growing rapidly wealthier. The Chrysler Corporation was founded that year, Ford Motor Company opened a subsidiary in Germany, and railroad mileage in the United States reached 261,000. And the only son of one of Chicago's wealthiest families, Emmett Burke Jernegan, celebrated his thirty-fifth birthday.

Emmett was an outpoken agnostic, a bachelor, and he had an acerbic sense of humour. He handled his share of the family business load with dispatch and brilliance and the rest of his time he devoted to the things he enjoyed most. Raising and training fine horses, drinking the best French vintages, and lying between the legs of young women.

Although he was admired and sought after by the daughters of Chicago's best families, Emmett openly preferred the company of actresses, waitresses, and chambermaids. No duchess or tobacco heiress, however, was treated with more tenderness or consideration or respect than Emmett treated these lovely found objects. 'You don't understand,' he once said to his father, '*kindness* is everything. It's important that we make people think better of themselves.'

How Margaret Ainslie wedged herself into that intricate grid of cynicism, hedonism, and idealism no one ever knew for sure. No scenario was ever presented that detailed how they met, what transpired, and how she managed to make the quantum jump from Margaret Van Arsdall, as she called herself, to Mrs Emmett Jernegan.

Everyone conceded, however, that from his covey of

27

shopgirls and waitresses he had married an outstanding one. Young and beautiful and well-spoken, as strong willed and imperious as if she were, indeed, well educated and wealthy. Bending the knee to no one, sensing early on who in the family held trump cards, and devoting most of her attention from then on to those individuals. Apart from her father-in-law, she was delighted to discover, no one in the Jernegan business and financial structure had greater autonomy than her husband, Emmett.

They were married in the summer of 1927. Between that time and the birth of Grace on October 17, 1929, Emmett was able to play Pygmalion on a grander scale than ever before. And he did it untiringly, with imagination and humour and generosity. Buying, ordering, acquiring, commissioning, building, and decorating. What later became known as the Jernegan compound, the walled estate in Lake Forest, was Emmett's official declaration of separation from his father's enclave ten miles farther south on the lake. In 1927 the compound began to come into being. The principal dwelling, three other homes, an indoor swimming pool, indoor and outdoor tennis courts, formal gardens, a horse ring and stables, and a deer park.

While waiting for their home to be finished, Emmett and Margaret travelled. For the first time in her life she saw great paintings, went to the theatre and the opera, ate in fine restaurants, travelled in luxurious suites on trains and ocean liners. In a few months, still not yet twenty years old, she had transformed herself, quite literally, and had become, in appearance and demeanour, in dress and speech, a cultivated and enlightened person, skilled with servants, at ease with her peers, gracious and kind to her economic inferiors. Her hunger for power and privilege and status had been suddenly gratified. A creature without a past, she feasted on her present delights and luxuriated in the future. Because, apart from her other good fortune, she had fallen in love with her husband.

When their daughter, Grace, was born, Emmett set up a massive trust fund in her name, payments to begin when she was twenty-one or on the day of his death, whichever came first. He also provided that she would inherit his entire estate, forty per cent at his death, the other sixty per cent when her mother died.

To everyone's astonishment, Emmett, the profligate bachelor and womanizer, became an extraordinarily devoted husband. As though he had prescience, he spent long hours instructing his wife about investments and business decisions. He sensed that she had financial skills and he helped her develop them.

Once his daughter was born, his attachment to her was remarkable. He carried her with him everywhere. For long walks. For drives. And almost every day he took her down to the stables and held her in his arms as he walked his favourite stallion, Hannibal, around the ring. Many days also he sat beside her crib as she took a nap. One golden October afternoon, ten days before her first birthday, he was watching her sleep, in a tangle of dolls and stuffed toys, when his body settled soft and heavy in his chair. And his heart, without warning or pain, simply stopped.

Chapter 9

*T*he morning after she'd telephoned her mother from Martha's Vineyard, Christine made complicated work trade-offs with Cuba and the other two girls she waited tables with and shared an apartment with, Lucy from New Bedford, and Margo, from Wayland, west of Boston, and freed herself for two days. She then arranged to borrow Lucy's car, threw some jeans and sweaters, a towel, and a bathing suit into the back seat, and drove south out of Edgartown toward the downside of the island. She turned west, passed the airport on her way through the farm country to West Tisbury, then angled southwest through Chilmark and on out to Gay Head on the farthest western point of the island, great clouds of gulls in the sky dipping and soaring and circling around their nesting and feeding grounds there.

She found a room for the night in a small frame guest house just above Gay Head; the proprietor, a white-haired man in his eighties, said, 'You're lucky it's midweek and I had a cancellation.'

The few things she'd brought with her she carried in from the car. She folded her clothes neatly and put them into a drawer in the low chest under the window, laid her toilet articles out on the shelf over the bathroom sink. Then she took off her clothes and took a shower. Steaming hot first, then cold, the water stinging her body like sleet. Rubbing herself dry with a rough towel, her skin flushed under her suntan, and tingling, she put on jeans and a shirt with no underwear, and slipped her feet into thong sandals.

She spent the rest of that day and all of the following morning, walking miles along the white beaches, swimming in sheltered coves, lying in hollows on the dunes, sleeping, browning her body, speaking to no one, isolating herself, stripping to her skin when she was really alone.

She let her mind drift. Demanded nothing of it. Held up no hoops for it to jump through. She knew why she'd come away; at least she sensed it. She'd done it in the past. Many times. Since childood, whenever tangles began to form in her head, she had simply climbed on her pony or her horse, later into her car, and gone off somewhere alone. Into a vacuum, a cocoon, a quiet place.

Christine was at home in the fields and the forests, in the ocean or on the beach. She was a student of flowers and ferns, shrubs and vines and trees. Birds fascinated her, butterflies and insects, and she loved animals of all sizes and species.

30

They in turn responded to her, came to her, had no more fear of her than she had of them. Sparrows fed from her hand, and squirrels and pigeons. There was a climate of communication, no question about it. She was able to lose herself, to blend with her surroundings in an animal way, to shuck off the layers of humanness that seem threatening, that *are* threatening, to other creatures. It was a transformation she was conscious of. She felt she was able to shed her skin, like a snake, and become, for the moment, a different sort of animal altogether. Selfless and fluid and unthreatening, a receptacle rather than a machine, a litmus to be acted upon.

So, for those two days on the beaches near Gay Head, Christine concentrated on the details of sea and sand, on the flying, flopping, crawling things around her; she felt that she came from nowhere and was going nowhere. Time had found a stopping place.

Her subconscious, of course, like a bank of underground computers, was whirring. Selecting and sorting, preparing to click forth some critical emotional printout. And at last, of course, it came. First things first. Fred Deets.

Fred was not a flawless and perfect creation. Even if he had been, he would have been the last person to recognize it. That was one of his best features. He was serious about a great many things, but he did not take himself seriously.

This is not to say that many people did not consider him perfect. Many did. His father, for example. Nelson Deets, a no-nonsense man and a self-made millionaire, believed that his son was close to perfection. 'He's just a kid that the angels kissed. He's got a good brain and a good body. He knows how to work and he knows how to play. He's got the world by the ass and he always will have, but he's not puffed up about it. I'm proud of him.'

The Deets family lived in Lake Forest, not far from the Jernegan compound. Christine and Fred had grown up together. When he was nineteen and Christine was seventeen, when it became obvious to anyone who was paying attention that their interest in each other was not platonic, Grace said, 'The only thing wrong with Fred, as far

31

as I can see, is that there's absolutely *nothing* wròng with him.'

Margaret Jernegan, in one of her regular visits with Christine, went straight to the core of things. 'That young man is absolutely first-rate. He has breeding from his mother's people, the Bishops, and money from his father. Unless I miss my guess, you've got a man there who'll be an outstanding husband and father. Also, when I'm gone, somebody will have to look after our holdings and investments and take over the Jernegan Company. So Fred is a perfect choice for you, no matter how you look at it.'

Christine, from age four, had never questioned that she and Fred were permanently attached. They ran and played and wrestled together. Climbed trees, rode horses, argued and fought and made up. They exchanged gifts and insults, swam naked as unselfconsciously as two otters, embraced like brother and sister and were, in fact, since each was an only child, very much like two children from the same family. When Fred, at sixteen, began going to parties and dances with girls his own age or older, Christine was fiercely possessive and wildly jealous. So she avoided him, insulted him when she saw him, and began, as soon as her mother permitted, to go out herself. She made a point, whenever possible, of dating young men who were older than Fred and making sure that he knew it.

All this ended when he went east to boarding school. Christine stayed home and attended the Halliburton Day School in Winnetka. They didn't see each other for months at a time. And when they did, his seventeen years seemed very old, at least to him, for her fifteen. And eighteen, of course, as everyone knows, is practically a generation older than sixteen. So for those several years he became an older brother, advising her against too much makeup, cautioning her about the dangers of going out with Northwestern undergraduates, and on rare occasions escorting her smoothly to family parties.

In the summer of 1966, however, when she was preparing for her first year in college and Fred had just finished his second year at Brown, their relationship changed. He had broken up with a truly gorgeous young woman from Providence and Christine's most attentive escort, Tod Brocki, had transferred from Northwestern to Stanford after his family moved from Glencoe to San Francisco.

One night, early in July, after a long sail on Lake Michigan, Christine and Fred, commiserating with each other, drank a magnum of champagne in his father's boathouse. Just before midnight, the moon burning white through the lakefront windows, they made love on the floor, he with all the tenderness he could manage, and with a near-incestuous guilt, and she with the lunatic energy and abandon of a forest animal.

They were together constantly that summer. Friends and relatives nodded their heads and smiled as though some lovely and inevitable third act had begun.

When Christine enrolled at Foresby that September, she told one of her newfound sorority friends that she had just spent the most perfect two months of her life. 'Nothing will ever be like that again. It doesn't even have to be. I had all the love and fun I'll ever need.'

When she and Fred said good-bye at the airport the day he flew back to Providence, she said, 'I'm gonna die without you.'

'No, you're not,' he said. 'you're going to have a terrific year. Every guy in the school will want to take you out.'

'Not me. I'm took.'

'That's right,' he said. 'But that doesn't mean you should lock yourself up in your room.'

'You mean you want me to have dates?'

'You *have* to. That's a part of going to school. But it won't change anything between you and me.'

'And you'll be going out with all the sexpots from those snotty girls' schools.'

'Are you jealous?'

'Damned right I'm jealous. If I start hearing stories about you, I'll come after you with a rusty knife.'

'You won't hear any stories. You know how things are with

us. We started out as little runts together and we're going to end up together. No matter what. Don't you forget that, because I won't.'

'I won't forget it,' she said.

That airport conversation stuck in their heads, it seemed, stayed with both of them, through the next two years. Separated by a thousand miles during their school terms, they managed nonetheless to see each other often. They wrote letters, talked on the telephone, and spent their vacations in Lake Forest together.

As predicted, Christine, in a very social school, was an extremely social person, much in demand, much pursued. A lot of young men asked her out, quite a few kissed her, and a few of them, two or three, sensed that if the circumstances had been slightly different, she would have held back nothing. They were right. She was vulnerable and she knew it. She had been physically awakened and she liked it. She'd seen, with Fred, the effect she could have on a man, she'd felt the effect he could have on her, and she adored everything about it. But she denied herself that ultimate pleasure with anyone else, kept herself far enough away from the top of the stairs so she wouldn't be tempted to dance all the way down and fall into the warm pool at the bottom.

During her third year at school their situation changed. Fred was out of Brown and had taken over part of his father's company, the division that constructed shopping centres in midwestern states. So they saw each other more often. Usually two weekends a month. Or three if he was really nearby.

Their love affair fell into a pleasant routine now. Like a rehearsal for marriage. They stayed in hotels as man and wife and began to have a relationship that went beyond wedding-night fireworks and acrobatics. At the end of those months as she finished her spring semester, they felt, each of them, as if they'd been married for a year.

'We've had our honeymoon,' Fred said. 'Now let's get married.'

'We've been like married for months,' she answered. 'When do I get my honeymoon?'

Her decision to go away that summer, to take a waitress job on Martha's Vineyard, had baffled even Grace. And Christine's grandmother had been immensely disturbed. Margaret Jernegan, that year, was still in shock from the riots at the Democratic convention in Chicago. She thought she saw a student radical behind every tree. 'That East Coast is a ferment of dissent and hooliganism. And Massachusetts is the centre of it all. Bombs and posters and girls without brassieres.'

Fred's reaction had been most maddening of all. 'Don't be silly,' he said when she told him. 'That's the dumbest thing I've ever heard of.'

'It may be dumb to you but it's not dumb to me. I was twenty years old in January and I've never worked a day in my life. Do you realize that?'

'So what? Most people wouldn't work at all if they didn't have to.'

'*You* don't have to work,' she said, 'but I notice you're working. You work yourself half to death. You must put in eighty hours a week.'

'That's different. It's my company and I'm a . . .' He stopped himself but not in time.

'You're a *man*,' she said. 'Is that what you were going to say?'

'I didn't mean it the way it sounds.'

'Well, I'm a woman. And I want to work. I don't want to sit in dreary Lake Forest for the rest of my life like my grandmother. A switchboard, three secretaries, a teletype machine, and a stock ticker. All that just to keep her informed about her investments, to tell her how much money we've made today. What kind of a life is that?'

Fred pulled back a bit but didn't fold. 'I understand what you're saying. You're right. But why work in a restaurant? Why not work in Chicago? Or Indianapolis?'

'Because I don't want a playpen job where somebody pays me five hundred dollars a week just because my name's Wheatley. I got this job on my own. They gave it to me because they think I need it. I want to earn wages and live on what I make. Most people do that all their lives. I don't know why everybody's so shocked that I want to do it for one summer.'

Later that night, when they were lying in bed together in a hotel in St Louis, Fred said, just before he went to sleep, 'You know something, I think you're right about that job. I'm proud of you.'

Christine lay awake for a long time, her head still on his shoulder, her arm across his chest. She felt warm and safe and relaxed. She loved having him beside her, loved feeling the steady thump of his heart, hearing his regular breathing. But for the first time she could remember, her imagination broke loose and ran ahead of her like an untrained spaniel. For the first time she considered a life for herself that was open-end, where all the pieces were not precut and carefully stencilled.

During those hours on the beaches near Gay Head, through much of the long night she spent in the tourist cabin she had rented, Christine's consciousness was crowded with snippets of sense memory and half-forgotten dialogues. She was trying still not to reach for conclusions and decisions, trying to let things wash over her and settle and find their proper niches. But in one area she was clear and specific. Like a litany, she kept silently reminding herself, '*You* are not Grace, Fred is *not* Harold Wheatley, Roy Lavidge is *not* Russell Atha. This is all about *you*. It has absolutely nothing to do with your mother's life, where she made mistakes and where she didn't.'

Early in the afternoon of her second day at Gay Head, she put her belongings in the car, paid her bill, and started back toward Edgartown. On the way she stopped at a store in West Tisbury, bought a basket, and filled it with food. Cheddar cheese, Swiss cheese, and a wedge of Roquefort. A salami, a pound of braunschweiger, and a half pound of Polish ham. A pot of butter, English mustard, two loaves of crusty Italian bread, kosher pickles, and green olives. And a still-warm, homemade cherry pie. At a liquor store across the road she bought a bottle of Muscadet, a Brouilly, and a Côte de Rhône. And she made sure the clerk put a corkscrew in the bag.

Roy had already left the construction site and was halfway down the street toward Mario's when she pulled up beside him at the kerb. 'Get in,' she said. 'We're going for a picnic.'

He got into the car and closed the door behind him. 'I thought you'd disappeared. Up in smoke.'

'I did,' she said, 'but I'm back.'

She drove south again to a tiny beach she'd found the day before, great craggy rocks shielding it from the road, rocks on either side cutting it off from the other sections of beach. Hiding the car in the trees near the road, they carried the basket to a grassy area and spread an old blanket she'd found in the car trunk. They sat watching the sun go down and drank the Muscadet. Roy built a fire as it started to get dark; they ate their food by the crackling driftwood and drank both bottles of the red wine.

'Are you drunk?' she said.

'I guess I should be but I'm not.'

'I'm not either.'

They took their clothes off then, ran down across the sand to the black, cold water, and dived in. When they came back, shivering, Roy heaped more wood on the fire, and they towelled each other dry as the flames blazed beside them. Then they lay down on the blanket and made love till the fire burned low and glowed deep red in the darkness. Tangled together in the blanket, they slept till the sun came up.

Chapter 10

*T*he day after her night on the beach with Roy, Christine wrote to Fred Deets in Indianapolis.

This is going to be a crappy letter. But I'm too cowardly to talk to you on the telephone.

I don't know how to start. I remember that it hurt my feelings terribly when I was fourteen or fifteen and you were starting to zip around with those beautiful, hateful girls I used to see you with. I don't mean you hurt me on purpose. But it hurt all the same.

Have I ever hurt *you* in that way? I don't think so. I certainly tried not to. The hard part is that I'm going to hurt you now. I know it and I can't avoid it.

I met a man here. A man, a boy, a guy . . . whatever. He's my age. Goes to school, in Maine. I'm not exactly sure how I feel about him or how he feels about me. But it's not something casual for either one of us.

My first two years in college, when you were still at Brown, both of us went out with other people. But there was never anything that trespassed on the way you and I were together, the things we did in the night.

God, all this sounds dreary and coldblooded, but it's the best I can do. I'm trying to be honest, Fred. I *am* being honest. And I don't feel cold about it at all. I feel miserable. You know how important you are to me. I've always loved you, even before I was *in* love with you. I was proud of the fact that I'd never made love to anyone but you. But . . . I can't say that anymore. I'm sure you guessed it from the way I'm carrying on.

I'm not sure what's going to happen with Roy and me. We haven't talked about it. When September comes he may tell me to get lost. But I don't think so.

I can't stop you from telephoning me but I'd like it

better if you didn't. At least for the moment. I'm telling you, in this letter, everything I know about the situation, *our* situation. And *please* don't come swooping out here in your Cessna. Everybody here, including Roy, thinks I'm a regular college girl working as a waitress because she needs the money. I'd like them to go on thinking that.

I'm not saying good-bye, this is the end, or any foolishness like that. As soon as I get back to Lake Forest I want to see you. But for now, you have to give me some time and some space to find out where I am and where I'm going.

Don't be mad at me if you can help it. I didn't want anything to happen to us. Not ever. But something *has* happened and I can't ignore it. And I couldn't not tell you.

Chapter 11

*L*ate afternoon. Roy and Christine sat in a corner booth at Mario's. Each of them had a stein of beer. 'How do you feel today?' Roy said.

'I felt terrific. I feel terrific. How did you feel?'

'A little bombed out. In bed at five. Up at six. Pouring concrete at seven.'

'I'm sorry I kept you up,' she said.

'No, you're not. Neither am I. I wasn't complaining.'

'That's good.'

'It was a very nice picnic,' he said.

She reached out and put her hand on his. 'You're not gonna say, "You're a nice kid but don't get any ideas"?'

'No. Nothing like that. You can get all the ideas you want.'

'Good,' she said. 'I've got a few already. Like how would you like it if I cooked you a terrific dinner tonight?'

'Don't you have to work?'

She shook her head. 'Angie put me on the morning shift. Breakfast and lunch. Up at six. Just like you. No nights, no weekends. Except for Saturday breakfasts.'

'How'd you wangle that?'

'It was easy. Nobody else wants to get up.'

When they got into a blue Pontiac sedan parked behind Mario's, Roy said, 'Whose car?'

'It's a loaner. Some people I met in the restaurant.'

When she drove east out of Edgartown, turned south, then west on the road to West Tisbury, he said, 'Where are we going?'

'Surprise. We're going to a surprise house where I'm going to cook you a surprise dinner.'

When she turned into a rough side road opposite the airport and drove across the low dunes toward the ocean, he said, 'Now what?' And she said, 'You'll see.'

After a ten-minute drive on the twisting road, no houses or buildings on either side, she turned sharp left and drove a hundred yards to the edge of a pond, a one-storey clapboard house sitting just beside it. She pulled into the carport and shut off the engine. 'Here we are.'

'Whose house?' he said.

'A writer named Adler and his wife. They had to go to New York. He's writing a movie for one of the networks. So they asked me to house-sit for a week.'

'Where do I fit in?'

'I look after the house. You look after me. I told them I had a friend. They liked that. They said they'd worry if I was out here alone at night.'

Later that night, when they were lying in bed, her head on his shoulder, night birds gurgling outside by the edge of the pond, she said, 'I'm not very good at playing games.'

'That's good. Neither am I.'

'Just because I don't flutter my eyelashes and blush pink whenever the toilet flushes, I don't want you to think that I'm some ballsy female marathon runner, somebody who has to make all the rules and manage events. Do you think that?'

'I don't know. I've never seen you run.'

'I'm serious. You know what I mean. All the women's magazines say that men are very threatened by a woman who goes ahead and does things. You think that's true?'

'I don't know. I never thought about it.'

'Then it's *not* true for you. If it were you *would* have thought about it. Lots of times.'

'What time is it?' he said.

She switched on the bed lamp and looked at her watch on the nightstand. 'Ten thirty.'

'God. It feels like midnight. What time did we go to bed?'

'Eight thirty,' she said. 'We had an early dinner. You said it would be good for us to get some rest since we were up so late last night.'

'Is that what I said?'

'Something like that. I was distracted. I wasn't listening closely.'

'You seem to get distracted easily.'

'I do with you,' she said. She raised up one elbow then, the sheet falling away from her shoulders, the bed lamp silhouetting her upper body. 'But don't get the wrong idea. Just because I can't keep my hands off you doesn't mean I'm Easy Edna from down the block.'

'I didn't ask you any questions. Did I ask you any questions?'

'No. But I'm giving you answers anyway. God, it sounds silly when you try to say it . . .'

'Then don't do it.'

'I want to. I've had the same boyfriend for three years. I've known him all my life . . .'

'You already told me about him. He gives watches away.'

'. . . I've slept with him. But nobody else. Not till now.' She switched off the light and snuggled close to him under the sheet.

'He's a nice guy,' she said. 'You'd like him if you met him.'

'You want to bet?'

'What about you?' she said then.

'You mean do I have a girl friend?'

'You got it.'

'I lost count when I got to three hundred.'

'Three hundred's all right. *One* is what I'm worried about.'

'Not to worry,' he said.

'No one?'

'No one special. You're the first girl who's ever really distracted me.'

Chapter 12

*A*mong Russell Atha's notes and research folders, in addition to the material I included at the beginning, I found some sort of beginning to the story of his meeting and falling in love with Grace Wheatley.

Why was I in France that summer? The logic of that period—I was twenty-two—seems arbitrary now. Paradoxical. Sensing that I was an empty container, I proceeded, nonetheless, to abandon whatever I did have that was solid and sure and financially promising.

First, after a year of classes, I abandoned Ohio Wesleyan. This decision left my father anxious and confused, until I explained that he must no longer expect me to function in any way in his business, located on the principal shopping street of Fort Thomas, Kentucky.

Big jump then. Across the river to Cincinnati. Almost two years there, working for a wholesale furniture company, selling carloads of chairs and sofas to retailers in Ohio and Indiana and Kentucky, practising charm and persuasion, earning a decent amount of money, saving most of it, living cheap.

Sliding also into a cruel relationship with a black cocktail waitress who had followed the Ohio River up from Louisville, where her husband managed the bar at Churchill Downs.

Out of an ugly marriage and a neglected childhood she had emerged, not with a desire for warmth and affection, but with an insatiable hunger for punishment. I hurt her in many ways, no doubt of it, both deliberately and accidentally, but never in the ways she wanted. I refused to degrade her or beat her so she felt worthless and unloved. If I hadn't abandoned her when I did, she would surely have abandoned me.

In that same week I abandoned Cincinnati. Sold my dreary furniture and my grey Plymouth, emptied out my savings account, and took a bus east to Atlanta. After only a week or so, I abandoned Georgia and hitchhiked to Miami. Then, with high spirits and a painful Bacardi hang-over, I abandoned the entire red-white-and-blue mother country and sailed on a Greek freighter for Lisbon.

When Russell went to Europe, I was already there. In January of 1949, after my fifth semester at New York University, I added up my credit hours and found I was a full semester ahead of myself. So I went to Europe. Sailed from Hoboken. Thirteen days to Antwerp, then by night train south to Paris. Through Harvey Stark, I got a room where he was living in Montparnasse, on rue Vavin, at the Hotel de Blois. And there in the lobby of that little hotel, the first four floors reserved for prostitutes and their clients, the top two for indigent students and other permanent residents, in March, I met Russell Atha for the first time.

The concierge was a tall, white-haired man in his sixties, silent and out of sight for the most part, clean-looking and curt. His wife, Claudine, a Breton like her husband, did most of the work. Oversaw the kitchen and the bar, was available to hand out towels whenever the *poule* bell tinkled in the entryway, collected the rents, and generally made herself pleasantly conspicuous. She was a tall woman, broad shoulders and hips, light on her feet, and very rare in the concierge profession, quick to laugh. Her hair was grey and thick and carelessly cut; she had strong white farm-girl teeth, a warm and absolutely irresistible smile, and hypnotic blue eyes.

Her cat was usually draped across her arm, a big and lazy soft-eyed animal with a grey coat that precisely matched Claudine's hair. And her dog, a smooth-haired black-and-white terrier named Honoré, was always at her heels as she made her endless trips up and down the six flights of stairs, supervising the *bonnes*.

One day at noon as I was going to lunch at Chez Wadja after a morning's work, Claudine was standing in the lower hall with a tall young man in a suede jacket, a leather valise sitting at his feet. 'I think this is one of your compatriots,' she said to me in French. 'When I talk, he understands nothing. When he talks, I understand less.'

'She only speaks French,' I said. 'Can I help out?'

'I'm looking for a room. Some guy in the café on the corner said maybe I could get one here.'

When I told Claudine what he wanted, she asked if he wanted a place by the day or the month.

'The cheapest way,' he said. 'I expect to be here for a while. Maybe a year.'

I passed this on to Claudine. She said there was only one room available by the month. I knew the place. I'd stayed there myself when I first moved into the Blois.

'There's a small room available,' I said. 'On the top floor. You may not want it. The bed's a disaster.'

'How much is it?'

'Three thousand francs a month.'

'How much is that in real money?'

44

'Nine bucks or so. If you change your money on the black market the room will cost even less.'

'I'll take it.'

'You'd better take a look at it first.'

'I don't have to. It's all right. I'll make out.'

'After that I didn't see him for several days. Then one evening when I was having a coffee at the Kosmos he came over and sat down at my table.

'How's the room?' I said.

'How's the room? Let me see. The window won't close so I freeze my ass every night. The bed's too short for me. The faucet in the sink never stops dripping. And the mattress is stuffed with corn husks. Also the armoire door comes off every time I open it.'

'If you tell Claudine you want something better, she'll move you as soon as another room opens up.'

'I don't *want* to move. You didn't let me finish. I think it's a great joint. Just what I want. The bottom rung. I feel like Raskolnikov. Looking for a pawnbroker.'

After I'd known him for two months or so, had seen him nearly every day, had talked with him many times, he admitted he was trying to do some writing.

'I'd like to see what you're doing,' I said.

'No. You wouldn't. It's just chicken scratches.'

'Did you ever take any courses?'

'No. I don't want any of that shit. What I need to know, nobody can teach me. It'll either come or it won't. I don't want to write something that's already been written.'

'Nobody does.'

'Bullshit. Most of the stuff you read, the guy who wrote it never had a gut idea in his life. If he did, he'd run away from it. Never been laid, never been in a fight, never swung a pick. Never did anything except read other people's books and try to copy them. No muscle. No bones and no blood.'

That night, in my journal, I wrote:

Atha seems to have some notion of himself as a raw,

creative force. Thomas Wolfe sideways. Primitive. Bare knuckles. 'Proust is a faggot and Conrad's a bore.' Guys like him, unless I miss my guess, are a dime a dozen. Talking and theorizing and throwing hand grenades to hide their own deficiencies. No wonder he doesn't want anybody to read what he's written. He probably hasn't written anything at all. He's always in the cafés, usually with a girl, or two, usually drunk. Doing research. I'm sure that's his rationale; gaining experience, gathering data. He doesn't have any conception of how to work on a regular schedule as I'm doing, as anybody else does who's serious. He's a talker, that's all. Pay no attention to him.

But I did pay attention. That night I got out the manuscript I'd been labouring on for months, slid a fifty-page section out of the centre, sat down and read it through.

Atha's words were still fresh in my memory. The more I read my worked-over pages, the more my stomach contracted. When I stopped reading at last and went to bed, I lay awake for a long time, questioning my judgement and my abilities. Questioning everything.

Chapter 13

*A*fter Russell discovered Micheline Pignot, I didn't see him very often. I was taking a class every day at the Alliance Française and the rest of the time I was grinding away on my manuscript, feeling queasy about it, not fully recovered yet from that sleepless night when I'd concluded that I was trying to duplicate Stonehenge with marshmallows.

When I did see him, he was loose and grinning always, drinking and talking and enjoying himself, his face suntanned now from sitting on café terraces. He was totally uninterested, it seemed, in anything more profound than which café served the best *croque-monsieur*, which bar had the best Alsatian beer.

One afternoon in early June, however, he knocked on my door. It was a welcome interruption. I had been staring at a blank page for two hours as the ink dried up in my pen and my eyes kept drifting across the room to the shafts of sunlight slanting down through the curtains.

As soon as he sat down he said, 'Avignon. How does that sound to you? I'm going down there tomorrow. Third class on the Blue Train. Thought you might like to come along.'

'Why Avignon?'

'Why not? I passed through there on the way up here from Portugal and the place startled me. In the words of Gully Jimson, it skinned my eyeballs. A bloody marvellous cathedral where the crusaders stopped to water their horses, the onetime palace of the Pope, and Villeneuve where the Romans lived. It's like a history book. And there's the Rhône River crawling along through the centre of town. And all those thousands of bottles of wine waiting to be guzzled. What more do you want? Don't tell me. I know. What *you* want is to stay at that table in the corner, very bad light there, incidentally, and finish your significant book. Am I right?'

'You're right.'

Five days later I had a postcard from him, a low-angle photograph, black-and-white, of Notre Dame des Doms in Avignon.

No disappointments here. No disillusion or failed hopes. All facets gleaming and rewarding. All faucets gleaming and regurgling. Wine flows red and girls drop dead when I pass by, clad in Papal robes, scattering the ashes of charred hymnals. Am I sober? Of course not. If

47

all goes well with the Châteauneuf-du-Pape, I may never be sober again.

Two weeks later I had a letter from him with a ten-thousand-franc note folded inside.

I am detained. I am fully occupied and gloriously detained. Please pay my rent for two months so madame Claudine will not reclaim my niche under the eaves. I may ask you to send along a couple of my shirts, too. Then again, I may not. I may, instead, commission the nuns of the lyceum (are there nuns in a lyceum?) to run me up a dozen garments of fine baize, my monogram embroidered on the pocket in virginal white.

If you promise not to bruit it about the quarter (consideration for the feelings and sensitivities of Micheline) I will tell you my schoolboy secret. I am in love. Childishly, totally, and desperately. I am a caricature. A stumbling cliché out of Molière. The village idiot smitten by the passing Princess. Except she didn't pass. She stopped. And she is as giddy and crazy and sweetly insatiable as I am. From Chicago. Can you believe that? How can it be? Did Botticelli ever visit Chicago?

Enough of this rhapsodic shit. I don't know why I feel driven to confide in you, but sometimes—have you experienced this—you have to confide in somebody. It's ironic to me that I, Mr Cynical Fast-and-Loose, should just now be cut down like a lodgepole pine. But I have been. An exquisite young woman named Grace.

I now have no plans that do not include her. In fact I have no plan at all *except* her. Nor do I expect to have. There are awkward details that I will explain when I see you. But nothing the two of us, me and Grace, can't deal with. If you are the kind of lamebrained asshole who goes around rejoicing in other people's happiness, then please rejoice in mine. Because that's what *I'm* doing. Night and day.

No word from him then, no communcation at all, till early August. Then one morning, unannounced, he showed up at my door. Freshly barbered, smartly dressed, with the aroma of last night's wine following him like a mist into the room.

'When did you get back?' I said.

'About ten days ago. I wanted to get over here sooner, but things have been hectic. Lots of things to do.'

'Where are you staying?'

'We're in an apartment out by the Bois-de-Boulogne. I want you to come out and have a meal with us when things get settled down.'

'You look a little hassled. Is everything all right?'

'Fantastic. Everything's great with Grace and me. But . . . there are some complications. She's married. And she has a little daughter. But it's not the way it sounds. She left her husband last summer. That's why she came to Europe, to get away from him. She had the baby in Avignon. She's not even in touch with the husband or her family. They don't know where she is.'

'Don't know or don't care?'

'Don't know. *He* cares all right, the son of a bitch. She's only twenty years old, for God's sake. She never could stand the bastard. I'm telling you, it's like something out of the Middle Ages. Two families with a lot of money and not much sense decide to merge their money. But the contract they sign is a wedding contract. They pressured her into a corner and before she knew it she ended up married.'

'Now what?'

'Just details. That's all. She has her own money so they can't squeeze her there. She'll get a divorce if she can. But if she can't, we'll just live together. It doesn't matter to us. Nobody can force her stay with a man she doesn't want to be with.'

Two weeks later, when I came home late one evening, Madame Claudine came out of her parlour behind the staircase and said, 'Your *ami*, Mr Atha, was looking for you. He waited for almost three hours. He was very upset.'

'Did he leave a telephone number?'

49

She shook her head. 'He was going to the airport. He told me he would fly to Chicago tonight.' She looked at her watch. 'He's up in the air by now.'

In September, less than a week before I was to leave for New York to start the fall semester, he came back. He was grey faced and thin and looked five years older than when I'd met him six months before. I was with him almost all the time for those few days before I left. That was the period when he couldn't eat, when he couldn't stop drinking and couldn't get drunk. He sat for long silent hours as the same table in the Kosmos, facing the street outside, his eyes staring, his cheeks flat and pale. When he spoke, he said the same thing, over and over. 'She tried to kill herself. They wouldn't let her alone. They kept after her till she tried to kill herself.'

Chapter 14

*I*n that year, 1969, when Christine and Roy met on Martha's Vineyard, more than a hundred US soldiers a week were dying in combat in Vietnam, a Czech student burned himself to death to protest the Russian occupation of his country, and Sirhan Sirhan was convicted for the murder of Robert Kennedy. In Chicago, eight young people were found not guilty of inciting to riot. Jack Kerouac died and so did Eisenhower, Sir Osbert Sitwell, and Mies van der Rohe. Charles Manson and his disciples were indicted for the murders of seven people, Neil Armstrong walked on the moon, and Mary Jo Kopechne drowned in a stream on Chappaquiddick Island. On Martha's Vineyard Cuba

Hostetler was pregnant and she was delighted. Tom Peddicord received his notice to report for induction into the armed services and he was delighted too.

'A lot of people in this country really have their heads up their asses,' he told Roy. 'They think we should just walk away from this thing in Vietnam and let the Communists take over. Not me. They have to be stopped someplace, and I figure Vietnam's as good a place as any. My dad fought in the South Pacific, and he says there ain't ever been a slant-eyed squat yet that could take on one of our guys and win. It stands to reason. We can outproduce and outfight anybody. Besides all the guns and rockets, we got the napalm. Dad says that's the answer. Burn up the whole fucking country. Turn it into a cinder. Then we'll see how quick the Russians will want to start up someplace else.'

To Christine, Cuba said, 'Tom and I are tickled to death we're going to have a baby. It ain't an accident either. We wanted it to happen. Everything free and natural. Like Adam and Eve.'

'Oh for God's sake, Cuba, are you wacky? Tom has no education, no trade, no profession, and now he's going into the army.'

'It's all right. We've got it worked out. We'll get married as soon as he finishes basic training. If they send him overseas, I'll stay on Staten Island with my folks and finish up my work at Columbia. Mom can help me with the baby when it comes, and everything will work out just fine. Tom and I couldn't be happier.'

'Happy? Don't you know what's going on in Vietnam? It's a madhouse over there. War games for lunatics. We can't *win*. There's nothing *to* win. All we can do is go on killing people. Why do you think we've got soldiers deserting by the thousands? Why do you think Canada and Sweden are crowded with guys Tom's age who either won't go to Vietnam or won't go back after their home leave is up?'

'Tom gets mad when anybody even mentions that. He says those guys are a lot of cowards.'

'Then God help him. He's going to get a big surprise.'

'I'll bet Roy wouldn't go running off to Canada with his tail between his legs. When the time comes, I bet he'll feel the same way about it that Tom does.'

'Maybe you're right. But I hope not.'

By this time, early in August, Christine and Roy had long since settled in, in the house by the pond. Five days a week they got up before six in the morning. By seven they were both at work, he at the construction site, she at the restaurant. On Saturdays Christine had to be at the restaurant to serve breakfast, but she was home before noon. The rest of that day and all day Sunday they had to themselves. They walked on the beach, lay on a blanket in the sun, swam and drank beer and read books on the screened-in porch overlooking the pond.

It was a quiet house. No radio and no television set. And except when they went to work, they almost never went into Edgartown or West Tisbury or Vineyard Haven.

They seemed settled and content. And they were. But ten days after the first night they stayed together in the house, before Christine had moved out of the apartment near the restaurant and Roy had left his furnished room on Grayfox Street, they had a discussion that almost ended their summer together before it had properly begun.

The conversation started calmly as they sat on the porch having coffee after dinner.

'The week was up a couple of days ago, wasn't it?' Roy said.

'What week?'

'Didn't you tell me the people who own this house . . . what's their name?'

'The Adlers.'

'I thought you said they'd be gone for just a week.'

'Oh,' she said. 'Yes, that's what they said. But I guess they had to stay in New York a little longer. She said she'd let me know exactly when they'd be back.'

'Maybe they won't come back at all,' Roy said. 'Maybe we'll get to stay here all summer.'

'Wouldn't that be nice?'

'It sure would. But I guess there's no chance of that.'

'I don't know. It could happen, I guess,' Christine said.

'You think so? You think there's really a chance we might stay here for the rest of the summer? Straight through to Labour Day?'

She didn't answer for a moment. Then she said, 'Why do I have the feeling that you're giving me the third degree?'

'I don't know. Why would I do that?'

'I'll bite. Why would you?'

'I wouldn't. Unless I thought you were playing some kind of a game with me and I couldn't figure out why.'

'What kind of game are we talking about?'

'I don't know. You tell me.'

'Cut it out Roy, don't gaslight me. I hate this kind of stuff.'

'So do I. I hate it when somebody looks me straight in the eye and hands me a line of crap.

'I don't know what you're talking about.'

'Yes, you do,' he said. 'You know exactly what I'm talking about. You told me the car we've been driving belonged to the Adlers. It doesn't. It came from the Avis agency in Edgartown.'

'I didn't say they *owned* it.'

'They didn't rent it either. *You* did. Ten days ago.'

'Who says so?'

'*I* do. This is a small island and Edgartown is a small town. Tom has a couple of sisters who know every girl who works in every store and agency on the island.'

'All right. So I rented a car. What difference does that make?'

'It doesn't make *any* difference. I just don't know why you'd want to lie about it. You rented this house too. From July Fourth till Labour Day. Wrote out a cheque for five thousand dollars.'

'You've really been busy, haven't you?'

'No, I haven't. But *you* have.'

'When did you find time to do all this private investigation work?'

'I didn't investigate anything. I sit down and eat my lunch out of a bucket every day and Tom Peddicord tells me all the gossip he's picked up from his sisters. When a college girl who's waiting tables for Angie Duncan starts writing cheques for five grand and leasing a car for three hundred and fifty a month, you shouldn't be surprised if people pay attention. When you make up a whole fancy story to tell me, you can't be surprised if *I* wonder why. It's open season on bullshit. I can find that anywhere. From you I thought I was getting something else.'

It was still light outside, but the evening sun was low now over the dunes and the pond was slowly turning from blue-green to black. Christine sat silent in her chair, looking out through the screen wire at the water. Finally she said, 'I've got the ball. I know that. I just wish I had something brilliant to say.'

'You don't have to say anything if you don't want to. You're not on trial.'

'Oh, yes, I am. You know it and and I know it. I tried to get away with something and I got caught.'

'Forget it. Let's forget the whole thing.'

'Oh, boy . . . you're really pissed off, aren't you?'

'What do you think? Figure it out.'

'You think if I didn't tell the truth about a couple of things, the car and this house . . . you think because of that, that everything else was fake, too?'

He sat looking at her in the dim light and didn't answer.

'Boy, are you dumb,' she said then.

'Yeah, I guess so.'

'Why do you think I made up that story? I *hate* to lie and I hate it when people lie to me. But I was afraid if I told you the truth, I'd scare you off. After that first night on the beach all I could think was that I didn't want it to end. I wanted us to have some time together. Go to sleep together and get up together. I love you. I love everything about you. But maybe I guessed wrong. Maybe if I'd said, "Look, I've got a little money. Why don't I find a house for us so we can have a nice summer?" you'd have said, "Gee, that's a good idea. Go ahead." Is that what you'd have said?'

'I'd have said five thousand dollars is not a *little* money.

Especially for somebody who's waiting tables for a peanut salary and tips.'

'All right,' she said, 'we can bury that one. In case you haven't guessed it by now, I took the waitress job because I *wanted* to work. I'm proud of myself for finding the job and for being good at it once I found it. But if I told you I *need* the salary and tips I'm earning, I'd be lying to you.'

'I got the message. That part I figured out for myself.'

'My father has a lot of money,' she said. 'And *his* father has a lot of money. My grandmother and my mother each have a lot of money. And I have a ton of money of my own. I knew you'd find it out sooner or later, but I wanted you to get to know me first. So I told you a fib. And under the same circumstances, I'd do the same thing again. Almost everybody I've ever met has a big reaction if they think you have money. Either they like you more all of a sudden. Or they like you less. In your case I was afraid you'd like me less. Or not like me at all. So which is it? Where are we?'

'What do you mean?'

'I mean are we going to go to bed tonight and be sweet to each other, or are you going to be different now?'

She crossed the porch, almost dark now, and sank down on the floor by his chair. 'I'm crazy about you, but it has to be good for you, too. Are you gonna run away now?' He didn't answer. 'Do you want *me* to run away?' she said.

She felt his hand on her cheek. She leaned forward and kissed him, holding his head between her hands. Then she stood up straight, pulled her cotton gown off over her head, and dropped it on the floor. Standing there silvery naked just in front of his chair, she said, 'Let's take a terrific swim.'

He leaned forward, put his arms around her hips, and pulled her toward him; he pressed his face against her stomach and held her close.

Chapter 15

*A*s soon as Fred Deets read the letter from Christine telling him about Roy, he tried to telephone her. For a week he called three or four times a day, at all hours. At the restaurant Angie Duncan, alerted beforehand, told him each time that Christine was too busy to come to the phone or that she wasn't there at all, that she was working another shift.

When he called the apartment, no matter how late at night, one of the girls always said that Christine wasn't home yet. Finally, very late one night, Cuba answered the phone and said, 'Christine's not living here anymore. She moved.' When Fred asked if there was a telephone number where she was living, Cuba said, 'No. They don't have a phone, but if you give me your number I'll have her call you.'

'This is Fred Deets. She knows the number.'

The next evening Christine called him, from a telephone booth at the Vineyard airport. His voice sounded calm and easy. 'There you are,' he said. 'The missing link. Boy, are you hard to find. I must have called thirty times.'

'I know. I asked you please not to.'

'I know you did. But you didn't expect to buy *that*, did you?'

'I meant what I said in the letter. I don't want to hurt you. But there's nothing more I can say. . . .'

'Sure there is. There's always something to say.'

'Then we'll say it in the fall. We'll talk it out then when I come home.'

'Where are you calling from now?'

'A phone booth. There's no phone where we're living.'

'Where *we're* living?' he said.

'That's right. *We*. Roy and I.'

'You didn't waste any time, did you?'

'No, I didn't. And don't try to lay some guilt trip on me. Because I don't feel guilty at all. I played it as straight as I knew how with you. I just wish I . . .'

He cut in then. 'How did you think I'd react to that letter you sent me?'

'I didn't know. I was hoping you'd understand.'

'Did you think I'd just roll over and play dead?'

'I thought . . . I tried to . . .'

'Well, I can't do that,' he said. 'I'm not made that way. Maybe *you* can just cut everything off like a piece of ribbon, but I can't. Maybe it's convenient for you right now if I just disappear. But I'm not going to do that. If I can get you out of this tailspin you're in, I'm going to do it. At least I'm going to try. You've heard about hard losers. Well, I'm the hardest loser you're ever going to see.'

The following weekend Fred flew from Indianapolis to Lake Forest to visit his mother and father. When he dropped in to see Grace late Saturday afternoon, she hugged him, kissed him on both cheeks, and gave him a Scotch and soda. But she gave him no information.

'Did she say anything to you about meeting someone?' Fred asked.

Grace took a long, slow sip from her drink, trying to balance honesty and loyalty. Coming down on the side of loyalty, she said, 'No, she didn't. But I have to be in Boston in a couple of weeks. I hope she can fly over to have dinner with me. Maybe I'll find out then what's in her head.'

When he left a while later, Fred drove out through the stone gates, turned left, and drove along the walls that encircled the Jernegan compound. At the east gate he turned in and parked in front of Margaret Jernegan's two-storey brick-and-timber house. She was delighted to see him, served him tea and scones, and listened carefully to everything he had to say.

Four days later, Christine received a registered letter from her grandmother.

I'm certain you will detest this letter and you will undoubtedly detest me for writing it. But when you're a few years older you will realize that I always act in what I think are your best interests.

I have always been candid with you about your mother. I love her, you know that, but she has been a disappointment to me and, I'm afraid, to herself. Because of that, perhaps, I have taken a greater interest in your life, your character, and your development, than one would normally expect from a grandmother. I know you have resented it at times, but all the same I have to continue to do my best for you. The only efforts that count are *best efforts*. I know you've heard me say that a thousand times, but it would be no less true if I had said it a million times.

Now . . . the business at hand. Fred Deets came to see me yesterday. He told me about the letter you wrote to him recently. When he asked me to read it, I said, 'Not as a spectator, Fred. If there's a problem with Christine, don't expect me merely to nod my head and do nothing about it. If you show me the letter, I will *tell* her you showed me the letter, and I will handle it with her in whatever way seems wisest to me.' So that's what I'm doing.

You're an intelligent young woman, Christine. You surely know somewhere inside that the life you want, the life you're intended for, is the life you've always had.

I think you know, too, that for you there's no better person than Fred. He'll be an excellent husband and father. Don't let some summer aberration on an island blind you to what is best for you. I know you don't think of me as a woman of the world, but nonetheless, please take this advice: have your fling, have your fun, and then leave it behind you. Your life is here in Lake Forest.

One last reminder. When Grace was your age, she made a spectacular error of judgement that coloured a large part of her life. Don't let that happen to you, Christine. Just remember who you are, where you came from, and where you're going.

Chapter 16

*I*t was the end of the first week in August, dry and deadly hot at the Martha's Vineyard airport. And in Boston, when Christine's plane landed there, it was even hotter, heavy with humidity and the rotten summer smells of the city.

She sat at lunch with her mother, by a window in the second-floor dining room of the Ritz-Carlton, the Boston garden green and steaming down below, the sky heavy and white and sunless, the tree foliage hanging low and limp and dusty green.

'You look sensational,' Grace said. 'All brown and pink and freckles on your nose. Can't you get me a job in that restaurant? I could save five thousand dollars on my Elizabeth Arden bill. How do you think I'd be as a waitress?'

'Terrible. You can't add.'

'That's true. I thought that's what cashiers did.'

'Not where I work,' Christine said. 'It's hometown style. Everybody does everything.'

'You told me you cooked thirty pounds of cottage fries one morning. I couldn't believe it. I told Carol Applegate and she was shocked.'

After the captain had taken their food order, Grace said, 'I hear Margaret sent you a poison-pen letter. She told me you were following in my footsteps. Right?'

'Something like that. But that was just part of it. She covered all the bases. She ended up preaching pot and promiscuity. "Take your pill every morning, don't give strangers your home address, and be back in Lake Forest before school starts." '

'Did you answer the letter?'

'Sure. You brought me up polite, didn't you? I wrote her a note the next day.'

'Saying what?'

'Saying I'm a big girl and I have to make my own decisions.'

'Any answer to that?' Grace said.

'Silence. Did she say anything to you?'

'Not since she told me she wrote to you. She only advertises her victories. She's very quiet about it when somebody slaps her down.' She lit a cigarette and sipped from her wine glass. 'Where do you stand at the moment with Fred?'

'I don't know. I feel rotten about that. I tried to be completely honest, and I guess that was a mistake. If I'd told him I was sleeping with a lesbian or turning tricks with summer tourists, maybe he could have handled that. He'd have got mad as hell, filed me away as a slut second class, and felt better about himself than he does now.'

'Nobody likes to be sluffed off. It's a rotten feeling.'

'God, I know that. And in this case it's worse. Because I really care about Fred. But I can't pretend that Roy never showed up. There's no way I can do that. Even if he kicked me out tomorrow . . .'

'Does Roy know about all this with Fred?'

'Sure he does. He says it's something I have to handle, and he's right. So I *have* handled it as well as I can. But I know I haven't seen the last of Fred. I know he'll show up on the Vineyard one of these days.'

'Then what?'

'Then I'll have to tell him in person what I've already told him on the telephone and in a letter.'

While they ate their lunch, she told Grace everything she knew about Roy. And what little she knew about his family.

'They're not like us, Grace. They're nothing at all like us or the people we know. And Roy's nothing like us. He's a plain regular guy. But he's smart and he's tough, and once he has an education he'll be able to compete anywhere and go after anything he wants. That's why he started running. Because he knew it would help him go to college. He's run five miles a day, *every* day, since he was twelve years old.'

'You say there's a chance he might transfer to Foresby?'

Christine held up her crossed fingers and nodded her head. 'He's having Bowdoin send his credit transcript to the admissions office at Foresby. And he wrote to Jim Hollenbeck, in the athletic department, to see if there's any chance he can get a track scholarship.'

'Do you want me to call Frank Ellerbie when I get home?'

'That's the first thing I thought of,' Christine said. 'Then I thought better of it. Roy doesn't like a lot of stuff going on that he doesn't know about.'

'That's easy to fix. *Tell* him about it. Tell him I know the president of the school and I'll call up and explain the situation. It can't hurt.'

Christine shook her head. 'I don't think so. I think he wants to handle it himself.'

Later in the afternoon, before Christine went to the airport to fly back to the Vineyard, Grace said, 'I have a lot of faith in you. You hardly ever go off half-cocked. And I don't think you're doing that now. But I have to ask you anyway. Are you absolutely sure you want to wind things up with Fred? It's easy to burn bridges. I'm an expert at it. It's not so easy to put them back up again.'

'All I know is how I *feel*. That's *all* I'm sure about. I've never met anyone before who took up all the air in my life. I've never had the feeling that I wanted to *fix* things, to make everything nice for someone. But I have that feeling now. And it's a marvellous, fantastic, *terrific* sensation. I don't want it to go away and I don't think it will. I don't think it's ever going to go away.'

Chapter 17

*R*ussell Atha's triumph, over me and everybody else, was a triumph of style. One drunken night in Montparnasse, after celebrating somebody's birthday near Alésia, we reeled home together down the avenue Général-Leclerc and Russell said, 'I am a man with a secret weapon. I'm an unassailable and impregnable bastard. I can't be hung up or shot down. There's nothing anybody can take from me that I'm not willing to do without.'

Was that a drunken joke or did he really belive it? *I* believed it. To a man like me who devoted a large share of his energies to avoiding failure or even the appearance of it, it was crippling to see Russell in action, tackling anything, taking on contrary theories and opinions, carousing and joking and bluffing his way through any situation or circumstance.

When he began to publish, the effect was the same. He leapfrogged from one project to another, tackled anything that caught his fancy, failed magnificently sometimes, but came away from those catastrophes with no apparent impulse to pull back or play safe. As I struggled forward, taking four years to finish a small novel, I was stunned by his productivity, baffled by his disdain of failure.

After I left Montparnasse that autumn to go back to school in New York, I didn't see him for more than six years. When we did meet again, in New York in 1956, he was divorced from Micheline and I'd been divorced from Sheila for six months. I was short of money and feeling guilty about living apart from my two daughters. Russell was prosperous from a recent book club sale, he'd just leased an apartment on Gramercy Park, and he felt no guilt about anything.

'Micheline's in great shape. And so is Jean-Claude. He's five years old and already he can kick a soccer ball out of sight. He's a tough little bastard. Looks like me. Except he's built like a fireplug. Takes after Micheline's dad. He was a footballer and a bike rider. Anyway the kid's great. He's on top of everything. And Micheline's setting the world on fire. She finished medical school and started practising pediatrics. Set up an office in St Malo. Now she's buying into a children's clinic. Money rolling in like rainwater. And she looks better than she's ever looked in her life. Prematurely grey. It runs in her family. Her old man was white when he was twenty-six years old. When he was a biker they called him Snowbird because of his hair. He lives out there in Bretagne too, in a town called Dinan just south of St Malo. He's a bird dog, still chasing the ladies. But he spends a lot of time with Jean-Claude. Running, swimming in the summer, kicking a soccer ball on the beach. The old man had three daughters. Never had a son. So he's having the time of his life. Micheline bought a big old house near the sea a year or so ago. And there's a guest cottage for me. So I fall in and out whenever I can. Sometimes I stay for a week. Sometimes, if I'm working on a book, I stay for two or three months. The kid likes it. He's always glad to see me when I show up. And when I leave he doesn't get nervous. Because he knows I'll be back.'

I asked him if Micheline was as happy with the arrangement as he and his son were, and he said, 'Sure she is. She doesn't hate me. We never did bad stuff to each other. We just decided not to be married anymore. Since then she's started a little arrangement with a doctor she works with. But nothing heavy. He's ten years older than she is. Married with four kids. They're not going anywhere and she knows it. So she likes it when I show up. We always have a lot to talk about. She reads my books and tells me what's wrong with them. And we still go to bed together once in a while. Why not? There sure as hell was nothing wrong with *that* part of our lives.'

When I left the West Village where I'd lived with my first wife, and moved into a big rent-controlled apartment on St Marks Place between First and Second Avenues, the divorce was far enough behind me so I could sleep through the night two nights out of three. I remember standing in that new apartment, looking down at the street, nothing in the room behind me but a bed, a wooden chair, and a telephone, and thinking that things would start fresh now. Walking the empty, spacious rooms from the parlour in the front to the huge bedroom in the back looking down on the garden, with four smaller rooms in between, I felt as if I'd found a solid work place, a home that made sense. Three days after I moved in I met Amy, at a friend's studio on Thompson Street. Ten days later she moved into my St Marks apartment, and two years after that we got married.

One night, a year or so after she'd met Russell for the first time, I told Amy how much I envied him. Her reaction was instantaneous. 'You're crazy. You *can't* envy Russell. He's too busy envying you. Do you think he really feels good about himself? All that jumping back and forth from one high-flash project to another. Do you think the situation with Micheline and his little boy is really the way he describes it? I don't. He feels awful about what he did to her. He married her for one reason—to try and cure himself of Grace. He knows it and Micheline knows it. They kept it in a box for as long as they could, and finally one day it jumped out. I guarantee it. Either *he* said something about it or *she* did. So they couldn't pretend anymore. They could separate or they could go on living together like zombies for the sake of the kid. I think they made the right choice. But it wasn't a perfect choice. There's never a perfect choice when kids are involved.'

'You may be right about *that*,' I said, 'but you're wrong about Russell. He's got a talent for dealing with things. He was born with it.'

'Boy, are you dumb. Russell can't deal with *anything*. Not really. I don't know what he was like before he got shot down by that rich chickie from Chicago, but since then he's been standing in a leaky boat. Did you notice that he never mentions her? Not ever. That means he's painted it over, bricked up that whole section of his life. Because he can't stand to look at it. He's drunk or half drunk every night, and he'll fall into bed with anybody who's breathing. Is that someone to envy? I don't think so.'

Chapter 18

*I*t was Tom Peddicord's last night on the Vineyard. Next morning he was due to report to New Bedford for induction into the Marine Corps. A week before, Christine had said to Roy, 'Why don't we ask him and Cuba to spend that last night here? There's that big bedroom in the back that we don't even use. I could cook a feast and we'll get a bunch of wine, and we can take them to the ferry on our way to work the next morning.'

'It's a nice idea. But they don't need company, do they? Why would they want us around?'

'I'll tell you why. Because they don't have anyplace else to go. They can't go to Tom's house with his folks there and all those kids. And she can't take him to the apartment. Because the landlady thinks screwing in her house is a Federal offence and she's the Attorney General.'

When Christine made the suggestion to Cuba, she began to cry. 'Oh, God, honey. That's the sweetest thing anybody ever did for me. We'd *love* that.'

The evening, however, didn't stay as simple as Christine had planned it. First off, Cuba invited their two waitress friends, Lucy and Margo. 'Their feelings would be hurt if we had a party without them.'

'It wasn't supposed to be a *party* exactly,' Christine said.

'I know it wasn't,' Cuba said. 'I know exactly what you're saying. But it'll be all right. I told them to come early. That means they'll go home early.'

On the party night, when Lucy and Margo drove in, both of them freshly bathed, shampooed, and cologned, Lucy wearing short shorts and a see-through shirt, Margo, in a pink muumuu, was leading by the hand a bearded young man named Lloyd Eitel, whose father sold real estate in Vineyard Haven. 'It's all right,' she whispered to Christine. 'He's a good guy. And we're leaving early. I don't want to screw things up for Cuba, her last night with Tom and everything.'

Tom showed up late, carrying three bottles of Old Crow, two unopened, the third half empty, and accompanied by his thirty-year-old brother, Leo, three times married, twice divorced. Leo made several trips to the truck, carrying into the house each time a twelve-bottle case of Heineken. 'If I'm gonna feel rotten tomorrow,' he announced, 'I want to feel bad from drinking something *good*.'

When Cuba introduced him to Lucy, he stared at her hard little breasts, bare and pale under her see-through shirt, rolled his eyes to the ceiling, and said in a husky whisper, 'Holy God, it's Christmas morning at the orphanage.' Lucy laughed, turned pink, but held her ground, and Christine said to Roy, 'I think we'll have to throw cold water on Leo before the night's over.'

Margo, already high after two glasses of Chianti, said, 'Gee, look how it turned out. Four and four. Boy-girl, boy-girl.'

They set up an eight-foot folding table on the screened-in porch overlooking the pond. While Tom and Roy found enough chairs and benches to seat eight people, Christine and Cuba and Lucy and Margo carried platters of food to the table. And whisky and beer and ice and half-gallon jugs of Soave and Chianti.

They stayed there at the table, like Elizabethan revellers, from seven thirty in the evening till almost midnight. No one left early, nobody got sick, and everyone drank too much. Tom's brother, Leo, punctuated the loud conversation with occasional toasts, beginning, as soon as they sat down, with an elaborate one to his brother.

'Here's a toast to my baby brother, Tommy. About to become a man. Gonna win us a war unless I'm mistaken. I've got a lot of respect for my bubba. It's hard for a young fella to keep his head together when he's stuck with a brother like me, a man who's got it all.'

Christine and Cuba and the other two girls held their noses then and began to boo. Leo started to laugh, a deep, infectious chuckle, took a long drink from his beer bottle, and went on talking. 'No disrespect, ladies. Nobody loves Tom more than I do. But I know his limitations. For one thing, the man cannot hit a curve ball. He's got a good arm, he can run you to death going from first to third, he can murder a fast ball or any slow stuff you throw up there, but give him a little soft jug-handle curve and he'll tie himself in knots. But who cares? The man deserves a lot of credit. So I say, let's drink to him.' He held up his beer bottle again, and everyone cheered and drank.

'Another thing,' Leo went on. 'The poor bastard has no luck at all with the ladies. Can't pee a drop. Look at him. Not a bad-looking specimen, is he? Shaves every day, takes a bath now and then. No dandruff or acne or dragon breath. But all the same, the girls stay away in droves. Up until now. Till Cuba took him over. Now it looks like she's got him in good working order. Jackpot the first time out. Gonna win a war and be a daddy all in one year. I say, "Hats off to my brother."'

The party didn't end at midnight but it changed directions. Abruptly. Leo and Lucy walked outside for a breath of air. While they stood at the edge of the pond, he deftly stripped off her gauzy shirt, leaned down and took one of her small pointed breasts into his mouth. When he put his arms around her then and kissed her he said, 'I've been wanting to do that ever since I got here.'

'I know you have,' she said. 'And I've been wanting you to.'

When Roy heard an Indian whoop he looked out the kitchen window and saw Leo running toward Tom's camper, swinging Lucy's shirt in a circle over his head like a lariat. Running along behind him, naked in the moonlight, came Lucy.

Tom and Cuba, as though responding to some silent signal, got up from the table, smiled sweetly at Roy and Christine, and walked hand in hand to the back bedroom.

Margo and Lloyd Eitel feigned sleep on the couch in the living room till Roy and Christine had cleared the table, put away the food, rinsed the dishes, and gone into their own bedroom. As soon as she heard the door close, Margo got up,

67

slipped out of her long dress, and led Eitel outside to the screened-in porch.

When she was lying in bed beside Roy, Christine said, 'It didn't turn out exactly the way we planned, did it?'

'Not exactly. But that's all right. Like the man said, "All's well that ends well." '

'You're a nice man. Did I ever tell you that? You're warm and sexy and very nice.'

'I thought you were sleepy,' he said. 'When we were in the kitchen, you said you couldn't keep your eyes open.'

'I couldn't. But that was then. This is now. Give a girl a break.'

Chapter 19

During the second week in August, Roy had a postcard from his uncle, Joe Medek.

> You're hard as hell to locate. You must be living in a cave. So call me up. Some guy from Illinois is trying to get in touch with you.

The following Saturday Roy took the early-morning ferry to Fairhaven and caught a bus going north to Boston. At noon he met Jim Hollenbeck, the athletic director of Foresby College, in the bar of the Revere Club on High Street. They had lunch and talked till almost three o'clock. Then Roy walked across the Common to the Greyhound station and took the four-o'clock bus to Portland, Maine, to see his aunt and uncle.

After supper Roy and Joe watched the Red Sox game on television. They were playing the Cleveland Indians at Fenway. The Indians won it in the tenth on two walks and a scratch single to right. Joe turned off the set then and said. 'You want a beer, or are you in a hurry to go to bed?'

'Let's have a beer,' Roy said.

Middle-sized, lean and hard and grizzled, Joe looked like an ex-welterweight who'd won most of his fights but had lost a couple of critical ones. The third son in a large family, he had assumed that he too would have at least six children. But his wife, Agnes, miscarried twice in the first year of their marriage, and when they learned that she was incapable of carrying a child to term, Joe simply put the notion of a family out of his mind.

Joe was a worker. His only natural skills were with tools. But he was also an omnivorous reader of technical and engineering books. He taught himself mathematics, through trigonometry and calculus, and was proud of his ability to multiply and divide in his head, without paper or pencil.

He powered his house with a windmill he'd built himself and heated it with solar panels he had designed and installed. And during one long Maine winter, with the aid of books and tape recordings, he taught himself to play the violin, mastering at last two selections, *Melody in A* and, for reasons known only to him, the first movement of César Franck's *Symphony in D Minor*.

Brought up in the Bohemian forest, in the mountain town of Sušice, living there, isolated, until he was sixteen years old, he knew nothing about athletic events, had no knowledge of them; he'd had no exposure whatsoever to American sports, baseball, football, and the like, when he came over in 1926. But as Roy was growing up, Joe schooled himself in athletics, the rules, the techniques, the records, so he could pass it all along to his nephew. By the time Roy had begun to compete as a runner, when he was thirteen years old, Joe, who was fifty-two by then, could tape ankles, treat sprains and charley horses, and give an expert massage. He knew all about calisthenics for runners, how to warm up and cool out, and how to avoid cramps at the first outdoor meets of the spring when the weather was still damp and cold.

'Tell me about this guy you saw in Boston. What's his name?'

'Hollenbeck,' Roy said. 'Jim Hollenbeck. He's the athletic director at Foresby College. In Illinois.'

'Yeah, he said something about Illinois when he called here. But I never heard of Foresby.'

'It's a good school. Not big but a great track programme. You've probably read about Hollenbeck. He ran the mile for Minnesota in the early fifties. Then he coached track at Santa Clara till four or five years ago. Since then he's been in charge of the sports programme at Foresby.'

'What's he want with you?'

'He wants me to come to Foresby. He wants me to run for them.'

'Is he offering you the moon or something?'

'Not exactly,' Roy said. 'Full tuition. Room and board. Transportation back and forth a couple times a year. And some walking-around money.'

'That's the same deal you've got at Bowdoin.'

'Not exactly. Tuition at Foresby is fifteen hundred more a year.'

'So what?' Joe said. 'When you get your diploma, they don't stamp on the front of it how much it cost.'

'I know that. But there are some courses at Foresby that I can't get at Bowdoin.'

'Take my advice,' Joe said. 'Don't jump around. Best thing you can do is hang on at Bowdoin. You're doing good there. You know the teachers. You know the coaches. And they know you. Why make anxiety for yourself? A new place. New people.'

'Nothing wrong with that. Once I'm out of school, I'll have to get a foothold someplace. I'm not gonna be able to stay in Portland all my life.'

'I didn't say you were. But jobs are one thing. School is something else. Just dropping one school for another one doesn't make any sense to me. Besides that, you'd make a lot of people mad at you.'

'What do you mean? What people?'

'People at Bowdoin. Archie Sattler. The other boys on the track squad. All those people are gonna feel like you let them down.'

'Archie Sattler's a *coach*, Joe. He's looking out for number one, just like everybody else. If I'm not there to run the half mile for him he'll find somebody else. If I fall off a scaffold next week and break my leg, do you think Archie Sattler's gonna get my scholarship renewed anyway? Not a chance. If I don't run, I don't eat. If I can't compete, I don't graduate. One, two, three. It's as simple as that.'

'Do you think it's gonna be different at some other school?'

'No I don't,' Roy said. 'I didn't say that. I'm just saying that if they can find a guy who runs faster than I do, they'll grab him. So if I can find a school that I think is better for me, there's no reason why I shouldn't grab that.'

Joe got up and walked to the icebox. 'You want a sandwich? I'm gonna make myself a sandwich.'

'Yeah. That sounds good.'

Joe carried the bread, the packages of meat and cheese, and a jar of mustard back to the table. He sat down and slapped together two thick sandwiches.

'Well, you must be making a reputation for yourself,' he said, 'if they came after you the way they did. Special trip all the way up to Boston.'

'They didn't come after *me*. I contacted them. I wrote Hollenbeck a letter and had Bowdoin send them a transcript. And he didn't come to Boston just to see me. He was trying to land a seven-foot basketball player from Brookline and a hotshot pole vaulter from Framingham. But he lost them both. The basketball player went to St John's and the pole vaulter picked Ohio State.'

Joe took a bite of his sandwich and began to chew slowly, taking a sip of beer every few chews. 'If you went after *them*, it looks to me like you've already made up your mind.'

'Almost, Joe. But not quite.'

'What made you so hot to switch schools all of a sudden?'

'I don't know. A lot of things, I guess. I met somebody from

71

Foresby, and the more I found out about the place, the better it sounded to me.'

'Who was this guy who told you about it? Is he a track man too?'

'It's not a guy. It's a girl. Her name's Christine Wheatley.'

Joe finished his sandwich and drained his beer glass. Then he carried the two plates and two glasses to the sink and washed them out. Roy stayed in his chair at the table.

Finally Joe turned to face him and stood leaning against the sink.

'What you're telling me is you got tangled up with some girl and she's got you to change schools so you'll be where she is. Is that right?'

'Not exactly. Christine didn't force me to do anything. As a matter of fact she's ready to transfer to Bowdoin. If I decide to go to Foresby, it will be because I want to, because I think it's a good thing for me. No other reason.'

'You can tell yourself that till you're blue in the face,' Joe said, 'but you'll never make me believe it.'

Roy pushed his chair back from the table. 'Come on, Joe. We've got nothing to fuss about. You know me. I'm not a fly-by-night. If I didn't think it was the best thing for me, I wouldn't do it. I've been making decisions for myself since I was fourteen. I haven't done bad so far, have I?'

'No. But this is different. I got a hunch it's somebody else's idea instead of yours. I just hate to see you make a jackass of yourself.'

The next morning after breakfast, Joe drove Roy downtown to the Greyhound station. As soon as they got in the car, Roy said, 'Are you still pissed off at me?'

'I'm not pissed off. I'm just saying it doesn't sound like a good move to me.'

'Did you tell Aggie about it?'

'Not me. I'll leave that job to you. Aggie thinks Illinois is halfway around the world. She's never been west of Buffalo.'

'Chicago's only a two-hour flight from Boston.'

'Don't tell me. Tell *her*. Since that scare she had coming back from Rome a few years ago she wouldn't get on a plane no matter what. If the Pope was the pilot she still wouldn't fly.' Then Joe said, 'What about this girl friend of yours? Where's she from?'

'Lake Forest. That's north of Chicago. She was born in France but she's spent all her life in Lake Forest. Till she started school at Foresby.'

'Is she pretty. Why do I ask?'

'*Pretty* isn't the word,' Roy said.

'Is she smart? Why do I ask?'

'*Smart* isn't the word.'

'What is the word?' Joe said.

'I don't know. There isn't any word. I just like her. I like her a lot.'

'You say she's working there at Martha's Vineyard? Same as you are?'

'That's right. In a restaurant. She's working as a waitress.'

'Working her way through school?'

Roy hesitated before he answered. Finally he said, 'Not exactly. Her folks are sending her to school.'

'Then why's she working as a waitress? That's a tough job.'

'She wants the experience,' Roy said.

'You mean she's working for fun?'

'No. She wants to have some work experience.'

'Why? A person who doesn't have to work doesn't need any work experience.'

'I didn't say she didn't have to work.'

'If she doesn't need the money, she doesn't have to work. I don't know any other reason to work.'

'Well, anyway. . .' Roy began.

'What about her father who pays all her school bills? What does he do?'

'I don't know. Her parents are divorced. I'm not sure he does anything.'

'And the mother doesn't work either.'

'No. Not as far as I know.'

'I see,' Joe said. 'So we're talking about rich people. We're talking about a family that is independently wealthy. Am I right?'

'I don't know much about them. All I know is what I've told you.'

'Do you want me to tell you about rich people? My brother was a gardener for a family named Butterfield, in Palm Beach, Florida. Seven years he worked there. You want to hear some stories about rich people, stories that would make your stomach turn over, you should talk to him. Not silly little things about people who don't know what to do with their money. Nothing like that. I mean spoiled people who never once in their lives had to worry whether there would be food on the table. So they turn into cannibals. They make a meal of each other. You think I exaggerate. You ask my brothers. Stories to curl your hair, he said. People who don't *have* to do anything so they make up things to do. Mean things. Bad stuff.'

Roy laughed. 'Christine's no cannibal. And she's not spoiled. She can cook and clean up a house and do laundry just like anybody else. She's a terrific girl who just happens to have a lot of money.'

'I hope you're right,' Joe said. 'But don't be surprised if you're wrong.'

Chapter 20

*B*efore he went to Martha's Vineyard to see Christine, Fred Deets discussed the trip with his father. 'I had three choices as I saw it,' Fred said. 'I could have gone there as soon as I got her letter, I could have waited to see her when she comes back to school next month, or I could give her some time to think things over and *then* go to see her. Before she leaves Martha's Vineyard. What do you think?'

'If I know you, you've already made up your mind to go. So go ahead. It's six of one and half a dozen of the other. You're either still in the ball game or you're not. When you see her you'll know for sure. You'll know right then if you've made the trip for nothing.'

Mr Deets was wrong about that. Fred wasn't sure of anything. When Christine drove to the Vineyard airport to pick him up, she put her arms around him and kissed him. 'Perfect timing,' she said. 'When you called the restaurant, we'd just stopped serving lunch.'

She drove back along the dirt road that led to the Adler house. When they got there she parked in the carport and took him inside. Standing in the living room, she swung her arm, taking in the screened porch and the pond. 'This is it. This is where I've been living all summer. What do you think?'

'It's nice.'

'What kind of reaction is that? It's not *nice*. It's *great*.'

She fixed him a sandwich then and some iced tea and brought it out to the screened porch. He sat on the couch with his food on the coffee table and she sat in a canvas chair facing him. While he ate, she asked questions about his work and about his parents and told him about her luncheon with Grace a month before in Boston. At last he put down his glass and said, 'Are we just going to be polite or are we going to talk about important stuff?'

'I'm not going to fight with you,' she said. 'If that's what you came for, you're going to be disappointed. I'm not mad at you and you have no reason to be mad at me.'

'I didn't say I was mad at you.'

'You don't have to *say* it. You have that look on your face.'

'What look?'

'Like I just came to apply for a job and I'm not going to get it.'

'I'll tell you the truth,' he said. 'I can't figure you out. I don't know what I expected, but whatever it was . . .'

75

'I'm not going to cry and scream. I won't do that. I don't want us to play some big scene. We've known each other too long.'

He sat there looking at her and saying nothing. Finally he said, 'I don't seem to be holding good cards in this game.'

'I'm sorry.'

'I don't want you to be sorry. That doesn't do any good. I sure as hell don't feel sorry for myself. But I'm confused. I can't figure out how we got from where we were three months ago to where we are now.' He looked toward the inside of the house, then out at the pond. 'The last time I saw you we had only one problem, to get the shower nozzle working so we could take a bath together. Now it's like all that never happened. Like *we* never happened.'

'I'm stymied, Fred. I don't want to hurt you. But I just can't . . . I mean something changed me. I'm not the same person I was at the beginning of summer. I'm never going to be the same again. You know what I found out? I like plain things. Plain stuff. I love those little drip-dry uniforms I wear at the restaurant. Ten dollars they cost. But every time I put mine on I feel like myself, *whatever* that is. Does that make any sense?'

'Sure it does. If nothing ever changes, what's the point? But the trick is to know what to throw away and what to keep. The good stuff doesn't come along every time the seasons change.'

Later in the afternoon when she drove him back to the airport, she said, 'You have a real edge on me and you know it. For a lot of years I hung on every word you said. You had me mesmerized. You still do. When I listen to you, I'm convinced. You convinced me today. I agreed with everything you said. At least my head did. But the rest of me still says I can't give up Roy.'

At the airport she parked the car in the lot and walked beside him out to his plane.

'So where are we?' she said.

'That's what I was asking you.'

'Now I'm asking you.'

'I'd call it a holding pattern. You're in love and I'm in

limbo. But I don't think we've seen the last of each other. In my book the odds are about ten to one we'll end up married.'

She stood by the wire fence watching his plane taxi to its takeoff and roar down the runway. As it climbed and turned in a wide arc toward the southwest, she started her car engine and drove slowly home.

Chapter 21

"*I* really made an ass of myself,' Christine said. She was telling Roy about Fred. 'I wanted to say, "I'm sorry but it's over. Even if something went wrong for me and Roy, it still wouldn't work now for us.' But I didn't say it. I didn't want to hurt him, so instead I did something worse. I let him leave with some idea in his head that we might get together again. I wanted it to be all clean and final, but it ended up uncertain and messy.'

'Don't worry about it. If I turn out to be a disappointment, you've always got Fred to fall back on.'

'You bastard.'

'A little security in your old age. You never know what's going to happen. You may age badly. Moles and warts and liver spots. Skinny little legs and tennis shoes. You might wake up some morning and I'm long gone. Off to Pago Pago with a baton twirler. On the other hand you might get tired of me. You know what they say about summer romances. By the time Thanksgiving rolls around, you might be tickled to death to see old Fred come cruising in from the airport in his Porsche station wagon. Leopard-skin seat covers, and six wristwatches on each arm. I think things are working out fine for you. It's always good to have a backup system, an ace in the hole.'

'If I didn't know you're kidding, I'd murder you.'

'Who's kidding?' Roy said. 'We're talking about survival systems. Battle tactics.'

Christine got up, crossed the room, and sat down on the couch beside him. 'Is this what you did up in Portland? Did you make a few calls? Leave all the doors open a crack?'

'Not me. I actually called a meeting of all my current girl friends, no casuals, just the ones I'm sleeping with, and I said, "Girls, you'll have to find a new body. I've been captured by a lady from Chicago. So I'm closing up shop here in Portland. Following this girl out to the cornfields and the meadowlands. A stitch in time and the world well lost. All that heavy stuff."'

'You're crazy.'

'I guess so,' he said. 'My uncle says I am. He said I should beware of people who have so much money they don't have to work. So what do you say to that?'

She lay back on the sofa and rested her head in his lap. 'You tell your uncle that he doesn't know the half of it. Tell him I'm going to spoil you rotten. Next time he sees you he won't even recognize you. First of all I think you should have a solid-gold tooth, like Jelly Roll Morton, with a diamond set in it. Then there's a barber in Lake Forest named Ambrose. He'll cut your hair. We don't pay him when he comes to the house. But once a year we send him a cheque for twenty thousand. How does that sound?'

'That should work out all right.'

'Your underwear I'll have made in a little shop on rue du Faubourg St Honoré. And your pyjamas.'

'I don't wear pyjamas.'

'I know,' she said, 'but it's good to have a few pairs handy in case of fire. Let's see now . . . what else? Your shirts will be made by Mr Breedlove, who used to run the shirt department for Turnbull and Asser before he opened his own place just down the way on Jermyn Street. Scarves and ties we'll get from Arboletti in Florence. But the best tailor in the world for suits is in Chicago, oddly enough. Mr Trevor-Whyte. He was chief fitter for Hawkes of Savile Row for twenty years.'

'You didn't say anything about shoes. I'll need shoes, won't I?'

'Alan McAfee. We'll have a cast made and they'll supply all your boots and shoes. They have a man who wears them for three months before they deliver so they're properly broken in.'

'Good. That's what I have against Sears, Roebuck and JC Penney—they expect you to break in your own shoes.'

She pulled his head down to hers and kissed him. Then, 'You tell your uncle I promise not to change you. I'll let you stay as tacky as you were when I found you.'

Chapter 22

*N*ear the end of summer, Russell, returning from a film location in Portugal, flew direct from Lisbon to Boston and from there to the Vineyard, where he spent two days with Christine and Roy.

After he left to return home to New York, Christine told Roy about the significant role he had played, twenty years before, in Grace's life. She tried to stick together all the separate pieces she had gleaned from her mother, from her grandmother, and from Russell himself.

'As near as I can tell, the problem with Grace's marriage to Harold Wheatley—that's my father's name—was that they should never have been married in the first place. And they never would have been if the whole production hadn't been engineered by my grandmother.

'I don't mean it could *never* have worked. Wheatley was older than Grace but not enough to wreck things. He's a pleasant-looking man, and he's not a sadist or pervert or anything like that. There just didn't seem to be any contact between them at all. After they came back from their honeymoon trip to Mexico City, Grace says she never spent another night in his bed. In fact, she may have got pregnant with me the first time she slept with my father. I have a suspicion that the first time was the *only* time. That was in June of 1948. In August she found out she was pregnant.

'A week later, without telling anyone where she was going, she flew to New York by herself, stayed in a hotel near the airport that night, and flew the next day to Geneva.'

'Were you born in Switzerland? I thought you told me France.'

Christine shook her head. 'Grace left Switzerland heading for Paris. She planned to find an apartment there and, when I was due, go to the American Hospital in Neuilly. But when she got to Avignon, she was having problems and she was afraid she was going to miscarry. And that's exactly what would happen, the doctor told her, if she didn't stay in bed. So Grace rented a house there, in Villeneuve, and hired a lovely old Scotchwoman to take care of her. Then she bought a bunch of books, crawled into bed, and stayed there till I was born. I was premature, so she only had to wait till January.'

'What about your father? Where was he all this time?'

'In Chicago. But he didn't know Grace was pregnant and he had no idea where she was living. All he knew was that Grandma got a letter once a month through a lawyer in New York. But with no hint of where Grace was living. They knew she'd transferred a large amount of money to a Swiss bank the previous summer; they managed to weasel that information out of her Chicago bankers. But beyond that they knew nothing.'

'Did she let them know when you were born?'

'Yes. But still no information about where we were living. Then, the next thing my father knew, a divorce lawyer called him up and said he'd been hired to represent Grace Wheatley in a divorce action. Wheatley told him there would be no discussion about a divorce until my mother came back to Lake Forest. Grace's lawyer countered by saying that unless divorce arrangements were finalized at once, Harold Wheatley would never be allowed to see his daughter. At this point, my father began to put big pressure on the Swiss bank through his bank in Chicago, and a few weeks later his people had located our apartment. By then we'd moved to Paris. One afternoon two men followed Nanny and me out into the Bois-de-Boulogne, took me out of my pram, and whisked us both away. Out to Orly, on board a chartered plane, and back to Chicago. So Grace had no choice. She had to come back too.'

'Where did Russell come into the picture?'

'They met in Avignon. In late May or early June. When I was about four months old.'

Christine got up and went into the bedroom then. When she came back she was carrying her billfold. 'Did I ever show you a picture of my nanny?'

'I don't think so.'

'Her name was Augusta Ross-Shannon; she came from Edinburgh.' She slipped a black-and-white picture that looked like a passport photo out of her wallet and handed it to him. It was the face of a seventy-year-old woman, pale eyes and a strong chin, a faint smile on her lips and her hair pulled back over her ears in a soft knot.

'She died four years ago, when I was sixteen, and it almost killed me. She'd been with me from the day I came home from the hospital. She taught me how to make cookies and fold the linen and pour tea. She used to say, "A real lady never asks a servant to do something that she can do herself. The wealthiest woman I ever worked for rinsed out her own underthings every night."

'She was like a mother to Grace, too. They didn't meet till Grace was grown-up but Nanny knew there was something very young about her. She's just that way. There's no toughness about Grace. She *trusts* people and I think she's right. I think it's better to get hurt than it is to . . . I don't know how to say it. You know what I mean?'

Roy nodded.

'Anyway, when Nanny died, Grace cried like a little girl. She didn't get over it for months. Even today I catch her looking at Nanny's picture with tears in her eyes. It all goes back, I think, to that time in France. Grace had cut herself off from her family, from everything. And Nanny filled in all those gaps. For the first time, Grace realized how much she'd missed from her own mother. All of a sudden she found out about tenderness. The real kind. And just then Russell Atha came on the scene. Maybe, at that moment in her life, it could have been anyone. Maybe any man who was decent to her would have caught that tide of love she'd been storing up. But I don't think so. I think some people *do* belong together. They can *see* things and *feel* things and *understand* things, by being together, that would have escaped them completely if they'd lived apart.'

She got up and walked into the bedroom again. When she came back, she was carrying a folded page of writing paper. 'I want to read you this note Nanny sent me when I was thirteen years old. Grace had just got her third divorce and there'd been quite a bit of noise in the paper about it, so I guess Nanny thought I needed to be propped up a little.' She sat down, leaned against one end of the couch, rested her bare feet on Roy's thigh, and began to read.

"Dear Chrissy,

"This is something I wanted to pass on to you, something important, I think.

"Grace is having a difficult time right now. And maybe you're embarrassed or upset by it because it all seems so public. But I hope you won't blame your mother. She may be at fault. All of us are sometimes. But it's important to remember that she has no impulse to hurt anybody. And she certainly would do anything to avoid hurting you.

"Some people are very lucky in their lives. Good things happen right on schedule. The proper pieces fall into place. But the rest of us, for reasons we can never understand, keep missing the things we really want. Just by a hair. When you have to give up something you need and you know you'll never get it back, it makes you do funny things sometimes. Think about it."

When they were lying in bed that night, a cool breeze blowing in across the pond, the curtains floating soft across the brass bedstead, Roy said, 'Let me get this straight. After your father sent those men to Paris to pick you up and fly you back home, your mother also went back to Chicago. right?'

'That's right.'

'And what about Russell? Did he go with her?'

'I'm not sure. But I don't think so. If I'm not mistaken he left Paris a few days after she did.'

'So she and your father got a divorce?'

'Yes they did.'

'And your mother was given your custody?'

'Yes.'

'Okay. Then why didn't she and Russell get married?'

'They couldn't.'

'Why not?'

'She married somebody else.'

'That doesn't make any sense,' Roy said.

'I know it doesn't.'

'Who'd she marry?'

'My father's cousin. A silly man named Evan Causey.'

Chapter 23

*H*arold Wheatley, Christine's father, had made his plans carefully. As soon as he was notified that his daughter and her nurse were on a plane over the Atlantic bound for Chicago, his lawyers, through their French associates, advised the Paris police of the circumstances. No kidnapping had taken place. A father had simply reclaimed his own child.

Consequently, as soon as Grace went to the police to report the disappearance of Christine and her nurse, she was informed by a captain of detectives that her daughter was en route to Chicago to join her father.

Grace made reservations on the next flight to New York for herself and Russell. But when she called her divorce lawyer, he said it would be better if she came by herself. 'We have some new developments. Your husband has counterfiled for divorce. The grounds are abandonment and adultery. And he's asking for full custody of your daughter, claiming you're an unfit mother. So for the moment . . .'

'I understand,' Grace said. To Russell, she said, 'It will just be for a few days. I'll call you from Chicago. Either you'll come there or I'll be coming back to Paris as soon as I get things straightened out. No matter what he says about me, there's no way he can keep me from having Christine.'

Her mother, however, when she met Grace at the airport, had other ideas. 'They say you've been living openly with some man, that he's shared a house with you and the child. Is that true?'

'Of course it's true. But do you think I'd do anything that would damage my own daughter?'

'It doesn't matter what I think. It will depend on what some judge thinks. And the facts don't make you look good. You've been carrying on a public love affair with some fly-by-night . . .'

84

'What does that mean? Russell's a terrific man and I'm crazy about him. The day I get my divorce, *one hour* after I get it, I'm going to marry him.'

'All I know is what's in Harold's dossier. In the Paris neighbourhood where your friend lived he is known as a drinker and a womanizer.'

'Oh, God, what do those words mean? I don't care if he drinks Sterno and sleeps with bearded ladies.'

'Suit yourself,' Margaret said. 'You're going to be divorced one way or the other. And then you'll be free to marry anyone you want to. But you will *not* have custody of your daughter. The only possible way you can keep Christine is if you put the matter completely in my hands.'

'I appreciate the offer, Mother, but I think I'd better let the lawyers handle things.'

Her lawyer, however, when she met with him the next day, was not optimistic. 'I was able to work out an interim agreement about your daughter. As I understand it, Mr Wheatley's house is not far from your mother's house.'

'It's *not* Mr Wheatley's house. It's *my* house and Mr Wheatley lives in it. It's just across the compound from my mother's house.'

The lawyer nodded. 'The assumption is that you will be staying at your mother's house.'

'Temporarily.'

'Good. I've worked it out that if you sign a bonded agreement promising you will not take your daughter out of the country, Mr Wheatley will permit you to visit her for two hours every third day.'

'Why should I sign anything? She's *my* daughter.'

'Also *his* daughter. He can't prevent you from moving back into your house if you want to, but he *can* prevent you from taking the child *away* from that house.'

'I'm suing him for divorce, for Pete's sake. I'm not about to move back in the house with him.'

'I assumed that. That's why we worked out the visitation arrangement.'

'I think it stinks.'

'So do I. But it's the best we can do at the moment. I could go to family court and try to get you temporary custody. But if they decided against you, it would work in your husband's favour when the final custody arrangements are being decided.'

When she called Paris that evening and talked to Russell, she was crying. 'I thought there was no way they could take Christine away from me. But I was wrong. There *is* a way, and they're going to do it if they can.'

At last, in desperation, Grace went to her mother. 'I'm sorry,' she said. 'You were right and I was wrong. I've been over this a dozen times with five different lawyers, and they all tell me the same thing. There's a good chance I could lose my daughter. I don't know what to think or what to do. I've even thought of going back to Harold if I have to.'

'Too late for that, I'm afraid. I talked to his father yesterday, and Cyrus says Harold doesn't want any compromise. He wants a divorce and he wants custody of Christine.'

'Can they really do it? Can a bunch of lawyers get together and shuffle a few papers and take a child away from her mother?'

'Of course they can. If they establish that you're unfit.'

'Unfit? What the hell does that mean? Just because I detest her father, just because I love somebody else, does that mean I'm unfit? Do *you* think I'm unfit?'

Her mother looked at her for a long moment. Then she said, 'I asked you the other day to put the whole matter in my hands and you said no. Do you still feel that way?'

'I'll do anything if I can keep Christine. But I don't know what to do.'

'Of course you don't. But *I* do. If you'll sit still and listen to me for ten minutes, you'll see that I have been doing my homework.'

She sat there, very straight in her chair, talking earnestly for almost fifteen minutes. After the first few minutes, Grace began to cry. She was still crying at the end when Margaret said, 'I think it's the only way you have a chance to keep

Christine. But it has to be *now*, before the lawyers start talking about the separation agreement. We have to move fast. Can you do it?'

Grace nodded her head. 'I can if I have to. If there's no other way, then I can do it.'

'Good. Then I'll get busy.'

For the rest of that day Margaret Jernegan was on the telephone. That evening, dark automobiles, carrying men in sombre clothes, pulled in and out of her driveway from seven thirty until almost midnight. And the following morning, her chauffeur handed her into the Mercedes limousine at nine o'clock. All that day and the following day she spent in downtown Chicago in the office suites of various white-haired gentlemen. On the third day Cyrus Wheatley came to her house for lunch.

Margaret, who had given birth to her own child when she was twenty years old, was even now, in the year of her granddaughter's birth, just past forty-one. Her sexual appetite had never been strong, even during her marriage. And since her husband's death, that appetite had almost vanished. This is not to say that she had become a celibate widow. She knew that she was sexually attractive and she knew the continuing power she could have over certain carefully selected men by simply pretending that their presence between her legs was as thrilling for her as it was for them. So she had had several lovers, each of whom assumed he was the only one and each of whom was also bound to Margaret in some business or financial way.

Five years after her husband's death, when Margaret was twenty-seven and Cyrus Wheatley was forty, she literally enslaved him for life. After a board meeting in Cleveland of a company for whom they both sat as directors, she invited him to her hotel suite, served him a drink, and stripped off his clothes. She then subjected him to an all-night marathon of oral sex that affected his motor reactions for several days afterward and left telltale discolourations in his genital area that kept him away from his squash club for two weeks.

When they were back in Chicago, however, when he tried

to call her on the telephone, he was unable to reach her. It was nearly a month before he was able to have a moment alone with her at a charity banquet in Wilmette. 'I've been tortured by guilt because of your wife,' she whispered. He thought he saw the glint of a tear in her eye. 'It's all I can do to stay away from you, but I must. If she found out, if we ever hurt her in any way, I'd kill myself.'

Since that time, almost fifteen years before, their relations with each other had been formal and restrained. She saw to it that they were never in a room alone. But occasionally, on very *rare* occasions, she let him see a fleeting expression in her eyes that told him she remembered.

As they ate lunch now, they agonized about the future of the country under the guidance of Harry Truman. Margaret questioned the sincerity of Albert Schweitzer and Cyrus questioned the judgement of the Nobel Committee in giving its prize to Faulkner. And both of them detested the Graham Sutherland portrait of Somerset Maugham, a man they had met and liked.

At last, as they were having pineapple ice and espresso, Margaret came around to the subject, the situation that existed between Cyrus's son and Margaret's daughter. She told him, crisply and concisely, what she had already done and what remained still to be done. When he mumbled that he was afraid it was something Grace and Harold would have to resolve by themselves, Margaret cut in and said, 'No, Cyrus, it won't work that way. The only way to handle it is the way I've just outlined for you.' Then, 'You mean a lot to me, Cyrus. You know that, I've never made any demands on you. Never asked you for anything. And I wouldn't be doing it now if this weren't a critical situation. I can't force you to intercede. But I promise if you do, you won't be sorry.'

Two days later, Cyrus had lunch with his son Harold. He came straight to the point. 'I saw Margaret Jernegan the other day. She is very upset about this divorce business and so am I.'

Harold had never been self-assertive. The youngest of three brothers, he had depended, for most of his life, on the decisions of other people. But marriage, even one as disastrous as his own, had given him a new self-confidence. And in the recent turmoil with Grace he had truly, he felt, come of age. He had made judgements, decisions, and threats that were all his own.

He never questioned that he was in the centre of a great calamity, but it was *his* calamity. And when it was over, he had strong confidence that he and his daughter, both of them terribly sinned against by Grace, would pick up the pieces and go ahead.

In addition to whatever other weapons she held in dealing with Cyrus, Margaret knew he didn't particularly like his third son. The first two boys, Duane and Britt, were blocky, rough edged, and athletic like their father. Like him they were yachtsmen and skeet shooters, shameless seducers of other men's wives. They were also fearless and ruthless in business, qualities their father admired. His third son was cut from finer stuff. Taller, leaner, more handsome than the other men of his family, he was no less masculine, but the things that absorbed him made him seem that way to them. He liked to play the piano in a closed room and fish in a boat by himself. He was not a competitor. But now, for the first time that anyone could remember, he was tooling up for a full-scale war.

'I've never heard of a divorce,' he said to his father, 'where *somebody* didn't get upset.'

The statement didn't surprise Cyrus. But the attitude was new. Cyrus was accustomed to seeing Harold ill at ease, on the defensive. But today, across the luncheon table, he saw a relaxed young man, pushed back a bit from the table, legs crossed, casually sipping his drink.

'You seem rather lighthearted about it,' Cyrus said.

'I'm not lighthearted at all. These past few months have been the roughest period I've ever gone through. But now I think I'm past the worst part. I've stopped feeling sorry for myself. I'm just thinking about what's best for my daughter.'

'I'm sure you are, and I admire you for that. But it's important to remember that Grace has some rights too. She's the baby's mother—'

'She should have thought of that. She might have behaved differently.'

'Maybe you're right. But the question now is: Are you serving Christine's best interests in separating her from her mother, or are you sacrificing her welfare just to have your vengeance against Grace?'

'Dad ... believe me, I have no intention of doing anything that will damage Christine. I'm convinced that I can bring her up with love and consideration and give her a better life than she would have with her mother. And that's what I'm determined to do.'

Cyrus Wheatley stirred his drink and looked out the window. Finally he said, 'What about Grace's mother? Have you thought how this might affect her?'

'I'm sure she won't like it. But this is something between me and Grace. We have to settle it ourselves.'

'I'm not so sure of that. The day you and Grace got married there was a lot more involved than a ceremony and a wedding cake. A lot of cross-fertilization took place between our holdings and Margaret's. It helped us both. It gave each of us a share of the market more than double what we'd had before. We have a loose confederation. An *understanding*. Something that can't be picked apart by the FTC. You see what I'm getting at? Goodwill is the key word. Trust and goodwill. Do you think you can get a smear divorce from her daughter and take over sole control of her only grandchild without knocking over a lot of dominos? If you think Margaret Jernegan will just pull down her flag and surrender, then you don't know her very well.'

He paused, took a slow drink from his sherry glass, and set it down carefully on the tablecloth. 'And if you think *I'll* let you jeopardize a business structure that Duane and Britt and I have put together like a Chinese puzzle, you don't know *me* very well.'

Harold, sensing the kind of confrontation he'd had with his father since childhood, recognizing the tone of voice and the speech rhythms that usually preceded an ultimatum, felt the blood rising in his neck and cheeks. 'Dad,' he said, 'I told you

I don't want to discuss this and I don't. This is *my* business. You and Margaret Jernegan may have engineered the marriage, but *I* have to engineer the divorce. No one else can do it for me.'

The waiter brought their food then. Both men picked at the cold salads on their plates, nibbled bits of bread, sipped water, and said nothing. At last Cyrus put down his fork, dabbed at the corners of his mouth with his napkin, and said, 'I know you don't have a high estimation of me. I know too, from your mother, that you think I don't have a very high estimation of *you*. But you're twenty-eight years old now . . .'

'Twenty-nine,' Harold said.

'That's right. And I'm fifty-four. So whatever we think about each other, it's the product of a lot of time that we've been together. Both of us have probably made some mistakes. Now there's nothing we can do but try to live with whatever we have left. I know this is a difficult time for you. But I thought if I presented some thoughts to you, you might see things differently, I thought you might be willing to compromise when you saw how all this is likely to affect other people.'

'I don't understand what you're talking about.'

'I was hoping I could persuade you. I've been trying to avoid a situation where all the decisions would be made by other people and just handed to you.'

'It's a divorce, Dad. That's all it is. It happens thousands of times every day. It's between me and Grace. Nobody else. In a few weeks it will be all over. If it was anything else, I'd listen to you. You know that. I always have. But this is something *I* have to handle. Just *me*.'

Cyrus signalled to the waiter for coffee, then lighted a cigar as their table was cleared. Finally he said, 'There's not going to be a divorce, Harold. Margaret Jernegan has arranged for the marriage to be annulled.'

'She can't do that.'

'Yes, she can. She's done it. Grace signed a sworn statement that the marriage was never consummated.'

'Never consummated? She had a baby. We have a child.'

'Grace says the child isn't yours. But she won't make that a part of the public record unless you force her to. The annulment will simply say *conjugal incompatibility*.'

'They're trying to bluff me.'

'No, they're not. I saw the papers. It may not be strictly legal, but it's legal enough. If Margaret says she's got an annulment, you can bet she's got one. You can fight it if you want to, but all you'll do is make a public ass of yourself.'

'I don't care about that. Whatever stories Grace decides to tell now, the fact is that we were married. And while she was Mrs Harold Wheatley, she had a child whose name is Christine Wheatley. She's my daughter legally no matter what Grace says, and I want her with me, whether we get a divorce or an annulment or whatever we get. Grace can live in Paris or Zanzibar or anyplace she wants to, with any derelict she picks out, but she's not going to raise *my* daughter like that.'

'She's not going anyplace,' Cyrus said. 'Margaret says she plans to stay in Lake Forest, in the house where she lived with you, as soon as you've moved your things out.' He paused and puffed on his cigar. 'She's going to get married again, Harold, as soon as the annulment papers are finalized.'

'That doesn't surprise me. I figured she'd marry that deadbeat as soon as she could.'

'She's not marrying the man she was living with in Paris,' Cyrus said. 'She's marrying your cousin.'

'What cousin?'

'Evan Causey.'

'I don't believe it,' Harold said.

'It's the truth. You know how Evan feels about her. He always liked Grace. Long before you two became engaged.'

Harold shook his head. 'I haven't even seen Evan for over a year. I don't know where he's been.'

'He's been in Palm Beach with his mother.'

'You mean he's been in Florida, Grace has been in France with some other fool, and now all of a sudden they're going to get married. It doesn't make sense.'

'It makes sense to Margaret. I guess she and Evan must have kept in touch.'

'Grace doesn't even like him. She thinks he's an idiot.'

'I didn't say she liked him,' Cyrus said. 'I said she's going to marry him.'

'But why? What's the point?'

'To keep you from suing for custody of Christine.'

'That's not going to stop me. Why would *that* stop me?'

'Think it over. Pretend you're the judge in the case. A man sues for custody of his child. But it turns out there was no legal marriage. It was unconsummated and annulled. In fact the child is not his child. But what if the judge says, "At the time of the child's birth, the plaintiff was legally her father, and she was christened with his name," what then? That means the plaintiff could try to prove his ex-wife was an unfit mother and perhaps pursue his custody fight. But let's look at the mother. She is a proper young matron, living in Lake Forest, married to a young man who is not only respectable and wealthy, but is a member of her first husband's family, the son of his mother's sister. Can you honestly see yourself in a court battle with the Causeys, making accusations against your cousin's wife?'

'I don't like it,' Harold said. 'But I'll do it if I have to.'

'No, you won't son. Your mother won't permit it. And neither will I. You will have reasonable visitation rights with your daughter but she will remain in Grace's custody. It's been decided.'

Only a few members of the family attended Grace's wedding at St John's Church in Lake Forest. During a small breakfast in her mother's house following the ceremony, Grace excused herself, locked herself in the powder room, and swallowed a bottle of sleeping pills. Christine's nanny called Russell in Paris that afternoon. Two days later he was in Chicago. But by then Grace, her doctor, and Evan Causey, along with Christine and her nurse, were on a private plane heading for San Francisco. A yacht was waiting there to take them for a three-month cruise among the remote islands of the South Pacific. A few weeks later Harold Wheatley left Chicago and moved to California. His mother visited him there once a year, but he never saw his father or spoke with him again.

BOOK 2

Chapter 1

*I*n October, after she was back in school at Foresby, Christine had a letter from Cuba.

Well, here we are, down south with the alligators. When Tom finished basic they told him they were sending him to noncom school for six more weeks. So I flew down to South Carolina and got myself a furnished room with a hot plate here in Port Royal.

My old man's really doing great. When he finishes this training period he's in, he'll be a corporal. Somebody told him they might keep him on here as a small-arms instructor. But he's got his heart set on going overseas. He can't wait to get to Vietnam. So we'll have to wait and see what happens.

I can hardly believe I'm pregnant. I haven't been sick to my stomach at all, I haven't gained much weight, and except for a gigantic bosom I don't look any different. The way I feel, I must have been born to be a mummy.

When she told Roy about the letter, Christine said, 'If being pregnant is such a kick, maybe I should try it.'

'Sure, why not? We might even be lucky enough to have twins. You could keep one at the Kappa house and the other one could bunk with me in the dorm.'

'I don't mean *now*. But it's nice to hear from somebody who really *likes* it. My grandmother only had one child, but to hear her tell it, it was like open-heart surgery without an anaesthetic. Also a couple girls my age in Lake Forest have babies already and they don't have anything good to say about it, What do you think?'

'I'm never going to have kids,' Roy said. 'I don't want to lose my figure.'

For several days after Cuba's letter arrived, it stayed in Christine's mind. It was impossible for her not to compare her own situation with Cuba's. If she'd been called upon to summarise it, she would have said, 'I have alternatives, all sorts of options and choices. I never have to wake up in the morning and wonder what terrible things are going to happen that day. I really do have some control of my life.'

In answering Cuba's letter, however, she made a conscious effort to minimise her own euphoria. She celebrated Cuba's good fortune, concentrated on the details of *her* life, and Tom's, on *their* future, on the baby. Only at the end of the letter did she make sketchy reference to what was going on at Foresby.

> We're plodding along here, Roy and I. It's a let down in a way from last summer. He lives in one place and I live in another, half a mile away.
>
> Still . . . we're tickled to death to be in the same school. If he was in Maine and I was here in Illinois it would really be the *pits*. So . . . that part is good. And Roy likes the school. So that's good too.
>
> Also, he's running cross-country this fall. He wasn't eager to do it. He prefers running on a track and he's never run such long distances before. Not in competition. But the track coach thought it would be good for him to build up his endurance and keep himself in shape for the regular track season when it starts. So Roy said he would. But he bitches and moans about it because in three races so far he's never finished higher than third place. He's not used to that. He likes to win.
>
> They run cross-country here on football game days. They time it so the race finishes between the halves.

You should hear me scream when Roy comes into the stadium and runs the final lap of the race around the cinder track. He's some cute guy in his little running shorts. Very sexy.

We had a scare two weeks after school started. There was a mix-up at Roy's draft board in Portland. They got the information that he'd withdrawn from Bowdoin, but they didn't know he'd transferred to Foresby. There was a hot scramble for a few days. But the track coach here and the school officials got into the act and finally it got straightened out. They put a *temporary* stamp on his deferment card, but I'm sure he'll be all right as long as he stays in school.

At the core of Christine's intricate system of right and wrong, plus and minus, there was a firm belief that every impasse had an exit, every problem a solution. She was chemically unable to lose heart, to throw up her hands, to toss in the towel. She was convinced that the cat could always be skinned, the fire put out, the tide turned. Experience had taught her that the first step toward progress was her firm conviction that progress could be made. She truly believed that if she thought she was lucky, she *would* be.

She felt very fortunate, for example, that the situation with Fred had resolved itself so smoothly. She had not come home from the east with great trepidation, but all the same she was conscious of a shadow lingering somewhere in the middle distance. She did not expect a dramatic confrontation. Pursuit without encouragement was not Fred's style. She was sure of that. Nonetheless, she was relieved when she found out that he had enlisted in an airborne unit of the Marines and had gone to California to train as a helicopter pilot.

Christine was informed and indignant about the United States' stance in Indochina. She had done extensive research for her political science course the previous school year, had written half a dozen short pieces on the relationship between the economic involvement of American banks and corporations in Vietnam and the military involvement of our armed forces. She'd been present in Chicago during the street riots in 1968, and she had been publicly vocal in her support of Dr Spock, the S.D.S., and the speeches of Jane Fonda. She decried the killing, the burning, the mayhem, and the public deception. To herself, but never to Roy, she had said, as soon as she came to know him, 'What would I do if he had to go there? How could I stand it?'

She would have expected to have some similar reaction to the news that Fred Deets would be piloting a gunship or a rescue ship over the half-jungle, half-moonscape surface of Vietnam. But the news, when Grace told her, did not jolt her. The reason was simple. It never occurred to her that anything bad could happen to Fred. She had always considered his destiny as secure as her own. In some way that defied reason, from the time of his enlistment, she thought in terms of two wars, the familiar much-photographed bombing and burning, *that* war, and the other one, *Fred's* war, a kind of warmly dressed adventure where expert pilots manoeuvred flawlessly engineered helicopters across a landscape where no guns ever fired. Later in her life, a few years later, she told herself that this bizarre attitude of hers had been a defence, that she had in fact been frightened to death that something would happen to Fred and that she could only handle that fear by fantasizing a playground war where no one ever bled, burned, or died.

But in its own time frame, she simply congratulated herself that Fred was safely elsewhere and did not represent any kind of threat to her life with Roy.

Chapter 2

Christine attracted attention at Foresby. She always had. From the day of her first enrolment as a freshman she had been one of the students whose opinions were listened to, whose remarks were quoted, whose clothes and hairstyles were copied. She had no drive to be a leader, but there were, all the same, a great number of young women who wanted to follow her.

There were some compelling contradictions about her. She never seemed to study hard, but she made high marks. She didn't fuss with her clothes or her appearance, but she always looked fresh and stunning. And she was as admired by her own sex as she was by young men.

At her young age, she had mastered the trick of being genuinely interested in other people. And most intriguing of all, of course, to most of her schoolmates, was her long-standing and very grown-up affair with Fred Deets.

Any rumour of a rift, however temporary, between Christine and Fred would have swept through the classrooms and residence halls of Foresby like a new strain of influenza. They were a tested commodity, a perfectly matched set.

So the news that Christine had chosen someone else was big news indeed. All the elements of high drama were there. Fred had gone off to a bad war that everybody else wanted to avoid, and Christine, after a mysterious faraway summer on an eastern island, had come home, back to school, with a new man. The girls who had admired her before were now stunned. And many of them, when they saw Roy for the first time, were baffled. One girl said, 'And the princess eloped with the gardener.'

A month or so after school started, Roy said to Christine, 'Well, what's the verdict?'

'What do you mean?'

'I mean the verdict must be in by now. Are they saying you

picked a winner, or are your best friends avoiding you in the street?'

'I don't know what you're talking about.'

'Sure you do. I'll bet your friends are looking at you funny. I'll bet they're saying, "Chrissy, you blew it. You sluffed off the beautiful aviator with an airplane full of wristwatches and came up with a yardbird." Is that what they say?'

'They'd better not.'

'By the way,' he said. 'I've been meaning to ask you something. If I buy you a beautiful forty-dollar Lady Timex with a battery you put in once a year so you never have to wind it, will you take off that Diamond Jim watch and put it away someplace?'

'I'll drop it in the Boone River if you want me to.'

'No. Let's not go that far. We may have to pawn it later.'

After his Portland draft board scare, when they got word that Roy was back on the educational deferment list, Christine began to cry.

'Hey, what are you doing?' he said. 'We just got *good* news. What do you do when things get bad?'

'I'm sorry. I can't help it. I was scared to death. I was lying awake nights trying to decide what we could do, where we could go.'

'They weren't going to draft you. Just me.'

'You're a first-class moron. Do you know that? Do you really think if something rotten happens to you it's not going to happen to me too? Do you think I'd let you go if there was any chance . . . I mean I don't think there's *any* problem that can't be solved if you care enough.'

'Maybe so. But there are a few thousand guys every month who can't solve *this* problem.'

'There are also a few thousand who *have* solved it. Do you know how many guys have refused induction?'

'No. But I'll bet you do.'

'Someplace between forty and a hundred thousand. You can't trust the government figures. A lot of people say it's closer to two hundred thousand.'

'And a bunch of them are sitting in jail talking to themselves.'

'That's right,' Christine said. 'But a lot of them *aren't*. There are also ways to fail the physical . . . People still go the C.O. route. Anything's better than getting your brains blown out.'

'Listen,' he said. 'I'm not nuts. I know what you're saying makes sense. You think I haven't thought about it? We talked about it all the time up at Bowdoin last year. And those guys I knew aren't chicken. They're not just thinking about saving their own skins. They don't want to drop napalm on villages or machine-gun a bunch of rice farmers. But then somebody always says, "I don't want to go to jail either. Or live underground for the rest of my life. I'll do my hitch and get it behind me. In a year or two I'll be back in school and everything'll be fine." '

'Does that make sense to you?'

'I didn't say it made sense,' Roy said. 'The whole fucking thing doesn't make sense. It never has.'

'I've been in some veterans' hospitals. I've seen those guys with no faces or arms or legs. Most of them said just what you're saying. 'Let's get it over with. It'll work out all right.' But it didn't. You think those guys wouldn't go underground if they had it to do over again? Or go to Canada? Or go to the moon? You're damned right they would. It's not an intellectual choice. It's a *survival* choice. But most people don't realize it till it's too late.'

Chapter 3

*W*hen the cross-country season was over and Roy's Saturdays were free, Christine began to make plans for a weekend at home. When she mentioned it to him, however, he said, 'I don't think that's a great idea.'

'Why not?'

'No big reason. I just don't feel like parading up to Lake Forest right now.'

'Forget about Lake Forest. I'm not going to put you on exhibition. I just want you to see my home and sleep in my house. What's so strange about that?'

'Nothing. I just don't feel like going.'

'I know what you think you're saying. But what are you *really* saying?'

'I'm saying I don't want to get into a big thing with your family. I don't want to confuse things by bringing in a gang of people.'

'There's no gang. It's just Grace and my grandmother.'

'Why would I want to meet your grandmother? You don't even like her.'

'But what about Grace? What should I tell her?'

'Tell her to come here. If she's so hot to see you and meet me, why didn't she come down for any of the weekends this fall?'

'Because she hates to come here. It gives her the heebie-jeebies. She went to school here for a year and she hasn't been back since. She says she'll come when I graduate and that will be it.'

'Good,' Roy said. 'If she doesn't want to come here, then she'll understand why I don't want to go there.'

'You're really hot about this, aren't you?'

'I'm not hot. I just don't see why you keep pushing it.'

'I keep *pushing* it because it's important to me. If the shoe was on the other foot, if you were asking me . . .'

'I'm *not* asking you. I *wouldn't* ask you. Do you think I'd ask you to troop up to Portland to meet my aunt and uncle?'

'God, you're bullheaded.'

'Fine,' he said. 'That explains everything. Let's leave it there.'

'I don't want to leave it there. You're the most sensible human being I've ever met in my life and all of a sudden you're not making sense.'

'All right. Let me put it this way. The thing I like about us is it's just *us*. A simple equation. Sooner or later, I guess, we'll have to open the doors and let other people in. I don't mean that nothing should ever change. But Jesus . . . we're just getting started. Let's not screw things up before we have to.'

At Thanksgiving time, when she told Grace about that conversation with Roy, her mother said, 'You're lucky. He sounds like a smart one. The best thing of all is two people by themselves. You should hang onto that for as long as you can.'

When Margaret got Christine alone the day after Thanksgiving, she said, 'When are we going to meet that young man of yours?'

'After that letter you sent last summer I thought you probably wouldn't want to meet him.'

'Nonsense. I always try to do what I think is best for you. But your life is your own. When I realised you'd really chosen someone, then he became my choice, too.'

'I thought your choice was Fred Deets.'

'I admire Fred. You know that. But if you prefer Roy Lavidge, then I can only assume that he is a first-rate fellow.'

When Christine told her mother about the conversation with Margaret, Grace said, 'She's regrouping, that's all. Falling back and getting ready for a new assault. I don't know if she *loves* either one of us—I'm not sure she *knows* about that word—but she doesn't want to give us up. After all, she gave birth to me and I gave birth to you, so whatever our flaws, she figures we inherited something swell from her.'

Christine went back to school early so she could spend an extra day with Roy.

'I have to admit it,' she said, 'but when I got home I was glad you hadn't come with me. I started looking at everything as if I were you, and I said to myself, 'Thank God he's not here.' I'm still dying for you to see Grace, though. Maybe she'll meet us someplace. On neutral ground. Would you do that?'

'You're relentless.'

'Only because it's important to me. Will you?'

'I guess so.'

Two weeks later she called Grace and said, 'Roy and I are going up to Chicago next Saturday. Do you want to meet us for lunch?'

'It's all set,' Christine told Roy that evening. 'And is *she* going to get a surprise! I saw in yesterday's *Sun-Times* that Russell Atha's in Chicago, so I invited him.'

'You have had some *terrible* ideas, but that's the worst one yet.'

'Why? You like Russell. You said you liked him a lot.'

'I'm not talking about Russell. I'm talking about your mother. You could really throw her for a loop.'

'Not a chance. You don't know her.'

'Do me a favour,' Roy said. 'Tell her about it. Give her a chance to say no.'

'Then it's no fun. That will spoil the surprise,'

'After twenty years, just seeing him will be enough of a surprise. Give her a break.'

Christine stood up. 'You're right. I'll call her up.' She walked into the next room. He heard her dial and there was a long conversation, soft and muffled. Just before she hung up, he heard her laugh. When she came back into the room, she was still smiling. 'Oh, was she floored. You were right. I think if she'd walked into the Tavern Club and seen him sitting at a table with us, she'd have keeled over. I've never heard her so shaky.'

'Is she coming?'

'Of course she's coming.'

Chapter 4

*A*fter Christine's telephone call, in the few days between that evening and the following Saturday, Grace felt alert and vibrant, her eyes and ears and sense of smell all unusually sensitized, missing nothing, all sights and sounds isolated, all surfaces and textures and objects defining themselves clearly and individually under her fingertips. Each movement of her body, each footstep, each lift of the arm, each meeting of thumb and fingers, she felt as though she was observing from a distance.

She left the house early those interim mornings, took long drives along the shores, ate breakfast in truck-stop diners, had lunch or dinner in restaurants she'd never seen in towns she'd never stopped in before. Like a child hiding her week's ration of candy, she was determined, it seemed, to keep those days of anticipation to herself, to stay off the phone, to avoid her mother, to break the routine of her normal life at home.

She made no lists, wrote no notes to herself, made no plans. She simply set herself free, allowed herself total freedom to live from moment to moment, to walk and drive, to eat and drink and sleep like a soft animal, to wander in and out of movie theatres, libraries, and department stores, freely, with no deadlines, no schedule, no clear line of destination. By a process of elimination she pulled herself back into an almost primitive pattern of simple movement and behaviour. And when Saturday came at last, she stayed in bed with the phone turned off till ten. Then she got up, showered and dressed in a plain wool dress and a cardigan, had coffee and juice while she read the morning paper, and left the house at eleven for a leisurely drive to Chicago, plenty of time to take Lake Shore Drive and probably enough time to browse in an antique jewellery store she knew on Wacker Drive before going up to the Tavern Club for lunch.

She drove south on Highway 41 through Highwood,

Highland Park, and Glencoe. Then suddenly, just below Winnetka, when she saw a sign that said *Kenilworth, four miles*, she pulled off the road into an emergency zone, stopped her car, and turned off the engine. She stared straight ahead through the windshield, her hands tighly gripping the wheel; her body shook under her trenchcoat, and tears streamed down her face. She sat there for a long time, till the tears stopped, and the trembling. When she started the car again, she drove back north a little way, then west, all the way to Rockford. She stopped there, in the centre of town, and drank two cups of black coffee. Then she drove southwest to Dixon, and slowly east again toward Chicago. At Geneva she turned north, bypassed Elgin, and picked up Highway 68 heading due east to Glencoe. By the time she reached Kenilworth it was almost three in the afternoon. She drove to Sylvester Street and stopped in front of a two-storey white house with black shutters and a gabled roof. On the mailbox at the kerb was the name Elizabeth Griggs. Grace got out of her car, walked slowly up the walk to the front porch, and rang the bell. When the door opened, a tall, grey-haired woman stood there, brown, freckled skin, and her glasses pushed up on her forehead.

'I'm sorry, Liz,' Grace said. 'I should have called ahead. Is this a bad time?'

'No. Come in. I'm clear till five.'

Elizabeth Griggs was born in East Lyme, Connecticut, in 1909. While she was attending Bryn Mawr she met Katharine Hepburn and they became lifelong friends. They didn't look alike, but they both had angular silhouettes and a directness of manner that made them seem more similar than they were. They also shared a love of literature and the theatre.

Both girls, after graduation, went to New York, shared an apartment, and launched themselves as performers. When Miss Hepburn was appearing in *The Warrior's Husband,* at the Morosco in 1932, Miss Griggs was two blocks away at the Denby in a comedy called *Laugh Lines.*

In 1937 Elizabeth married a young theatrical lawyer. Both she and her husband expected that she would continue with her career. But by 1939, when Katharine Hepburn was appearing on Broadway again in *The Philadelphia Story*, Elizabeth was the mother of one child and was expecting another. Three years later, when her husband was run down by a taxi on Lexington Avenue, she was left with a modest annual income and four sons. In a letter to her friend Kate, who was busy making a film called *Keeper of the Flame*, Elizabeth wrote:

> As you know, I am now a young and lusty thirty-three. Not even in my prime yet. I could go back into the theatre. A part of me is longing to do just that. But . . . cooler heads, as they say, have to prevail. I have four little boys running around my apartment. And the oldest one isn't ready for school yet. So I'm afraid the only part for me to play is *mama*. I was very happy those five years with Philip and I never stepped on a stage once. So there's no reason why I can't go on as a non-actress.
>
> Here's what I plan to do. As you know, Ralph Atterbury, our old teacher at Bryn Mawr, is at Northwestern now. Head of the acting department. He wants me to come out there to help him, and I've decided I will.

For twenty-seven years, till she retired at age sixty, Elizabeth Griggs counselled and directed and bullied and consoled young actors at Northwestern. She lectured them in the art of the theatre and the science of themselves. When they found a way to connect those two areas, they knew everything she could teach them and they were ready to begin work as professionals.

From her interest in psychology as it relates to the theatre, she had gradually become involved in psychology as an end in itself. In 1948, when Carl Jung had opened his institute in Basel, she'd wangled a semester's leave of absence and attended those training sessions for five months. From then on, in addition to her teaching she had worked independently toward her own advanced degree in psychology. She received her doctorate at last in 1964, from the University of Chicago.

Her first patients, when she opened an office in her new home in Kenilworth, were former students and faculty members from Northwestern, people whom she had counselled and advised as friends, non-professionally, through the years. She decided, from the beginning, to restrict her patient list to women. One of these women was Grace Wheatley.

Chapter 5

'*I* really feel like such a horse's ass,' Grace said. 'I thought I was long past all these traumas and emotional jags. I'm forty years old, for Pete's sake. I should be able to handle things by now. But I fell apart like a total fool. Crying and shaking like a sad old drunk. It's bad enough I didn't get there after I promised I would. But I didn't even have the guts to call. I dialled the Tavern Club number twice. And both times I hung up before anybody could answer. What a boob.'

Elizabeth never took notes. None of their remarks were recorded. But she had in her mind, nonetheless, a full and very lovely portrait of Christine. She felt, listening to Grace, as if she'd watched a daughter grow up, seen the mother and child grow closer as the years passed.

Her perceptions of Margaret Jernegan were equally clear, she felt. An obsession with standards and behaviour and an inability to recognize the wisdom of warmth and touching, the priceless gift of a physical self.

And, of course, there were portraits of the men. Russell

Atha in the main gallery. And Grace's three husbands in a shadowy hallway at the rear.

'Everyone assumed that I detested Harold Wheatley, but I didn't. Except when he was trying to take Christine away from me; I hated him then with a passion. But when the dust settled and we weren't married to each other, when I knew I wasn't going to lose my daughter, then I saw things differently. I could admit to myself that I'd done him more damage than he'd done me.

'Harold wasn't a monster. Not at all. Potentially, he was a nice man. But that was the catch. He didn't know *how* to be a man. All he was able to be was a son.

'When we got married, I knew only that he came from a nice family, he was taller than me, and my girl friends thought he was cute. We had a short courtship. I can't remember any time when we were alone together. Not really. When I think about him now I feel sorry for him. I think he really did want to break loose from his father and his brothers but he didn't know where to start.

'I remember standing in front of the altar the day of the wedding. I was carried away by the whole production. I stood there, Little Miss Mushhead, and made a secret pact with myself that I would be the best wife that anybody ever saw. Then the minister said, "You may kiss the bride," and I turned back my veil and turned to Harold. He put his arms around me and his face was so close his nose looked magnified and distorted. There was perspiration on his upper lip and a sickening sweet smell from the lilies of the valley pinned to his lapel. He was holding me so tight it was hard to breathe, and when he put his lips on mine they felt wet and cold. Then he put his tongue in my mouth. I felt the blood drain out of my head and I almost fainted. I'd never been kissed like that before, not by him or by anyone, and I hated it. His tongue felt wet and slippery and fat as a goldfish. When he let me go and I looked up at him, he was smiling and his face was flushed. And there were trickles of saliva at the corners of his mouth.

'Don't misunderstand me. I don't mean that one kiss at the

altar set a tone for our whole relationship. It wasn't that simple. On our honeymoon, Harold was almost apologetic. He was fumbling and unsure of himself. We slept together three nights before he made love to me. It was very brief. I didn't feel anything. The next day I bought a box of Tampax at the hotel pharmacy and pretended I had my period. By then I had developed such a physical aversion to him I could hardly spend the night in the same bed. I hated to sit across the table from him and watch him eat. The sound of him brushing his teeth and gargling made me feel sick. If he had been a different kind of man, if he'd paddled my behind or got drunk and screwed me silly, I might have responded differently. But as it was, the worse I treated him, the more tentative he got. When we got back to Lake Forest and I said I wanted a bedroom by myself, he didn't let out a peep.

'When I found out I was pregnant I couldn't believe it. I was in a panic. All I could think was that a child would give permanence to something that I knew had to be temporary. So I left and went to France.'

About her second husband, Evan Causey, she said, 'God knows nobody ever got married for worse reasons. I did it because Margaret forced me to. I knew it was the only way I'd be able to keep Christine. And he married me because . . . I don't know . . . I guess because he wasn't married to anybody else at the time. Evan's been married to somebody ever since he was eighteen. It's the only way he can keep his mother out of his bed. She is really a piece of work. One of those delicate little numbers in pastel silk with a bosom out to here and ankle-strap pumps like Joan Crawford.

'Evan has a sense of humour about her, though. He has a sense of humour about everything. When I was drunk—I drank a lot during those five years in Palm Beach—I used to say to him, "Don't tell me you've never slept with her. Have you ever gone to bed with her or not?" And he'd say, "Hardly ever."

'Being married to Evan was like going to an expensive summer camp where they start serving drinks at breakfast and stop in the wee hours when the last body falls. In my frame of mind it was a perfect life for me. The only way I could blot out the memory of Russell was to saturate myself with booze, beginning with champagne and fresh orange juice on my breakfast tray and going on from there. It was a perfect life for everyone. Evan had his Siamese cats and his model airplanes, his mother had her mirrored bedroom and whatever beach creatures she could lure into it, Christine had her dog and her Nanny, and I had my Dom Pérignon.

'When Chrissy was old enough to start school, when I told Evan I wanted to take her back to Lake Forest and put her in school there, he said, 'Jesus, kid, I don't want to struggle through those Chicago winters.' So that summer we got a divorce, and three days later, he married an Australian girl he'd met at a horse show in Dublin two months before.

'For the next seven years, till I was thirty-three and Christine was thirteen, I devoted myself to her. Not for *her* sake, but for mine. I needed her in those days more than she needed me. She was solid and secure and full of beans. I spent every minute I could with her from the time she started school till she entered high school. We really enjoyed each other. She was the most interesting person I knew. I was contented with my life, enjoying my days and feeling good about myself. I was crazy about my daughter and she was crazy about me. I couldn't, at that time, envision a better life for myself. Then one day Mrs Ross-Shannon sat me down and said, "I'm concerned about Christine. She's turning into a young woman, she's very grown-up for her age, and I think it's important for her to try her wings, to meet other people. I think she should go away to school." When I said that Chrissy and I had discussed that subject a lot and that she preferred to stay at home and go to day school, Augusta said, "Of course she *thinks* that. She's very contented here. But that's just my point. She needs to see things now that are not so easy, not so comfortable. She's spent her life so far in a world of women. Girls' schools, girl friends, women teachers, and nothing but women in her home."

'I said she would have plenty of time in her life to meet men, and Augusta said, "I'm not talking about *that*. She's a beautiful girl. Men will always find her. I'm talking about balance. *Now* is the time when she should begin to get a feel of the way the world works, how men and women work together and play together and live together. She doesn't need boyfriends, but she very much needs to have friends who are boys."

'Christine did go away to school that September. And I missed her terribly. There was never a specific moment when I decided that I might get married again, but I became gradually aware that I was open to the idea in a way that I hadn't been since my divorce from Evan.

'One thing I was sure of. I was anxious to avoid the kind of men I had married before. Harold and Evan were as different as two people could possibly be. But somewhere, in their soft centres, there was a kinship. They were, as *I* am, children of privilege. That is difficult for anyone to survive, but it is particularly difficult for a male child. It's no accident that so many of them end up as drunks.'

Elizabeth Griggs sat listening, slouched in a deep chair with her legs crossed. She smiled and said, "So did all this . . . what shall we call it . . . this assessment of the men you'd married before help you in selecting your third husband?'

Grace nodded. 'Enter Vincent Weigle. A different species altogether. His father and both his brothers are steelworkers in Erie, Pennsylvania. German father. Italian mother. They're a terrific family. They were wonderful to me.'

'How long were you married?' Elizabeth asked.

'Three years.'

'Not a long marriage.'

'No. Not at all. Vince had been married before. He had two kids living in Pittsburgh.'

'He was an athlete, wasn't he?'

'That's right. He played four seasons with the Steelers.'

'What about his children? How did he handle that?'

'He was crazy about them. But he believed they were better off living with their mother. At least that's what he said. The truth was he didn't think he was good enough for them. I think that's why he left his wife, too. She'd been his girl friend

113

since high school. She'd been with him through all the football glory days. I never thought it was a coincidence that they split up two months after the Steelers let him go as a player. He didn't know how to start over.'

'But he did it with you.'

'He *tried* to. But feeling the way he did about himself, the last thing he wanted was any kind of demanding relationship. I don't think he was in love with me when we got married, but I *know* he was in love with me when he left.'

'What did he say to you? Why did he leave?'

'It was pathetic. Vince was a terrible liar. He said he knew I was in love with somebody else so he didn't want to stand in my way. He said he'd already talked to a lawyer and he was going to give me a divorce.'

'What did you say?'

'I told him I *wasn't* in love with anybody else and I didn't want a divorce. He thought that over for a few days, then he told me the real reason he wanted a divorce was so he could go back to his wife and kids in Pittsburgh. A week later his lawyer served papers on me.'

'Did he go back to his kids?'

'No. I don't think he ever expected to. He just wanted out. Later I got one note from him with no return address. It said, "You gave me better than I gave you back. You meant a lot to me, but I couldn't handle it." '

Chapter 6

*E*arly in December, at six o'clock one morning, Roy had an accident. Startled by a ground squirrel that appeared suddenly on the running path in front of him, he stepped to one side, hit a soft spot of mud and rotted leaves, and slid from the ridge crown down the steep bank of a ravine. Halfway down his left foot wedged itself under the ground root of a walnut tree, his body continued to twist and slide, and the ligaments in his left knee tore loose.

Quite apart from competitive running, which Roy had done since age thirteen, he had becomed addicted to the daily agony of five miles before breakfast. Pushing himself till it hurt. In an oilskin jacket with a hood when it rained, in a wool hat, sweat suit, and thermal underwear when the weather began to freeze.

He was always, wherever he was, the first one up, the only man in the streets, on the road, in the woods. He became accustomed to that grey and silent world of first light before engines coughed and roared, before the ugly music of bells and horns and sirens floated through the streets. It was his time. It anchored him, soothed him, cleared his head.

All Roy's plans about college, about work, about the future, had germinated in his mind during his morning runs. As long as his legs were pumping, as long as the breath was gusting in and out of his lungs, he felt no restrictions on himself, no limitations. He had the courage to hope and plan, to project his future image on whatever screen he might select.

And from the time when his senses and his energy began to change the temperature of his body, when soft floating images of women began to crowd into every corner of his life, when no hour or even a ten-minute segment of time slipped by without some silver flash of sexual impulse nudging him, all those solitary running times gave him freedom to indulge his senses, to see white flesh undulating in every clearing and cove.

115

Between the ages of thirteen and sixteen, when his sexual frenzy was most acute, the act of running coupled with the female images that flickered in his mind was enough to bring him to climax. As he felt it coming on he ran faster and faster, forced himself to stay at full speed. The more shattering the orgasm, the faster he ran, resisting collapse, trembling and gasping, but running through it. Exorcism of the beast. Act of atonement.

After he met Christine, her presence and her reality monopolized his running hours. Only to himself, alone in the silence, his feet beating a steady rhythm on the ground, only then could he let down the barriers, recognize and accept his vulnerability, admit to himself how linked to her he was, how dependent on her.

She said to him, 'I know how you feel about me, but only because I'm a good guesser. If I had to go by what you *say*, I'd feel like a poor rejected soul.'

'No, you wouldn't,' he said. 'Besides, if I sat you down and told you how I *really* feel, I'd scare you off. You'd say, "God, he's pitiful." You'd be on the first bus to New Orleans, looking for a merchant seaman with a tattoo of an eagle on his arm.'

'There you go again,' she said. 'Laying down a smoke screen.'

It was true. He was afraid of stumbling, of breaking all the way loose, of turning to her in bed some night and saying, 'I didn't think there *were* any women like you. At least not for me. It makes me go slow. I don't want to get so far out I can't swim back.'

He never spoke to her like that, of course. He wasn't able to. Instead, he said, 'I hope you're not getting too serious about me. I mean you're a nice girl and we have a lot of laughs together, but a guy like me, you know, I'm really in demand. Women after me all the time. God knows when some lady might make me a fantastic offer. Take me to Argentina or something.'

'If that happens,' Christine said, 'I wouldn't want to stand in your way.'

116

'Good. That's what I hoped you'd say.'

'On the other hand, if you go off to Argentina with some chippie, I promise you will go as a soprano.'

The plans he had made for himself in the past took on new urgency now. Time was against him. Even if circumstances remained ideal, Christine would be out of college a year before he would. So it would be two years, perhaps three, before . . . before anything.

When he mentioned these things to Christine, she refused to discuss them. 'Are you a worrywart? Am I going to spend my life with a nervous person? We have the world by the proverbial curls. Love conquers all, Lavidge.'

The morning he fell into the ravine by the running trail, it was almost an hour before he managed to extricate himself from the root where his leg was pinned and drag himself up the slope. His leg was stiff by then, his knee swollen and throbbing. Supporting himself with a stick, he hobbled for more than a mile to the nearest house. By midmorning he was on his way by ambulance to Springfield. Just after noon, they operated on his knee.

Chapter 7

'*I* know you feel lousy about it. So do I,' Roy said, 'but it won't help any to cry.' He was sitting in his hospital bed, his left leg, heavily bandaged, stretched out straight in front of him on the mattress.

'I didn't say it would *help*,' Christine said, 'but I can't just turn off the way I feel. And the worst part is that you've given up.'

'I haven't given up anything. But I'm not gonna sit here and tell myself fairy stories. My only shot at going to college was using my legs. Running. Now I *can't* run.'

'You're not *crippled*, for Pete's sake. Your knee will heal up.'

'That's right. I'll be able to walk. I may even be able to run. But that doesn't mean I'll be able to compete. It's a cinch I won't be running next spring.'

'So you'll lay out of competition for a season. They're not going to pull the plug on you after one semester. Do you really think they're going to cancel your scholarship?'

'What do *you* think?'

'I don't think they will.'

'Good. I hope you're right. But I wouldn't advise you to put any money on it. Why should they carry somebody who can't produce? I wouldn't do it if I were in Hollenbeck's shoes.'

She folded her handkerchief and slipped it into her jacket pocket. 'It's not even Christmas yet. And I'll bet you're a fast healer. I don't know why you're so sure you won't be able to run in the spring.'

'I said I wouldn't be able to compete. Did you ever see an anatomical drawing of a knee? It looks like the insides of a computer, wires going off in all directions. When those ligaments or tendons get ruptured or split or tangled up, it takes a genius surgeon to piece them all together again. Any athlete would rather have a broken leg, or a fractured skull even, than a bunged-up knee.'

'You make everything sound hopeless.'

'I told you. I don't want to kid myself. And I don't want to kid you.'

'If you don't come back to school after Christmas, you'll be in the Army before you can turn around.'

'I know that. I think my best bet is to enlist before I'm drafted. Then I can get the Navy maybe. Or Army Engineers.'

'Are you crazy? Half the people in the world are out in the streets carrying posters against the Vietnam thing, and you sit there and say you're going to *enlist*? What kind of sense does that make?'

'It makes a helluva lot more sense than being drafted.'

'No, it doesn't. Do you think they send all the enlisted men to Disneyland? Everybody's going to the same lousy place. They just need bodies. And once you sign your name, They've got *yours*.'

'What's the use of talking about it?'

'We *have* to talk about it. The only answer for you is to stay in school. I don't think they'll take your scholarship away, but if they do, you still have to stay in school. You'll have to pay your own way.'

'Brilliant. How do I do that?'

'Borrow the money. Take out a loan. There are hundreds of companies who do nothing but lend money.'

'Not without collateral.'

'Then borrow from private sources. From an individual.'

'Great idea,' he said. 'Like who?'

Looking at him, something told her that he knew what she was about to say, that his answer would shoot back at her like an arrow as soon as the words were out of her mouth. 'I don't know,' she said slowly. 'I wish I did.'

Chapter 8

On December nineteenth, the last day of classes before Christmas holidays, Roy still had a light cast on his knee and was using a cane. He and Christine rented a car at noon that day in Lincoln and drove north to Bensenville, just west of O'Hare Airport. They spent the rest of the day and that night there in a motel called Itasca Gardens.

As soon as they checked in, the evening already grey and

thick outside, the constant hum of jet engines in the deep sky overhead, they got into bed, ordered ham-and-egg sandwiches, two each, from the coffee shop, and called for a large bucket of ice to cool the bottles of champagne they'd brought with them. They sat in bed then, eating and drinking and watching mindless programmes on the television set.

After they finished their sandwiches, she said, "Dessert now or later?' and he said, 'Now.' She got up, cleared away the plates, and came back to the bed with two forks, two hand towels for napkins, and a cake they had bought in a German bakery just off Highway 55 in Bolingbrook, a heavy chocolate cake with raspberry jam between the layers and thick bitter-sweet chocolate frosting.

They sat shoulder to shoulder in the bed, the covers pulled up to their waists, their backs against the padded headboard, the iced champagne on a chair within reach, the cake balanced on a Chicago telephone directory resting on the mattress between them.

'We're eating the whole cake,' she said.

'Not leaving a bit of it.'

'Guzzling champagne and gobbling down every single crumb of this marvellous cake.'

'Just like grown-ups.'

He held out his glass and she filled it, then filled her own draining the bottle.

'*Voilà*,' she said. Then, 'I think we're drinking too much.'

'It doesn't matter.'

'You told me one thing a distance runner mustn't do is drink too much.'

'What's the other thing?'

'The other thing is what we always do so much of when we drink too much.'

'It doesn't matter.'

'What does this remind you of?' she said then.

'What?'

'Sitting here like this, eating like animals and drinking till our heads spin. What does it remind you of?'

'I give up.'

'No, you don't. You know what I'm talking about.'

'Martha's Vineyard. That picnic we had the first night.'

'You got it.'

She carefully lifted the cake plate and the telephone book off the bed and put them on the floor. Then she switched off the lamp on her side of the bed, slipped out of her pyjamas, and lay close against him under the blankets.

'I can't reach my lamp switch,' he said.

'That's all right.'

'The television's still on.'

'There's a Randolph Scott movie later,' she said. 'I thought you might want to watch it.'

'You taste like chocolate cake.'

'Count your blessings.' Then, 'Did you ever think that it takes a very agile and creative girl to make love to a man with his leg in a cast?'

'Shall we send out for one?'

'You bastard,' she whispered.

'Maybe I should have got a note from the doctor.'

'Tomorrow.'

'What does that mean?'

'You know what it means. *Tomorrow* you'll need a note from the doctor. Tonight you're in fine shape.'

Late the next morning, as they drove toward the airport access road, she said, 'I need some promises from you.'

'Like what?'

'Like you won't go crazy and enlist in the Navy or the Canine Corps or something while you're home in Portland.'

'I don't want to enlist,' he said, 'but I can't promise.'

'Yes, you can. We're talking about ten days. You can wait till you're back at school.'

'I never got anything but maybes from Hollenbeck. I don't know if I'm coming back to school.'

'Don't be a dope, Roy. No matter what happens, you have to finish out the semester.'

'No, I don't. Not if the draft board's sitting on my tail just waiting for my deferment to fizzle out. I have to enlist before they grab me.'

'That's not going to happen.'

'Who says so.'

'I do. The next thing you know, you'll be into your senior year and the whole crappy Vietnam thing will be over.'

'Jesus, I'm glad to hear that. I was starting to get worried. You should travel around the country with a sound truck so all those guys who are burning their draft cards will know they can relax.'

'Don't be a smart ass. Just don't go home to Portland and do something cuckoo. Okay?'

'Okay. I'll be good.'

Chapter 9

'*I*'m worried about Agnes,' Joe Medek said. He and Roy were driving north from Boston toward Portland. 'She's always had the migraine headaches. You remember that from when you were a kid. And she's always had asthma attacks. But lately, it seems like everything's going wrong. Her blood pressure went sky-high and she's got terrible back pains. And as if that wasn't enough, her circulation ain't what it ought to be. Her ankles swell up.'

'What's the doctor doing for her?'

'He's got her pumped so full of pills she doesn't know where she is. Just sits up in a chair in front of the TV, half asleep. When she comes to, she pops another pill and away she goes again.'

'Jesus, she's not very old—'

'Fifty-two next month,' Joe said, 'but you'd never guess it to look at her. She's really failed.'

Later that night as he stood in his windowed room looking out at the sea, Roy felt tentative and off-balance, poised between this world he knew so well and a new one he didn't know at all. He told himself it was his aunt's illness, her half-drugged silence, that was throwing him off. Then he blamed his stiff leg. Or was it being away from Christine? He reached several different conclusions. But the depression did not go away. He stood in his room, stared out at the sea, and floundered.

Chapter 10

Christmas Eve, while Agnes slept in her chair, Roy and his uncle put up the tree, strung the lights, and hung the decorations, many of them handmade, passed down through generations of Czech and Italian peasants. Then Joe went into his workshop to wrap gifts, and Roy, upstairs in his own room, wrapped the gifts he had brought for Joe and Agnes.

After they'd put the packages under the tree, they sat down at the kitchen table with a bottle of I W Harper, and worked out the menu for Christmas dinner the next day, checking the refrigerator as they went down the list to be sure they hadn't forgotten anything at the market.

They got up early the next morning, ate some ham and eggs in the kitchen, drank half a pot of coffee, and started preparing the dinner. At ten o'clock, when Agnes got up, they waited while she drank a glass of juice and swallowed her morning line of pills. Then they all sat around the Christmas tree in the living room and opened their gifts. By the time they finished, Agnes was drowsy again.

At two in the afternoon, when everything was waiting on the table in the dining room, Agnes was sound asleep, heavy in her chair. When Joe shook her awake she said she didn't feel like eating.

So the two men sat across from each other at the table with the platters of food between them. Joe said, 'It's not the way Christmas usually is, but I'm glad you came home.'

'Me too.'

They drank the wine and ate huge amounts of food, each of them, as though they were trying to reassure each other that everything was all right. When they finished at last, they put away the leftover food, washed the dishes, and straightened up the kitchen.

It was a quarter past four when Roy said, 'I feel like the Goodyear blimp. You want to take a walk?'

'I'll walk you as far as the car. We'll drive up north and I'll show you some of those condominiums that Rigby's putting up.'

They went in to see Agnes before they left. Her eyes were open, but when Joe asked if she'd like to come with them she said, 'No, I'll just stay here. You two go ahead and have a nice time.'

When they were inside the car, heading north along the coast, Roy said, 'I think we should have waited till tomorrow. We're losing the light pretty fast.'

'That's all right. I just wanted to get out of the house for a while. There's something I wanted to talk to you about and I didn't want Agnes to hear it.'

'Is something wrong with my mother?'

'No. Maria's fine. Agnes hears from her regular. But you're getting warm. It's your dad. He was here in Portland a couple weeks ago.'

'No kidding.'

Joe nodded. 'Big as life. *Bigger*, as a matter of fact. He's put on maybe thirty pounds since the last time I saw him.'

'What did he want?'

'What do you think? He was looking for you. Came to my office down by the lumberyard. Caught me bright and early. I was loading some stuff in the truck, getting ready to go out to the edge of town, where I had a couple of men putting up a garage, when he strolled up, with his hand held out like he was running for office.'

'What did he say?'

'He said he wanted to talk to me. But I had a ready-mix truck on the way to my construction site and I had to meet the driver there. So I told your dad I was under the gun, but if he wanted to come out where I was working at noon, I'd talk to him while I was eating my lunch. So that's what he did. When I pulled out of the lot in my truck, I saw him at the kerb getting into a car. There was a blond-haired woman sitting behind the wheel—T.J. always had an eye for blondes.'

'What did he want to see you about?'

'Like I said. He was trying to locate you. But it took him a while to get around to the subject. He sat in my truck with me while I ate my lunch and he was blabbering away like a travelogue, telling me about every place he's been in the last fifteen years. Hawaii, Tokyo, Singapore. Worked on the pipeline up in Alaska. Six months in New Zealand. A year in Australia. Always a little fuzzy about what he was doing, but one thing I'll say for him, T.J.'s not afraid to work. He can drive any kind of truck ever built, and he handled a bulldozer for me one summer. And he's been a bartender off and on since he was twenty, so he can always do that. I think that's what he likes best. He likes to get dressed up and bullshit with the customers, especially the women. He thinks they're all after him. And quite a few of them are. He always seems to have one in the bed and one in the air. But he's a crumb, no matter how many females he has chasing him. I figured he'd straighten out like any other decent guy when he saw that he had a wife and a kid to look after. But I didn't know the kind of bird I was dealing with. He knew all along there was a bus heading south from Damariscotta every day. And he knew someday he'd be on it.

'I've thought about him a lot, through the years. Lots of

times I've felt like killing him, but mostly I decided he wasn't worth killing. Your mother would have been better off if she'd had her baby, given birth to you, and just gone on living with Agnes and me. And later marrying some decent guy who cared something about her. But she was scared to death of the priest, afraid of the church. With her and Agnes after me, I didn't have any choice but to do what I did. Anyway, your mother got a husband and you got a father, in the church records at least. But he wasn't worth a damn to either one of you. I'm sorry to talk that way about your dad, but what I'm saying is the truth.'

'You're not hurting my feelings,' Roy said. 'You're more of a dad to me than he'll ever be. I don't even know why he'd want to find me after all these years.'

'He probably wants you to love him. T.J. wants everybody to love him. He thinks he's America's boyfriend. Always did think that. If you ever meet him you'd better throw your arms around him and give him a big kiss, because that's what he expects. He even had the guts to say to me, "Roy's got a right to know his own father." I was all ready to say, "Listen, you silly bastard, you should have thought of that fifteen years ago." But I let it pass. I just sat there eating my sandwich. When he asked me where you were, I said I didn't know.'

'Did he believe you?'

'Course not. But he knows better than to call me a liar. I said for all I know you were out in Vietnam someplace. But he was heading for Damariscotta from here, like I said, and I'd be surprised if he didn't stop at Bowdoin on the way to do his long-lost-father act and see if he could weasel some information out of them. So don't be surprised if he shows up out there in Illinois.'

'I still can't figure why he's so hot to see me.'

'Proud father, he says. Somebody sent him some clippings about you from the sports pages. He said he'd like to see you run.'

Roy tapped the cast on his knee. 'Maybe I can get him to sign my cast instead.' Then, 'Did you tell him about Mum? Does he know she's married again?'

'He knew it all right. Also knew she has two daughters. Maria had a couple of close friends in Round Pond. So if she's been in touch with them through the years, I guess the news leaked out.'

Joe had turned the car around and they were halfway back to Portland before either of them said anything more. Finally, Joe said, 'T.J.'s a big kid in a lot of ways. Something about him never grew up. New places. New faces. A different bar every night. I always thought that was why he liked the Air Force so much. I think those years during the war were the best ones he ever had. I told him once that he'd made a big mistake when he left the service. And he said, "You hit it, Joe, That's where I blew it." '

'He was a bombardier. I saw pictures of him standing by the plane. A sharp-looking kid. Like I said, I think he started sliding downhill the day he took of that lieutenant's uniform. All he knew was to keep the party going any way he could. And when the going gets tough, you pick up your marbles and run. That's the way he was twenty years ago, and that's the way he'll be the day he dies.'

Chapter 11

*T*hree days before they left school to go home for their Christmas holidays, Christine began sending letters to Roy's home in Portland. 'This way you'll have mail waiting when you get there and a letter every day till you come back.'

While he was in Portland she called him every day, usually

at night, after Joe and Agnes had gone to bed. And at some point, during each phone conversation, she asked, 'Any word from Hollenbeck?'

'Nothing so far.'

'Well, don't worry. I've been doing my witch routine. I have good feelings about it.'

Two days before he was due to go back to Foresby, Roy received a telegram message from Hollenbeck.

SCHOLARSHIP PICTURE LOOKS GOOD.
SEE ME AS SOON AS YOU'RE BACK.

That same morning Roy had an overseas airmail letter from Tom Peddicord.

Saigon

Dear Roy:

Talk about shit luck. You remember how I couldn't wait to get over here so I could wade through the jungles and shoot a few gooks? Well, guess where they put me. In the fucking Military Police. Stationed in Saigon. Walking through the streets, trying to keep a hundred thousand freaked-out G.I. assholes from killing each other. I had the second-best firing-range record of any dog-ass who ever went through Parris Island. By the time I finished basic I was hard as a rock and mean as a snake. So where am I? Billeted in a hotel with a French restaurant on the main floor and working eight hours a day like a fucking accountant. Except I work nights. And instead of adding up figures, I'm adding up bodies. They say there's a hundred American combat deaths in Vietnam every week. That's bullshit. There's a lot more than that. But whatever the figure is, there's just as many getting killed behind the lines. The ones that don't O.D. on heroin get cut up by some little whore or her pimp. Or else they kill each other. Officers and noncoms get killed by their own men every day. Back here it's worse than it is in the combat zones. All the guys in uniform in Saigon are bucking for just one thing. A discharge. Any kind they can get. There's a less-than-honourable discharge called a 212. They hand them out over here by the hundreds. My captain told me that rear-area guys get fifty percent more 212's than combat soldiers do. How do you figure it? There's more discipline at Parris Island before breakfast than there is here in a week. If these black dudes and S.D.S. assholes and pill poppers get pissed off at an officer or a noncom, they just kill him, *frag* him they call it. A captain and two lieutenants were fragged here last week, and nobody keeps track of the noncoms who get a grenade rolled under their bunks. They pin a purple heart on them before they ship them home and list the cause of death as a 'nonmilitary accident.'

So that's my war, buddy. Not what I bargained for, but I'm stuck with it. Nobody ever gets transferred out of the MPs. Mostly I stroll the streets at night with my partner, visit the whorehouses and the nightclubs, and try to be someplace else when trouble starts. It's like a carnival here. You can buy anything you want. Or anybody. Down by the wharfs you see the slopes selling brand-new American refrigerators and television sets. Air conditioners and record players. Anything. It all gets shipped here with the war hardware. And that stuff's for sale too. You can buy a new M 16 anyplace. Or any other weapon. Hand grenades by the case. They say the Vietcong guys are in here shopping all the time. It's all graft and pussy and booze and dope. People getting rich and your life's not worth a nickel. The latest rumour I heard is that Nixon has a percentage deal with the South Viet government. When he sends them a hundred million in aid, they deposit ten million in his name in a Chinese bank. I don't believe that shit. I voted for Nixon and I'd do it again. But that's the kind of stories that float around over here. The worse they sound, the better chance they have of being true.

I sure miss my wife. I don't mess with any of this

129

Saigon gash 'cause I wouldn't want to carry something home to Cuba and the kid. I'd really like to be there when she has the baby, but since it's due in April I know I'm out of luck. Drop me a line. And stay out of the fucking Army. It's a joke.

Chapter 12

*H*is first day back at school, Roy went to Hollenbeck's office.

'You got my telegram, I guess.'

'Yes, I did,' Roy said. 'So where am I?'

Hollenbeck grinned. 'You're *in*. We're sticking with you through the spring semester. Then we'll see how things look for next year. How's the leg feel?'

'I'm still hobbling. I'm supposed to go to Springfield day after tomorrow to get the cast off.'

Hollenbeck nodded. 'I've had a couple chats on the phone with Jack Kenzler, the doctor who operated on you. And Monk Gilby, our team doctor. We don't want you to push yourself. Monk will bring you along slow. We want to make sure that knee is completely healed before you try to give it any speed work.'

'What if I'm not ready to run when the track season starts?'

'Then you won't be,' Hollenbeck said. 'We don't even *want* you to compete till we're damned sure you're ready.'

When Roy told Christine about the meeting with Hollenbeck, he said, 'I thought they'd want me to lay out next semester so I wouldn't lose a season of eligibility.'

'They're not dopes. They know if you're out of school you're in the Army.'

As they sat in a booth later in the coffee shop, she said, 'It was the strangest Christmas of my life. I really hated it. Always before, for as long as I remember, I couldn't wait for the holidays to start. But this year . . .' She picked up her cup of cocoa and drained the last swallow.

'What went wrong?' he said.

'Nothing went wrong. I mean Grace had the house all lovely and decorated like every other year, and we stayed up and trimmed the tree as usual. But there was something missing. *You* were missing. I was thinking all the time about you. And I know Grace sensed that. And the other thing was, we both started to feel bad about Nanny. When we were doing the tree I opened a box of ornaments she had made. Little animals made of fine needlework. As soon as Grace looked at them she started to bawl. And as soon as she started, so did I. We sat there sobbing like a couple of fools. Before we went to bed that night, Grace said, 'I'm glad we had the crying jag. It was five years overdue. We owed her one.' And we did. At least *I* did. Ever since I met you, I've been thinking more and more about Nanny. As much as I love my mother, the person I really would like to show you off to is Nanny. I've tried a thousand times to imagine just how she'd look at you and what she would say.'

'She'd say, "Where'd you find that bum?" '

'No, she wouldn't. She'd ask you if you'd like some tea. Or a glass of stout. She loved her Guinness. Then she'd sit you down for a nice talk. She was an interesting woman. She'd travelled all over the world. She'd spent her whole grown-up life working for conservative people but she ended up with liberal ideas. She used to say, "It doesn't make sense for some people to accumulate more than they'll ever need when every night there are millions of children who go to bed hungry." '

'Was she ever married herself? Did she have children?'

'I'm not sure. She was almost sixty when she started to take care of me, so she'd lived a lot of years. But she never talked about her own family or what her personal life had been like. After she died, though, when Grace and I were sorting through her things, we found a box of pictures, all photographs of children. And mostly there were pictures of a little boy and girl. And when we opened the gold locket Nanny wore around her neck, there were pictures inside it of those same two children. So who knows? Maybe they *were* her children. But if they were, it was something she didn't want to talk about. She treated Grace and me as if we were her only relatives, as if she were a mother to both of us. And that's the way we felt. Especially Grace. Nanny was the one who kept her afloat.'

'Did your mother ever tell you why she didn't show up for lunch that day?'

'Nope.'

'You didn't ask her?'

'I didn't have to. I knew without asking. She just chickened out. As long as she doesn't see Russell, she can remember what she wants to remember. The illusion stays intact.'

'Did you ever read that story by Faulkner where a woman's lover dies and she sleeps with his skeleton for the rest of her life?'

Christine nodded. 'She was crazy. But Grace is *not* crazy. Just the opposite. She went as far down the well as a person can go when she had to make a choice between Russell and me. She had to give him up if she wanted to keep me. Even after she'd *made* the choice she couldn't face up to it. I told you about that. That's when she tried to kill herself. And finally, I think she said to herself, "They can keep me away from him, but *nobody* can wreck what we had together." '

'I know what you're saying,' Roy said. 'But it still doesn't make sense.'

'To me it does. Why are you shaking your head?'

'I think I'm tangled up with a family of crazy ladies.'

'And don't you forget it,' Christine said.

132

Chapter 13

*T*en days after he came back to Foresby, Roy had a letter from his draft board in Portland ordering him to report for induction February ninth, 1970. The papers had been forwarded by his uncle with a note attached.

What's the matter with these bastards? Don't they know you have a deferment?

As soon as Roy opened the envelope and saw what was inside, he went upstairs to his room and typed out a letter to the draft board, explaining his situation. 'If you refer to my file, I think you'll see that some mistake has been made.'

He put the papers, envelope and all, into a fresh envelope. Then he walked downtown to the post office and mailed it, certified, to the Portland draft board. At noon, just after his eleven-o'clock class, he took the bus to Springfield to meet with Dr Kenzler. The cast had been off his leg for a week and he had begun his daily therapy programme in the weight room of the Foresby gymnasium.

When Roy was up on the examination table in his shorts, Dr Kenzler said, 'How's it feel?'

'Tight. No pain when I work out. But it never really gets loose.'

Kenzler manoeuvred the knee gently. 'Any twinge when I do that?'

'No'

'How about that?'

'Nothing.'

'And when I flex it?'

'It steel feels a little tight, but it doesn't hurt.'

'Good. That's good.'

Late that afternoon, when he got back to his dormitory,

Roy found a message in his room. 'Call Jim Hollenbeck.' When he came on the phone, Hollenbeck said, 'Why don't I buy you some breakfast in the morning? I want to hear how it went with Kenzler.'

The next morning Roy met Hollenbeck in a restaurant just off campus. He told him about the examination. 'He took some new X rays and said he'd be in touch with you.'

'He called me last night, as a matter of fact,' Hollenbeck said. 'He says he didn't talk to you about the X rays.'

'He hadn't seen them when I left.'

Hollenbeck studied the coffee in his cup. He picked it up, swirled it slowly, and took a drink. When he set it down, he said, 'I'd give fifty bucks if somebody else was sitting here instead of me.'

Before the words came, Roy could feel his palms get cold suddenly and his stomach start to tighten. Finally Hollenbeck said, 'I think Kenzler's full of crap on this one. At least I *hope* he is.' He spoke very slowly then, as though he was fighting an impulse to blurt out all the words at once. 'He says your leg's looking fine. If you take care of it it should be good as new by summer.'

'That means I won't be able to compete this spring.'

Hollenbeck shook his head. 'Not *any* spring, according to Kenzler. He says the surgery was a success. The ligaments and the tendons and the cartilage all got sorted out and put back in place. But there were some damaged nerves. They were alive during the operation, but between then and now about forty percent of them died.'

'Why does it feel the same as it did then? I told Kenzler it still feels tight but it's not numb.'

'That's right. And he says the tightness will go away too. Your leg should be as good as it ever was. You can dance and jump and run. What you'll never be able to do, according to Kenzler, is run *fast*. At least not fast enough. It's a matter of quickness. You'll feel like you're running the way you always did, except your left leg will never be able to match the right one. In the eight eighty he says you'd be lucky if you ever came within ten seconds of your best time.'

134

After his ten-o'clock class that morning, Roy went to the administration building and had a talk with the assistant to the registrar. After lunch he talked with the dean of male students, and from there he went to Theoni Clegg in the office of grants and scholarships.

That evening he told Christine about his conversation with Hollenbeck.

'I don't believe it,' she said. 'By next year you'll be beating everybody. The main thing is you still have your scholarship.'

'I wasn't too sure of that. So I decided I'd better check it out with Hollenbeck.'

'What did he say?'

'No problems. Not only am I locked in till the end of the year, my scholarship's extended till I graduate.'

'That's terrific.'

'It's *too* terrific. We're talking about a free ride for a runner who may not be able to run anymore. It either has to be a mistake or something's fishy.'

'Fishy? What could be fishy?'

'That's exactly what Hollenbeck said. But I kept after him. And finally he admitted a few things. After I hurt my knee, the athletic department had some reservations about renewing me for the spring semester. So they made an adjustment in my status.'

'What kind of adjustment?'

'I still have a scholarship, but it's not under the athletic department anymore. Hollenbeck said there are special endowment funds that can be used at the school's discretion to permit certain students to stay in school. And I'm one of them.

'Wow. That's too good to be true.'

'That's what I thought. It's like some stranger decided to hand me a check for nine thousand dollars. That's what three semesters here would cost me if I had to pay everything myself.'

'That's right. But endowment money is different. A lot of it just lies there year after year, collecting interest. Foresby's a rich school. Sometimes they create new awards and scholarships just to use up that income.'

Roy didn't answer for a moment. Then he said, 'But why keep it a secret? Why did they give me the impression I'm still on an athletic scholarship when I'm not?'

'Just some screw-up in the administration building, probably.'

'That's what I thought. So I went over there to see what I could find out. Everybody was very nice. My scholarship was on the books all right, but it didn't have a name. And nobody knew what fund it came from. In the department of grants and scholarships it's listed as an *extension* scholarship. But when I asked what it was an extension *of*, Mrs Clegg didn't seem to know. Finally she said she thought it was a fund administered through the university president's office. What do you think of that?'

'I don't think *anything*,' Christine said. 'President Ellerbie's office administers all kinds of things, I guess.'

'Yeah, I guess so. But all the same it seemed strange to me. When I left the administration building, I went and sat in the library for over an hour, trying to figure out some kind of an answer.'

'Did you find one?'

'No,' Roy said. 'So I decided to run a bluff. I went to see Hollenbeck again. I told him what I'd found out and finally he told me the rest. He told me who's paying to keep me in school.'

'Hollenbeck doesn't know . . .' Christine said. She stopped, but not in time. Finally, she said, 'Oh, God . . . here we go again. Why do I feel as if we've had this conversation before?'

'Because we have. Last summer.'

'All right. So you know. If I'm supposed to sniffle in my handkerchief and say I'm sorry, I'm not going to do it. I'm *not* sorry. I was trying to do something positive, trying to solve a lousy, complicated problem. You were in a corner and your idea of a solution was to enlist in the Navy. I thought my idea was better. I still think it's better.'

'Then why all the secrecy? Why didn't you come out and tell me about it?'

'I'll tell you why. Because you're a hardheaded pain in the

neck whenever the subject of money comes up.'

'My uncle used to say if you loan money to a friend, you'll turn him into an enemy.'

'I don't care what your uncle says. I don't think of you as my *friend*. We're a thousand light years beyond that stage. And I'm certainly not *lending* you money.'

'What would you call it? An investment?'

'I wouldn't call it anything,' she said. 'Something had to be done and I did it.'

'Where did the money come from? Seems to me you said there was a Jernegan Foundation and a Van Arsdall Foundation. Is there a Wheatley Foundation too?'

'Yes, there is. Am I supposed to feel guilty about that?'

'No. God no. People never feel guilty because they're loaded, do they?'

'I don't know *how* people feel and I don't give a damn. All I care about is you. You and me. Most people have fights because they don't have enough money. You and I have fights because I have too much. So what? When I'm naked in bed do I feel *rich* or do I just feel like me?'

Ray sat looking at her. When she looked away finally, he said, 'I had a friend named Rico when I was in high school. He had a girl friend named Connie whose father was a successful doctor. Whenever they went to a dance, Rico would scrape together a little money and send her a corsage. But when he went to pick her up the corsage was always three times as fancy as the one he'd paid for. It turned out that Connie's mother had a standing deal with the florist. He would always send Connie more elaborate flowers than Rico ordered and her mother would pay the difference. It seemed harmless enough. A mother wanting her daughter to have nothing but the best. But to Rico it wasn't harmless. When he finally found out what was going on, he stood in Connie's living room one evening with her mother and father watching, carefully unpinned the corsage from her dress, tore it in a hundred pieces, and left it there on the carpet.'

When Christine didn't say anything, Roy went on. 'I don't care how much money you have. As long as it doesn't change things for us. As long as it doesn't screw things up.'

'It won't,' she said. 'I promise.'

'Good. Now, let's finish talking about the scholarship thing.'

'Oh, God . . .'

'Don't tighten up,' he said. 'I'm not gonna drop out of school and run off to my draft board just to prove how independent I am. I would have accepted the money from the school or from a stranger, so it doesn't make sense to turn it down just because it comes from you. But . . . two conditions. One . . . it has to be official, like a student loan from the government or any place else. You have a lawyer draw it up and I'll sign it.'

'You said there were *two* conditions. What's the second one?'

'Starting now, I don't want any help from you that I don't know about. No secrets. No more mysterious summerhouses and no more phantom scholarships. None of that crap. I don't need a fairy godmother.'

Chapter 14

*E*arly in February, Fed Deets, newly commissioned as a first lieutenant in the helicopter division of the Marine Air Force, was invited to Foresby to address the student body. As a recent college graduate himself, as a young man who had volunteered for service in Vietnam, the convocation committee theorized that he might serve as some sort of antidote to the dissension that had begun to spread to formerly peaceful schools like Foresby.

He never made his speech. When he was introduced and approached the lectern, a hail of eggs and snowballs came down from the balcony, splattered on his uniform and on the platform around him. Simultaneously, a series of paper fires in metal wastebaskets began to smoke at various points around the auditorium, and a sizeable percentage of the audience stood up, began chanting, 'Hell no, we won't go,' and marched out of the building. Outside, a huge bonfire had been lighted. It melted a great circle in the snow and scorched the linden trees that bordered the walk leading to the auditorium. Hundreds of students marched around the fire, carrying placards, the same message painted on each one— *Vietnam Sucks*.

Christine did not attend the convocation or the demonstration outside. Neither did Roy. Each of them had talked with Fred Deets when he arrived at the school the day before. Christine, when she came out of the sorority dining roon after lunch, had found him in the guest lounge. And Roy, when he went to the weight room for his therapy session an hour or so later, had found Fred waiting for him at the athletic centre.

'I thought you'd be wearing those fancy Marine pants, the ones with red stripes down the legs,' Christine said to him.

'That's the dress uniform. It doesn't get worn much.'

'I guess not. Look at you. Corduroys and a sweater.'

'Low profile,' he said. 'They don't encourage us to wear uniforms when we're off duty. But the school wants me to put it on tomorrow when I make my little talk.'

'I hope you're not trying to recruit anybody. When anybody mentions Vietnam, things heat up fast. Lots of pissed-off people here.'

'You can't blame them. Nobody wants to get shot at if they can help it.'

'Then why are *you* going?'

'I don't know. Because I know how to fly, I guess. People don't realize that there are more rescue ships and hospital ships over there than there are gunships.'

'If there weren't *any* gunships,' Christine said, 'if they brought everybody home, they wouldn't *need* any hospital ships.'

'Easier said than done.'

'Does that mean they brainwashed you when they gave you that short haircut?'

He smiled. 'Don't you like my haircut?'

'I love it. I'm just a little shaky about some of the things I'm picking up from you.'

'You shouldn't be. I didn't turn into Dr Strangelove. But we have to draw the line somewhere. We can't just walk away from a fight like this.'

'Why *not*? *Somebody* has to walk away. *They* can't walk away from *us*. It's their country, for Pete's sake.'

'But you have to admit there's a principle involved.'

'No, I don't. I think there's pride and greed and arrogance involved. A bunch of lunatics decide to play soldier games and everybody nods his head and starts talking about national honour. We don't *have* any national honour. If we did, we'd stop killing all those people who don't even know why we're there.'

When she went across campus to her next class, Fred walked along with her. 'I think I know the answer already, but is there any chance we could have dinner together?'

Christine shook her head. 'I don't think that would be a brilliant idea.'

'Maybe you're right. I guess Roy wouldn't go for it too much.'

'It has nothing to do with Roy,' she said. 'If I told him I was going to have dinner with you, there wouldn't be any problem. What I said was exactly what I meant. *I* don't think it's a good idea for us to sit down across the table from each other and talk about old times.'

'Why don't the two of you have dinner with me then?'

'I already saw that play. Noel Coward. Sorry, but I'm not that sophisticated.'

'I'm beginning to think there's no such guy as Roy Lavidge. I've never met him, your grandmother's never met him, and she says Grace hasn't either.'

'Is Margaret keeping score?'

'Don't ask me. She just told my mother that they'd never met Roy. Mum was surprised.'

140

'All right. I'll tell you what,' Christine said, looking at her watch. 'In about fifteen minutes, Roy will be showing up at the gymnasium to work in the weight room. Why don't you stroll over there and introduce yourself to him? Then at least one person will have met him.'

Fred grinned. 'You're kidding me, aren't you?'

'No. Why would I do that?'

'I mean I've never seen him. I don't know what he looks like.'

'I'll tell you. He's about two inches shorter than you and about twenty pounds lighter. He has brown curly hair and a broken nose. When I saw him this morning, he was wearing grey corduroys and a sheepskin jacket.'

Twenty minutes later, just inside the main entrance to the gymnasium, people coming and going, Roy didn't notice Fred till he fell in step beside him and said, 'Are you Roy Lavidge?'

'That's right.' Still walking toward the stairway that led down to the weight room.

'I'm Fred Deets. Chrissy sent me over to find you.'

Roy stopped walking and they stood facing each other, precisely in the geometric centre of the big square room.

'Why'd she do that?' Roy said.

'She just thought . . . I mean I'm here to give a talk in convocation tomorrow, so she said it seemed like a good chance for you and me to meet.' He held out his hand.

'Yeah . . . sure,' Roy said. He shook Deets' hand. 'It's nice to meet you.'

'Same here.' There was a silence then, and Fred said, 'I noticed you're limping a little. What happened?'

'Operation on my knee. Nothing too serious.'

Another silence. Finally Fred said, 'Chrissy thought it might be a good idea for the three of us to go downtown and have a steak together tonight.'

Roy studied the sun-browned clean-featured face in front of him. 'That's nice of you,' he said, 'but tonight's a bad night for me.' He looked at his watch. 'I have to get downstairs for my workout. Thanks for coming over. I'll take a raincheck on the steak.'

141

Walking out of the gymnasium into the cold air, Fred could feel the blood in his cheeks, and an angry pulse throbbed on his forehead. But the anger was inturned, directed hotly against himself. He had made two choices that ran counter to his own instincts. When he had accepted the invitation to speak at Foresby, there had been no question in his mind as to how he would behave toward Christine. His instinct told him he should make no move to see her or talk with her.

He had discussed the situation with his father. Nelson Deets had said, 'I think you're right. At least that's the way *I* would handle it.'

Fred expected the same type of advice from Margaret Jernegan when he talked with her. But she surprised him. 'Sometimes it's very effective to do what people are *not* expecting. I'm sure Chrissy doesn't expect to hear from you. So if I were you I would surprise her. Kill her with friendliness. It may be embarrassing to you, but I guarantee you it will make her think. Most of what men and women do together has a strong element of gamesmanship in it, and you never know how much a tiny psychological edge can help you in the future. So I say—play innocent. There's something very intriguing to a woman when an ex-lover says, "It's all right. I don't mind. I'm just as happy to be your friend and find my fun elsewhere."'

It had also been Margaret's suggestion that he try to meet Roy. 'Why not? The most potent adversary of all is an invisible one. No man ever existed who can match his own description as told by a woman who loves him. Look him up. I promise you he'll turn out to be a scruffy young person wearing dirty tennis shoes. Kill *him* with friendliness too. There's nothing quite so disarming as love from the enemy.'

Walking across the frozen campus in the glare of midafternoon, Fred felt only awkwardness and humiliation. And when the eggs splattered against his chest in the auditorium the following morning, he felt, in a flash of panic, as though, by choosing the role of victim the afternoon before, he had tattooed the word brightly on his forehead. He'd made himself a clear target for contempt, for eggs thrown from balconies, or for antiaircraft shells bursting in the cockpits of helicopters.

142

Chapter 15

*E*arly in the morning of March eighth, Tom Peddicord and his partner Cesar Aguila broke up a fight between two soldiers, one of them a white corporal named Merle Stanforth from Laurel, Mississippi, and the other one a young black man named Arthur Bohannon from New Haven, Connecticut. It was a senseless and bloody drunken fight outside a whorehouse on avenue Pétain in downtown Saigon. When Peddicord and Aguila stepped in, it became even more senseless. Without missing a stroke, Stanforth and Bohannon wheeled away from beating each other and attacked Tom and Cesar, flailing away, kicking and punching till they fell senseless under the two nightsticks.

Three nights later, early morning, almost dawn, when Tom and Cesar had finished their seven-to-three tour and come back to their barracks, two men waiting in the latrine overpowered Cesar and cut his throat. Tom, already half asleep in his bunk, didn't know anything had happened. When the same two men slipped into his room twenty minutes later, he didn't hear them. The taller man released the trigger of a grenade, placed it on the floor under Tom's bed, and ran for the nearest door. He and his companion were halfway to the outside entrance when they heard the explosion.

The shrapnel from the blast ripped up through Tom's mattress, tore open his lower back, and shattered his spine.

As soon as the Army notified Cuba, her sister called Christine. The following afternoon she went to Chicago and took the first available flight to Baltimore.

Christine was gone for six days. During that time Roy's father came to Foresby, inquired at the administration building about his son, and went that evening to find him at the dormitory where he lived. Roy was studying in his room after dinner when one of the freshmen who worked at the desk in the lobby came upstairs and said, 'There's a guy downstairs wants to see you. Says he's your dad. Do you want me to send him up?'

'No. That's all right. Tell him I'll be down in a couple minutes.'

Roy took his time. He walked down the hall to the lavatory, washed his face and hands, and brushed his teeth. Then he stood there at the sink, alone in the long, white-tiled room, and looked at himself in the mirror. He was determined to have no emotional reaction. The man was a stranger. He had chosen to be a stranger. He would simply treat his father the way he would treat any other stranger.

But when he came into the main-floor lobby, when he saw a man get up from a chair far across the room and come toward him, Roy's face felt warm suddenly and his heart changed its rhythm. The man, square and blocky, his grey-blond hair slicked back with water, moving with a kind of awkward rolling motion, as though somewhere along the way he'd had a back injury, came all the way to where Roy was standing, stopped in front of him, and stared at his face. Finally he said, 'I guess you wouldn't have known me if you'd passed me in the street, would you?'

'No, I guess not.'

'I've got a head start then, because I've seen pictures of you. A pal of mine in Round Pond used to send clippings from the sports pages when you were running everybody ragged there at Bowdoin.' He moved back a half step and looked Roy up and down. 'You're built like a racehorse, all right. You must get that from your mother's people. All the Lavidges are set up like tree trunks, the men and the women both.'

Feeling awkward suddenly, Roy gestured toward a couch over by the window and said, 'Why don't we go over and sit down?'

'To tell you the truth, I missed my supper and I'm hungry as a dog. Is there anyplace we could go for a sandwich and a bottle of beer?'

'Sure. There's a saloon called Winkler's. Just down the street. We can walk.'

'If it's all the same to you, I'll drive. Living in California has thinned out my blood.'

They drove to Winkler's in T.J.'s Chrysler, stereo music sobbing softly as soon as he turned on the ignition. And leopard-skin seat covers. 'People will tell you not to go near a Chrysler car. I know people who would rather hitchhike. But I've had nothing but good luck with them. A Chrysler's not that quick on the pickup, but neither is a Mercedes. Once they get the juice flowing, though, they'll take you right to town.'

When they walked into Winkler's and sat down in a booth in the second room, T.J. said, 'Nobody here. There must be doing something wrong.'

Roy glanced up at the clock. 'Everybody's studying. We've got exams next week.'

'Am I screwing you up? If you're supposed to be home working . . .'

Roy shook his head. 'I'm in good shape. I try to keep ahead of it so I don't get snowed under at the last minute.'

'Well, that makes sense. Not that I know anything about it. I hated every day I ever spent in school. You talk about dumb bastards, I was the champ. Didn't take me long to find out how important an education is. But by then it was too late. I was on the road, laughing it up, and burning rubber. Thought I knew everything and didn't know shit.'

They ordered steins of beer and T.J. ordered a roast-beef sandwich, baked beans, and potato salad. 'Jesus, I'm hungry. You sure you won't have something to eat?'

'No thanks. I had a big dinner.'

'You're skinny as a snake and you're eating nothing. I'm the size of a phone booth and I'm the one who's shovelling it in.'

After he finished eating and the dishes were cleared away, T.J. said, 'All these years, I've been thinking if I ever got to see you, you'd probably be pissed off at me. But now that we're sitting here, I think either you're a actor or you're not as sore at me as I expected.'

'I'm not sore. I used to be but I'm not anymore.'

'What happened?'

'I don't know. I grew up, I guess.'

'Well, I have to hand it to you. Most people, if their dad ran away and left them and then a few years later their mother took off, they'd figure they got more than their share of shit.'

'I didn't say I liked it. I didn't like it at all. When I was thirteen or fourteen I had all kinds of plots in my head about how I'd get even with you when I grew up. And I didn't have a very high opinion of Mum either.'

'Nobody blames you. I was surprised myself when I heard Maria went back to Italy and left you here. But I'll tell you something about your mother. She would never have done what she did if I hadn't done what *I* did. You said something before about growing up. Well, some people, it takes them a helluva long time. And a lot of other people never manage it at all. When you were born I was twenty-seven years old with the gumption of a kid of eighteen. I'd fought a war and risked my ass and I'd seen guys get their faces blown off, but it hadn't sunk in. To me life was one big party, start up the music and bring on the girls, and I didn't want it to end. I'm sure Joe must have told you—I never would have married your mother if he hadn't scared me into it. The last thing I wanted was to be *responsible* for somebody. I used to sit there and watch you in your crib, and I'd think, "Jesus Christ, I don't know anything about being a father. This kid's gonna count on me and I'm gonna let him down." I had my head cocked around so much, I decided I was doing you and Maria a favour by taking off."

'I got the idea you left because you thought I wasn't really your kid.'

'I know Maria thought that's how I felt. And I let her think it. But the truth was I always knew I was your father. Maria was an innocent kid when I met her. She'd never been near another man.'

When Roy and his father drove back to the dormitory, Roy said, 'I'm sure I can find you an empty bed if you want to sleep here tonight.'

'Thanks anyway, but I've got a motel room out on the highway west of town.'

Just before Roy got out of the car, T.J. took a small gift-wrapped package out of the glove compartment and handed it to him. 'Here's something for your twenty-first birthday. I know I'm a few weeks late, but I didn't know where to send it exactly. You don't have to open it now. I'll tell you what it is. It's a belt. Hand-tooled. With a silver buckle. An old Yaqui Indian I know made it up for me. I wasn't sure what size waist you'd have, so he didn't punch any holes in it. You can find some shoemaker who'll do that for you.'

When he was upstairs in his room, Roy unwrapped the package and took out the belt. Inside the box was a card with his father's name and address on it. On the back he had written:

Here's my temporary permanent address. If I hear from you I'll write back. If I don't I'll know you'd rather not stay in touch. Either way I wish you the best.

Love,
T.J.

Chapter 16

*T*hree years later, after the Vietnam cease-fire, in a long piece in the *Sewanee Review*, Russell Atha wrote:

In 1970 President Nixon announced that fewer than four hundred thousand U.S. soldiers were then in Vietnam. But the casualties continued to escalate. And the Paris peace talks, after two years, reported no progress. Also, around the world, great masses of people continued to demonstrate and burn effigies of Uncle Sam that looked remarkably like Nixon. Then, within one week, two events took place that so enraged the young people of America that an end to the fighting became an inevitability. It took three years for a cease-fire to happen, but the last vestiges of popular support vanished in that spring-time week in 1970.

On April 30, the President announced that American forces were being sent into Cambodia to flush out the Cong and N.V. forces hiding there and thus, by his rationale, hasten the conclusion of the Vietnam conflict.

The paint had scarcely dried on the angry signs being painted on walls throughout the world when another obscenity occurred. On May 4, in Kent, Ohio, National Guardsmen fired on a crowd of protesting students and murdered four of them, Allison Krause, Sandra Lee Scheuer, Jeffrey Glenn Miller, and William K. Schroeder.

I was in California that Monday afternoon when the news first broke about the Kent State killings. Russell was there too. I had just driven in from the airport and checked into my hotel when the telephone rang. As soon as I answered, he said, 'Turn on your television set. I'll call you back in an hour.'

He didn't call. But at four thirty they rang up from the desk and told me a Miss Wisner had left a message saying Mr Atha would pick me up at seven o'clock.

We went to dinner at a Greek place in Santa Monica. On the way we stopped at a bar on Montana Avenue to see the evening news on television. There was a short item about the shooting at Kent State. The commentator, in closing said, 'President Nixon expressed it best. When he was informed about the unhappy events in Kent, Ohio, he said, "When dissent turns to violence, it invites tragedy." '

'Can you believe those bastards?' Russell said when we were sitting in the restaurant. 'Ten minutes after those kids were killed, Washington already had an official propaganda line. "The young National Guardsmen fired in self-defence. When sniper fire started and they were charged by a mob of angry students, these inexperienced part-time soldiers used their weapons to protect themselves." '

'It could happen, I guess.'

'It could, but it didn't,' he said. 'I have a buddy, Sid Kantz, who's the city editor on *The Plain Dealer* in Cleveland. They've had a team of reporters down in Kent since Saturday when the R.O.T.C. building was burned. Kantz says the whole thing stinks. Those troops weren't being charged by anybody. Of the four students who were killed, the closest one was twenty-five yards away from the guardsmen.'

In his *Sewanee Review* piece three years later, Russell wrote:

I think the Vietnam experience will stay with us. I suspect that it will haunt us, those of us who were witnesses, for as long as memory functions. And most haunting of all will be the deaths of four young people who never marched in cadence, fired a weapon, or put on a uniform, the four students who were killed by riflemen on the campus of Kent State University in 1970.

Chapter 17

*O*n Tuesday, May fifth, the students at Foresby, protesting against the Kent State killings, boycotted all their classes. President Ellerbie, in a gesture of solidarity with the students, named that date Kent State Memorial Day and ordered all classes cancelled. A religious service was held at noon in the university chapel, and a student rally with music and speeches took place that afternoon on Kingham Bluff overlooking the Boone River. For the first time ever at Foresby, several students burned their draft cards. And a lovely girl named Penrose from St Louis, whose father was a long-time member of the Missouri legislature, burned an American flag. A Nixon effigy was doused with gasoline, set on fire, and thrown off the bluff, still burning, into the river. Students who never drank at all got very drunk that afternoon. And hundreds of girls were crying.

When he came back to his dormitory at four o'clock, Roy found a telegram there from his uncle.

CALL ME. IT'S IMPORTANT.

When he called, his aunt answered the phone and said Joe wasn't home from work yet. 'He should be here by six the latest.'

Roy called back at six. He talked to his uncle for almost twenty minutes, until they started to yell at each other. Then Roy hung up and called Christine. Fifteen minutes later she met him at the student centre and he told her what had happened. The day before, two Federal marshals had come to Joe's house in Portland. They said they had a warrant to pick up Roy Lavidge for refusal to answer an armed services induction order.

'What order? You didn't get an order to appear.'

'Yes, I did. Right after Christmas.'

'But you sent that back to them. I thought that was all straightened out.'

'So did I. But I guess it wasn't.'

'What did your uncle tell them?'

'He said I was in Illinois going to college and I had a deferment. They said it was a good story but if I'd had a deferment I wouldn't have been called up.'

'But what about the Portland draft board?'

'Joe went there this morning. And finally he got to talk with Dr Hemmings, the guy I talked with at Christmastime. He looked through my file and pulled out the new deferment card they sent me when I transferred from Bowdoin to Foresby. He pointed out that the word *temporary* is stamped on it. He said a temporary deferment can be cancelled at any time.'

'But they can't just *do* that?'

'Sure they can. According to Joe, they've already done it. He says if I'm not back in Portland by the end of the week, they'll send some marshals here to pick me up. The guy at the draft board really did a number on Joe. Maximum sentence if you refuse to submit to induction is five years in the can or ten thousand dollars fine. Or both. The average sentence is three years. By their definition I've already broken that law, so I'm indictable. Joe says if they let me go into the Army now, they'll be doing me a favour.'

'That's crazy. There are lawyers who love to take on cases like this. By the time this gets to court the draft will be over.'

'Maybe you're right. But all the same, three thousand guys were prosecuted last year and almost two thirds of them are locked up now.'

'So where are we?'

'The same place as last summer. The same choices. I might as well let them draft me. It's two years out of my life. At least I'd come out clean that way.'

'Who says so? Look at Tom Peddicord. Do you still have that letter he sent you?'

'I guess so.'

'Well, read it again. It's a no-win game, Roy. Even if you came back in one piece, with ribbons and medals and a slimy handshake in the White House, how do you ever get those pictures out of your head? It's enough to see them second-hand, in the papers or on television. Naked kids running down the road, old men on fire, pregnant women with bayonet gashes in their bellies. How could anybody ever forget stuff like that if they saw it firsthand? How do you live with yourself if you've helped make it happen? They're finding it out already in the V.A. hospitals. The worst

151

casualties are the soldiers who never got a scratch.'

'I know all that,' Roy said, 'but what's the answer? I don't want to go underground and live in somebody's barn, I don't want to refuse induction and go to jail, I don't qualify as a conscientious objector, and I don't want to blow people away in Vietnam. That doesn't leave many alternatives.'

'One good one.'

Roy nodded. 'That's what Joe was yelling about. He said I shouldn't let anybody talk me into running off to Canada.

'Why not? Does he know there are more than sixty thousand guys who went north rather than go to Vietnam? There must be twenty or thirty from Foresby alone.'

'He didn't want to hear. He said he'd rather see me dead.'

'He's crazy. Where's he been living the past five years?'

'He's a naturalized citizen. So's my aunt. They have patriotism coming out of their ears. Respect for authority. *Any* authority. It's all black and white to Joe. When the government whistles, you run.'

'So . . . you tell me. What's the answer?'

'I'm going to Canada,' he said.

'You're *what*?'

'I'm going to Canada.'

'When did you decide that?'

'Just now.'

'I can't believe my ears.'

'You can believe it. I'm going.'

'*We're* going.'

'No, we're not. *I'm* going. You're going to finish out the semester. You graduate in a month.'

'I don't care about that.'

'*I* do,' Roy said. 'One of us has to have a degree. Otherwise we'll end up driving laundry trucks.'

She put her arms around him and kissed him. 'I've been hoping and praying this is what you'd decide to do. You're doing the right thing. It's the *only* thing to do.'

'I wish I was as sure as you are. What do I know about Canada? I don't know what I'm getting into.'

'It doesn't matter. It's a temporary solution. That's all. A means to an end. In two years all you guys who walked out on the war will be back home. By then you'll be heroes. As soon as there's a cease-fire, the government will declare an amnesty. They always do. Washington did it, Lincoln and Wilson. And so did Truman.'

Two days later they took the noon bus into Springfield. They stayed that night at the Salem House Hotel, and the next morning Roy took a northbound bus to Moline—final destination, the city of Calgary in the province of Alberta.

Chapter 18

'*W*hat are you crying about?' Roy asked.

'What do you think I'm crying about?'

They were lying in bed in their Springfield hotel room the night before he left for Canada. Very late.

'I don't know. Some girls cry when they're happy. Some girls cry when they're sad.'

'Listen to the expert.'

'I'm not an expert. I just read a lot.'

'I'm crying because I'm happy,' she said, 'and I'm crying because I'm sad. I'm happy you're here and sad your leaving.'

'It won't be long. If you're not in Canada in six weeks I'll come back to get you.'

'I'll be there. Don't worry about that. As a matter of fact, I've decided we shouldn't worry about anything. We have nothing to worry about.'

'Then why are you crying all over me?'

'I'm not. I just stopped.' She dabbed at her eyes with a

153

corner of the sheet. 'See—no tears.' She snuggled down beside him and rested her head on his shoulder. 'Survival,' she said, 'that's our only problem. Since we're pretending I'm poor and destitute, that all my money got blown away in a storm . . .'

'Does that bother you?'

'Not at all. But I'll admit I have fantasies sometimes about how we could live if we wanted to. I catch myself thinking how nice it would be if we just spent a few years travelling and enjoying ourselves, having a baby every now and then, and just *living*. No schedules, no deadlines, no one to answer to.'

'Scott and Zelda.'

'That's right.'

'And we all know what happened to them.'

'I told you they were fantasies,' she said. 'What I'm saying is I think we could make almost *any* choice and it wouldn't wreck us. We could play and party and wear fancy clothes and raise a gang of dogs and kids and we'd be fine. I think we could be very happy being fat and indolent and self-indulgent. But I know that's not going to happen. So what I really want is whatever *you* want. I just want things to be good for you. If they *are*, then they'll be good for me.'

'That's a big statement. I wish I had a tape recorder running.'

'Not necessary. I'll remember.'

'So will I.' He kissed her. 'I wish you were coming with me.'

'Don't even *say* it. I'll come apart like a two-dollar shoe.'

'Come with me. We'll have a terrific time. We'll sit in the back of the bus and fool around a lot.'

She raised up on one elbow, switched on the bed lamp, and looked down at him. 'Don't tease me. Because I'm taking you seriously. Are you saying you want me to come with you or you want me to stay here and graduate?'

'I want you to come with me, but my head says you should stay here and graduate.'

'So you *are* teasing me?'

'No. I wouldn't call it that. We just shouldn't have serious discussions when we're in bed.'

154

As he pulled her close to him, she looked at the clock over the door. 'Do you know what time it is?'

'I don't care.'

'It's almost four and we have to get up at six. Aren't we going to get any sleep?'

'I hope not.'

Chapter 19

*R*oy sold almost everything he owned before leaving Foresby. He got on the bus in Springfield like an itinerant cowhand, carrying a sheepskin coat, a rolled slicker, and a small bag of clothing. In his pants pocket was a sheaf of dollar bills, eating money for the trip, and in his shirt pocket three hundred dollars in traveller's cheques, the income from the cut-rate sale he'd held in his dormitory room.

He changed buses in Moline and La Crosse, Wisconsin. But the bus he boarded in Minneapolis took him all the way north and west, through Fargo and Bismarck and into Montana; across the great empty plains, then through Lewistown to Great Falls. He slept all night there, in the bus station, and next morning took the first bus north, crossing the Canadian border north of Shelby, showing his passport and going in on a visitor's card, then on north through Lethbridge and Fort Macleod to Calgary.

Feeling no sense of doom or banishment, Roy, on the contrary, devoured every detail of the long and twisting, stop-and-go trip. The forests and rivers, the villages and cities, the endless fields that later in the summer would be yellow with wheat. He recorded in his mind the weathered faces, gnarled hands, and flat voices of the people who got on the bus, listened for local lore and gossip in the lunch stops along the way.

He was moving from one place to another. That's what he told himself. It was as simple as that. Unanchored and weightless. Travelling light. Everything he owned in the baggage rack over his head. It gave him a startling sense of freedom.

Book 3

Chapter 1

*A*t the office for the Calgary Committee to Aid War Immigrants, Roy sat across a desk from Bobby Slayback in the corner of a large room with dirty windows, the area cluttered with tortured metal desks and chairs, stacks of cartons, racks of used clothing, a coffee maker, several typewriters, and an ancient duplicating machine.

Bobby Slayback was not a figure of authority or rebellion. No fires of anarchy burned behind his eyes. He was slender and pale with thinning blond hair and discoloured teeth. Clean shaven. Wearing well-washed jeans and a work shirt.

'Any hassle with Immigration?' he said.

'No. I came in on a visitor's card,' Roy said.

'What kind of I.D. did you show them?'

'I've got a passport.'

'That's smart. You must have planned ahead.'

Roy shook his head. 'Not exactly. I didn't know I was coming till a few days ago. I've had a passport since I was sixteen. I thought I might be going to Italy, but I never went.'

'Well here's the deal. You can come in as a visitor the way you did. Or you can come as a student. Or you can apply for landed-immigrant status. That's the best deal you can get. After five years you're eligible for full citizenship if you want it.'

'What about the student thing?'

'No problem if you have plenty of money. You have to prove you have enough bread to support yourself through a full school year. Can you handle that?'

Roy shook his head. 'I have to work.'

'Then you'll have to forget about the school bit. How long's your visitor's card good for?'

'Only a month. I was lucky to get that. The Immigration guy was pissed off because I didn't have a return ticket.

'Some of those birds are real assholes. They make up their own immigration laws. But the good thing is, once you're in Canada, you're pretty safe. They're not hot to deport anybody. Even if your card's expired'

'If they don't police the visitors cards, what's the point of going for the permanent resident thing?'

'One big reason. If you're not a landed immigrant you can't work. And if you can't find somebody who'll promise to hire you, it can be rough to make landed immigrant. The problem right now is that jobs are tight. Almost eight percent unemployment in Quebec, over ten percent in British Columbia, and nine percent here in Alberta. The other problem is that United States money has taken over more than five hundred Canadian companies. American industry owns three quarters of all Canadian assets now. So those companies can be tough to connect with. The Canadians don't give a shit if you're a resister, but with the American-owned firms it's a different story.

Slayback took a yellow pad out of the desk drawer and uncapped his fountain pen. 'Let's get some dope on you. How about work experience?'

'Well . . . I've been working since I was fourteen. Construction work mostly. General labourer, cement worker, carpenter's help, that kind of stuff.'

'I haven't been able to steer anybody into a construction job in almost a year. What else?'

'I worked with a sign painter for a year, did some house painting, worked for eighteen months in a meat market, waited tables, fry cook, cashier. You know, jobs you take when you're going to school and trying to make some money.'

'You think you could handle a bunch of kids in a summer-camp situation?'

'I guess so. But to tell you the truth, I'd rather not be out in the woods someplace. My girl friend's coming up in a month or so when she gets out of school. We'll both be working and we'd like to be in the same place. Get an apartment maybe.'

'Yeah, I know. We all have the same problem. My wife takes a bus down to Nanton five days a week. Over an hour each way. She's got a job in a supermarket there. We don't like it much, but until she can latch onto something here in Calgary we have to live with it.'

That night, Roy wrote a letter to Christine.

Well, I'm here. It was a good trip on the bus. I saw some terrific country. I arrived in Canada with a numb rear end, but outside of that everything's fine.

How do I feel? I don't know. I don't think it's started to soak in yet. All the way up here on the bus, I kept telling myself not to blow everything up giant size in my head. I didn't want to feel as if I was burning bridges. I mean I hate all that shit about people starting their lives over. But as I was walking through the streets this evening, I couldn't kid myself. Whatever I've done before doesn't count for much up here.

There's still a frontier atmosphere in the province of Alberta. You only get what you work for. And that's all right with me. But first I have to find some work.

Here's the situation. I went to the office of the Calgary Committee to Aid War Immigrants and talked with a guy named Bobby Slayback. He looks like a guy who's never worked up a sweat in his life. But one of the other guys up here told me Slayback did a full tour in Vietnam, reenlisted to get home leave, then deserted as soon as he hit Fort Dodge, Iowa, his home town. They caught him and stuck him in a military prison in Idaho. But after a year and a half he put on a woman's dress somebody had smuggled in to him and walked out through the visitor's gate. Next day he was in Alberta, and he's been here ever since.

Anyway, he got hold of an old run-down house, on Charleswood Drive out near the University of Calgary campus. He and his wife, Doris, live there, and they've been gradually fixing it up. When new guys like me hit town, he takes them in, lets them stay at his place till they get squared away. Everybody chips in whatever he can afford for food. It's share and share alike.

Right now there are twenty people living in the house. That's about average, Bobby says, but he's had as many as thirty-five at one time. Two thirds of them are deserters, he says. Only one third are resisters like me. He expects ninety thousand deserters to come to Canada this year alone. He says there are four or five hundred thousand guys who deserted, resisted the draft, went underground, or went to jail. There are guys coming now who did their service in Vietnam and got honourable discharges. And guys who were classified 4-F but just didn't want to stay in America.

To become working residents of Canada we have to become 'landed immigrants'. To qualify, they judge you on a point system in nine different categories. Fifty points needed to become a resident. Here's the list, along with the points Slayback thinks I could get.

1. Education and training. One point for each year of formal education or professional work.

I get 14 points. You'd get 16.

2. Adaptability, motivation, initiative, resourcefulness, assessment of personal suitability to life in Canada. Maximum points: 15.

This is a crap shoot. Slayback says I could get 8. You could get more, I think.

3. Occupational demand. Points granted according to the demand for occupation applicant will follow in Canada.

We have no occupations so *no* points.

4. Occupational skill. Assessment of occupant's highest skill. 10 points for a professional. One point for the unskilled.

Slayback says I would rate 5 points but I don't see how.

5. 10 points if applicant is between eighteen and thirty-five years of age.

Big breakthrough. 10 points. You too.

6. 10 points if applicant has arranged for a definite steady job in Canada.

Zip. No points here either.

7. 5 points if applicant, reads, writes, and speaks either French or English. 10 points for both.

I get 5. You get 10 because you know French.

8. If you have a relative in Canada, etc. . . .

No points.

9. 5 points if applicant intends to go to an area in Canada where there is a strong general demand for labour.

Slayback says we nod our heads on this one and pick up 5 points.

By my count you would get 56 points and I *might* get 47. You're in and I'm out. But there's an answer, Slayback says. He'll help me round up some kind of job, *any* job I can land, and I go back to the border with a letter from my employer. That will add on 10 points. Then I'm in like a burglar.

It's not going to be a fancy life here, Chrissy. From what I can see it's a lot of people in the same boat trying to keep from drowning. But I like it so far. I think you'll like it too.

Chapter 2

*S*layback's assessment of the employment situation turned out to be true. By the end of the first week in June, when his tourist card had almost run out, Roy still had no job.

There had been encouraging interviews. Even some friendly ones. Oscar Muchow, a tiny bald man with a Dachau tattoo on his forearm, was a Polish immigrant. He had pulled himself up from a sausage stand near the bus depot on Centre Street to the ownership of three twenty-four-hour coffee shops, one on Sixteenth Avenue Northwest, one on Memorial Drive near the zoo, and the largest of the three, also on Centre Street, just across from where his original sausage stand had been.

Mr Muchow had seemed reluctant to end the interview. 'You can see, I'm not busy now. They don't let me work so much. Just when I got to the point where I could afford Hennessy brandy and Cuban cigars, the doctor made me stop using them.'

At last he said what he had postponed saying for as long as possible. 'I would like to do something for you. But . . . there is a business slowdown now. We had to lay off half a dozen people. And when things pick up, those people must be taken back before I can hire any new help.'

Jay Tippet, a man who ran a sign-painting shop, was less encouraging 'You got any samples with you?'

'No,' Roy said. 'I haven't done any sign work for three years or so.'

'What did you do? Big stuff or little stuff?'

'Mostly window cards, show cards. Single-stroke lettering.'

'Well, you can see I don't have anybody on staff here except my gold-leaf man. And I've got two billboard guys who have their own loft where they work. The kind of stuff you're talking about I usually knock out myself. You got a working setup where you live?'

'Not yet,' Roy said. 'I've only been in Calgary for a couple weeks.'

'I'll tell you something. You're not gonna get rich painting show cards in Calgary. A free-lancer has to work night and day to make sixty bucks a week.'

When he was discussing his interviews with Slayback, Roy said, 'They have minimum wage here, don't they?'

'Sure they do. But it's only a buck seventy an hour. And they take tax out, the same as they do in the States. So if you're working forty hours a week minimum wage, you'd better like the taste of cat food. Also, if you're hungry for a job like all of our guys are, you'll find an employer every once in a while who'll try to cock you around and pay you *less* than minimum. They come up with piecework, unit work, part-time, any scheme they can think of to save a few dollars. They know we're not about to blow the whistle on them. So how you doing? Still no luck?'

'I finally got a nibble at that packing plant out of Crowchild Trail. Magnuson's place. Wholesale meat suppliers. You know. You sent me there.'

'Who'd you talk to? Art Feeney?'

'No. He sluffed me over to a guy in a bloody apron. A guy named Herman Esterhazy.'

'Any action?'

Roy shook his head. 'But he said there might be something opening up in a few weeks. A lot of good that does me. I need to latch onto something now.'

'You can always buy yourself some time,' Slayback said. 'I told you about Meredith Duffy.'

'No, thanks. I'll keep looking for work if it's all the same to you.'

When Roy wrote to Christine two days later, he told her about the work situation.

If something else doesn't turn up soon, I'll have to take a bus down to Coutts, cross over to Sweetgrass, and then come back into Canada with a fresh tourist card.

My other alternative is Meredith Duffy. Did I tell you

about her? She's famous up here among the resisters. She's a fat little cartoon somewhere in her fifties who works for the Department of Immigration, lives with her invalid mother, and likes to have a few blasts of Canadian Club at the end of the working day. Slayback says she specializes in American guys who are having problems with their visitor's cards. If she invites you to her house to discuss the situation, you know your card's going to be extended. For a straight screw downstairs in the living room you get thirty days extension. Add some oral sex to that, either giving or receiving, and you've got sixty days. Miss Duffy's also a little kinky. A Chinese guy from San Fransicso who used to live here in Slayback's house took her upstairs and banged her on the floor at the foot of her mother's bed. He got landed-immigrant status a week later. So . . . do you think Meredith Duffy might be the solution to my problems?

Chapter 3

*L*ess than a week after her graduation, Christine arrived in Calgary. Two days later she found work. She went to the largest downtown hotel, the Martin House, applied for a job as hostess in the mezzanine dining room, and was hired that same afternoon. Doris Slayback, when she heard the news, said to Bobby, 'That's some fast action. Talk, about luck.'

'It's not just luck. She played it smart. She applied for her residence papers by mail over a month ago. So when she

165

crossed the border at Sweetgrass she already had landed-immigrant status. Also, she's a sensational-looking mama. That didn't exactly hurt her chances.'

Doris was a delicate and pretty girl, but her hair was curlier than she would have liked. And her legs displeased her. So she was almost always in slacks or jeans. She had been in love with Bobby since they were both fourteen years old, freshmen in high school. They had married at seventeen, and as far as she knew he had never strayed from her.

She was fiercely possessive, all the same, intensely aware of the wives and girl friends who came with the resisters to their house on Charleswood Drive. She studied each of them carefully, like a stockman buying heifers, and quickly be-iended the most attractive ones. As soon as she learned their flaws, she pointed them out to Bobby.

The thing that disturbed her most about her daily trip to Nanton and the hours she had to spend there was leaving Bobby alone in Calgary. She envisioned him in sexual combat with every woman they knew. Including, now, Christine.

There was no way to meet Christine Wheatley for the first time and not be stunned. No one ever said, 'Hello, how do you do?' and simply went back to what they were doing. In addition to her startling appearance she had a sense of self that turned people's eyes toward her and kept them there.

So it was difficult not to be ensnared. And for Doris it was impossible to believe that Bobby would not be ensnared.

Some jungle instinct told her, however, that in this circumstance a careful attitude was necessary. Sugar in the cup. Honey in the horn. Not long after Christine arrived, Doris lay in bed beside her husband and said, 'Sometimes I wish we didn't have to live with new people *all* the time. I'd like to have a woman friend for a change, one who didn't take off for Edmonton or Medicine Hat or someplace just as I was getting to know her. Just once I wish some nice couple would stick around for a while. Like Roy and Christine, for instance. I'll bet they'd stay on if you asked them.'

'It's all right with me. But I thought maybe you weren't too crazy about her.'

'I was jealous at first because she got that job. But that went away. I've had some talks with her and she's really nice.'

'Well . . .maybe I'll talk to Roy and see what he says.'

Roy liked the idea. 'I appreciate it,' he said. 'It really helps us out. Christine won't get her first cheque for a couple weeks, and maybe by then something'll come through for me.'

He was right. Three weeks after Christine arrived in Calgary, Roy had a card from Art Feeney at Magnuson's Meat Suppliers.

REPORT FOR WORK AT 7 A.M., MONDAY, JUNE 15.

Two days later, carrying a letter from Sweeney, Roy went by bus to the border station at Coutts-Sweetgrass. After an interview with an Immigration official there, he was awarded fifty-six points and given his landed-immigrant card.

That night, after Christine came home from work, she and Roy and Bobby and Doris celebrated in the kitchen. A bottle of whisky, scrambled eggs, and a day-old cake that Doris had carried home from the supermarket in Nanton.

Chapter 4

Five days a week Christine worked both the lunch and dinner shifts. On Monday and Tuesday she did only dinner, didn't have to report for work till five forty-five. Working three-hour shifts, her total hours, without overtime, were thirty-six. But she had no evenings off. And if the dinner business was heavy it was eleven o'clock or midnight before she got home.

167

Roy worked only five days a week. But he had to get up at five thirty to be at work by seven. He got off work at four, but by the time he cleaned up and came home on the bus it was usually five thirty.

So they had no evenings together. Only mornings, Saturday and Sunday. On those days he usually stayed downtown until after she'd finished with the luncheon crowd. Then they would take a walk or sit in a coffee shop till it was time for her to go back to work.

'I hate to see you working such screwed-up hours,' he said. 'I'll be glad when we're both working day jobs.'

'Me too. But for now, this is the best we can do. I want to put some money aside so we can start looking for a place of our own. I don't care how little it is, just so we can be by ourselves.'

'Doris and Bob think we're planning to settle in with them for a while. I wouldn't want to hurt their feelings.'

'Don't worry. It won't be a problem. I've been looking at apartment rentals in the paper, and it's going to be quite a while before we'll be able to make a move.'

'We might decide we don't want to stay in Calgary. Now that we both have residence cards, we can go anywhere we want to. Toronto or Vancouver or anyplace.'

'It's all right with me. But let's get our feet under us first.'

They lied to each other about their jobs. She said, 'It's a breeze. What I have to do is smile a lot, hand out menus, and try to give everybody the table they want. Sometimes I pour coffee or water. And if we're really rushed I'll help to clear some tables. All the waitresses are nice and the boss is a good guy, so I have no problems.'

If she had told the truth, she would have said, 'It's boring and degrading. At least half the men who come in for lunch are either on the make or want everybody to *think* they're on the make. After they've had a drink or two they make suggestions to me that would make a hooker blush. They sort of ooze it out in your general direction as you're passing by. Or two of them discuss what they'd like to do to you as you're pouring water into their glasses. And in the kitchen it's almost as bad. The salad chef is an authentic lunatic. His routine is flashing. Every time the door to the dining room swings open and one of the girls comes into the kitchen, up goes his apron.'

About *his* job, Roy told her, 'I really lucked out. They put me in the retail service section. Another guy and I are in charge of hamburger and sausage. We trim the bones and hack up the cheap cuts of meat and feed them into the grinders and mixers. We fill up big pans, maybe forty pounds to the pan, then put the pans on the conveyor belt and send them along to the packaging girls. It's an easy job. No wear and tear on the brain.'

These things he told Christine were true. Other things he chose not to tell her. Most of the men he worked with were illiterate alcoholics who cursed and fought with each other and spit black streams of tobacco juice on the floor. Roy's partner, a forty-year-old, grossly fat Piegan Indian named Wesley, never washed himself or changed his clothes. In the damp cold of the refrigerated cutting room, he coughed and sniffled constantly, and his nose ran a double trickle down across his long upper lip to his mouth. An earphone radio was always fastened on his head, and he lumbered through his work like a foul-smelling robot receiving secret instructions from some interplanetary satellite.

Through the months, every day he worked in the meat-cutting room Roy was cold. The floor was slick with blood and water between the sawdust patches. The hunks of meat were slippery and cold to his fingers, the cast-metal sides of the grinders were cold, and the water he mixed with the ground meat to give it weight was as cold as ice. He worked always with two sweaters under his apron and long johns under his pants. Rubber-soled boots and wool hunting socks.

But the real killer, in contrast to what he had told Christine, was the sameness, the animal simplicity of it. And Wesley, most of all, was a reminder of the nature of the work, a mindless brute without words or thoughts or reactions, a throwback to some medieval cellar, a feeble-minded fool cutting up meat for the master's coach dogs. 'That's *me*,' Roy would mutter to himself. 'A different face and a different name but that's *me*. Doing my chosen work. And Wesley gets twenty cents an hour more than *I* do.'

Chapter 5

Christine had never been a dependable letter writer. But since her arrival in Calgary, she had begun to write to her mother once or twice a week. She was careful in her letters to paint a positive picture of life in Alberta. Bright, primary colours. But late in August, she opened up and told the truth.

You know something, Grace? I feel lousy today. And I feel like saying it. I'm not crying on your shoulder. I don't want to upset *you*. But on the other hand, you're no dope. I know you realize that my life is not all sugar and spice.

I'm not talking about Roy. Thank God. When I met him a year ago, during those first weeks we spent together, I thought I could never love him more than I did then. But I found out different. Every week it gets better. Every day I realize all over again how much I depend on him and need him.

As for everything else . . . am I delighted? No. I had no illusions when I came to Canada. But still, somewhere in the back of my mind I was planning a little dream life. The Martha's Vineyard summer was still dancing around in my head, trying to duplicate itself.

But . . . that hasn't happened. Not only are we not in a place by ourselves, we are in the equivalent of a fourth-rate hostel.

Don't misunderstand me. Slayback's house is a godsend to people who arrive here short of money and short of information. Nowhere to go and no way to get there. But the idea is that once you're landed and stabilized, you move on to other quarters. And that's what we should have done. But the Slaybacks wanted us to stay on for a while, and Roy thought we should. He's grateful to Bobby for helping us and I understand that, but Jesus, I get tired of sharing a bathroom with strangers.

Then we have the Slaybacks themselves. Doris Slayback says things like 'We're so tickled you're going to stay on with us. You're such a terrific couple. We *envy* you guys. Both of us do.' Did anybody ever tell you they *envied* you? It's only happened to me a couple times. But *both* times I discovered that the envy was really hatred. Or at least that's what it turned into.

So I don't feel too relaxed with Doris. She smiles too much. And when she's not smiling she's staring. I feel like I'm Rebecca and she's the wicked housekeeper. Mrs de Winter, wasn't it?

Now we come to Bobby Slayback. For all his admirable qualities, there's something girlish about him that puts me off. But I suspect there's nothing girlish at all about his attitude toward me. Get it? He's a starer too, like Doris. There's a certain kind of jerk who thinks that if he stares at you hard enough, if you see that his heart is pouring out through his eyeballs, you will take pity on him, step sweetly out of your panty hose, and put his soul at ease.

Am I being a pain, bitching and moaning about a world I never made? Probably. But it's not a habit with me. And it won't become one, I promise. Still . . . sometimes, not often, I get to the point where I have to blab about everything that's bothering me or I'll blow up and burst. End of lament.

Did I tell you Russell might come to see us? Well, he came. He was here for two days. On his way to God-knows-where. I saw him one afternoon when I was between shifts and the next morning for breakfast. And he had dinner one night at the house with Roy and the Slaybacks and half a dozen other people, exiles like us. It was a terrific gab session, Roy said.

It was great seeing Russell. In between times I forget about all that energy. Ideas crackling out of his brain like an electric charge, words and images and hilariously funny mixtures of things and sounds that aren't supposed to go together but which end up perfectly meshed. Somebody said a sexy man is one who is very much what he *is*. Does that make sense? It does to me. And it certainly fits Russell.

Only one problem. How does he dare to be so free, to be so smilingly in charge of his own life? I read once where a cat is the only animal that has no time lag between the impulse and the action. That's Russell. And it's a lovely thing to see.

Chapter 6

From the moment Roy and Christine agreed to stay on with them, Doris Slayback had a premonition that she had outmanoeuvred herself.

Her rationale had been clear and correct in her mind. It was a kind of passive resistance she had used successfully before. Based on her own sexual self-confidence. Like many delicate, small-breasted young women who are pretty but not beautiful, she knew that her clothes, no matter how carefully selected and fitted, did not serve her well. Like an actress who becomes, before a motion-picture camera, a glowing and idealized version of her regular self, Doris, pale and naked, every vestige of hair removed carefully from her soft and rounded little body, became, in her own mind, a lush Ingres woman, eager to demonstrate that in spite of her smallness, *because* of it perhaps, she was a sexual match for any male, able to arch her slender back and stay the course with anyone.

Only Bobby, however, had been the beneficiary of her sensuality. He had deflowered her when she was fifteen, in her mother's sewing room, and since that time she had had no impulse to share herself with any other man. On the contrary. At the time of their marriage, both of them still in high school, she made a silent pledge to herself that she would provide her husband, and *only* him, with a variety of sexual delights that he had never imagined.

Of all the people in their town who knew Bobby, only Doris saw something special in him. He was ordinary-looking and timid. When he graduated from high school, he went to work in a radio repair shop and lived in a one-room flat with Doris over his parents' garage. Drafted and sent to Vietnam, he went without a murmur.

But combat changed him. He received three field promotions in two years, was decorated twice, reenlisted, and was sent home on furlough. He was welcomed as a hero. At a banquet in his honour he announced that he was deserting from the service and going to live in Canada. Three days later he and Doris were picked up in Utah, heading north on a motorcycle.

The military court, because of his record, gave him a chance to honour his enlistment. He refused, attacked the Vietnam War in a press conference that made him a hero to every draft-age man in the country, and was sentenced to five years in prison.

During his year and a half in detention he wrote articles encouraging young men to defy the draft. They were smuggled out of the prison, published in underground papers, and reprinted in *The Village Voice*. When he escaped from jail and made his way into Canada, it was reported on network news programmes.

From her schoolgirl years, from the very first day of her physical relationship with Bobby, Doris made a pact with herself. When she saw the power she had over him, when she learned the splendid havoc her tiny body could wreak, when she saw him time after time tremble and gasp and collapse beside her, she promised herself that she would refine and develop that power she felt inside, that mysterious mix of subordination and domination.

When she was seventeen, she confided to her wide-eyed friend, Alma Hubbard, 'I do things to Bobby that make him crazy. I tease him and hurt him and say dirty things to him so he's hard all the time when we're by ourselves. I wear him out every night. Since we're married he never goes to sleep. He *collapses*. I read in a doctor book that the more a man does it, the more he's able to do it. And I've got Bobby going so he can't *think* about anything else all day. He can't wait to get home so we can start up again.'

While Bobby was in Vietnam and later when he was in prison, Doris became a tireless reader of erotic books. Her name appeared on every sleazy mailing list, and she pored over each fresh piece of filth like a student studying for midterms. Every description, every position, every drawing and photograph, she recorded on the front of her brain, carefully substituting Bobby's face and her own on the coupled bodies, filing everything away in the sensual dark till she could turn it loose when she saw him again, till she could touch him, suck him, straddle him, and carry him along with her through the slow hours of the night into soft unconsciousness.

The man who came home to her from Vietnam, however, was a different person from the man she had married. And the subsequent months in prison changed him even more. He had stretched his consciousness and redesigned his ability to reason, to draw conclusions, to take action. The man she

174

followed to Calgary in 1968 was in many ways a father to the boy she married in 1963. He had broken out of the cocoon they shared into a world of concepts and ideals, of projects and programmes. In that world Doris could be supportive, but she could not contribute. He realized that and so did she. But it didn't alter or diminish their one-to-one contact with each other, that trusting, sharing, mutual dependence that had begun when they were fifteen years old. In triumph or disappointment he still turned to her. And she to him. Whatever changes they had gone through, whatever changes might be ahead, they thought of each other as permanent, thought of themselves as an indestructible unit. And their life in bed together went its crazy headlong way, fuelled by Doris' ingenuity and endless energy and scented by the perfume of sly perversion she gave off like a mist whenever the door to their room closed behind them.

Their nights all ended the same. Drunk or sober, sick or well, they knew, as sure as the sun, that they would roll together at last, naked in their soft bed, whisper, laugh, and devour each other.

So Doris, when she decided that Roy and Christine should stay on with them through the summer, had been dealing from strength. She had confidence in herself, confidence in her power over Bobby. She had seen him look at other young women the way he looked at Christine, and she had seen it come to nothing. Still, as she spent the days behind her checkout counter, sexual images of Bobby and Christine together continued to flash and flicker in her mind. She was painfully aware that from six in the morning, when she and Roy left the house to go to work, to eleven o'clock, when Christine went downtown, for five hours, she and Bobby were there in the house, together if they chose to be, in bed if they wanted to be.

If she expected to find some clue to Bobby's daytime activities in her own bed at night, Doris was disappointed. He was as ardent as ever, as insatiable as she was. If anything, he was more aggressive than she had ever known him to be. And leading her in a way that was new. From the time when she had begun carrying her erotic research into their bed, whispering, suggesting, showing him pictures and positions, they had taken delight, each of them, in her acting as teacher, aggressor, seductress, harlot, he as a willing victim. They played out roles in the night. The nun seducing the gardener. The nurse seducing the patient. The teacher seducing the schoolboy. She took the lead always. It excited her to do that. And it excited him.

But that summer he changed the game. Where before they had teased and played, laughed and dallied and punished each other, had interlocked and tangled and switched positions, rung a thousand changes on hands and mouths, fingers, toes, tongues, and genitals, now she found herself always on her back as soon as she was undressed, a pillow thrust under her hips, her legs tight around his waist, as he pounded and battered at her, driving and unrelenting, until they had rocked and groaned through a chain of orgasms and he tumbled flat beside her, exhausted and asleep.

She tried to tease him out of this new rhythm, tried to slip back into the sweet, extended, and intricate pattern of touching and tasting she was accustomed to, all smooth and tantalizing and painfully ecstatic. As she slid out of her clothes and stood by the side of the bed, her pelvis thrust forward, her breasts cupped in her hands, she said, 'Why don't we skip the missionary position tonight? All we've done for two months is the gorilla rapes the flower girl. Just lie back with your hands behind your head and I'll take you on a sweet trip.' But as soon as she leaned over him on the bed, he rolled her on her back, spread her legs, and thrust deep inside her.

Another change. They made love in the dark now. All their years together they had preferred lights in the room. Full light often. Some light always. Now suddenly he switched off the bedside lamp and kept it off all the time they made love.

Her sexual preferences, through the years with Bobby, had become sophisticated and intricate. His body never failed to arouse her, but her imagination aroused her more. She loved to linger, to hesitate, to stop and start, to hold herself back, to come just to the brink of a climax, then slow down, come to the brink again, as many times as she could, until her body would no longer be denied, till she shook suddenly and suffered with painful contractions, her hips jackknifing out of control, her body slamming against his with lunatic force. She had often said to him, 'I don't want us to fuck like anybody else. Or ever exactly the same as the last time. I want to surprise you every time. And I want you to surprise me. Coming is great but it's not everything. It's too easy. When we were in high school I used to come sometimes when I saw you walk into study hall. I'd feel all warm and swollen down there, I'd sit at my desk and cross my legs, never taking my eyes off you, and I'd come in my panties.'

Still, Bobby's nightly assault on her served a fine purpose. It took her mind almost completely off Christine. When she stood at work, with her soft little mound which was always sore and sensitive now pressed against the counter, when she envisioned Bobby driving on top of her as he had the night before, when she realized that in a few hours he would be pounding and punishing her again in the same way, it made her quiver. And the threat of Christine seemed like no threat at all.

One night late in August, however, the fears she'd felt early in summer came back to bedevil her.

It was a Saturday night. Roy had gone downtown to meet Christine after work and had come home with her on the bus. They found Bobby and Doris still downstairs in the kitchen. The four of them sat around the table, talking and drinking beer, for nearly an hour. When they went upstairs together, Bobby and Doris to the second floor, Christine and Roy to the third, they were whispering and trying not to laugh, trying not to wake the other people in the house who were already asleep, and Doris thought, 'This is really nice. This is what I wanted all along. Another couple we could be friends with and talk to and have some fun with.' When they said good night in the hall, she said, 'I hope you guys never move away from here.'

'I mean it,' she said to Bobby as they went inside their bedroom. 'I hope they . . .'

When she turned back from closing the door, he slapped her hard across the face, switched off the ceiling light, and pushed her back against the wall.

'Jesus, Bobby . . . what's the matter? What did I do?'

He slapped her again, held her against the wall with his body, and ripped away her skirt and panties.

'It's all right,' she said. 'It's all right, honey.' With one arm around his neck she lifted herself, wrapped her legs around his waist, and with her other hand guided him inside her. As soon as she closed around him, he shook and bucked against her and came immediately.

'Let's get on the bed,' she said. 'Let me take off my shirt.' But he kept her there, her back against the wall, his fingers digging into her soft bottom, pounding at her, long, hard strokes that made her gasp, 'Honey, Jesus, you're killing me.'

At last he eased away from the wall, staying inside her, lowered her to the floor, and crouched there on his knees between her legs, thrusting inside her like an iron and awkward machine built to resemble a man, keeping it up, no pause or break in rhythm for more than an hour, till at last a raw and rasping cry tore out of his chest, his body shook in a final burst of spasms, and he collapsed on top of her.

After she got him to the bed, took his clothes off, and covered him with a sheet, she went, still trembling, into the bathroom to inspect herself. She took off her wet, wrinkled shirt and stood naked in front of the mirror.

Her face was flushed still, with pale welts on her cheek where his hand had struck her. Her eyes looked large, the pupils black and dilated, and her lips were full, puffed and red, from the pressure of his mouth. She felt violated in a way she had never felt before, and it thrilled her. Staring at her own white nakedness, she felt strong and in control in a new way.

It was only when she was lying in bed in the dark, with Bobby breathing evenly beside her, as she reviewed the evening, examining the moments like beads on a string, it was only then that some of the questions she had asked herself all summer suddenly found searing answers in her head. She knew suddenly why Bobby for weeks had made love to her as if she were a pickup in an alley; she knew why the lights were always turned out, and she knew why he had hit her tonight.

The answer, when it came, was clear and undeniable. It echoed back and forth in her head like a cry against the mountains. 'He's pretending I'm Christine. All summer he's been using me to rape Christine. All that craziness in the dark was for her, not me.'

She lay there, frightened and cold suddenly, and tried to refute what her senses were telling her. But the truth kept chiming in her head; the vibrations travelled slowly down through her body and settled with a jolt in her stomach. She got out of bed, ran into the bathroom, and was sick on the floor.

She was still awake when the light started to filter in around the window shades. Down in the kitchen someone had begun to make breakfast. She lay in bed feeling drained and light as parchment, but she was past the desperation that had chilled her through the night. She was frightened still, and apprehensive, but she was determined, too.

Chapter 7

'*W*hose turn is it to go downstairs for coffee?' Roy said.

'Mine,' Christine said. They were lying in bed, nine o'clock in the morning, a warm wind blowing through the open window, church bells ringing in the distance.

'I don't think so. You went yesterday.'

179

She reached under the sheet and took his hand in hers. 'That's all right. That's my fun. Saturdays and Sundays are my only chances to spoil you. Bread and coffee in bed. When we have our own kitchen I'll make you famous breakfasts. Fruit and cereal and fresh orange juice. And sausage and ham and eggs and toasted English muffins with strawberry jam. And a big pot of cowboy coffee to make your hair stand on end. Then we'll get back in bed with the Sunday papers and stay there all day. How does that sound?'

'Terrific. But you made me hungry.' He got out of bed and pulled on his jeans and a sweat shirt. Then he leaned down and kissed her. 'Go back to sleep for ten minutes. When you wake up I'll put a cup of coffee in your hand.'

Downstairs, in the community kitchen, someone had already started the coffee maker. As Roy took cups and plates out of the cupboard, Doris Slayback came into the kitchen wearing cutoff jeans and a T-shirt, her face scrubbed and her hair pulled back with a rubber band.

'Good morning,' Roy said. 'How'd you sleep?'

'Not so good.'

'Too much beer or not enough?'

'Nothing like that. Just bugs in my head.'

'A couple quarts of coffee will fix that,' he said.

'I don't think so.' Then, 'Can I talk to you for a minute?'

'Sure. I've got a hungry lady upstairs, but –'

'I'm serious,' Doris said. 'This is serious.' She poured two cups of black coffee. When she sat down at the table, Roy sat in the chair opposite her.

'I hope you're not gonna tell me you're hot for my body,' he said. 'And you want me to take you off for a long weekend or something.'

'You won't think it's so funny when I tell you what – Oh, shit . . . now that I've got you here I don't know how to start.'

'Maybe you shouldn't start at all. I'll tell you the truth – if you need advice about something, I'm a bad guy to talk to. I have trouble finding my shoes in the morning. Chrissy's the one with the cool head. Maybe you should talk to her.'

180

'I don't want to talk to her. I want to talk *about* her. Are you two having problems?'

Roy grinned. 'Our problem is we don't get to spend enough time together. But outside of that . . .'

'It's tough on Bobby and me, too, the crazy hours. Me down at that cow town supermarket five days a week and him up here trying to handle a million things all by himself. So I guess we can't blame Chrissy too much.'

'Blame her for what?'

'Don't get mad at me. I mean so far nothing's happened. But Bobby's like any other man. He's human. And Chrissy's a sexy-looking girl.'

'What are you talking about?'

'Jesus, Roy, don't be dense. Don't make me lay it out on the table.'

'I *am* dense. I *want* you to lay it out on the table.'

'Oh, boy,' she said, 'why do I always get the crummy jobs?' Then, 'Chrissy's been coming on to Bobby. She's been doing it for weeks now.'

'Who says so?'

'*I* say so. I can see it. And you'd see it if you opened your eyes.'

'I *do* open my eyes. And I see Bobby staring at Chrissy like a lovesick goat. He's been doing it ever since she came up here.'

'Oh, God, are you dumb? Is that what she told you? Do you believe *anything* she says? She told Bobby that you guys have an understanding. You do what you want to and so does she. She said she's been balling some guy down at the place where she works ever since she came to Calgary.'

'Where's Bobby? I want him to tell me that to my face.'

'He won't *do* that. He likes you. He would *never* tell you what I'm telling you now. He'll be mad as hell at me if he finds out *I* told you. But that doesn't mean it's not the truth. He's told *me* plenty. He says she's after him almost every morning. After you're gone and I'm gone. She follows him here to the kitchen, she comes into his room. She shows up anyplace in the house whenever he's by himself. She presses up against him and tells him everything she'd like to do to him. Every time he turns around she's got her shirt open so he can see her—'

Roy stood up suddenly. 'I don't know what you're up to, Doris, but you're lying in your teeth. And if Bobby told you all that crap, he's a bigger liar than you are.' He started around the table toward the door, but Doris was across the room like a cat blocking the door to the stairway. 'Don't go after Bobby. That won't do you any good. It's not his fault.'

'The hell it's not. If he said what you say he did . . .'

'But he won't admit it. I told you that. He doesn't want to cause any trouble between you and Chrissy. And neither do I. I was just talking to you so maybe you could talk to her and get her to back off from Bobby.' She was crying now and had braced herself, arms and legs against the frame of the doorway. Roy took hold of both her wrists and tried to pull her away without hurting her. 'Don't go up there, Roy. Please. I didn't want to make trouble between you and Bobby. He'll *kill* me if you tell him what I said. *Please*. Pretty please. I was trying to help. I was trying to do something *nice*.'

When Roy pulled her hands away from the door, she screamed, tried to kick him between the legs, and fell backward on the floor at the foot of the stairs. But before he could step over her, she scrambled to her feet and raced ahead of him up the steps, screaming, 'No, Roy . . . no . . . *please*.' Running down the hallway toward her room, she put both hands inside the collar of her shirt and ripped it open so it hung like a tattered waistcoat, exposing her naked breasts.

With one last ear-shattering scream that wakened everyone in the house, she slipped inside the bedroom she shared with Bobby, slammed the door behind her, and slipped the bolt just as Roy hit the door with a thud and began pounding on it with his fists.

Bobby turned away from the sink in the corner, a razor in his hand, lather all over his face. Before he could speak, Doris was across the room, her arms around his neck, sobbing and babbling. 'Don't let him in, Bobby. Don't let him get me.'

'Don't let *who* in? What's the matter?'

'It's Roy. He's gone crazy. He caught me in the kitchen and tried to . . . He pinched me and hit me and tried to . . .'

Outside the door, Roy kept shouting, 'Bobby. Open the door. I want to talk to you.'

'What's he mean?' Bobby said to Doris. 'What's he want with me?'

'I told you . . . he's crazy. He doesn't want you. He wants *me*. He wants to fuck me.'

'I'll fix his ass,' Bobby said. He put Doris down on the bed and covered her up. Then he crossed the room, slid the bolt, and opened the door. As Roy stepped forward through the doorway, Bobby swung his right fist and hit him on the side of the head, just above his ear.

They wrestled each other to the floor then and rolled back and forth, swearing and grunting and punching. Doris, her head propped on a pillow, watched them. With no expression, no hint of a smile or a frown, she simply lay there and watched.

Chapter 8

*L*ate that afternoon, the weather sultry and overcast, their clothes, books, and other belongings stashed in an inexpensive room in a motel on John Laurie Boulevard, Roy and Christine walked slowly along Lacree Trail and sat down on a grassy slope overlooking the golf course. From where they sat, the golfers looked like brightly dressed dolls; their voices carried up from the fairways like thin bird calls.

They sat there for a long time, resting back on their elbows, their legs stretched out in front of them. Finally, Christine said, 'I can't get it out of my head. It's the strangest thing. Something scary about it. Like those stories you hear about where somebody goes clear out of control.'

'I don't think she was out of control,' Roy said. 'She knew what she wanted and she got it. She wanted us out of the house and we're out.'

'But my God, why would she do a whole opera? All those lies. And then after the damage is done, after you and Bobby are ready to kill each other, she admits she was lying, that she made it all up. What kind of sense does that make?'

'None.'

Bobby had knocked on their door late in the morning, a blue welt on one cheekbone and a strip of tape acoss his nose. When Roy opened the door, Bobby said, 'Look, I feel like a horse's ass. I want to talk to you.'

'Forget it. Doris wants us out of here. We're getting out. That's all there is to it.'

'I don't blame you for being sore. Just let me tell you what happened. Then you can do what you want to.'

Roy stepped out into the hall and closed the door behind him. He followed Bobby down to the end of the hall, and they stood by a bay window looking down on the street. 'I've been talking to Doris for over an hour. She just admitted that she made up all that shit.'

'I could have told you that. I *wanted* to tell you that. Why do you think, I was pounding on your door?'

'All right. I was stupid. But what would you do if Chrissy came tearing into your room with half her clothes torn off and said somebody was trying to rape her?'

'I'd probably do what you did,' Roy said. 'But what's that have to do with all the crap she was feeding me about you and Chris? What was that all about?'

'You're really pissed off, aren't you?'

'You're damned right I'm pissed off. I don't like to have people cock me around. When somebody looks me in the eye and lies like a thief and it's just for meanness, just to make trouble, then I'm long gone, Bobby. On the bus. Out of sight.'

'Everybody's entitled to a mistake.'

'Doris didn't make a mistake. She knew what she wanted and she got it. If she's shedding tears now, I guarantee you she's doing a bigger number on you than she did this morning.'

'What did he say when you said that?' Christine asked. She turned over in the grass and put her head in Roy's lap.

'What could he say? He knows she's a wacko.'

As soon as they'd checked into the motel, around the middle of the day, they'd bought a Sunday paper and searched the classified section for apartments. With two dollars' worth of change, Christine had then spent more than an hour in the phone booth by the registration desk. Back in the room with Roy, she said, 'Not too encouraging. There were three little apartments that sounded like possibilities, but one of them is out north by the airport and the other two are on Anderson Road at the south edge of town. With our work schedules, we'd need to have *two* cars.'

'It's all right,' Roy said. 'If we keep checking the papers, something will turn up. Every vacant apartment in Calgary can't be out at the edge of town.'

'They're *not*. There are apartments in every section. But either they cost too much or they're too far from the bus lines.'

That evening they had coffee and a sandwich in a diner down the street from the motel. They sat for a long time in a booth in the corner, going over their choices, trying to make their alternative seem plentiful and pleasant. But at last they sat quiet, like cranky children, drinking endless cups of coffee and staring out of the window at the night. Finally, Christine said, 'I know you can't blame a place. You can't get a gun and start shooting at trees or fireplugs. But all the same, I'm not too much in love with Calgary right now. It may not be *against* us but it sure as heck isn't *for* us.'

'Maybe not. But we're stuck with it.'

'No, we're not. You said so yourself. Just because we came here first doesn't mean we have to *stay* here. We could go to

185

Edmonton or Toronto. Any place we want. Vancouver's supposed to be great.'

'So's Tahiti. But we're not there.'

'Oh, come on, Roy. We had a bad day, but it's not the end of the world. Since we're moving, maybe we should make it a *big* move.'

'Then what? We've got jobs now. If we go someplace else we have to start from scratch.'

'So what? We'll get *better* jobs.'

Later that night as they lay in their motel bed with the lights off, Roy said, 'You know something – you're right. Let's get a couple of bus tickets and relocate.'

'Where do we go?'

'How about Vancouver?'

'Sounds good to me.'

'They say it's a beautiful city. The winters aren't so cold, and there are lots of Americans there in case we want to play softball or listen to Count Basie records.'

'Can we go through Banff and Jasper? That's supposed to be terrific country.'

'No problem. We'll go wherever the bus goes.'

They decided to leave at once, the following day. But they left themselves an escape hatch. From the bus station next morning each of them called their places of employment and said they had been called to Edmonton by the central office of Immigration. Christine bluffed her supervisor by saying, 'If there's any problem about my getting the time off, they said they would call you direct from Edmonton.' She was given a week off without pay. Roy, using the same tactic, was also given a week off.

'In case we lose our nerve, that gives us seven days to scramble back to where we are now. All we lose is a week's pay. So at worst we have a vacation and at best we change our luck.'

They booked their bus trip to Vancouver via Banff and Jasper. Straight west to Banff, then northwest on Highway 93 to Jasper, due west to pick up Highway 5 in British Columbia, south to Kamloops, and on to Vancouver Island on the Pacific coast.

186

But they never reached Vancouver. And they didn't return to Calgary. After four days in the Banff-Jasper area they had no desire to go anyplace else.

They cashed in their Vancouver tickets at the Jasper bus station, bought new tickets for Banff, returned there the following afternoon, and before another week passed had met Abe Singleton and his splendid wife, Annie.

Chapter 9

*O*n the bus heading south from Jasper to Banff, Roy said, 'Why do I feel so great all of a sudden?'

'Because you have the instincts of a *clochard*.'

'What's a *clochard*?'

'A bum. A hobo. A man who sleeps under bridges in Paris,' Christine said. 'You feel good because we have no jobs, not much money, and great expectations. We have taken the future into our hands and we are headed, nonstop, for the poorhouse.'

'Not a chance. Banff is the answer. I like a town that's not too big. I predict that we will make a strong impression in Banff. A lot of people are bound to wonder where we came from and why it took us so long to get here.'

'You're right. I think we should go to the biggest bar in Banff, buy drinks for the house, and announce that Lavidge and Wheatley are in town, ready for action, willing to discuss business propositions. Any offer considered as long as it's respectable and looo-crative.'

'Lucrative. That's the word. No more throwing ourselves away on unrewarding work.'

'Absolutely. In exchange for a nice apartment, a handsome salary, and three meals a day, we will give them a guarantee that we are truly outstanding. For an extra fee they can photograph us and use the pictures in their advertising.'

'We'll find a public typewriter and make a résumé of our qualifications. We might even spend a few bucks and have pictures taken. Very sober. Me in a shirt and tie. You with your hair pulled back.'

Their plans hit a snag as soon as they were back in Banff. The hostel where they had hoped to stay, more than two miles west of Banff, was closed for the season. When they hiked back into town, they found at last a bed-and-breakfast place on Big Horn Street near the railroad station. *Jesus Saves* was set in pebbles in the concrete of the walk leading up to the door, and a sign in the window read, *Have You Told the Lord You're Coming?*

The tiny white-haired woman who opened the door said, 'I've got a bed but it's no playpen. You know what I'm getting at?'

'We're married,' Christine said. 'Mr and Mrs Roy Lavidge.'

She looked them over thoroughly. 'I don't see no rings on anybody's hand.'

'It was a single-ring ceremony,' Christine said, 'But I'm allergic to all kinds of metal. Can't wear jewellery at all. Not even my wedding ring.'

The woman thought it over. 'I don't think so.'

'We'll be in town for a week at least. We'll pay you seven nights in advance,' Roy said.

When they were upstairs in their room with the door closed, Christine put her arms around him, kissed him on the chin, and said, 'Clever. Very clever.'

'First principles. Money talks.'

Two days later they sent off their résumés, thirty-five of them, photographs enclosed. At the end of a week after twice-daily trips to their post-office box, they'd had only one reply. A barely legible handwritten note on the stationery of the St Albert Hotel.

Dear Lavidge and Wheatley:

I'm impressed. But here is my problem. You caught me between seasons. The skiers won't start arriving till November. If you can hang around till then, maybe we can work something out.

The signature, a slanting scrawl, was totally illegible.

'It's not a turndown exactly,' Christine said. 'It's more like a postponement.'

'Same difference. We can't camp out here for two months.'

'I'm really surprised,' Christine said. 'I was sure we get some action from those slick résumés.'

'*Too* slick, I guess. We should have wandered in with a blank look on our faces and just said we're looking for work. That must be what they're used to up here.'

'Then that's what we'll do now. We'll follow up the résumés with a personal call. You take half and I'll take half. If we can't get jobs together, we'll get jobs separately.'

But there were no jobs. Together or separately. The same story everywhere. Between seasons. Come back in two months.

'Now what?' Christine said.

They chose Vancouver. But the day before they were scheduled to leave Banff, Abe Singleton came to look them up. Early in the morning. They'd just had coffee in their landlady's kitchen. When Abe came to the door and identified himself as the man who'd written them a note on St Albert Hotel letter paper, Roy went outside to talk with him, away from Mrs Guinnup's inquisitive ears.

'How'd you locate us?'

'This is a little town. I inquired around and somebody steered me here.' He leaned back against the fender of his Land-Rover. 'After I wrote to you, I thought you might drop in to see us.'

Roy shook his head. 'The St Albert was the only place we *didn't* follow up on. I figured there was no point to it after we got your note. Because we can't wait two months to start work. We're going out to Vancouver tomorrow. Unless maybe . . . I

189

mean the situation hasn't changed at your hotel, has it?'

'No, I'm afraid not.'

Abe offered Roy a cigarette and lit one himself. 'To tell you the truth, I've been driving myself nuts ever since I got the résumé of yours. When I saw the name, *Lavidge*, I almost looked you up right then. I thought you might be related to a guy I knew in New Zealand.'

'Maybe I am. What's his first name?'

'Thomas. But everybody calls him T.J. He's a big guy. Easygoing. Used to live in the state of Maine.'

'That's my dad,' Roy said.

Chapter 10

*T*wo weeks later, Christine wrote a long letter to her mother.

Like I told you on that postcard I sent, we lucked out. Up here in the Canadian nowhere, we run into a guy who used to work with Roy's father in New Zealand. This man, Abe Singleton, manages the St Albert hotel here in Banff. And it just so happens that he and his wife, Annie, needed a first-rate couple to help them run the place.

Actually, they didn't need anybody for a couple of months, till the ski season starts, but Roy and Abe made a deal. We work for just our room and board till business picks up, then we go on salary.

What about the St Albert? Here's what it says about

us in *Travel Alberta*, the booklet that's put out every year by the tourist office. I've cut it out and I'll stick it to the page with a piece of Scotch tape.

St Albert Hotel – 555-2565
Caribou Street Box 7246, Banff TOL OCO
52 rooms. Some TV. 31 washbasin only. Central bath.
Elevator. Tavern. View of river. Near bus depot.
Off-season rates. Single:
$12-16. Double: $14-20. Twin: $16-21.

As you can see, the place is not expensive and not fancy. But it's clean and solid and well run and the food is good. The St Albert has been here, just at the edge of the Bow River, since 1903. Skiers come in the winter and tourists and fishermen when it's warmer.

So . . . we're in residence. I've never lived anyplace where I could look out the window and see mountains, and it really turns me on.

And then we have the Singletons, the people we work for. And that's the best part. They're a nice, attractive couple who really like each other. Two kids. A boy, Victor, who's six years old, and a daughter, Stephanie, who's four. Abe is forty but looks fifty, and Annie is thirty but looks twenty-five. They've been married for seven years, and in that time they've lived in three or four different countries. They have itchy feet and they're proud of it. They know that anyplace they wind up, they can always make a decent living. Abe has worked in bars and hotels and restaurants all his life, and Annie's family has a little bed-and-breakfast hotel in New Zealand. So they know the ropes.

'Clean beds, large portions on the plate,' Abe says, 'and a schooner of beer for a decent price, and you never have to worry about the trade. You'll have customers coming at you like mosquitoes.'

Annie says it's all Abe, that *he's* the one who makes

things work. 'He could tap a barrel of beer out in the wilderness, nobody living for miles around, and in two days there'd be people standing in line. He's an international attraction.'

I think she's right. He's got that thing that all Irishmen are supposed to have but don't. When he talks the words come out good.

He drinks a lot, but Annie says she's the only one who can tell when he's had too many. The tip-off, she says, is when he wants to get into his car at three in the morning and race around the mountain roads.

He never wants to go to sleep. He's the first one up in the morning and the last one to bed. He sits up reading and writing letters till all hours.

So that's Abe. We all have a crush on him. Annie, his two kids, me and Roy. Roy especially. He's found a hero. They sit and talk and drink beer together as if they'd been friends for years.

I'll have to write a special letter later on about Annie. She fabulous. Not beautiful, I guess, not like you, but really handsome, like a barefoot peasant who also ended up with a brain and a sense of humour.

She's tall, for one thing, taller than all of us, including Abe. Great legs. But with hips and a spectacular bosom. A real earth mother.

The wildest thing about her is her colouring. She has a mop of beautiful dark-red hair. Cinnamon coloured. But with dark eyebrows and lashes. Not all white and washed-out like some redheads. Her skin isn't pale either. It's sort of brown and tawny, and she has some freckles sprinkled across her nose. And her eyes are almost exactly the same colour as her hair. So she's really something to see.

On the last page of her letter, Christine told Grace she was going to have a baby.

I just found out for sure three days ago and I'm so

excited I can't sleep at night. I can't make a big thing about it because it's still a secret. Outside of Annie, who took me to her doctor here in Banff, you're the only person who knows. I haven't even told Roy yet. I want to pick a great moment. Everything's been so perfect for Roy and me, I want this part to be perfect too. And it *will* be. I can't tell you how happy I am.

Everything she wrote to Grace was true. But it was not the *total* truth. Although she and Roy had agreed that they wanted children, the question of *when* was another matter. In all their talks about it there had been a heavy use of the future tense.

So although Christine told herself it was perfectly acceptable for her to savour the experience for a few days or a few weeks before telling Roy, the truth was she was not sure that he would be pleased with the news.

She had insisted, from the start, that avoiding pregnancy was her responsibility. Both of them had relied on her. And she had forgotten only once. On the final morning at the Slayback's house in Calgary, sleeping late, lazing in bed while Roy went downstairs for coffee, she had failed to open the prescription vial in her handbag and swallow the tablet.

Distracted all day, she had continued to forget, until late that night, after their decision to leave Calgary and travel west to Vancouver, when they were laughing and congratulating themselves, planning and teasing and playing, only then, when they had rolled naked together, and she was trembling on the edge of orgasm, only then did the truth flash through her mind. And at that instant it was already too late. There was nothing to do but lie on her back and whisper to herself a simple child's prayer.

Chapter 11

*L*ater that autumn, when Russell met Abe Singleton, his assessment of him differed, in almost every respect, from the one Christine had given Grace.

'A strange apple,' Russell said. 'Odd and complicated. I never trust a guy who likes everybody. Making friends can't be a man's main occupation. It's not a profession, for Christ's sake. So when I see somebody who seems to be ingratiating himself to everybody, my first reaction is—'What's the son of a bitch *really* up to?" '

'*Cynical*,' I said, 'you're getting cynical as hell.'

Russell shook his head. 'Trust me. I've seen guys like him before. Usually they've pissed away every opportunity they've ever had. They've been halfway around the world. Or *all* the way. They've been drunk in all the famous bars and screwed everybody in sight. And if you look close, you'll find some wives and a few kids left behind. Wondering where Daddy went.

'Great talkers, too. Always. A lot of inside dope on anything that comes up. First-name references to guys you never heard of but who know somebody *everybody* has heard of. Guys like Singleton always bring up somebody who knew Howard Hughes like a brother, or a hooker in Bristol who spent weekends with J Paul Getty. Or somebody who had breakfast with Jack Ruby the morning he shot Lee Harvey Oswald. A lot of mystery. A lot of sly winks and finger snaps. It's a politician's trick. It's what politics *is*. Mass seduction. I saw Franco speak to twenty thousand people in Madrid. I was in a conference room in a bank in Zurich when Perón sat at a table and talked for an hour to fifteen bankers. Those guys were fucking snake charmers. If they were burglars, people would save them the trouble. They'd walk out into the street and hand them the family silver.'

'What's all that have to do with Abe Singleton?'

'I'm not sure. I just know he's one of those assholes who for one reason or another hates himself. So he's found a way to turn himself into a central figure, to lead the parade, to call the tune.'

On the subject of Annie Singleton, Russell's views had a different tone. 'It never fails,' he said. 'Guys like Singleton always end up with first-rate women. You see his wife come strolling across the lawn with one kid draped across her shoulder, another one riding her hip, two dogs and a cat following her, and you say to yourself, 'Jesus, what have I missed? What kind of a woman is *that*?'

Chapter 12

'*I*'ve been scrambling since I was eleven,' Abe told Roy. '1941 . . . the year my mother died. Those were tough years in Sligo. Poor times all over Ireland, but especially in the northwest. "When there's a feast in Dublin, nothing but table scraps make their way to Donegal." That's what the people say.

'My mother, Mary Dockery her name was before she married, came from the Aran Islands, stuck out in the ocean off Galway, and her people, even if they'd claimed me, which they didn't, had nothing extra in the cupboard to feed another mouth.

'As for the Singletons in Cork, they'd disowned my dad in April 1916, when he fought in the Easter Rebellion. He was only fourteen and he was shot twice that day. Carried a bullet in his thigh the rest of his life.

'He was a tough little bugger, my father. A member of the IRA before it had a name. He was a tiny man, half my size, not even as big as my mother. But he was all knuckles and guts and sinew. And a tongue like a flamethrower. They say he could whip up a crowd so priests went home to make gasoline bombs and old women volunteered to throw them.

'Martin Singleton his name was, there's a street named after him in Derry, and another one in Bundoran. It's a famous name in Ireland now. But from the time of the Easter Rebellion till he died in 1935, he was always in jail or on the run to keep from going there.

'He was a stonemason by trade, learned it from his dad in Cork, but between the ages of fourteen and twenty-seven he did most of his stonework in one prison or another. And even after I was born, in 1930, I spent all the time with my mum. We seldom saw my dad.

'His greatest strength was his greatest failing. He didn't know how to compromise. He believed in unrelenting pressure till he got what he wanted. A united Ireland and total separation from England. But all he got in his lifetime was prison cells, bad food, and at last a hundred bullets in his body.

'When I was two years old we moved north from Sligo to Raphoe. That's only a short drive to the border of Ulster and the town of Strabane, which was an IRA stronghold. So my dad moved back and forth, from one place to another in that area, sometimes on one side of the line, sometimes on the other. My mother would ride out on horseback at night and meet him in the fields near Raphoe. When I was three or four years old she began to take me along. I remember those meeting places more clearly than I remember my father. Wooded spots most often, glades in the forest, very early morning or evenings just at dusk. My mother always carried food with her, and I remember sitting on logs, or on the ground in dry weather, outdoors, eating, just the three of us.

'After one of those times, when we'd met out in the woods, after my mother and I had left and started back to Raphoe, my dad was ambushed and killed. But I didn't know what had happened till several years later. All I knew was that the picnics had stopped.

'When I was eleven, just before my mother died, she told me my father had been dead for more than six years. She hadn't told me before because she still hoped he was alive, hiding out somewhere. But at last one of his mates came to see her and told her that he was the one who had buried my dad after he was torn apart by bullets from the Orange.'

Abe's story didn't come in a smooth flow. As he and Roy worked together in the hotel, or as they sat with mugs of beer after the tavern had closed and was cleaned up, bits and pieces of Abe's life and experiences came out and were enlarged upon.

Often he discussed his role as a publican. 'First-rate life,' he said. 'It's the calling for dreamers and poets and thieves. When I was a kitchen lad in the Central Hotel at Raphoe, working sixteen hours a day for my food and a corner to sleep in, sweating my brains out, straining my young back and scalding my hands, taking the jolts and the knocks of any kitchen drunk or barmaid or patron who wanted to test his knuckles on my skull – even then, cold and wet, aching muscles and all, I felt as if I was in a magic business. Nice smells always, of bread and crumpets baking, or stew, or kidney pies, and the beer sloshing into big mugs behind the bar. And new faces always. New help in the kitchen. New customers at the tables or standing long hours at the bar. Jokers and singers and windbags. Discussions and quarrels and ragging sessions that would start on a Saturday in April and peter out in early October. *Change* always. That's what I liked best, I guess. And I *still* like it.

'Even being sacked is no great worry, because you know that down the line there's a manager or an owner who's just sacked somebody himself. And he's looking for a lad just like you. It's a bloody carousel. A nice warm plate of food always ready for you and a party in the pub every night. And upstairs or downstairs or somewhere on the premises there's a soft clean bed with a warm little woman in it to get you through the night.'

197

About T. J. Lavidge, Abe had stories and anecdotes and pungent quotations. 'He had a life that ought to be written down in a book. It wouldn't be a book I'd want my daughter to read, but it would be a hell of an experience all the same. T.J. is an original creation. He invented himself. He's a man who said to himself, 'I think I'll have some fun.' So he did. And he does. It's like a holy crusade to him. I'm no bloody angel, but compared to T.J., when he gets the bit in his teeth, I'm Saint Francis of bloody Assisi.

'The thing about T.J. is he has to do whatever he sets out to do or he'll explode. So that's what he does. And somehow he gets away with it. There's nobody like him. He'll have women chasing him through the streets when he's eighty.'

And very often Abe talked about his wife. 'Since I met Annie, I haven't laid hand or foot or anything else on another female. She was just eighteen then. So it was a big difference between where *she's* been and where *I'd* been. I'd been married and I'd tried everything else I could think of, animal, mineral, or vegetable. But when I laid eyes on Annie, I said to myself, "She's the top of the mark, the class of the breed. If she can't turn you into a one-woman man, then nobody can."

'Even your dad, whose idea of monogamy was to shack up with no more than three women at the same time, said to me, "Abe, if you don't like *her*, I don't like *you*." He thought Annie was the *best*.'

In the folder in his files labelled *Singletons*, Russell Atha had detailed notes about Abe's father, Martin; his mother, Mary Lois, and the early days of Abe's life in Sligo and Raphoe, before and after his father's death, the material that I've just covered in the dialogues between Roy and Abe.

In addition his notes spanned the period between 1941, when Abe's mother died, and 1960, when he married Annie Granger in New Zealand.

Between 1941, when he was eleven, and 1946, when he was sixteen, Abe worked in hotels and pubs and restaurants in Raphoe and Letterkenny, Ballybofey, and Lifford. When he was sixteen he went to Strabane, looked up some men who had known his father, and tried to join the IRA. Too young, they said.

So he worked for several months on fishing boats out of Killybegs. Then he shipped out from Galway on a Libyan freighter bound for Manila. For the next two years he sailed a regular route, from San Francisco to Singapore to Australia. In 1950 he jumped ship in Sydney and found a job as a bar-tender. Married a girl named Sybil from Perth, but after six months he left her, went to Queenstown, on the South Island of New Zealand, and worked as a waiter in the Hotel Esplanade on Peninsula Street overlooking Lake Wakatipu.

In 1951, when the United Nations began sending troops to Korea, he enlisted in a New Zealand unit and went along, trained as a commando.

Discharged in Tokyo in 1953, Abe flew from there to London, spent six months in St Albans living with a Pakistani woman named Rhangi. The child she had, a daughter named Pia, may or may not have been his. During this time he was arrested twice. At an 'Ireland For the Irish' demonstration during coronation week and at a rally in Leeds protesting the executions of Julius and Ethel Rosenberg.

By 1955, having left Rhangi behind in England, he was in Ireland again, operating a pub on Inishmore in the Aran Islands, living with a woman named Sarah Dockery, his third cousin on his mother's side.

In 1957 he shipped as a deck steward on a British cruise ship bound for Honolulu via the West Indies, Panama, and Acapulco. In Honolulu, in the grill room of the Royal Luana, he worked first with T.J. Lavidge. When Abe got a chance to go back to New Zealand in 1958, to manage a bar in Christchurch, T.J. went with him. The following year they both went to Wellington, on the North Island, to work at the St George. In 1960 Abe flew to Nelson on a three-day holiday. He stayed at a small bed-and-breakfast hotel just off Bridge Street. The hotel was run by Ruth Granger, Annie's aunt. Abe and Annie met that weekend and were married the following Christmas.

Footnote: Maybe there's no significance to this, but in every place that Abe settled, he seemed to have two sets of friends. The seamen and barmen and waiters he worked with on the one hand. And another higher-level, higher-income group, some of them Irish, some not. All of his girl friends and his drinking companions came from the first group. But the others, wherever he established even a temporary residence, were always there, too. Odd.

Chapter 13

*I*n Banff September and October are filled with magic days. Between seasons, between the heat of summer and the aching cold of winter, also between the crowds of summer visitors and the crowds of winter people, the year-round residents can revel in the self-deception that their town belongs to them.

Christine, that 1970 autumn, felt an exhilaration that was almost frightening to her. As much as possible, she kept this excitement inside, hoarding it like candy wrapped in gold foil and stored in a cool drawer.

Later in her life she would abhor the quirkish, perverse sentimentality that had possessed her during those weeks, causing her to conceal something that was crying to be shared. But at the time she was rosy cheeked and sure of herself.

Annie was her only confidante. And Annie told her, repeatedly, that she was making a mistake. 'I know what you think you're doing. You're trying to make it better. Dressing it all up. It's a sweet idea but it's cuckoo.'

'You're probably right,' Christine said. 'But don't spoil my fun, Annie. I feel like I've got the sun in my belly, and it's a crazy sensation.'

She studied her body in the mirror for any change and saw none. But her eyes shone, her skin glowed, and her lips were full and red, as though she had made love through the night. Also, contrary to the theories she had been exposed to in a college course called *Marriage and the Family*, she found herself inexhaustibly passionate during those autumn weeks. It excited her somehow that being pregnant, she could not possibly *become* pregnant; she could spread her legs for Roy anytime, anywhere, like a barefoot slut with no thought for anything except physical gratification.

Her hands were on him always, in any private moment, in the hotel corridors, in the pantry, in the car; she took delight in enticing him to their room in the afternoon when they had sometimes only a ten-minute break, lifting her skirt and pulling him down on the floor, neither of them removing their clothes.

'Can it hurt the baby,' she said to Annie, 'if Roy and I make love a lot?'

'Not unless you do it on the roof and roll off.'

'I mean if I come so much I'm exhausted, it won't have any effect, will it?'

'It will have an effect on *you*,' Annie said. 'Happy mothers have happy babies.'

'I should have brought you to Banff a long time ago,' Roy said one night as they lay side by side in their bed, Christine's head on his shoulder, her leg heavy and still trembling over his. 'You're too much.'

'You're not complaining, are you?'

'Not me. I never planned to live past thirty anyway.'

'How about twenty-five?' she said.

'I may not make that either.'

She raised her head up and kissed him under the chin. 'You didn't think I was going to get tired of you, did you?'

'You never know.'

'Well, I'm not. I have all kinds of plans for you.'

Chapter 14

*A*nnie's six-year-old son, Victor, tall for his age and straight-backed, looked like his mother. Brown hair and yellow-flecked eyes, and coppery skin with freckles. Stephanie, the daughter, was blocky and square like her father, very fair, with pale-blue eyes, and soft dimples wherever dimples are likely to be seen. Her baby teeth were tiny and pearl white; she had a sweet nature, tender little hands, and a laugh like a swift run on an ocarina. Still a baby she was, all the same, graceful in her movements, and very much a female in her vanities about dainty dresses and blue bows in her hair.

If their mother resembled a sleek lioness lying in some island of shade under the trees, and if their father was a bear, equal mixtures of fierceness and fun, the children were half-breed cubs, soft and tumbling, giggling and eager to be touched and held, lifted on laps, hidden by great hugs. Their first memories, surely, were of physical love. They had been handled and pummelled, smooched and snuggled, cuffed and caressed, fondled and tickled

and cuddled and kissed, bathed and towelled and pow-
dered, nursed and muzzled and held in the air like
trophies. Before they could make intelligible sounds or feed
themselves or walk or even crawl, they had begun to learn
the language of their bodies, to fall into outstretched arms
with total freedom, confident of finding joy there, warmth
and comfort.

Stephanie and Victor had been attracted to Christine
from the beginning. Stephanie, who never tired of leafing
through her picture books or of having their stories repeated to her, who was fascinated by castles and dungeons,
trolls and knights and dragons, said to her mother not long
after she had first seen Christine, 'Chrithy lookth like a
printheth.'

Like a cat adopting another cat's kittens, Christine
became a surrogate mother to Annie's children, spending
as much time as she could with them between her early-
morning shift in the coffee shop, her supervision of the
chambermaids, her stint at the front desk every day, and
her cashier's chores in the tavern at night.

'Being a mother is no mystery,' Annie said. 'If you really
like your kids it's no problem to take care of them. The
main thing is how you *feel*. Kids pick that up first of all. If
you resent them in some way, if they're a burden to you or
an inconvenience, if you can't wait for them to grow up so
you can get on with your own life, then you're in trouble.
They'll *know* it before they can walk or talk, and they'll find
ways to get even with you all their lives. If you're *willing* to
give them everything, then they'll never demand it. But if
they sense that you're a part-time mother, that you're holding back, only willing to go halfway, they'll go to their
graves convinced that you've cheated them.'

The more time she spent with Annie, the more Christine
admired her. There was a nine-year difference in their
ages, but it was a long nine years. Annie was, in every
sense, a woman and Christine was, in many ways, still a
girl. If they had concentrated on their differences – and
that could have happened easily – they might never have

found any real meeting ground. Instead, everything that was precociously mature in Christine made contact with areas in Annie that were permanently young, and they became, very quickly, close friends.

As soon as Christine picked the time when she would tell Roy she was pregnant, she told Annie about it. 'Thanksgiving Day,' she said. 'That's perfect, I decided.'

'Sounds good to me. The four of us will have a feast upstairs. Champagne and a roast goose. And I'll make a fattening dessert. We'll eat too much and drink too much and have a proper celebration.'

So they planned the details like two schoolgirls; they bought special napkins and table decorations and made place cards. They went to the cellar, selected the wines they would drink, and put the bottles to one side with cards tied on them reading *Do not sell*.

Two days before Thanksgiving, Annie said, 'We've done it all now. We've thought of everything. Now all you have to do is compose your announcement speech.'

'Don't say that,' Christine said. 'You make me frantic. All I plan to do when the time comes is blurt it out.'

That night Banff had its first heavy snow. In the morning the town and the surrounding mountains were white and silent. When Roy and Abe left, just after breakfast, for Calgary, the motor for the hotel's auxiliary water heater loaded in the back of the truck, Christine kissed him and said, 'I can't wait till tomorrow. We're going to have a storybook day.'

At noon, when the coffee shop was filling up with customers, Christine felt nauseous suddenly and began to stain. Within minutes Annie had hurried her to the car and driven her across the river to the hospital. But before she could be admitted, she began to haemorrhage.

It was nearly two o'clock before Annie managed to locate Abe and Roy in Calgary, and almost four when Roy came into Christine's room, bent over her bed, and put his cheek against hers. She was very pale and she started to cry as soon as she saw him. 'I'm sorry,' she said. 'I'm so sorry.'

*E*arly in December Christine flew from Calgary to Chicago to be examined by her own doctor. When Grace met her at the airport, she said, 'How we doing?'

'Not great. A little let down.'

'No way to avoid that,' Grace said. 'That happens even when you *have* a baby. When you lose one, it's worse.'

'I just keep thinking that if I'd taken better care of myself, maybe . . .'

'You mustn't second-guess yourself. I'm sure you'll be able to have a dozen kids if you want them.'

Dr Obendorfer agreed. 'No problems, Chrissy. Everything looks normal.'

'Why did it happen?'

'No way of knowing that. Women have been giving birth for thousand of years and we like to think we know all about it, but we don't.'

When she left the doctor's office that day, Christine called Elizabeth Griggs in Kenilworth. 'I met you only once,' she said. 'I'm not sure you remember me. I'm Christine Wheatley, Grace's daughter.'

They made a date for the following afternoon. Before she hung up the receiver, Christine said, 'I don't know why I want to keep this a secret, but I do. Can this be between us?'

'Of course. If you hadn't suggested it, *I* would have.'

The next day, as soon as she was comfortably settled in Elizabeth Griggs' sun-room, Christine said, 'Now that I'm here I don't know what to say. I'm not even sure I should be taking up your time.'

'You mustn't worry about my time – it's no more valuable than anyone else's. There are very few world-shattering events that take place here.'

Christine explained to her then about the miscarriage and the fact that she had not told Roy she was pregnant. 'In my

205

head I don't think I did anything so wrong. But all the same I can't help feeling guilty. I've never felt like such a failure.'

'Do you feel as if you're to blame for the miscarriage?'

Christine shook her head. 'Everything my doctor said convinced me it was something I had no control over. But I still feel lousy and I can't shake it.'

'Maybe doctors feel that when a woman has a miscarriage, especially a young woman, it's a blessing in disguise.'

'I know that. The doctor in Banff explained all that to me; sometimes it means that something would have gone wrong later.'

'That's right.'

'I guess that's supposed to be a consolation,' Christine said, 'but I don't see it that way.'

Elizabeth offered her a cigarette, then lighted one herself. 'Guilt is a strange three-legged creature,' she said. 'It's not something we stumble on at age twenty-one. Not usually. It comes early and stays late. People with a history of emotional stability can have lapses or bad patches, but by and large they tend to remain emotionally stable.'

'I didn't mean I'm getting wacky,' Christine said.

'Of course not. I understand exactly what you're saying. An unusual event has happened to you and you don't feel as if you're handling it well. It's causing you to question yourself. You're trying to redefine yourself and it's tough going.'

'Something like that.'

'How about Roy? Does he blame you for anything that's happened?'

'He doesn't *say* anything, if that's what you mean. But I sense . . . I don't know, once you start looking on the gloomy side of things, you see shadows everywhere . . . I get the feeling there are things in his head that haven't come out yet.'

The fact was that some of those things *had* come out. The morning she left Banff to fly to Chicago, when Roy drove her to the Calgary airport, Christine said, 'You're not holding out on me, are you?'

'Why do you say that?'

'I don't know. But ever since I came home from the

hospital, since I lost the baby, I can't shake the feeling that you're behind a wall, someplace where I can't get you.'

Roy shook his head. 'No secrets.'

'You're not still mad at me because I didn't tell you I was pregnant?'

'I never *was* mad at you. I felt funny about it, but I wasn't mad. Besides, it's over now. There's no point in talking about it.'   'Yes there is. If you've got some kind of a bug in your head, then we *have* to talk about it.'

Roy pulled off the highway suddenly and stopped in an emergency zone at the side of the pavement. He turned off the ignition. 'Look, Chris, let's not beat this to death. I thought –'

'You only call me Chris when I've screwed up. You *are* mad at me. You've been mad at me ever since –'

'I told you before, I didn't understand why you didn't tell me. I don't understand it yet. But it's past history. It's *over*.'

'No, it's not. I look at your face and I know it's still on your mind.' She started to cry. 'You have to tell me the truth, Roy. It's important.'

He took out his handkerchief and handed it to her. Finally, he said, 'All right, I'll tell you what I think. I don't want to *own* you and I don't want you to *own* me. Nobody wants to share *everything*. Nobody's *able* to. On the other hand – when something concerns *both* of us, then I expect to have a vote. I don't want to be manipulated or programmed, even if you think it's for my own good. You know what I'm thinking about. We've been on this subject at least twice before. I like to know what's going on. No secrets and no surprises.'

'I know that. I know how you feel. I just have this drive to *fix* things and make everything nice. I always think I can iron out the wrinkles and solve the problems. I try to save you from fretting about a lot of silly stuff.'

He sat there, half turned in the car seat, looking at her. Finally he grinned. 'You know something? I've been housebroken for a long time. I don't need to be led around the block on a leash. So anytime you have an impulse to shelter me, let's talk about it first. Okay?'

'Okay.'

Just before Christine left that afternoon, Elizabeth Griggs said, 'It isn't easy to do what you and Roy are doing. The most difficult thing for any of us is to change rhythm, to go in a new direction, to move at a different pace. And when you're in a strange environment, it makes things twice as tough. You've had a difficult year. But I think things will look different to you now. I think they'll be better.'

Chapter 16

'*I* suppose your mother told you about Fred Deets,' Margaret Jernegan said.

'No, she didn't,' Christine said. They were sitting in her grandmother's morning room, having breakfast; later that day Christine would be flying back to Canada.

'There was a long piece about him in the *Tribune* last month. He's been decorated three times. He's made an outstanding record over there in Vietnam.'

'That's nice.'

'A credit to his country, the paper said. They called him a hero.'

'Good for him.'

'His mother and father are very proud of him. And I can understand why. He's a credit to all of us.'

'He's not a credit to me,' Christine said.

'You know what I'm saying. Just when it looks as if courage and bravery have gone out of style, a few young men come forward and make us all proud.'

'*I'm* not proud. What's so brave about shooting people from a helicopter? Or dropping napalm? What kind of courage does that take?'

Margaret sipped her coffee carefully and touched the corners of her mouth with a napkin. 'I don't lose my temper, Christine. You know that. So there's no point in your trying to get me angry. I was simply talking about Fred Deets and his courage. When the news seems to be filled with stories of cowards and deserters . . .'

'I don't want to hear any more, Margaret. You're getting warmed up to take a swipe at draft resisters in general and Roy in particular, and I won't—'

'Not at all,' Margaret said. 'I have never said anything against your young man and you know it. I'm sure he has excellent reasons for doing what he's done.'

'He didn't want any part of the whole mess. If you call that cowardice, then Roy's a coward.'

'Chrissy, sweetheart, don't be so upset. If Roy has your approval he automatically has mine.'

'Good. I'm glad to hear that. Because every time I see you I get the feeling you're still trying to arrange a wedding between me and Fred.'

Margaret smiled and carefully folded her napkin. 'If I told you that I don't admire Fred, I would be lying to you. I was delighted when you two were planning to get married.'

Anticipating a quick reply from Christine, she held her hand up and said, 'I know . . . circumstances change. I accept that. But you can't expect me to be pleased when my only granddaughter runs off with someone who's a total stranger to me.'

'You just said –'

'I know what I said. And I meant it. But my feelings say something else. It hurts me that your mother and I never see you. It hurts me that you're not able to take advantage of the special kind of life you're entitled to.'

'Maybe I don't want a *special* kind of life. There's something about the word *entitled* that makes me sick to my stomach. What you can't see is that I *love* what I'm doing. I

209

love where we're living. I love everything about it. I can't wait to get back there. We may never leave Canada, and if we don't I'll be perfectly content.'

As she said it, it became true. Galvanized by her grandmother's opposition, she put behind her the doubts and indecisions she had brought home to Lake Forest. As she boarded the plane for Calgary, as she settled into her seat, she understood totally Elizabeth Griggs' final words to her: 'Freedom is the strongest prison of all sometimes. Nothing can shackle a person more than total freedom of choice. Your mother has had to deal with that and so will you.'

'So how do I handle it?'

'You simply play a trick on yourself. If Roy is the most important thing in your life, you simply tell yourself he is the *only* thing in your life. The work you're doing is the *only* work available to you, your home with him is your *only* home. Make no other plans, consider no alternatives. I think you'll be surprised with the results.'

She told herself, on the flight north from Chicago, that when they drove down Banff Avenue and turned into Caribou, when she saw the St Albert again, she would say to herself, 'I'm home. *This* is where I live.'

When the moment came, however, no persuasion was necessary. She felt a rush of blood to her head and she was eager, suddenly, to see Annie and Abe and the children, to go upstairs with Roy to their warm room, unpack her bag, and take up the rhythm of her life again. Before they got out of the car, she said to Roy, 'I know I was a pain in the neck before I left. I had a lot of things scrambled up in my head. But now I'm perfect again. Flawless and sweet smelling and no wet towels ever on the bathroom floor.'

Chapter 17

On New Year's Day 1971, Russell Atha got married. It was a surprise to the columnists who reported it in the New York newspapers, it certainly was a surprise to Amy and me, and when I finally spoke to Russell about it, he told me it had also been something of a surprise to him.

Amy and I had spent the holidays on Sanibel Island, in Florida. It was the third of January, two days before we were scheduled to go back to New York, when we read about the wedding in the Miami paper. 'I can't believe it,' Amy said. 'All the women in the world to choose from and Russell marries a *German*.'

'Who says so?'

'*I* say so. *You* should read *Women's Wear Daily*. Then you'd know about these international types.'

'It says here in the paper she's from Uruguay.'

'Sure she is. So are a lot of other Germans. Her last husband was Dieter Gortmann. Does that ring a bell? Before that her name was Könter. Before that she was married to August Stracke, the film director who made all those superrace films with naked stormtroopers diving into mountain lakes.'

'How old is she?'

'She has to be fifty. Maybe more. She was acting in German films in the late thirties and early forties. Pietra Hanz. That was her name then.'

I handed her the folded newspaper. 'If this is an accurate picture, she looks pretty good.'

'It's accurate, all right,' Amy said. 'What do you think I'm yapping about? Not only is she a Kraut, she's gorgeous. She was gorgeous when she was twenty and she'll be gorgeous when she's eighty.'

When I placed a long-distance call to Gale Richmond, Russell's agent, she said, 'Where have you been? Russell's been trying to contact you for two weeks.'

There was no way I could reach *him*, she said, because he was on his way to the airport. 'They're flying to Montevideo at two this afternoon. He promised to call me from Kennedy. If he does, give me your number down there so I can have him ring you up.'

Half an hour later Russell called, full voice and high energy. 'I know you called to congratulate me, but that's a damned poor substitute for being here. I was expecting you to give me away or carry me down the aisle on a velvet pillow. Or whatever you do with shopworn bridegrooms.'

'You should have given me some warning. Last I heard you were in Amsterdam. No mention of a wedding. It must have been a fast decision.'

'Not at all. I've known her for nearly a month.'

'Gale says you're off to Montevideo.'

'Taking off in eleven minutes. Tomorrow I'll be in Punta del Este, naked in the sunshine, sipping a tropical drink, and counting my toes.'

'It sounds as if you already sipped a few tropical drinks.'

'No question about it. What good is a sober honeymoon? We have been semialcoholic and totally contented since One January. And in Uruguay, where Pietra is a resident and I am an alien, we plan to institutionalize our present condition. Dozing by the sea, looking east toward Capetown.'

'How long will you be there?'

'How long is life? I plan to take root like a frangipani plant. Vegetate and luxuriate and pick up where Mr Maugham left off.'

'Bullshit, Russell. If you pass up St Patrick's Day at McSorley's, I'll be surprised.'

'That's the old Russell you're talking about. I've recast my life. Booze and fresh air and the love of a not-so-good woman. How can you beat it?'

Four days later I had a letter from him. Airmail. Special delivery.

Dear Ben and Amy and Posterity:
With that salutation I charge you to save this letter and

all the ones that will follow. History will thank you, my biographers will thank you, and I, in advance, thank you.

Pietra and I are settled in here, trying to survive in her modest twelve-bedroom playpen by the sea. Cold roast fowl on silver platters and beakers of Lafitte-Rothschild. And lap robes for early evening when the cool winds come in off the water.

Are you mystified? Do you imagine that I've abandoned everything worthwhile, that I've chosen, at this middle moment in my life, to be a profligate? The answer is *yes*. I'm packing it in. Other than letters to you, to Christine, my almost daughter, and a very few other friends, I have no further plans to write. I have, as you know, made a few dollars here and there. So I could live in reasonable comfort, I suppose, from my investments. But now that is not a consideration. *Money* is not a consideration. Because my new wife, Pietra Hanz Stracke Könter Gortmann Atha, has wealth that is as limitless as it is obscene.

So it began, that odd, parenthetical period in Russell's life. Triggered by what impulse? God knows. But whatever prompted him to lose himself for almost four years, first in Uruguay, then in Switzerland, and at last back at Punta del Este again, I was, in some bizarre way, the beneficiary. He wrote me long letters, at least once, sometimes twice a week. As I page through that stack of correspondence now, it reads like a bitter history of those years.

It would be logical for you to assume, Ben, that from my present benevolent position, from this beautiful location where I have forsaken all the pressures of life and love and work, that the world would look misty and tender. Not true. There is a lot to be depressed about.

As much as the Mansons and the Calleys and the Juan Coronas disturb me, Nixon with his white shirts, turd-bird neckties, and damp hands disturbs me infinitely more.

213

Consider, on the other hand, Louis Armstrong, who died this week. Remember what he said when somebody asked him to explain jazz—'If you have to ask what it is, you never get to know.' You think that's not a life lesson? None of the really singular stuff can be defined or duplicated. The top-notch people like Louis and Matisse and Camus can't be cloned. Only the assholes find ways to reproduce themselves in multiples. So here we are, nearly two thousand years after Jesus Christ got born and showed us the error of our ways, and Idi Amin is in power in Uganda, the British decide to imprison people in Northern Ireland without trials or formal charges, the police slaughter thirty-two prisoners at Attica prison, Rolls-Royce is bankrupt, and the Roman Catholic bishops reaffirm celibacy for the clergy. No comment from the nuns.

'It's interesting that he never says anything about his spooky wife,' Amy said.

'Sure he does. Remember when they first arrived down there? He said, "We have a perfect marriage. Founded on mutual distrust. She doesn't trust my brain and I don't trust her body."

'If I live to be a thousand I'll never understand how he could live with that horror.'

'Forgive and forget, Amy. That's the watchword. The Krupps are back in fashion. Buchenwald's a public picnic ground.'

'It all makes me sick.'

When Nixon was reelected in the fall of 1972, Russell wrote:

If I needed a reason to stay away from the United States, I now have one. Jesus. They used to call me Laughing Boy. Now I see dreck and desolation every-place I look. Only 24,000 US troops left in Vietnam, they say. But every one of those turkeys must be flying a plane. Because the bombs keep falling like rain. In

Nicaragua ten thousand poor bastards die in an earthquake, eleven Israeli athletes go to Munich and they end up dead; the president of ITT is paid one point six million a year. Does that make sense? Not to me. The supply of world oil is starting to peter out and nobody wants to talk about it, some lunatic decides to express himself by hacking away at a Michelangelo statue, and last but not least keep your eye on that little inconsequential burglary story, the break-in at the Watergate. If that doesn't grow into something smelly, I will be very surprised. It has CIA stamped all over it. And I smell *money*. Mark my words.

By Christmas of that year, Russell was writing from Montreux in Switzerland:

I had a minor medical problem – equivalent of a hangnail – so my doting and well-organised wife brought me over here to have it attended to. We are living in a hillside chalet overlooking the lake and it is a handsome situation indeed. But I am saddened to hear that my dear Auden is gravely ill. He is a valuable man and a fine poet. When he goes he will leave a hole in the lives of all of us who know him. My book about him, which should have been out long since, is now scheduled for next fall. My long-time editor, Albert Tolliver, suffered some kind of emotional collapse last year and his replacement, a brilliant young girl with short experience but excellent instincts, began snorting cocaine to cure herself of incipient alcoholism and was, at last report, unable to stay at her desk and concentrate for more than twenty minutes at a time. Nerves shot. Hands all atremble. Why do we artists stay so healthy as the world around us crumbles?

Speaking of that, I will be forty-five years old next February ninth. Does that depress you? Doesn't bother me. All systems still function reasonably well and women of all ages try to lay hands on me whenever I'm left unguarded. But I have noticed that very young people, both male and female, have begun to treat me with a kind of deference that turns my stomach. So . . . time marches sideways. None of us will deceive, *enfin*, the hourglass. Or will we?

While we're on the subject of *tempus fugit*, my excellent son, Jean-Claude, has been spending some days with me here in the snow. He's lean as a tiger, very adept with skis and automobiles. He is also prototypically French, which means he drives like a maniac and smokes Gauloises *sans arrêt*. We like each other, respect each other, and we have very involved philosophical and economic discussions. He's bright as hell and tirelessly contentious. I'm proud of him but I don't *know* him very well and I guess I never will. Because we've spent a lot of years living apart and because he's French. I take most of the blame for our being apart but none of the blame for his being French. The wisdom of my middle years persuades me that very few parent-child-relationships are what they're cracked up to be, broken homes or no. I suspect that today's young whippersnappers feel toward their parents as certain female insects feel toward their mates. Once they've performed the breeding function, they should be killed and eaten as quickly as possible. It is ironic but perhaps inevitable that I have a much closer quasi-parent relationship with Christine than I do with Jean-Claude. She writes to me from Alberta with warmth, good humour, and astonishing regularity. Bless her.

In another letter he wrote:

Christine doesn't mention leaving Canada. She used to, but no more. That surprises me. Especially since the Vietnam thing is getting close to a cease-fire, they've abolished the military draft, and most of the reasonable people I talk to think that as soon as they get Nixon's ass in jail or at least out of office, *somebody*, whoever gets the job of cleaning up after him, will start talking about an amnesty for the draft resisters. If I were an expatriate person, that would be uppermost in my mind. But Christine seems to take no notice, pays no mind, and makes no mention.

In closing, I salute Pablo Picasso, Joe E. Brown, Noel Coward, Kid Ory, and Betty Grable. All dead now. Dead this year. And I salute those poor courageous bastards at Wounded Knee.

After he left Switzerland, the letters continued from Montevideo, all through the early summer of 1974. Then, late in August, after Nixon had been forced to resign and Gerald Ford had replaced him in the White House, I had a long final letter from Russell.

In spite of all my threats about remaining here in benevolent exile, I am returning to my native land. Late in September or early in October. Not because of the demise of my *bête noire*, RMN. But I do concede that it will be a sweeter-smelling country now. Unless Ford gives him a full pardon. And I suspect this was part of the deal. If that happens, then once again the perfume of garbage and offal will permeate our Eastern Seaboard air.

I have some stupid news. I would keep it from you if I could but I can't. I'm dying. I have cancer of the bone marrow and I've had it since before I came to Uruguay. It is treatable but incurable. My wise and expensive Montreux doctors say that I could continue to lead a reasonable active life for as long as ten years. On the other hand I could be dead a year from now. It is a capricious form of malignancy. That may be its only attractive feature.

Three years ago, when I believed I was an instant goner, I chose to spin out my days in a mist of Veuve Clicquot and indolence, a pale-skinned, slightly *vicieuse* woman in my arms, bright macaws on bedroom

217

perches, and half a dozen Dobermans pacing the veranda outside the French windows. I don't regret that choice. For a compulsive worker like me it has been a revelation to do nothing. But now I've had enough of it. Rather than kowtow to the angel of death by adjusting my life-style to hers, I have decided that I will ignore her and proceed as I did before. I will live my life, as much or as little as I have, get on with my work, and let the Devil take the hindmost. There's a book idea I've been chewing over that I am particularly anxious to wrestle with, a complicated stew involving Grace, Christine, myself, and all sorts of secondary characters.

How will my return to work and sanity affect my marriage to Pietra? Badly, I should imagine. Terminally, I suspect. My wife is less flexible than me. She chose her life-style long ago. And since she is wealthy, she has less freedom of choice than those of us who are not blessed in that way. This is not to intimate that she is lacking in either loyalty or devotion to me. She is not. She has been unselfish and supportive through all the exploratory months in Montreux, and has announced that she intends to stay by my side whether I want it or not. I do *not* want it, of course. I won't permit it. If I am going to disintegrate physically, and I *am*, I intend to do it privately, with as much dignity as possible. I do not want to be watched or monitored or wept over. I will not see my own deterioration mirrored daily in someone else's eyes.

As you can see, in a totally negative circumstance, I am dynamically positive. I will simply do what I can for as long as I can and then I will stop.

Footnote: You and Amy are the only people in New York who know about my condition. I don't expect to tell anyone else. My physical appearance is unchanged. I'm a little thinner maybe, but no scabies or leprous swellings. What I'm struggling to say is that I hope you'll be able to look at me as myself, as the person I've always been and not as an imminent obituary. I told you the

218

truth because I needed to tell somebody who could handle it. Above all do not treat me with kindness and consideration. Our relationship has always been built on insults and savage criticism. I'd hate to see us lose that. When you see me, you'll see that I am as charming, handsome, and hateful as ever.

Chapter 18

On the twenty-third of April, 1974, Christine and Roy decided they wanted to have a child. In August she discovered she was pregnant. The doctor she talked with in Banff told her she would have to be extremely careful, especially during the first months. 'No stairs. As little walking as possible. If you expect to have this child, consider yourself an invalid. Stay in bed.'

'It's nothing to fret about,' Annie told her. 'I had to do the same thing when I was carrying Victor. It doesn't hurt to baby yourself a little. You might even get to like it.'

For the rest of her life, Christine would remember those quiet weeks in her bed, the trees changing colour outside her window, the snow accumulating gradually on the far mountain crests while the valley floor where Banff rests was still clear and sunny, the grass still green under the fallen leaves.

She would ask herself over and over if the events of the following weeks had been preordained somehow, if the cushioned and bright-painted future she had envisioned from the beginning for her and Roy was never what she had imagined, if it was always flimsy and frail, more dream than substance.

Or had it all been simply a matter of incorrect choices at critical moments, a failure to recognize proper priorities? It was a tangle she would never straighten out, a maze through which no path could be found, but all the same, it could not be ignored or hidden away. She could not put it out of her mind.

All other considerations aside, one thing she was sure of. When Grace's car spun crazily across the Tri-State Tollway that October afternoon, between Riverwoods and Lincolnshire, skidded through four lanes of traffic, and slammed against the chain-link fence that separated northbound from southbound, at that instant the pattern of her daughter's life changed. Not abruptly, not clearly and finally, like death or desertion, but gradually and painfully, an inch at a time, in a teasing, veering way that defied either acceptance or adjustment, that held out promise of relief or triumph but provided neither.

It was a stretch of highway that Grace had driven hundreds of times. At all hours. In all kinds of weather. It was a fine straight road, designed for heavy interstate traffic, and it was the fastest route north from the Chicago airport to Lake Forest.

On this particular day, clear and bright at two in the afternoon, the traffic was light. Grace had just passed the Riverwoods turnoff, driving in the far-left lane, her speedometer needle holding steady at the speed limit, when a mammoth tractor-trailer thundered even with her in the lane to her right. As she glanced toward the cab of the truck, all she could see was a great expanse of painted metal. When the truck pulled ahead, when she picked up the cab through her windshield, the driver's side window was still above the top line of her vision, no one in view behind the wheel.

Sensing, suddenly, that the truck was edging into her lane, Grace sounded her horn. But the side of the trailer seemed to press in still closer on her right. Her first instinct was to slow up and let the truck take the lane; but glancing over her right shoulder, she could not see the back end of the long trailer. Fearing that even if she slowed down, the tail end of the truck

220

could catch her front end as it kept drifting into the left-hand lane, she jammed down hard on the accelerator and shot ahead, trying to speed past the truck and get into a free stretch of highway before her car was squeezed off the road.

It was the best choice she could have made. Her only choice, in fact. The state police, when they investigated the accident, agreed on that point. But there was no way to compensate for the design flaws of the truck. The cab sat so high off the highway that the driver's vision, except for straight ahead, was always impaired. Even with an elaborate system of rear- and side-vision mirrors there were blind spots. And Grace's car, just behind and far below the truck driver, on his left, was dead centre in one of those spots. With his radio blasting Merle Haggard, he didn't hear her horn or see her car as he eased steadily left. His first awareness of the situation was at the second when his left front bumper hooked her right rear bumper as she speeded up trying to pass him. From that instant he saw everything clearly as Grace's car skidded and spun across his path, and on across all four northbound lanes, miraculously missing the other cars; turning slowly a hundred eighty degrees till its headlights were facing south, it slammed into the highway divider and hung there, crushed, its horn stuck and wailing.

Chapter 19

*T*hree hours after her grandmother telephoned her from the hospital, Christine was on a plane heading for Chicago. 'I know how lousy you feel,' Roy said as he drove her to the Calgary airport. 'But the more you can keep a handle on yourself, the better off you'll be.'

'I know it. At least my *head* knows it. But I'm scared to death. I know I shouldn't be out of bed.'

On the plane Christine tried to read, tried to listen to recorded music, tried to write a letter to Roy. But her concentration failed her. Her mind kept wandering, trailing away.

This was unlike her. Her instinct was to deal with specifics, handle them one at a time. She genuinely believed that life was a series of problems and solutions. Either you handled the details or the details would handle you. She had no patience with those who complained about ill winds or stars in unfortunate positions. She believed that people got what they deserved, harvested what they sowed. In short, Christine refused to concede that the major plot points and curtain lines of her life were outside her control. Good fortune could be improved, bad luck could be tempered. Only those who lacked energy and imagination could rail against the gods and complain that their destinies were not their own.

Knowing all this, accepting it as true, genuinely believing it and living by it, Christine, on the plane, flying to see her mother in the hospital, could nonetheless, not dismiss the feeling that chance had begun to take over her life. In the next few days that feeling would become a fixation.

At O'Hare Airport outside Chicago, when she came off the plane, she saw Fred Deets waiting for her. She hadn't seen him since that morning at Foresby four years earlier, but she knew, from Margaret's careful briefings, that he divided his time now between Lake Forest and California, that he had established a company there, offices in Los Angeles and San Jose, and that he himself lived in Santa Barbara. Married two years ago to a wealthy girl from Seattle and recently divorced.

After the world of rough boots and lumber-jacketed beer drinkers that Christine had become accustomed to, seeing Fred was a sudden glimpse into a place she had known and left, where men wore fine soft jackets, neat shirts, and striped ties. When Fred put his arms around her, it was an absolutely proper gesture from a man she had known since childhood. She welcomed it. After the fantasies that had unsettled her on the plane trip, that familiar platonic touch steadied her and brought her back to earth.

'How is she?' she asked.

'Still in Intensive Care. But out of danger, the doctors say.'

Grace's doctor was a small, wiry man named Donald Maslin. He took Christine just inside the door of the Intensive Care section so she could see her mother. She was sleeping on her back, with intravenous tubes taped to her right arm and a heavy bandage, from elbow to fingertips, on her left.

When they were sitting, a few minutes later, in the doctor's office, Christine asked, 'Is she still unconscious?'

'No. We just gave her a sedative and some anti-infection drugs and she's sleeping. It's the best thing for her. She wasn't unconscious when the paramedics brought her in, but she'd lost a lot of blood. No serious head injuries, however, and no shock symptoms.

'Her face didn't even look bruised. I was afraid—'

'That's because the car hit sideways. She got scalp lacerations and a minor concussion just behind her left ear. She also broke three ribs. But no organ damage and no internal bleeding that we can detect.'

'Is her arm broken?'

'That's the nasty part. If we hadn't been afraid of delayed shock, we'd have taken her straight to the operating room for that arm. From what we can tell, her car door must have swung open as the car was sliding, and her arm was outside. The police think she may have grabbed for the roof to steady herself, to keep from being thrown out. So when the car crashed, the door slammed shut and caught her arm. We've had it packed in ice and we expect to be able to work on it'— he looked at his watch—'by late this afternoon. Dr Jeschke from the Naval Hospital in Glenview will be working with me. And Dr Eisler, the head of plastic surgery at Passavant, will be up here to help us too. Her vital signs are good now. Once we patch that arm up, we expect her to recover quickly.'

As soon as she'd left the doctor's office, Christine called her grandmother, who, it turned out, had already talked with Dr Maslin earlier in the afternoon. 'He told me they expect to operate this afternoon.'

'That's right,' Christine said. 'About five, I think.'

'My doctor doesn't want me over there at the hospital unless it's absolutely necessary.' Margaret said. 'I had a stubborn virus last spring and he doesn't want me exposed to any people who might be contagious.'

'It's all right. I'm here. I'll call you as soon as she comes out of the operating room.'

'I just hope it doesn't turn out she was drinking.'

'Oh, for God's sake, Margaret, it wasn't *her* fault. It was the truck driver's fault. There were all kinds of witnesses. Fred says they may even charge him with reckless driving.'

'Well, that's good. I hope you're right. But you can imagine what I thought . . .'

Christine broke in. 'I have to go now, Margaret. I'll call as soon as I know something.'

Chapter 20

$\mathcal{J}$ust after they wheeled Grace into the operating theatre, Christine found a pay phone and called Roy. She told him about Grace's condition, and as much as she could about the operation in progress. When she finished, he said, 'How about you? Are you all right?'

'I feel fine. I haven't even had time to think about myself.'

'Is somebody there with you just in case?'

She hesitated, almost told him that Fred Deets was there, then said, '*Everybody's* here with me. It's a big hospital. Nurses and doctors coming out of your ears.'

They began operating on Grace's arm at five twenty. At nine forty-five they took her into postop. For those four hours and a half, Christine and Fred Deets sat in the lounge nearest the surgery wing, talking and waiting.

'I'm scared stiff of any operation that takes four hours,' she said.

'She's lucky. They're not going into the chest cavity. There are no vital organs involved. I saw a lot of shot-up guys in Vietnam, and believe me, everybody was praying that if he got hit it would be a leg or an arm.'

He kept them supplied with fresh coffee from the canteen down the hall. And at eight o'clock he went down to the cafeteria and brought back sandwiches. After they finished eating, Christine said, 'I really appreciate everything you're doing, but you don't have to hang around here all night. I mean I'll be all right by myself.'

He grinned and said, 'I'm not doing you a favour. I'm here because of Grace and your grandmother. You've got a severe shortage of men in your family. I'd be here whether you were here or not.'

He asked no questions about Roy, made no reference to Canada at all. And neither did she. Nor did she mention his marriage. But at last he brought it up. 'I guess Grace must have told you I was married.'

'Yes, she did. I'm sorry it didn't work out.'

'It worked out. It just didn't last. I mean . . . listen . . it happens. Thank God we didn't have any kids.'

'You didn't want children?'

'*I* did. But she didn't. Actually, it wasn't that she *didn't*. It was just that she didn't want to *yet*.'

'Well, anyway, I'm sorry. I hope it wasn't too grisly for you.'

'It wasn't. We didn't fight or cheat on each other or any of those fun things. We had plenty of money and a nice house and lots of friends to play with. We had a great time for a couple of years and then it just sort of petered out, like a New Year's Eve party at six thirty the next morning.'

'Do you mean . . . Never mind.'

'Do I mean what?'

'It's none of my business,' she said.

'Sure it is. I brought it up. What did you start to say?'

'I don't understand. The way you're describing your marriage, it sounds like a blind date that didn't quite jell.'

'Let me put it this way,' he said. 'Among the people Gwen and I knew, nobody thinks twice about buying a million-dollar house that they know they'll only be living in for six months.'

'Are you saying that's how you got married?'

'Not me. I was shooting for something permanent. But it didn't work out that way. Now . . . I don't know . . . nobody likes to feel like a failure.'

'What's become of . . . Gwen . . . is that her name?'

'She's living with a lawyer in Montecito. He handled the divorce for her.'

'Does *she* feel like a failure?'

'I don't think so. And I don't either. Not now. I just meant that when we were signing the final papers I was having a little trouble figuring out what we'd been up to. I thought, "Well, if that's what marriage is all about, I'd like to be excused." '

'You still feel that way?'

'Not exactly. Now I just feel cautious.'

'Do you plan to stay in California?'

'Oh, sure. I like it. It's a great place.'

'It sounds terrible to me. I think I'd hate it.'

'No, you wouldn't. There are some strange people out there, but that's because of the palm trees. Any place where palm trees grow always attracts the crazies. The only place with a high percentage of lunatics and *no* palm trees is Lake Forest. Lake Forest people feel right at home in California. You would, too.'

'Thanks for nothing.'

'I mean it. You'd feel the same way *I* do. It's an outdoor life, with animals and fruit trees and good weather most of the time. If you stay away from the hustlers and the dopers and the sexual acrobats, you can have a great life. Once a month you go to San Francisco or Los Angeles to hear some music or look at some paintings, every few weeks you check out New York, and once or twice a year you go to Europe.'

It was almost ten o'clock when a black nurse wearing tinted glasses came down the corridor to find Christine.

'Are you Christine Wheatley?'

'Yes, I am,' Christine stood up and moved quickly to the door of the waiting room. 'Is everything all right?'

'Everything's fine. Dr Maslin wants to see you before he goes home.'

Christine hurried down the corridor with the nurse and Fred trailed along behind. Up ahead he saw Dr Maslin, in his shirt sleeves, carrying his jacket over his arm; he came out of his office and met Christine. As they talked, Fred found a bench thirty feet away and sat down, waiting and half watching, not trying to hear the conversation, Maslin's voice droning softly like a cello and Christine's cutting through in short sharp accents. Suddenly Fred heard her say, 'Oh, my God,' and there was a hollow sound as though her lungs had emptied. As Fred stood up, he saw her half turn away from the doctor. Her eyes looked flat and unfocused. Suddenly they rolled back white and she slumped to the floor.

Chapter 21

*I*t was after midnight when Dr Maslin called Roy in Banff. He and Annie had just closed the tavern for the night. Abe was in Ottawa for two days.

Roy took the call in the phone booth in the lobby. When he came back into the tavern, he said to Annie, 'She lost the baby.'

'Oh, my God,' Annie said.

'She's in the hospital. The doctor said she really went to pieces. He said it would be good if I could come there.'

'Did you tell him you can't do that?'

'No. I told him I could. I'm going. As soon as I can get on a plane.'

At eleven forty the following morning, Roy's flight landed at Chicago's O'Hare. When he came into the terminal, he was being paged on the public-address system. At the Air Canada customer-relations desk, Fred Deets was waiting for him. 'I don't know if you remember me. I'm a friend of Christine and her family's. We met a few years ago when you were at Foresby.'

As soon as they arrived at the hospital and went upstairs to the third floor, a nurse took Roy to Dr Maslin's office.

'I'm glad you're here,' the doctor said. 'She needs a lift.'

'She's all right, isn't she? I mean she's not—'

'She lost a lot of blood in a short time. I think I told you that when I called you last night. But we've got her back up to normal now. All her signs are good. In two or three days she should be able to go home. But she's had some psychological jolts that won't heal up quite so fast. I understand she miscarried once before.'

'That's right. Three or four years ago.'

Dr Maslin nodded. 'She's convinced herself there's something wrong with her. Something that can't be fixed.'

'You mentioned on the phone that she was upset by some news about her mother.'

'We had bad luck with Mrs Wheatley. If we'd been able to operate as soon as they brought her in, the result might have been different. I had the best team of surgeons in Chicago working on her, but we could tell as soon as we started the operation that we had only an outside chance of saving her arm. And the longer we worked, the slimmer those chances got. We had to amputate the left arm at the elbow. That's when we . . . When I told Christine about her mother, she collapsed. If we'd known she was pregnant, we could have handled it differently. But as it was, by the time we saw what was happening, it was too late.'

Roy sat at the side of Christine's bed for more than two hours before she opened her eyes. Her cheeks were pale and she looked very young, like a sick child kept home from school and tucked up warm in her bed.

Roy moved over, sat on the edge of the bed, and put his arms around her. Her body felt thin and fragile under the hospital gown. She was sobbing, her face pressed against his chest. Over and over she said, 'Don't be mad at me. Please. Don't be mad at me.'

Chapter 22

*R*oy checked into a motel three blocks from the hospital. But for two days he spent all his time with Christine.

There were moments when she responded, smiled, and seemed very much herself. But each time she slipped back into silence. Then she would start to cry again.

'I can't help it,' she said. 'Every time I think of her, in that room by herself, with one of her arms half gone, it drives me crazy. Why Grace? That's all I ask myself. With all the absolutely worthless people in the world, how did she get singled out to be maimed and crippled?'

Then she would say, 'I know I won't be able to have a baby now. I feel empty. Like the wind's blowing through me.'

The first night, feeling depressed after his afternoon and evening at the hospital, Roy called the Singletons. When Abe came on the phone, he said, 'You're really gonna get yourself in a crack. You're a fugitive, for Christ's sake. You'd better get back across the border as fast as you can.'

'I can't do it, Abe. Chrissy's in bad shape.'

'So are you,' Abe said. 'Your name's on the spook list. And your picture's right beside it. Take my advice. Get your ass on a bus and head north.'

That night in the motel, Roy couldn't sleep. The second night he couldn't sleep either. He lay on his back in bed, a pillow bunched under his head, and watched an old film, George Brent and Bette Davis, on television. When it was over he switched off the set, turned off his bed lamp, and moved to the other side of the bed, where the sheets were fresh and cool. At last, at nearly three in the morning, he began to slide off into sleep.

When the telephone rang, when he picked it up after the third ring, he felt groggy. As soon as he said hello, the line went dead. Suddenly he was awake. He hung up the receiver, then picked it up again and called the switchboard.

'This is Mr Lavidge in 104. I just had a call and I was disconnected.'

'No, sir. Your party hung up.'

'Well, if they call back . . .'

'Yes, sir.'

'Never mind. If they call again, I'll talk to them.'

Ten minutes later, the phone rang again. Roy picked it up after the first ring. A man's voice said, 'Roy Lavidge, please.'

'Who's that you're calling?' Roy said. Country accent.

'Is this Roy Lavidge?'

'No, it's not. What room were you calling?'

'Room 104.'

'Sorry. This is room 401.' Roy hung up, got out of bed, and put on his clothes. Leaving his room door double-locked from the inside, he unlatched the sliding glass doors leading out to the pool area, stepped outside, and slid the door shut till he heard the lock click. As he moved away toward the pool-

230

enclosure gate leading to the street, he heard his room phone start to ring again.

At the hospital he went upstairs to Christine's floor, walked through the dim-lighted corridors, passed the half-open door of her room, and found a visitors' waiting room fifty feet down the way. He sat there in a deep chair and waited for the night to end.

At five in the morning he went down to the main floor, found a pay telephone, and called his motel. 'This is Mr Lavidge. I'm in 104. Are there any messages for me?'

A short pause. Then, 'Mr Singleton called long distance from Canada. Wants you to call. Says you know the number.'

'What time was that?'

'Four thirty a.m. Forty minutes ago.'

'Any other calls?'

'A man called several times, but he left no message.'

Abe answered the phone immediately, as if he'd been sitting beside it waiting to hear it ring.

'Where are you?'

'At the hospital,' Roy said.

'Good. You're getting smart. Don't go back to the hotel.'

'What about my stuff?'

'Leave it there. You're hot, kid. After I talked to you yesterday, I got in touch with a guy I know in Chicago. Told him to sniff around. He works for the Treasury Department. He knows all the other agency guys. He called me back a couple hours ago and said they've got a bee on you. Somebody blew the whistle. You're on the pickup list for today.'

'There's a plane for Calgary at noon. I'll be on it.'

'No good. As soon as you make a reservation, it'll be government information.'

'Then I'll cash in my ticket and take a bus.'

'Better. But not good enough. Here's what you do. There's a car-rental agency at the corner of Lake and Wabash in the Loop. Go downtown, go to that agency, it's called Rothrock's, and say you're there to pick up Mr Barker's car. That's all you have to say. They'll give you the keys and you're home free.

231

Get on the expressway and drive north to Duluth. There's a Rothrock agency there too, on the corner of Evergreen and Halliburton. Pull into their lot at about six tonight. I'll meet you there.'

'Wait a minute. What is all this? Are you telling me I can't cross the border into Canada by myself?'

'I'm telling you they're out to nail your ass. If they miss you in Chicago, they'll figure you're heading back to Canada. One phone call and they alert every Immigration office on the border. If you think you can beat that with a big grin and a couple of jokes, go ahead. I'd say it's about a fifty-to-one shot. If I'm with you, you sail through like you're Prince Charles. Take your choice.'

When the nurse told him Christine was awake, Roy went into her room and sat with her while she ate breakfast. After the nurse had come back and taken her breakfast tray away, Roy said, 'You look better today. How do you feel?'

'I won't know till the sleeping pill wears off. I hate those damned things. But I also hate to lie awake all night fighting off the dragons.'

'That won't last long. You're the world's champion sleeper.'

'Used to be. Now I can't turn off the noises in my head. But last night it was better. It's better when I know you're around., I'm glad you're here.'

'So am I,' he said. 'I wish I could stay.'

'You can stay, can't you? You've only been here two days.'

He shook his head. 'Somebody's been calling the motel checking on me. I talked with Abe on the phone a while ago. He says they're planning to pick me up today.'

'What does he know about it? He's in Banff, for Pete's sake.'

'He knows a lot. And even if he's wrong, I can't take the chance.'

'But it doesn't make sense. How would they find you? How would they know you're here?'

'Abe says somebody told them.'

'Who would tell them? Nobody knows about you except me.'

'Fred Deets knows I'm here. I'm sure your grandmother knows.'

'But they wouldn't call the police. They wouldn't—'

'I didn't say they would. I'm just saying that other people know I'm here. It's not a secret.'

She sat staring at him, her eyes looking vacant and hurt. Then, 'Please don't go. I'm really shot right now.'

He came over and sat on the edge of her bed. 'I'm not going because I want to. I hate to leave you by yourself. But I'd hate it a hell of a lot worse if you had to wait five years for me to get out of jail. So would you.'

Again she was silent. At last she said, 'I wish I knew what's happening to us.'

'Nothing's happening to us. I knew I was taking a chance coming down here. And it didn't stop me from coming. But now—'

'I don't mean that. I mean *us*. I thought . . . I always thought we had a big golden umbrella protecting us.'

'Nobody has anything like that, Chris. Everybody has things they have to deal with. And sometimes they come in bunches. But they don't solve anything by throwing up your hands and baying at the moon.'

'Is that what you think I'm doing?'

'No. I don't think that. I think you had a couple of lousy shocks, one right after the other. And you're not going to snap back in twenty minutes. Nobody expects you to. But it's not gonna wreck your life either. Nothing's changed between you and me and nothing's going to. I'd give anything if I could wipe out what happened to your mother, but I can't. Neither can you.'

As soon as he mentioned Grace, Christine started to cry. She was still crying when he left the hospital to take a bus down to the Loop.

*I*t was nine thirty in the morning when he picked up the car at the Rothrock, Agency. The man at the desk was thin and balding, with wire-rimmed glasses and an Irish lilt to his speech. 'It's a Buick we're giving you. Mr Barker likes to drive a Buick.' He walked out to the car with Roy. 'There's a map in the glove compartment. I've marked the best route for you. Take the Northwest Tollway out to Rockford. Then go north on Ninety. At Madison, Wisconsin, you'll pick up Ninety-four to Eau Claire. From there you jog north on Fifty-three right into Duluth.'

It was twenty minutes past six when Roy turned into the Rothrock lot in downtown Duluth. There was fresh snow on the streets and a great dirty mound of snow at one end of the parking area where the bulldozers had pushed it. As Roy got out of the car, Abe Singleton came out of the office building across the lot and walked to meet him.

'You're late, you bum.'

'Not much,' Roy said. 'Twenty minutes.'

'No problem. Let's go.' He walked across the lot to a two-ton Ford truck and Roy followed him. 'We're heading straight north,' Abe said. 'We'll cross into Ontario at International Falls, then drive west to Winnipeg. Are you hungry?'

'I'm starving. I didn't stop between here and Chicago except to take a leak and gas up.'

When they were inside the truck cab, moving out of town on Highway 53, Abe said, 'I'm just as hungry as you are. I haven't had a bite since morning. But we'll eat big at Eveleth. That's not too far up the road. From there it's a hundred-mile straight to International Falls. We'll be home free at midnight.'

'Who's Mr Barker?' Roy asked then.

'No such animal. It's just a name we use.'

Dead centre in Eveleth, they stopped at a tavern called the

Lifford House. As they got out of the truck, a light snow began to swirl across the parking lot. A young man came outside, took the car keys from Abe, and drove the truck into a large shed in the rear.

Inside the tavern a grey-haired man wearing a loose Aran sweater came forward to meet them. After he and Abe shook hands with their free hands clasping each other's wrists, Abe said to Roy. 'This is my oldest friend, James Duggan. The day he left Sligo, twenty ladies went into mourning. None of them were his wife, but they mourned all the same.' Turning back to Duggan, he said, 'And this is Roy Lavidge, the man I told you about. Half Italian an half Airedale, judging from the looks of his dad, but I have a hunch he's got an Irish heart. If he's not careful, Annie and I will take him along to Donegal when we go. My wife thinks he's the finest young man she's seen in her lifetime. Didn't know that, did you, Roy? Annie's your staunchest admirer. Thinks you're the class of the breed. If you didn't have a young woman of your own, I expect Annie might throw you over her shoulder and carry you up the stairs.'

Roy felt the blood come into his face suddenly and Abe, noticing it, said, 'My God, the man's blushing. Maybe I've hit on something. Maybe he admires my wife as much as she admires him. I'll have to tell Annie that. It might give her courage.'

They sat for almost two hours in a corner booth, with James Duggan and two other tousled young men. Roy and Abe ate thick steaks with fried potatoes and all the men shared a deep-dish apple pie covered with heavy cream. The mugs of stout kept arriving in a steady rhythm from the bar, and in the background the Clancy brothers sang sweetly from the record machine.

When they left and walked through the light snow to their truck, Abe said, 'I need a little nap. Wake me up when we get to the village of Ray. Just stay on Fifty-three and hold it steady at fifty. That'll get us there at the proper time and it won't attract the speed police.'

Driving north through a sifting of snow that was melting as

235

soon as it fell on the highway, with Abe sleeping in the seat beside him, Roy tried to make sense of the almost twenty-four hours since he had returned to his motel room the night before.

He and Christine, when they had first gone to the St Albert to work, had wondered about Abe's frequent trips away from Banff. But each time, whether he went for one day to Edmonton, three days to Vancouver, or a week to Ottawa, there was always a simple explanation. Abe was continually buying goods, selling services, or attending conferences. 'It's more than a bung starter and a bar rag that's needed to go into business. A publican nowadays wants six legs, six arms, and a head like a bloody computer.'

All the same, there was something foreign and fascinating about Abe as Roy had seen him in the past several hours. Something reckless and chancy. Did trained house dogs run through the fields suddenly, with no warning, and begin killing sheep? Where did the truth end and barroom humour take over? What did it mean when he referred to Annie in a way Roy hadn't heard before? What in God's name was he implying? Was it just the Irish tongue unhinged and flapping, the Irish ears listening to the sound of words strung in loops and caring not at all for the sense of it? Probably.

Still, it was unsettling, the bulk of it taken together, a sense of the familiar turning suddenly strange, of the stone sprouting flowers and the brook gurgling claret.

At the far edge of the village of Ray, Abe, behind the wheel again, consulted his watch, regulated the speed of the truck, and arrived at the International Falls border crossing at precisely midnight. The Canadian Immigration officer who strolled out to the side of the truck said, 'Hey, Abe. You're a stranger.'

'I'm tied down now, Jack. A domesticated animal.'

'Still out in Alberta, I understand.'

'Still in Banff. Beautiful scenery and no time to look at it.'

As he took Roy's residence card and Abe's papers and stamped them, the officer tilted his head toward the back of the truck and said, 'Driving empty?'

236

'Not at all. I've got three rolls of paper towels back there, half a dozen light bulbs, and a box of wee candles for my daughter's birthday cake.'

'Personal gear,' the officer said, writing in a notebook.

'That's the size of it.'

'Don't stay away so long. Abe. And give my love to Annie.'

'I'll do it. And a big hug to Marjorie.'

They passed through the border station, turned west and then north on Highway 71. They pulled up and stopped at last behind a parked car, just south of the town of Finland. Leaving his headlights on, Abe studied the two men who got out of the car and stood waiting at the side of the road.

'What's going on?' Roy asked.

'We may do a little swap. Wait here while I check it out.' He got out of the cab and walked to where the two men were waiting. Roy watched them through the windshield. Abe was talking earnestly and the men were listening. Suddenly one of the men began to laugh. Then all three of them were laughing.

Abe walked back toward the truck, saying something over his shoulder that made the men laugh again. When he opened the door on the driver's side, he said, 'Let's go, Roy. We're trading cars. And we're getting the best of the deal.'

As they drove on north in the grey Mercedes sedan, Abe said, 'This beats hell out of riding in a truck, doesn't it?'

'Can I ask you a question?' Roy said.

'Shoot.'

'Where were the US Immigration guys? When you slowed down at International Falls, nobody even came out of the shelter. They just raised the gate and let you through.'

'It's a cold night. Maybe they—'

'Come on, Abe. Stop cocking me around.'

'What do you think, genius? Why do you think we came this way? I told you we wouldn't have any problem. This is James Duggan territory. And James Duggan is a particular friend of mine.'

'In other words I should mind my own business.'

'Not at all,' Abe said. 'The fact is you're entitled to some

237

answers even if you don't ask good questions. I'm a soldier, Roy. I'm a member of the provisional wing of the IRA, the only IRA there is that's worth a damn. We're the backbone of the United Ireland movement. Without us people would lay back, go to confession once a week, curse bloody England in the pubs every evening, and do nothing at all about it.'

'I thought you hadn't been in Ireland for years.'

'I haven't. I was home a few months after I finished my stint in Korea, and since then I haven't been back. But now I'm going. Taking Annie and the children and going back. The man you met tonight, James Duggan, and his mates, are all Provisionals. Terry White as well, the lad in Chicago who fixed you up with a car. And the Immigration officer at International Falls, Jack McBride, immigrated to Canada from Derry twenty years ago. But he's still a Provisional.'

'That's why he didn't inspect the truck tonight?'

'That's right.'

'What were we carrying?'

'Automatic weapons. Plus forty cases of ammunition and three hundred pounds of plastic explosives. We can buy anything we want in the States, but sometimes it's tough to ship it out. So we bring it to Canada, and our friends in Quebec ship it from Montreal.'

'Is that what you've been doing all along, every time you've made a trip away from Banff?'

Abe laughed. 'Not me. I only made the run tonight so I could bring you in. Usually James Duggan engineers those operations. What I do is raise money. Since 1960 I've raised over four million dollars. In Hawaii and Australia and New Zealand. And these last years in Canada. And we've got people in the States who've raised three times that.'

'And all that money goes for guns?'

Abe nodded. 'Guns and explosives and legal fees.'

'If you're so good at raising money, I'm surprised they don't want you to stay here. Why do they want you back in Ireland?'

'They don't. But I'm going anyway. I think we could win the battle in the next year, and I want to be there for it. I would never have left in the first place if we hadn't had some weak-hearted pussies at the head of the Provisionals just then. But now we're back on the track. Two hundred fifty dead in the Six Counties last year, we've bombed the London Tower this year and the bloody British Parliament, and now Wilson's in office as Prime Minister. We always get a better shake when Labour's in power.'

'When are you planning to leave Canada?'

'I told the hotel owners I'd stay on till after Christmas but not longer than February first.' He looked over at Roy and added, 'If you're wondering how Annie feels about it, I'll tell you. She's dead set against it. She wants to go back to bloody New Zealand.'

'I thought you liked it down there?'

'I do. But now I've got other things that need to be done. There's a country pub that I can take over in the village of Malin. That's just south of Malin Head, the northernmost point in Ireland. I'm hoping you and Christine will come along with us.'

'What the hell would I do in Ireland?'

'The same as you're doing here. You work and have some fun and live your life.'

Roy shook his head. 'Christine wouldn't go to Ireland if I tied her up with ropes.'

'Sure she would. Once Annie and I and the kids are gone, you'll find that Canada is a dull proposition. When Abe Singleton leaves the room, all the lights go out.'

'We'll be going back to the States soon. Everybody says there'll be an amnesty before long.'

'Not for you, there won't.'

'Why do you say that?'

'Because I know you a little bit by now. I don't think you're about to go crawling back, kiss some judge's ass, and say you were sorry you were a bad boy. When you read Ford's amnesty proposal, it won't be what *you* want. I guarantee it. *Then* you'll say. 'Abe, I think I want to go to Donegal, eat fresh trout every day, drown myself in Guinness, and paddle around on Lough Swilly.'

'I'm not planning to do anything *by myself*, Abe. If it's no good for Christine, it wouldn't work for me.'

'Oh, my God, what a sweet trap you're falling into. Nobody admires women more than I do. But they have no talent at all for deciding what's *best* for them. If they did, most of them would have selected different husbands. If you don't think that's true, just ask Annie. She'll give you an earful.'

Chapter 24

*T*he amnesty programme, when it was trumpeted at last from Washington, turned out to be a *clemency* plan. Although nine previous presidents, including Washington, Adams, Lincoln, Wilson, Roosevelt, Truman, and Roosevelt had granted amnesties or pardons during their terms in office, Gerald Ford could not push himself beyond an 'earned reentry' programme.

Acknowledging that more than half a million young men were elibile for repatriation, the plan made separate provisions for draft resisters and deserters.

As civilians, the draft resisters had been indicted in absentia. Upon returning to the United States, they would be required to report to the nearest US Attorney and identify themselves. After the resister had been interviewed and had sworn an oath of allegiance, the Attorney would then determine exactly how much alternative service he must put in. He would be sent along to his original draft board to be assigned a suitable job. Salvation Army, community projects, welfare workers, playground attendants, and similar work. After fulfillment of his work commitment, after the draft board had filed a satisfactory report, the returnee would be given a dishonourable discharge and his indictment would be lifted.

In addition to the loyalty oath and two years or so alternative service, the individual would be required to give up his constitutional rights to due process, a speedy trial, the statute of limitations, and protection against double jeopardy.

Although the clemency programme was extended beyond its original time frame, at the end less than five percent of those eligible had applied. Nine international exile organizations had voted unanimously to boycott it. Attempting to explain later why the programme had so little appeal to draft resisters, the Amnesty Action Information Centre in Los Angeles published the following conclusions:

THE CLEMENCY PROGRAMME'S LIMITED SCOPE IS DISCRIMINATORY, ITS PENALTIES FOR MANY PEOPLE WHO UNDER PRESENT LAW HAVE COMMITTED NO CRIME ARE SHOCKING, ITS 'CLEMENCY DISCHARGE' IS STIGMATIZING, AND ITS FAILURE TO PROVIDE FOR LEGAL REPRESENTATION IN THE INTERESTS OF THOSE WHO QUALIFY IS SEVERELY PREJUDICIAL. PERHAPS MOST IMPORTANT OF ALL IS THE DEMEANING CHARACTER OF THE LOYALTY OATH, AND THE FACT THAT SIGNING AN AGREEMENT TO PERFORM ALTERNATIVE SERVICE AMOUNTS TO AN ADMISSION OF GUILT. SUCH AN ADMISSION IS ABHORRENT TO THOSE WHO RESISTED THE WAR FOR REASONS OF CONSCIENCE AND WHO FEEL WHAT THEY DID WAS MORALLY RIGHT AND ETHICALLY CORRECT.

Christine, however, felt differently. As soon as she heard the news from Washington, she called Roy. 'I can't believe it,' she said. 'I thought we were doomed to nothing but bad luck. You remember how down in the dumps I was last week?'

'I sure do,' Roy said. 'How about your mother? Have you seen her yet?'

'Yes, twice.'

'How long will she be in the hospital?'

'Her doctor says she could go home now, but she doesn't want to. She doesn't want to do anything. She just sits there in that half-dark room staring at the wall. I'm worried sick about her, but I don't know what to do.'

'Don't they have therapists at the hospital, psychological counsellors or whatever they call them?'

'She won't talk to anybody, she won't let anybody visit her except me.'

'What's she going to do when you come back up here?'

'That's the problem. I *can't* come back till I get her home and quieted down. It's had me crazy. Dying to get back to you but not being able to leave Grace. Now, like a miracle, this amnesty thing happens. You can come here. You can go back to school. We can pick up where we left off almost five years ago.'

'It's not that simple, Chris.'

'What do you mean?'

'Just what I said. When you read the fine print it's not that simple.'

Two weeks before Christmas Christine brought her mother home from the hospital. As they sat that evening in Grace's half-dark bedroom, she talked, for the first time, about the future.

'I know you think I'm feeling sorry for myself. But I'm not. I feel sorry for my poor sweet arm, cut off and tossed away somewhere. I always wonder what they do with those leftover hands and arms and legs and feet. Who's in charge of disposing of the pieces that aren't needed anymore? Is it someone with medical training or just a couple little Mexican ladies who clean up the operating room?'

When Christine said that Roy wanted her to come to Banff for Christmas, Grace said, 'You're going, aren't you?'

Christine shook her head. 'Not a chance. I'm not going to leave you by yourself over the holidays.'

'Yes, you are. Because I want you to. I don't need a *companion*. And I don't *want* one. Not even you, Chrissy. I said don't feel sorry for me. That's why I haven't wanted to see anybody. Not even Margaret. I know already that she's decided the best way to handle the situation is to look me squarely in the eyes all the time, never look at my arm or refer to it. I'm just not ready for that yet. I'm not sure I ever will be. I can't see myself with a mechanical arm like Captain Hook, and I don't want to spend the rest of my life swathed in chiffon. But I don't know yet what my other choices are. I plan to take some time to think about those. I've always spent a lot of time by myself, so I think I'll go on doing that. You're the only permanent thing I have. I adore every moment we spend together. But I will not allow you to redirect your life just because I had a stupid automobile accident and lost my stupid arm. If I decide to live like a recluse, it has nothing to do with you. The best gift you can give me is to go ahead with what you're doing. Marry Roy if you want to, have some kids if you want to, and bring me back some firsthand gossip from the outside world. I promise you I won't shoot myself and I won't turn into a drunk.'

The day before Christine left Chicago to go back to Banff, her grandmother said to her, 'I'm surprised you're going away now. I thought perhaps . . . because of Grace . . .'

'She wants me to go. She *insists* that I go.'

'Naturally, she would *say* that.'

'She means it. She knows I'll only be a few hours away.'

'Of course,' Margaret said. 'I keep forgetting how close you actually are.' Then, 'You won't be staying in Canada much longer, will you?'

'I don't know. We haven't made up our minds yet.'

'*You* haven't or *he* hasn't?'

'*We* haven't.'

Margaret sat immobile in her chair, a gentle smile on her lips. Christine assumed that a new topic of conversation was in order. But Margaret said, 'May I ask you a personal question?'

'What if I say no?'

'Then I won't ask you.'

'Go ahead and ask, but I don't promise to answer.'

'I sense something changed about you. You seem uneasy. Are you and Roy having a problem?'

'My God, Margaret, where have you been living the past few weeks? Of course I'm uneasy. I'm a basket case. I lost a baby, a baby I was very anxious *not* to lose. And on top of that I've been worried sick about Grace. I lie awake at night thinking about her, trying to fix things in my head. But I can't fix anything. Something painful and ugly happened to her and it *can't* be fixed. So when you say I've changed you're right. I've changed a lot. A few weeks ago I was as confident as a child. I thought nothing bad could ever happen to me. But now I know different. And I hate it.'

After Christine left, Margaret remained in the chair that looked out on her flower garden. She sat erect as always, a crystal glass of port on the table by her hand. But suddenly, against her will, tears glistened on her cheeks. She bit her lip and tried to blink them away, but they wouldn't stop.

She sat there by the window for a long time before she was able to control herself. When she was calm at last, a winter dusk settling on the garden outside, she picked up her telephone receiver and placed a call to Fred Deets in California.

Chapter 25

*W*hen Roy met Christine at the Calgary airport three days before Christmas, as they stood with their arms around each other in the rush of deplaning passengers, he said, 'I think we should stop fooling around and get married.'

Doing her W.C. Fields voice, she said, 'I'll marry you, sweetheart, but I won't stop fooling around.'

As they walked toward the baggage claim area, he said, 'When shall we do it?'

'How about for our birthdays?'

'Sounds good. Big wedding or small?'

'Just you and me and the preacher.'

For the next ten days, their lives at the St Albert were like a carnival. The hotel was filled with skiers, the tavern opened early and closed late. People ate too much and drank too much, and everyone stayed up till they dropped.

'We're killing ourselves,' Annie said one morning at three. 'Why don't we ever go to bed?'

'Because it's Christmastide,' Abe said. 'We're celebrating the birth of the Saviour. We'll rest when we're older. We'll sober up after Epiphany,'

On the morning of January sixth, the hotel nearly empty now, Roy said to Christine, 'Comb your hair and brush your teeth and I'll take you out for a fancy lunch.'

They went to the Banff Springs Hotel. They sat in the vast dining room by a window looking out toward the west, drank wine, and had an elaborate meal.

'Just what I need,' Christine said. 'I've been eating like an animal for ten days, so for a change of pace we guzzle a ton of wine and eat a huge lunch.'

'This is an engagement party. I'm going to make an honest woman out of you.'

'You're going to make a fat woman out of me. The powerful Katrinka. Famous side-show attraction.'

'Don't worry. Tomorrow we'll be good. Tomorrow you can be skinny again.'

'It was a fine Christmas,' she said then. 'The best one I can remember since I was knee high.'

'You sure laid it on with the presents. You spoiled all of us.'

'That was my fun. I felt as if I hadn't spent any money for five years and I wanted to splurge a little. I wanted everybody to have something special.' She reached over and touched the watch on his wrist, a wafer-thin Universal Genève. 'How's it running?'

'Watches like this one don't just *run*. They make speeches and start wars.'

Christine looked around the dining room. 'Can we stay here all afternoon?'

245

'Sure, why not? The headwaiter's a buddy of mine. We can even stay through and have dinner if you want to.'

She smiled. 'That's funny. Reminds me of when I was four or five years old. Whenever Grace or my nanny took me someplace, I always wanted to stay longer. I used to cry and say, "I want to stay more days." '

'How *is* your mother? What's the word?'

Christine shook her head. 'I can't answer that. because I don't know. I can't even think about her because it gets me too crazy. But I can't stop thinking about her either. I lie in bed at night, and all I can see is that beautiful body with only half an arm on one side. It's like some ugly punishment that goes on hurting forever. I've never felt the way I've felt these past few weeks. You know me . . . Sally Sunshine; I could always find the bright side of things. But now I've done a whole turnaround. I see havoc everyplace I look. Abe and Annie for instance. I always thought they were solid as a wall. No wrinkles or blemishes. Both of them bright and funny and crazy about their kids. But the last ten days I've been looking at them and I see something different. I sense some kind of bubble beneath the surface, something struggling to break loose. I see her looking at us, looking at *you*, as if she's trying to remind herself of what she had. Trying to remember where she lost it. I know it's my cuckoo imagination. I know I'm wrong—'

'No you're not. There's something in the wind. He says it's because he's taking her to Ireland. He says she doesn't want to go. But I think it's something else. They've lived in half a dozen places since they were married. What difference could one more make?'

'Maybe it's one place too many. To tell you the truth it doesn't make much sense to me. What's his big drive to go to Ireland all of a sudden?'

'He's going to manage a country pub in Donegal.'

'Does he really want us to go along?' Christine asked. 'He keeps mentioning it, but I thought he was joking.'

Roy shook his head. 'He's not joking. He wanted us to come all right, But I told him we like it in Banff and we'll probably stay here.'

After a long moment Christine said, 'Is that what you told Abe or is that what you're telling me?'

'That's what I told Abe. I'm not telling you anything. We're just having lunch.'

'Don't get fancy with me, Lavidge. Is there something I don't know about?'

'There wasn't till this morning. Mr Knowles, the owner of the St Albert, flew out from Montreal a couple weeks ago to go over things with Abe. And to make arrangements for somebody to take over as manager when he leaves. So this morning he called and said we could have the job if we wanted it.'

'We?'

'You and me.'

'What did you say?'

' I said it sounded good to me, we talked about the money, and I promised to let him know by the tenth.'

She pushed her chair back and stood up. 'Excuse me a second. I'm going to the ladies' room.'

When she came back to the table and sat down, she said, 'I feel as if you're slipping away from me and there's nothing I can do to stop it.'

'Not true,' he said. 'Nothing like that.'

'Then you're going to have to bring me up to date on a few things. Like why we came to Canada in the first place. I thought we came here so you wouldn't be drafted. Is it only in my head, or did we discuss the fact that as soon as it was safe for us to go home, we would?'

'We discussed it,' Roy said. '*That* was the idea. We would only stay in Canada as long as we had to.'

Christine nodded her head. 'Good. That's what I thought. But now you've changed your mind.'

'Not necessarily. I said we have a chance to stay on and manage the hotel if we *want* to. But I never planned to make a decision until you and I talked about it.'

'All right, let's talk about it. I'll tell you straight out what I think. I don't want to stay in Canada.'

'Then we won't stay.'

'Wait a minute. I don't trust you. That was too easy.'

'No, it wasn't. If you're saying you *have* to go back to the States, then I go with you. If *I* have to stay here, then you stay with me. Isn't that the way it works?'

She nodded. 'That's the way it works. But it doesn't solve anything. We're back where we started.' She reached across the table and touched his hand. 'We'll both be twenty-six this month. Whatever we decide now will affect our whole lives. Do you really see yourself as the manager of a resort hotel for the rest of your life?'

'Five years ago I'd have said no. But now I'm not so sure. We'll be eligible for Canadian citizenship this year, and I can think of lots worse places to spend my life. What do you think?'

'I think it's terrific here. But it was always a means to an end. I never thought of it as an end in itself. I just think you're too good and too smart to spend your life supervising fry cooks and chambermaids. If you handle yourself right, I'll bet you could be making a hundred thousand a year by the time you're thirty.'

He grinned. 'Only if you decide to pay me that much to drive your car.'

'You know what I mean.'

'I don't think you read the fine print of Ford's clemency programme. If I go back to the States tomorrow, I have to go straight to Maine. Then I do my alternative service. Probably two years. No income to speak of. Then, if I can scrape together the money, or borrow it from you, I go back to school. Two years to go. I graduate when I'm thirty. If I still want to go to business school, that's another two years. So when I'm thirty-two or close to it, I'll be ready to look for a job. Willing to go wherever the company sends me. Pittsburgh, Houston, or Albany, New York. Does that make sense to you? It doesn't make sense to me. I'm spoiled. I don't want to give up the kind of life we've had for the last five years. I like to *see* you during the daytime, not for just a couple hours at night. When we have kids, I want to be able to spend some time with them. I know I'll never get rich as a hotel man, but

I'd have a life that makes sense to me. I see people coming to Banff who spend fifty weeks a year beating their brains out so they can come here for ten days. I look at them and I think, 'You poor sap. I *live* here year round. And I get paid for it besides. I mean what are people after? I want to have a good life. And that's what I want for you. Doesn't that sound reasonable?'

'Of course it does. I just . . .'

'What?'

'I just hate to see you settle for something that's not good enough for you. I want to see you go for the moon.'

'I'm *on* the moon already,' he said. 'We're both on the moon.'

Just before they left the dining room to go back to the St Albert, he said, 'I meant everything I said. I'm trying to tell you what I think is best for us. But if it's no good for you, it wouldn't be any good for me.'

Late that night, lying in bed in the dark, he said, 'The truth is, there's nothing down there for me. I'm an embarrassment to my aunt and uncle. They don't want to see me. I don't have a school to go back to. And on top of all that I'd be a second-class citizen, with a chicken-shit discharge from an army I never served in.'

Long after he was asleep, Christine lay there composing a rebuttal she'd been too stunned earlier to deliver. Silently, wordlessly, she let herself pour out all the resentment she was feeling.

'I don't want any medals for coming to Canada with you. You couldn't have kept me away with a gun. But it wasn't for life. At least it wasn't supposed to be. It's not fair to give me a list of all the reasons we should stay in Banff and then tell me none of those things matter, that if I want to go back you'll come along regardless of your own convictions. How do you think that makes me feel? Either way, I lose. The trouble is, the *main* trouble is, that I agree with you. Everything you say is logical. Everything makes sense. But my feelings keep screaming out something else. I'm *homesick*. I kept it under control all those months when we had no choice. But as soon as I knew we could go back, *anytime* we want to, it all flooded over me. I saw how much I'm a product of where I came from. Even Lake Forest. I joke about it and make fun of some of the silly people who live there. But I can't just blot out the years I spent there, the things I learned, the people I knew. I think Canada's a terrific country, but I don't feel as if it's *my country*. *Feelings*, that's all I keep yapping about. But the're *real*, Roy, they're real to me. I don't know how to deal with them and it's driving me crazy. I don't know how to deal with Grace either. I don't know how to deal with *myself*. And for the first time since I met you I feel awkward with you. Both of us say we're willing to give in, but neither of us is able to ask the other one to do it. We're out of the deep water. Finally. And now we're trying to keep from drowning in the shallows. God, what an idiotic joke.'

The next day and the following days, when they discussed what answer they would give Mr Knowles, they were sensible and dispassionate. They reasoned and speculated, agreed at last, or seemed to, and smiled at each other. When Mr Knowles called from Montreal on January tenth, Roy told him they would accept the job.

Roy's birthday was January twenty-first, Christine's was the twenty-third. They made the wedding date the twenty-second.

'Good choice,' Abe said. 'Twenty-two's a lucky number. Any number that can be divided by eleven is money in the bank.'

On January twelfth, Christine flew home to Chicago.

'We have to do this right. I need my mother's wedding dress and a blue garter, plus something old and something new.'

When they kissed goodbye at the boarding gate, he said, 'What are you crying about? You'll be back in seven days.'

'I always seem to be getting on planes and going away from you. I hate it.'

When her plane took off, she looked out the window at the ground, keeping the air terminal in view as long a she could, till it disappeared under the cloud cover. Then she called the stewardess and ordered a drink. When Wilson met her with the car at the Chicago airport, a flight attendant came off the plane with her, one hand on her elbow. When he handed her over to Wilson, he said, 'She's all right. But she had quite a lot to drink.'

Christine smiled sweetly and said, 'Ish true. I had quite a lot to drink. When I get home I expect to have quite a lot more.'

Chapter 26

The morning after her arrival in Lake Forest, her head still throbbing from the alcohol in her system, Christine pulled on corduroys, boots, and a heavy sweater and went to Kenilworth, to Elizabeth Griggs' house. There, sitting comfortably, drinking from a large mug of coffee, she succeeded in saying things about herself that she had never admitted before, not even in silence.

At last Elizabeth said, 'If you could bring off a miracle, if you and Roy could do anything you wanted to, what would it be?'

'If I could have things *exactly* the way I want them, I'd like to see Roy come back here, live with me in our house in Lake Forest, and finish school at Northwestern. I'd like to see him have an easy life for a change, to have no worries at all except going to school. Maybe I'd take some graduate work myself and we could be school kids again. I mean, we got cheated out of that and I'd like to have it back. Then, when he has his degree, I'd like it if he took a job in Chicago. With the connections that Margaret and Grace have, he could take his pick of the best companies. He could start at a high-enough salary so he'd really feel good about himself; we could live in Lake Forest and have a terrific life.'

'Would you want to stay on in your own house?'

'Of course I would. Why not? It's the greatest house I've ever seen, and there's room enough for twenty people. And especially since Grace's accident it would be ideal if she and I could be in the same house together.

'Have you and Roy discussed all this?'

'There's no point. He has a fetish about doing everything for himself. Finding his own job, buying his own house, supporting his own family.'

Elizabeth smiled. 'That's not unusual. Most men feel that way.'

'I'm not so sure of that. I think lots of people, if they had the chances that Roy has, would be a little more flexible than he is. He doesn't understand, or he doesn't want to understand, that the money is just *there*, it will always be there, and if we don't spend some of it, it won't get spent.'

'Do you resent that?'

'*Resent* isn't the right word. It baffles me. I don't give a damn about money. The only good thing about having money is that it permits you to pick the life you want. I never even noticed what my income was till I met Roy. Then all of a sudden it started to interest me. Because I said to myself, "Boy, oh boy, just think of all the terrific things we can do together." That just seems sensible to me. But . . . it's not going to be that way. I just think he's putting a silly ceiling on himself.'

'I know how upset you've been about Grace,' Elizabeth said then. 'All of us feel the same. If you've decided to stay in Canada –'

'Don't ask me that. I don't know the answer. When I think of being away from her, of not seeing her for weeks or months at a time, it makes me sick.'

'How does she feel about it?'

'She's as bullheaded as Roy is. She tells me she doesn't

want me hanging around. But she doesn't fool me. I know how important it is for her to spend time with me. She never leaves her wing of the house. Except for the servants she sees only me. Have *you* seen her since she came home from the hospital?'

'No. We've talked on the telephone and I've offered to drive up there, but she always says another time would be better.'

'That's what I mean. It kills me to see her like that.'

'Does Roy know how you feel about Grace?'

'We've talked about it,' Christine said, 'but it's hard for anybody who doesn't know her to understand. When there are so many people who are *really* disfigured, it's easy to assume . . . I don't know – I guess a lot of people would say she's lucky to be alive. And maybe she is. But *she* doesn't think so.'

They sat talking for more than four hours, up to and past lunchtime. Elizabeth made a pot of tea and some cheese-and-tomato sandwiches, and they ate at the glass-topped table in her kitchen. Then they went back to the sun-room.

'I don't feel as if I'm being very helpful,' Elizabeth said.

'It's not your fault. It's a bramble patch.'

Elizabeth lit a cigarette and settled herself in her chair. 'One thing I would like to caution you about. It's critical to remember that one accident does not mean you're accident-prone. One failure doesn't mean that you're a failed person. Symptoms are one thing. Sickness is something else. It's dangerous to mistake one for the other.'

When Christine answered, it was as though she hadn't heard what Elizabeth said. 'I lie awake at night and things race back and forth in my head. All the bad things that have happened during the past five years seem to fall into a pattern. Sometimes I think that when I decided to go off to Martha's Vineyard to work that summer, I triggered a whole chain of events that screwed up a lot of people. Roy most of all. If I hadn't influenced him to leave Bowdoin and come to Foresby, would the draft board in Portland have fouled up his status? Would he have got his draft notice when he did, when he was still in school? I doubt it. If he'd be running in Maine that morning instead of in some woods in Illinois, would he have fallen and wrecked his leg the way he did? It doesn't seem likely. Was I responsible in some way for my first miscarriage? Could I have avoided the second one? Am I like one of those children with white eyes in horror movies? Did I put some kind of a whammy on Tom Peddicord and Cuba? Was I responsible in some remote way for Grace's accident? I certainly screwed up Fred Deet's life. There's no doubt about that. You see what I'm getting at?'

'No, I don't see what you're getting at,' Elizabeth said. 'You're doing exactly what I said you mustn't do. You're not a witch, Christine. None of us are. The children with white eyes exist only in the movies.'

'But if Roy hadn't met me, he wouldn't have come to Foresby; if he hadn't come to Foresby he wouldn't have been called up in the draft. That means he wouldn't have gone to Canada and he wouldn't be there now. Planning to spend his whole life there. It's a pattern, Elizabeth. You can't ignore it.'

'Yes I can. If he hadn't met you that summer, he could have married a Chinese girl and be running a laundry now in Boston.'

Christine shook her head. 'You're talking about what *could* have happened. I'm talking about what *did* happen. It gives me a creepy feeling. It makes me hate myself.'

'Christine, darling, you have to stop this. You've had some hard knocks. And they've come in bunches because that's what they do sometimes. But you have to deal with them as they are. You mustn't blow them up to giant size and paint monster faces on them.'

Christine sat with her hands in her lap, a listening expression on her face. But her eyes had clouded over. Her mind was off somewhere, gathering other information and drawing its own conclusions. When she was ready to leave she made a telephone call. Fred Deets drove over from a nearby restaurant, where he'd been waiting, and picked her up.

Chapter 27

*T*wo days after Christine left Banff for Lake Forest to get her wedding things together, Roy called Mr Knowles in Montreal and told him he wouldn't be able to take the hotel manager's job after all. 'I'm sorry to hang you up,' he said, 'but it's a family situation. We're going back to the States to live.'

'January fourteenth,' Abe said when Roy told him about the decision. 'Mark that down in your daybook. For the rest of your life you're going to be telling yourself. "That's the day I made my big mistake." '

'I don't think so,' Roy said. 'I've decided I want to go back to school so I can get a degree and ace myself into a real job.'

'I'm not talking about jobs. Jobs are a dime a dozen. I'm talking about where you're going to live. If you're leaving Canada, then come with us to Ireland. Don't go back down there to cardboard land and get yourself a cardboard job. They'll wring you out like a rag for thirty years and then fire you so they won't have to pay you a pension. That's providing you can get a job at all. Those guys who fought in Vietnam aren't heroes. They're like lepers. Nobody wants to hear about that fucking war or police action or whatever you want to call it. So you can imagine the reception you guys who came up to Canada are gonna get. They'll crucify you.'

Roy grinned. 'Thanks a lot, Abe. You're really getting me all excited. Can't wait to cross that border and wrap myself in the Stars and Stripes.'

'I'm not trying to screw you up. I'm trying to do you a favour. I just hate to see you make an ass of yourself. If you think *leaving* was tough, wait'll you see what it's like when you try to go back. You're too good for that place.'

'That's funny. Christine says I'm too good to stay up here.'

'Don't listen to her. Christine's a nice girl, but women have their own axes to grind. What did she do? Give you an ultimatum?'

'Nope. She thinks we're staying in Banff. I didn't tell her I was calling Knowles to turn down the job. That's gonna be her wedding present. I'll tell her just before she cuts the cake.'

'Well, all I have to say is keep your passport up to date. You've got the address where I'll be and it's an open invitation. We'll be waiting for you in Donegal.'

Annie reacted differently when Roy told her what he had done. 'I hope you're not doing it just for her. It won't be any good if you don't want it too.'

'I'm gonna miss living here in Banff. But in the long run we'll be better off. Things will settle down and Chrissy will have a life she's used to.'

'You didn't answer my question. Are you doing it for her?'

'Yeah, I guess I am. But that's all right. She's a good kid. Lousy at sewing on buttons, but she's got a good heart.'

Chapter 28

*R*ussell came to have dinner with us the night of January nineteenth, the day before he was flying to Canada for Christine's wedding.

'How do I look?' he asked as he walked into our living room with Amy, who'd met him at the door.

'I don't know,' I said. 'How does he look to you, Amy?'

'Very healthy. He used to look dissipated. Now he looks like a man who sleeps eight hours every night and takes his vitamin pills in the morning. Good colour. Bright eyes. Steady hands.'

'Never mind the medical examination,' he said. 'Feed my vanity. How do I *look*?'

'Gorgeous,' Amy said. 'If anyone says you're not gorgeous, they'll have to deal with me.'

He had refused chemotherapy and all other medication. 'I will ride it out with my own natural resources. I'd rather die beautiful in January than ugly in May. Meanwhile, I'm happy to report that a side effect of my ailment is heightened sexuality. I am suffering from an almost inexhaustible potency. So spread the word, please. I'm asking all my friends to publicize that particular aspect of my condition.' He glanced at his watch. 'I'm sure that this evening's queue has begun to form already outside my apartment door.'

He told us in detail about the impending wedding. 'When you start giving brides away or being selected as a godfather, you know that people are beginning to regard you as someone who is venerable and serious. Last year two couples presented me with godsons. I was humiliated but I didn't know how to get out of it. Do you know what the official duties of a godparent are? I looked it up. To supervise the religious education of the child in question. Give me a break, folks. I can teach the little buggers the Lord's prayer, but after that they'll be on their own. Giving brides away is more in my line. I get to wear a nice suit, drink a lot of champagne, and maybe even scurry into the cloakroom with one of the bridesmaids. No bridesmaids at Christine's wedding, however. A very small wedding party. Singleton the best man, his wife the matron of honour, and yours truly representing the bride's family. Not officially, you understand. Just filling a vacuum. But . . . this is as close as I'll ever come to seeing a daughter married. Christine is as close as I'll ever come to *having* a daughter. So I want to make the most of it.'

The next day at noon, Russell called me. 'I thought you'd be on your way to Canada,' I said. 'Weren't you taking a morning plane?'

'Cancelled the flight.' His voice sounded as if he'd been drinking. 'Cancelled Canada. Cancelled the wedding.'

'What are you talking about?'

'No wedding. The wedding's called off. Christine married somebody else last night.'

Book 4

Chapter 1

*T*he day before the Singletons left to go to Ireland, Abe and Roy sat up all night in the tavern downstairs, a bottle of Irish whiskey on the table between them.

'Don't be a jackass,' Abe said. 'It's not too late. All you have to do is put those tacky clothes of yours in a paper sack and we're off to the races.'

'Jesus, Abe, you never let up, do you? We've been over this ground twenty times.'

'And we may go over it twenty more if that's what it takes to drum a little sense into your head.'

'I've *got* a little sense in my head,' Roy said. 'Not much maybe. But enough so I'm able to make up my own mind.'

'Any fool can make up his mind. The trick is to make it up *right*. When you said that Donegal was no place to take Chrissy, that made sense to me. But the situation is different now.'

'Forget it, Abe. I don't want to go over it again.'

'Neither do I. There's nothing anybody can do about that. But what *you* decide to do *from now on* is another matter. I feel like hell, packing off and leaving you here by yourself. I want to help, damn it.'

'I know you do. But I don't need any help. I'm not gonna fall apart.'

'Maybe you are and maybe you're not. If you think it's gonna be a picnic being here by yourself . . .'

'I don't plan to stay in Banff. I told you that.'

'That's even worse. I'd rather see you go back to the States than bum around up here in Canada, living in furnished rooms and getting drunk every night.'

Roy grinned. 'I only get drunk when I'm with you, you bastard.'

'I'm not getting through to you, am I?'

'You're getting through to me, but you're not changing my mind. I told you what I want to do. I'm going up to Grande Prairie and latch onto a job in the oil fields. Or maybe in a lumber camp. I want to put in a lot of overtime and stash away some money. When I get a few thousand in the bank, I'll go back to college, probably in Edmonton. Or if I feel like it, I'll go back to Maine, kiss the US Attorny's ass, and finish up at Bowdoin. Who knows what I'll feel like a year from now?'

The next morning, after Abe and Annie and the children had left to drive to the Calgary airport, Roy carried his duffel bag over to the bus station on Caribou Street and bought a ticket for Jasper.

On the bus going north he sat in the front seat on the right, the same seat he and Christine had sat in when they'd made that trip more than four years before. In Jasper he stayed in the hotel where they had stayed. He asked for the same room and slept there for seven nights.

In the daytime he went to places where he and Christine had gone, ate in the same restaurants and coffee shops, walked the same streets, tramped the same trails. At night he sat in the tavern of the hotel, in the corner where they had sat, listened to the country music, watched the local young men play pinball machines and struggle with the electronic games.

He never got drunk that week in Jasper. Never came close. Every night at nine or nine thirty he went upstairs, watched television for an hour, and went to bed.

In his mind there was nothing sentimental or tender about this trip to Jasper. He saw it as a rite of passage, a way to put an end to something that for reasons outside his control had not ended properly. There had been just her barely coherent words from a pay telephone at the airport outside Chicago, then sobbing, then silence. At last someone had replaced the receiver there, Roy had replaced the receiver of the hotel telephone behind the desk at the St Albert, and all connections with Christine were broken. No anger, no recriminations or accusations. No explanations. Nothing.

Abe and Annie, to a large degree, had kept their feelings to themselves. Even during their late-night drinking sessions, Abe avoided talking about Christine. And Annie, after that first night, did not mention her at all. So Christine went uncondemned and unpunished. Until Jasper.

With no intention of trying to match her cruelty with some after-the-fact voodoo of his own, Roy felt, all the same, a need to particularize her, to bring her back to life in an isolated situation, in a place where he had no associations that had not been *her* associations also, where every building and street keyed some memory of the days they had spent there together.

He was in the process of rescuing hemself. A shoring up was necessary. General repairs. But he was wise enough not to tell himself that a bad ending proved that everything before the ending was also worthless. When he felt most bewildered and betrayed, he never questioned the value of what they'd had together, never wished it hadn't happened, never imagined that either of them would have been better off it they hadn't met.

He detested what she had done, the way she had done it. But he didn't detest her. He had learned long ago that he could survive under impossible circumstances, could do without people who were precious to him. He knew he could survive without Christine, too, no matter how painful it was or how empty and painful it might continue to be. Still, something inside him continued to look for that final missing piece, of drama if not of logic, some teeterboard that would propel him up and out of the warm valley he'd shared with her, across some border, and into some new place. Before he could begin, he desperately needed an ending, one he could have a role in, something more definitive than that final phone call when he had only listened.

So he made the trip to Jasper and brought her with him. In

every way he could. Using his memory and his imagination, he stuck together every physical detail, every touch, every word, and every conversation. Talking to no one else, he devoted the entire seven days in Jasper to re-creating Christine. And when he reached the point where he could see her everywhere he looked, hear her voice, and feel her beside him in the bed at night, when she was real and warm to him, and three-dimensional, he left her. He got on the bus alone and rode south to Park Gate. From there he hitchhiked east on Highway 11 to the town of Rocky Mountain House.

Chapter 2

*I*n Venice, where Christine and Fred stopped on the first leg of the extended wedding trip, she sat by herself one grey afternoon on a terrace overlooking the Grand Canal and wrote a letter to Roy.

What can I say to you? You have a right to think that I have done the most careless and selfish thing one person could possibly do to another. You have a right to think anything you like. But when I tell you I wasn't thinking of myself, that's the truest thing I can say.

I used to think that if two people loved each other enough, they could handle any problem that confronted them. I don't believe that now. Sometimes two particular people, no matter how strong their feelings, just can't make it together. All kinds of things creep in. Families, money, other loyalties. And all of a sudden you're shocked to find you can't divorce yourself from what you've always been. I know you never made unreasonable demands on me and I tried to make none on you. But more and more we could both see that we were pulling in opposite directions.

If Grace hadn't been hurt the way she was, if that hadn't happened . . . but it *did* happen. Before that, I had chosen my life with you over the life I'd had before. But when Grace needed me, I had to choose again. I didn't want to give up anything. Certainly not you. I tried to find a way to make it work so it would be perfect for you and perfect for Grace. But I couldn't do it. I was making myself sick with trying. So I . . .

Christine stopped writing. She read through what she had written, read it again, then deliberately tore the pages into small pieces. When she left the terrace, she leaned across the railing and scattered the confetti she'd made on the water.

Everything that was sensitive and lovely about her Christine had inherited from Grace. But there was a sliver of Margaret in her too. She sensed it and was not proud of it. In certain isolated moments, however, she was grateful for that tough-mindedness. In a life studded with triumphs, Christine had endured her occasional defeats by simply saying to herself, 'I did my best, it didn't work, so screw it.'

This was not, of course, her attitude toward Roy. Nonetheless, when she found herself halfway around the world from Chicago, when she realized that for good or ill she had made a painful choice and seen it through, when she accepted the fact at last that nothing more could be done, no wreckage salvaged, she drew then on whatever genetic thing it was that had been passed on to her, and promised herself that she would try to make the best life she could for herself and her husband.

Her failed letter to Roy gave her the final bit of reassurance she needed: there was nothing more that could be said or done.

From Venice she and Fred went to Siena. It was cool in

264

Tuscany, with winter rains still falling. But the servants kept the fires glowing and they had dinner each night in front of a great marble fireplace that had been transferred from the doge's palace in Verona.

It was as though they had played a trick with time, as though they had married six years before, before Christine had gone off to Martha's Vineyard. In Italy they simply bypassed and erased Fred's marriage in California. And Christine's years in Canada with Roy. It was as though some instinct told them, each of them, that their strength was in their childhood, their friendship, their early courtship. There was a wealth of common experience there. Shared memories, shared families, a thousand familiar and pleasant contact points.

Their sexual life together was also like a warm reprise, an easy resumption of what it had once been. Expert and considerate and satisfying. They performed together like two fine athletes who complemented each other perfectly.

After three days in Rome they flew to Lisbon, and from there they drove south to Algarve, to Portimão and on out to the beach at Praia da Rocha, where they stayed in a suite at the Bela Vista, on a high bluff looking down across the beach on the blue-green waters that moved back and forth between southern Portugal and the northern-most edges of Africa.

At least twice a week, usually every other day, Christine wrote a long letter to Grace. About Praia da Rocha she wrote:

This place is like dying and going to heaven. Like living in a castle a hundred years ago. The hotel is small and elegant, with the best dining room on the Algarve. So we're eating like irresponsible fools. And drinking the lovely Portuguese wines.

Because it's still winter here, bright sun most days but too cold to swim, there's almost no one in the hotel but us. It's as though we have our own seaside home with a staff of twenty. As I said the ocean is cold, but Fred goes in anyway; he also plays golf every morning, and we walk for miles up and down the beaches.

In the morning, the thing that wakes us up is a pony cart driving into the hotel courtyard with the day's supply of fish just off the Portimão boats. What a peaceful sound that is, the pony's hooves on the cobblestones.

In the daytime there's a band of raggle-taggle dogs that prowl the beach looking to make friends. You know me and dogs. I'm having a great time. I also walk down the road sometimes, when Fred is playing golf, and visit with a shepherd who has a flock of sheep and goats out past the edge of town. He lets me play with the lambs and baby goats.

Fred is brown as a nut, full of beans, and very vain at the moment about his golf game. He sends his love to you. And I send mine.

All the weeks she was away she reported the quality of her days to Grace. She had no feelings that she was selecting details or editing her experiences. There were no shadows in her hallways and no water in the wine. She felt no need to deceive or manipulate herself. She was a genuinely happy young woman, recently married to an affectionate and decent man. She assured herself that their marriage had been predestined.

Then one day the illusions ended. The self-hypnosis wore off as abruptly as it had begun. She didn't know then, nor was she able to determine later what had triggered it. She only knew that her resolve left like an exhaled breath. From quiet self-assurance she dissolved, in what seemed a matter of minutes, into panic, trembling and looking for a place to sit down.

Out of context in her stream of thought, unbidden and unwanted, a clear picture of Roy settled into her consciousness one beach morning and would not be dislodged. Like a cleverly edited montage, then, scenes from their years together flickered behind her eyes and would not be turned off. Trying to distract herself, she called the beach dogs to her, tried to involve them in a game of throwing and retrieving a stick of driftwood. But the dogs would not cooperate. As if they'd heard a signal, they turned and trotted away down the beach, leaving her with Roy.

She took off her beach robe and walked into the cold surf, swam out a quarter of a mile then slowly back. She took a taxi into Portimão and wandered through the shops for the rest of the morning. At lunchtime while Fred told about his triumph on the golf course, she drank a bottle of vino verde all by herself. When they left the table she led him upstairs and made love to him on their bed in the sunshine.

That afternoon they drove to Faro, prowled the streets there, and stayed over for dinner. On the way home they stopped at a low club in Albufeira, danced, and drank cognac till two in the morning. Back at the Bela Vista, they made love again till the sun began to streak yellow through their window shades. But as she lay on her back in bed, her head throbbing and Fred asleep beside her, Christine's thoughts were fully occupied with Roy. Even when Fred's arms were around her and hers around him. Especially then.

They stayed ten more days in Portugal, the last three in Lisbon. By the time they got to Lisbon, the guilt she'd felt about Roy sharing their bed had left her. Now she welcomed it. She opened herself to Fred not to help her forget Roy, but to help her remember. With her eyes closed, it was Roy's weight she felt on her. She made love with a ferocity that startled and delighted her husband. But it frightened her. Time after time she could feel Roy's name just at the tip of her tongue, ready to burst free as her body trembled and contracted and released.

At last, one morning, she walked into the writing room of the Hotel Lisboa, sat down, and in a letter to Roy told herself the truth.

> I can't hack it, Roy. I thought I was being grown-up and responsible, doing what was best for everybody. But God, was I mistaken.
>
> I hope it's not too late. I hope you don't hate me so much that you'll just tear this letter up and drop it in the

toilet. I wouldn't blame you if you did. But *please*, don't try to get even with me.

I'm sure this letter won't make sense to you. If it sounds like the rantings of a crazy lady, that's what it is. I don't feel sorry for myself and I'm not trying to make *you* feel sorry for me, but I really have been nearly out of my skull these last days.

You know how upset I was about Grace and how disappointed I was when I realised you wanted to stay in Canada. But dear sweet Jesus, whatever made me think that *anything* could be solved by our breaking up? By my getting married like a stupid jackass?

Like I said, I must have been crazy. I *was* crazy. But now I'm not. Now all I can think of is how to straighten out the mess I made. I know I can do it. But not without you.

I'm asking a lot. I know that. But don't say no without thinking it over. I just want you to forgive me if you can. At least forgive me enough so I can see you and talk with you.

I don't know what I expect. I don't even know what I deserve. But I know what I *want*. I want us to find a way, *any* way, to get past these last months, to put them behind us, to take up, as much as we can, where we left off. Is there some way we can do that? There must be.

I'm not trying to pretend that Fred doesn't exist. He does. And I detest the thought of hurting him. But the worst possible thing I could do would be to live some false life with him when every part of me is aching to be with you.

I'm not going to say any more now. All I'm asking for is a chance to plead my case. I'm sending this to the St Albert in Banff. I assume that if you're not there, the new managers will know where you are.

I guess it would be a miracle if you still want me back. But it was a miracle that we met each other in the first place. It was a miracle that things worked out so we could stay together. So if we had *two* miracles, why not a third one?

Please write me as soon as you get this so I'll know where you are. Send it to Elizabeth Griggs, 904 Sycamore Place, Kenilworth, Illinois. Mark it *Hold for Christine Wheatley. Do not forward.*

For two weeks after she and Fred were back home, living in the Wheatley house in Lake Forest, Christine called Elizabeth Griggs every afternoon when she knew the day's mail had been delivered. Nothing came for her.

She called the St Albert in Banff then, spoke to the manager, and asked if he had a forwarding address for Roy Lavidge.

'I'm afraid not,' he said. 'He's had two or three letters since February, but we had to give them back to the post office to be returned.'

As the manager indicated, the letter she'd sent to Roy had been returned to the Hotel Lisboa. The mail clerk there had compared Christine's name on the back of the envelope with the hotel guest list for the day the letter was postmarked and had sent the letter along to Fred's California address, the one he'd signed on the Lisboa register. The letter came to Fred at last in his Chicago office. His secretary gave it to him unopened and said, 'This looks as though it has bounced around a bit.'

Fred picked up the envelope and studied it, the date, Roy's name on the front in Chrissy's writing, and her signature on the back. He considered opening it and reading it. But he didn't. He considered taking it home and giving it to Christine. He didn't do that either. At last he put it into his wall safe with a sheaf of shock certificates and production contracts.

For three days he pondered what he should do about the letter. Finally he took it out of his safe one morning, walked into the stenographic area outside his office, and dropped it into the paper shredder. At that moment he sincerely intended never to mention the letter to Christine.

Chapter 3

*W*hen Abe flew from Montreal to Shannon with Annie and the children, he expected some of his friends to meet him at the air terminal. He particularly expected to see Arthur Ross. He had written him three weeks before to tell him his arrival time.

But Arthur was not there when the Aer Lingus flight touched down. When Abe called his home in Letterkenny, a young girl answered and said, 'Mum's gone to the school to see about my brother, Alfred, who's been naughty, and me dad's in Derry.'

'Do you know when he'll be back?'

'Not precisely . . . no.'

'Well, when you hear from him, tell him Abe Singleton called him. Can you remember that?'

'Yes. I've written it down.'

'Tell him I'm driving up to Sligo and will be staying there tonight at the Ballincar House.'

There were no messages waiting at the hotel in Sligo and no one called that evening. Before he went to bed, Abe telephoned Arthur again. The woman who answered sounded distraught. 'Arthur's away on a journey.' She hung up then before Abe could ask any questions. When he called the number again a moment later, no one answered.

It was ten days before he heard from Ross. In that time Abe and Annie had put the Malin public house in working order and opened for business. Their first customer, a tall ascetic man who wore a limp wool hat and army leggings wrapped around his calves, gave them his assessments of their prospects.

'You've taken on a sorry specimen here. Most of the trade goes over to Bristow's in Culdaff. And the young people have taken a shine to The Yellow Gull, a place that's just between Malin and Carndonagh. They've a saucy barwoman there

270

who says whatever comes into her head and a music machine that plays the kind of tunes I'd pay a lot not to listen to.'

'We'll get our share of the trade,' Abe said. 'As soon as people see that we know how to run a good house.'

'I hope you're right.' the man said. 'Have you bought the place outright or just taken it on for the owners?'

'For now we've just taken it on for Gogarty, but I intend to buy it within the year.'

'I wouldn't be in a hurry. If I was you I'd wait to see how it works out. There's extra people up here in the summer, but once the chill comes on and the rain starts, you'll be hard put to find any cutomers. Except for the walking trade.'

When Arthur Ross showed up at last, early one morning, Annie fixed eggs with bacon and sausages and soda bread and the two men ate alone in the snug.

'Your hair's gone white as a pigeon,' Abe said, 'and it's changed you'.

'We're all changed, Abe.'

After breakfast Arthur said, 'I'm to take you across the line to meet with the committee. They want to bring you up to date on certain circumstances and affairs.'

'What does that mean?'

'I don't know myself. All of a sudden it's a new organization. The leaders are college men now, bright young fellows from Trinity. Philosophers. They understand everything.' He took a packet of documents out of his jacket pocket. 'Here's your new papers. For you and the family. They've kept pretty close to the facts, your name and all. But forget you ever spent time in Canada. They've got you coming straight here from New Zealand.'

'What's that all about?'

'I can't tell you, Abe. Somebody decided. So that's the way it is.'

They drove down through Buncrana, crossed the border west of Derry, passed through three roadblocks manned by British soldiers, and stopped at last in the village of Claudy. There, in the storeroom of an auto supply station, Abe sat at a round table with Arthur, a young man named Lillis, and two other men who were introduced as Smith and Timothy. The three men were in their mid-twenties. Lillis looked like a university student. He was abrupt and humourless.

'As you know, Mr Singleton, our people in Dublin were not keen on your leaving Canada to come back here. Dangerous, they felt, for you *and* the movement.'

'Well, I'm here now,' Abe said, 'safe and sound. So I guess that part of it's settled.'

'No. It won't be settled till we've discussed it.'

'I don't mind discussing it, but I went over it all by mail with Pearse.'

'Pearse is not in charge now. He's in prison outside Belfast.'

'I know that,' Abe said. 'I had a letter from his wife.'

The man named Smith said, 'According to our records, Pearse told you you were more valuable to us where you were.'

Abe nodded. 'He told me that, and I told him I was determined to come back to Donegal, closer to the fighting. So we decided that I would run the pub in Malin and keep a safe house for whoever might want it on short notice. And I'm close enough to the border so I can do my bit in the Six Counties whenever I'm needed.'

Smith and Lillis exchanged a look, and the young man named Timothy, square and bulky, with thick red hair, said, 'We work in a different way now. It's a disciplined operation we've got.'

'Timothy's right,' Lillis said. 'If I'd been in Pearse's shoes I would have encouraged you to stay in Canada.'

Abe grinned. 'It's pretty hard to keep a man who's spending his own money from getting on a plane and coming back to his own country.'

Lillis nodded. 'Maybe you're right. But it's not hard at all to dismiss a man who won't take orders.'

Abe turned to Arthur Ross. 'You've got to help me out here, Arthur. Who are these people? Why'd you bring me down here?'

'Ross brought you here because we asked him to.'

'So we could have this discussion we're having now.'

'I don't call it a discussion. So far all you've done is threaten to have me thrown out of the Provisionals. And even if you had the authority to do it—'

'He has the authority,' Timothy said.

'Then do it, for Christ's sake,' Abe said, 'and let's get it over with. I was making gasoline bombs when you three were in nappies. People like Ross and me . . .'

'People like Ross and you aren't making the plans now. In case you missed it on the telly, we've just agreed to an open-end cease-fire. And *all* our members are going to observe it.'

'That won't last long,' Abe said. 'I give it two weeks. My dad started fighting the bloody crown sixty years ago and it's not over yet. And it won't *be* over till they call home their soldiers and give us back our country. A cease-fire means nothing. A cease-fire means shit.'

There was a heavy silence in the room. Finally Lillis said, 'What we *want*, Mr Singleton, is for you to run that pub in Malin. And that's *all* we want you to do. No trips to the Six Counties, no contacts with our people in Strabane or Sligo or Dublin. From now on you're a country publican, a non-political. That's your value to us. Can you handle that?'

'You mean can I sit on my ass and do nothing?'

'No. I mean can you take orders? We're giving you a chance to prove that.'

Twenty minutes later, in the car with Arthur Ross, heading north-west toward Malin, Abe said, 'Arthur, I was all alone back there. You were silent as a mute. What's happened over here? Art those three thumb suckers the whole movement now? Where are the men we had? Where did they all go?'

'Where do you think they went? They're dead. Or they're sitting in jail. Or else they wore out and gave up. A man with a family . . .'

'*You've* got a family. *I've* got a family.'

'That's right. And no day passes when I don't tell myself I'm a lunatic to keep on fighting. You think I like to knuckle under to those snot-nose lads with schoolboy ink still on their fingers? I hate it. But that's the way it is now. It's them and people like them who make the plans.'

'Then maybe it's better not to fight at all,' Abe said.

'No, it's not. There's just two sides in this thing. There's our side, thinking the way we do, and there's the Ulster bastards, not thinking at all, just hating us and everything we stand for. For every one of us who gives up, they gain a bit of ground. I've got an eighteen-year-old boy who's itching to get into the Provisionals. I tell him he's daft. But he won't listen to me. I know he'll go his own way just like you did and I did. And I'm proud of him for it.'

Later that day, sitting at his own bar, the only customer there, with Annie behind it wiping off bottles and polishing the mirror, Abe said, 'Here we are, at the end of the fucking world. Out in the country, away from everything, our kids twenty miles from their school. Rooms to let and nobody to sleep in them, hot food in the kitchen and nobody to eat it. Nobody even wants to drink our whiskey. Anyplace else in Ireland you can open a pub in your grandfather's outhouse and *somebody* will show up. But not here. Not Malin in the winter. So why are we here? So I can get pissed on Jameson and Guinness every afternoon? Not at all. We're here because my friends are fighting a war and I figured they couldn't win it without me.'

Months later, in a letter to her aunt in New Zealand, Annie wrote:

You know Abe. You met him when I did. Perhaps you saw things in him, even then, that I was blinded to. But no matter. I'm not complaining and I don't regret anything. I think I made him as happy as anyone could have and he made me as happy as he was able to. I gave all I had and he gave as much as he could. He loved me in his way, as much as an emotional cripple can love anyone.

I think he might have held himself together if we'd stayed in Canada. Or if we'd gone back to New Zealand when I wanted to. One thing I'm sure of. Nothing could have been more damaging to him than coming to Ireland. From the day he drove to Claudy with Ross and came back with all the colour washed out of his eyes, from that day till the day he died, all his frustration and anger and self-contempt, all those things, burst through the shell of fun and energy he'd built around himself, and took full charge of his life. He drank and howled and railed against the world, and at last he swallowed death like a thirsty man gulping water.

Chapter 4

*L*iving in Lake Forest again, Christine's life pattern became as smooth as a sheet of marble. Fred, after adjusting his business schedule to fit their choice of residence, assured her that he preferred Lake Forest to Santa Barbara or anywhere else. He flew to California every Tuesday morning and flew back Thursday night. So they were apart only three days and two nights each week. Every third or fourth week she flew to Santa Barbara with him and amused herself by riding or swimming or poking through the shops in Montecito while Fred attended to business.

She began also to take an active interest in her investments. She separated a certain amount of money from one of her trusts, called it 'play' money, and began speculating. Real estate, commodities, and high-flash stocks that her advisors would have normally avoided. She spent two hours each morning reading, researching, and educating herself. Six months later she had tripled the capital she started with.

For the first time she began to feel that the assets listed under her name were really hers. So she enjoyed her speculations. She began also to enjoy *spending* money, buying things for Fred or Grace without hesitation, without questioning the price, without guilt. She had never been profligate with her wealth. She'd had no flair for ostentation. Now, suddenly, it came to her that for the past few years she had been ashamed of her ability to buy whatever she chose. She had persuaded herself that *privilege* was, in some way, an evil, something to conceal. But now even some of Margaret's dicta began to make sense to her. 'Our families didn't keep slaves or exploit immigrants. There's no blood on our money. It was carefully planned for and honestly earned. It's as much a part of you as your straight legs or your strong teeth.'

So in almost every way Christine was contented and in command. Her friends told her it showed in her face, in her colouring, in the way she moved on the tennis court. 'Don't go to Chrissy's backhand. She'll make you swallow it.'

But for all this, for all her activity and warm surroundings, the central fact of her life was that Roy followed her everywhere she went. The physical truth of him would not go away. Time healed nothing and changed nothing.

Her daily life, the nights and days, were a graceful performance. But behind the facade she continued to lead an uninterrupted life with Roy. It maddened her. At the same time those memories, that ghost life, were the best thing she had, like a lucky coin she could carry in her sweater pocket and touch with her fingertips.

When she'd telephoned the St Albert upon returning from Portugal, when she'd learned that her letter to Roy had been sent back, it had disappointed her at first. Then she was encouraged. It meant that channels were still open. If only the proper channels could be found. After her call to Banff she tried to telephone Roy's father in El Centro. But there was no listing for T. J. Lavidge. She then called Portland and talked to Joe Medek.

'Do you mind telling me when you heard from him last?'

'Five years or more,' Joe said. 'When he first went up to Canada.'

'And in all that time you haven't heard a word?'

'We don't *want* to hear from him and he knows it.'

When she confided in Grace several weeks after her return from Lisbon, when she told her in detail about her dilemma, she was surprised at the reply she got.

'Forget it, Chrissy. You have to close the door on Roy. It's over. It has to be. Why are you looking at me like that?'

'Because I'm floored. I didn't expect that from you.'

'I love you, Chris, and you know it, ' Grace said. 'But when your head's not working right, you can't expect me to agree with you.'

'It's not my *head*. I'm trying to sort out how I *feel* and what to do about it.'

'If you're telling me you don't want to be married to Fred and you're going to get a divorce, that's one thing. Is that what you're saying?'

'No. I didn't say that. I just—'

'Then you're saying you'd like to locate Roy and see if he'll take you back. If he *will*, *then* you'll decide what to do about Fred.'

'It's not like that. You make it sound so rotten.'

'I don't make it sound any way,' Grace said. 'I'm just feeding back what I'm getting from you.'

'Are you trying to get me mad? Or hurt my feelings or something?'

'No, I'm trying to help you. But if all you want is for somebody to agree with you, I can't do that.'

'All right. I surrender. What do you think I should do?'

'I told you. You have to find a way to cut it off. You're a grown-up. You can't play games with people.'

'I don't want to play games. Nothing like that. Are you telling me the only choice I have is to spend the rest of my life with Fred just because I'm married to him?'

'No, I'm not saying that. I'm saying you should divorce him if that's what you want to do. What you shouldn't do is shop around for somebody else while you're still with him.'

Chrissy didn't answer for a moment. Then she said, 'Didn't *you* do that?'

277

'No, I didn't. And you *know* I didn't.'

'I'm sorry. I don't want to hurt your feelings. But it's *true*, isn't it?'

'No, it's *not* true. Your father and I were separated when I met Russell. We'd been separated for months.'

'Maybe so. But *he* didn't know you were separated. So I don't see why you're coming at me so hard. I don't know what I said or did—'

'I'll tell you what you did and what I think you're doing now,' Grace said. 'When you met Roy you were planning to marry Fred. So you and Fred broke up. A few years later, when you're about to marry Roy, you change your mind at the last minute and marry Fred. I'm not sure what that was all about and I don't think it's any of my business. *None* of it's my business unless you want it to be. Do you want me to go on?'

'Yes.'

'*Now* . . . unless I've misunderstood everything you've said, you've decided that you made a mistake, that you really want to be with Roy. So you're going to make an effort to locate him. And if you do—'

'I told you, you make it sound so cold-blooded.'

'I'm sorry. Maybe I've got it wrong. Let me ask you a question. What if you never find Roy? Or what if you find him and he's married to somebody else? Then what? Are you saying that if you can't have Roy you'll be happy to stay with Fred?'

'I don't know,' Chrissy said. 'Is there something terrible about that?'

Grace sighed. 'I guess it depends on how you look at it.'

'That's what I'm trying to figure out. How do *you* look at it?'

'I don't *want* to look at it. I think it's terrible. You're trying to have it both ways and that never works. If you're not careful, you'll put yourself in a spot where nothing will be good enough. *Nobody* will be right for you. And after that comes a kind of desperation and self-hatred that *nobody* can handle.'

The conversation with her mother had a penetrating effect on Christine. She decided that Grace was right. Whatever her feelings, she could not lie beside her husband every night and dream of some way that would enable her to take up again the life she had led with Roy.

She solved the problem by promising herself that she would make no further efforts to locate him. She made no pledges, however, about what she would do if he showed up on her doorstep, or if she found out by chance where he was. She told herself it was unlikely that either of those two things could happen. But she didn't believe it. She never questioned that somehow she would see Roy again.

Chapter 5

*L*iving alone, away from Christine, first in a lumber camp north of Rocky Mountain House, then in a boarding house in Grande Prairie, Roy came to believe that he had been an interim lover, that the connection between Christine and Fred had never been broken, not really, that both in spirit and in fact they had continued together through the time that she was with Roy. He didn't examine her motives. It served his purpose to draw the conclusions that he drew, it fuelled his resentment and triggered his anger.

It all worked for him. And nothing worked. Through the end of that year and on into the next, as he put in long hours at back-breaking jobs in the forests and in the Grande Prairie oil fields, as he drank and fought and whored, all through that long and lonely time he told himself that he was a fortunate man; he was well out of it.

All this provided a perfect mind-set for his purposes. It

walled him in totally, kept out everyone, friends and strangers. And most important, of course, it kept out Christine. Or so he told himself.

But the memory and the senses were not so easily fooled. They could not be so neatly manipulated. However he defined Christine in his thoughts, his fingertips disagreed. No matter how tightly he controlled his mind, his skin remembered. The sweet nights and soft afternoons they had spent together, the moments, the words, the details, refused to be erased. No fresh assessment of her character, no new pinned-on label could change or destroy what had already been. Everything female, whether on a poster, on a television screen, or on a real naked woman in a real bed, became an inperfect version of Christine's femaleness, he had memorised her and the memories refused to go away. He could condemn her or denigrate her in his mind, but he could not forget her.

Having no sure grasp of tomorrow and eager to forget as much as he could of yesterday, Roy concentrated on present pleasures. Instant gratification. When he wasn't working, pulling as much overtime pay as he could manage, steadily accumulating money in his bank account, when he was not thus occupied, he played cards, drank with his work friends, went to the movies, and slept with any female under forty who could be persuaded to come to his place or take him to hers or stretch out on the grass in the summer.

None of these women—some of whom he saw only once, others who became friends—ever imagined there was any future with Roy Lavidge. But as one brown-haired, slightly overweight waitress, Lois Tucker, put it, 'If you want to have a lot of laughs, get bombed, and bounce around in bed with a sweet, clean guy who loves to screw, you'd have to go a long way to find anybody nicer than Roy. He's a sweetheart.'

Avoiding newspapers and all the current information programmes on television, Roy survived handsomely through those months. Not realising that an earthquake had rocked Guatemala, that Patricia Hearst had been convicted, that the British had decided to drop all pretence and openly rule

Northern Ireland. He didn't know that a mysterious fever had killed twenty-eight conventioneers in Philadelphia or that North and South Vietnam, after all the bloodshed, had consolidated again as one nation. The Chowchilla children escape from a buried bus, a number of West Point cadets were discovered cheating, and the state of New York ruled that Richard Nixon could not practise law there, all without Roy Lavidge's knowledge. He knew, of course, in November that an odd and unlikely man named Carter had been elected President, but it did not in any way interest him or concern him.

He thought often of his aunt and uncle in Portland, wished he could see them or be in contact with them. But he always stopped short of writing or calling. He suspected their feelings had not changed, that they would not welcome hearing from him.

He didn't write to his father either. But for different reasons. More complex. He had long since ceased to hold T.J. responsible for things that had happened years ago. He thought of him as a man he had spent an evening with, someone he had liked, someone he still liked. He did not feel fatherless in the same way he felt motherless. Because of that one evening, T.J. was specific and real in Roy's head.

He began to think of going to El Centro and spending some time there, thought of finding a university close by, in San Diego perhaps.

So at last he did write, middle of November, a raunchy, picaresque letter that explained nothing about his silence, that dwelt almost exlusively on the humorous side of his work and the carousing, unhinged other life that existed in Grande Prairie.

At the close of the letter, however, he went straight for a few lines and told as much of the truth as he was capable of telling about Christine and himself.

You probably guessed that things didn't work out between me and Christine, the girl I was with at Foresby and who came up here to Canada with me. I mean things just didn't *last*. She married a guy who's as rich and beautiful as she is.

So I'm a solo flyer now, working hard, saving money, and trying to decide what I want to do with myself for the rest of my life.

Did you know that Abe and Annie took their kids and went to Ireland? I haven't heard from them because they don't know where I am, and they haven't heard from me because I'm an indolent arsehole. But ... I plan to correct that one of these days.

Roy did begin a letter to the Singletons not long after he wrote to his father. But before he finished it, he had a reply, special delivery, from T.J.

Crazy timing. I was about to call the Canadian Mounties to try and get a line on you. I wrote you a time or two almost a year ago, but the letters came back.

When I did hear from you finally, after I'd almost given up, your letters came *one day* after a letter I got from New Zealand. News about Abe and Annie from a lady I used to know who's a friend of Annie's aunt in Nelson.

You're not gonna like this any more than I did. But as soon as I read that letter I knew you had to be told.

Abe's dead, Roy. And both his kids with him. It happened a few weeks ago, something about a car accident, but my friend was fuzzy about the details. There may have been some shooting involved before the car crashed, she said. Annie wasn't along, but ever since it happened she's been in the hospital. Half crazy, I guess. I hope she has friends in Ireland who'll look after her.

Chapter 6

*L*ess than forty-eight hours after the letter arrived from his father telling of Abe Singleton's death, Roy had left Grande Prairie, had left Canada entirely, and was on his way to Ireland.

The man he worked for, the woman from whom he rented a room, and the people at his bank, all accepted without question his explanation for leaving Grande Prairie. Only Lois Tucker, as she drove him to the airport in her red Datsun truck, demanded more details.

'Ireland?' she said. 'That's a long way to go for a funeral.'

'It's not a funeral. The man's been dead for a while, the way I understand it.'

When she gave him a questioning look, he said, 'They didn't know where I was. They couldn't get in touch with me.'

'Are they your relatives or something?'

'No. They're people I worked with down in Banff. I lived with them for several years.'

'I don't know,' she said then. 'If the man's dead and his kids are dead and the funeral's over and everything's settled down, I don't know what you can do.'

'I don't know either. I just know Annie's in bad shape and I don't like the idea of her being by herself.'

'Annie's the wife—right?'

'That's right.'

'I just don't see what you can do for her. When a woman's just lost her husband and two children . . .'

'I know that. Maybe I can't do anything.'

'How old is she?'

'Annie? I don't know. Thirty-six or thirty-seven, I guess. Maybe a little older.'

'Older than you, though.'

Roy grinned. 'Everybody's older than me. I'm a baby. Twenty-seven years old and never been kissed.'

'Is she pretty?'

'Pretty? I don't think so. She's a great-looking woman but I wouldn't call her pretty.'

'Is she prettier than me?'

'Nobody's prettier than you, Lois.'

'Don't give me that. I'm fat and I know it. Is she fat?'

'No. She's not fat but she's big. She's twice your size. She's as tall as I am.'

'No kidding.' Then, 'But some guys like horsey women. You sure you don't have a little crush on her?'

'Is that what you've been driving at?'

'When a guy drops everything and flies halfway around the world, gives up his job and sells his car, there has to be some reason besides paying your respects to the dead.'

Roy shook his head. 'Abe was the one who was my friend. I don't even know Annie very well.'

Lois looked at him. 'What if I get killed on the highway next week? Will you come back to Grande Prairie and bury *me*?'

'On the first plane, Lois. Like a shot.'

Roy's flight from Montreal arrived in Shannon at seven thirty in the morning. While he waited for the travellers' information desk to open up, and the car rental offices, he had breakfast in the airport cafeteria. Later he talked to a brisk young man at the travel desk about the problems of getting to Malin.

'Is it a short visit you're planning or a long one?' the young man asked.

'I don't know for sure. At least two or three weeks, maybe longer.'

'Well, here's the situation. We're in the low season now and we will be for several months. We can't provide the same services we do in the smmer. And especially where you're going, far north in Donegal. This time of year some of those villages in the mountains get bus service only once a week.'

They decided at last that Roy's best bet was to take a bus from Shannon to Sligo, spend the night there, and on the following morning take a bus to Letterkenny. 'It's only forty miles or so from there to Malin. You can rent a car in

Letterkenny, the rates will be lower than here, and you won't have so far to go to return it.'

He arrived in Letterkenny the following afternoon, later than planned, because of a three-hour layover in Raphoe. He booked a room at Gallagher's Hotel, then walked down the street and rented an English Ford for a week. On a highway map he checked the twisting road, heading unevenly north through towns like Speenoge, Burnfoot, Buncrana, and Drumfree, arriving at last, by way of Carndonagh, at Malin, looking west across Trawbreaga Bay.

That night, lying sleepless in his dark room, voices floating up from the public house downstairs and cars screeching past on the main street in front of the hotel, Roy began to doubt himself. Everything Lois Tucker had said or implied seemed sensible to him now. Why *was* he here? What *could* he possibly do? Surely Abe had had many friends in Ireland who could be truly supportive of Annie. Wouldn't she look at him with bewilderment? Wouldn't she think a carefully thought out letter would have been preferable? To appear suddenly, as casually as a neighbour strolling over from next door, wasn't that theatrical and nervous making and out of tune?

He decided it was. He lay there feeling juvenile and inept, wishing he had not left Grande Prairie.

In the morning he felt better. He concentrated on the details of the day and attempted no conclusions. After shaving, taking a shower, and carefully packing the cowhide satchel he'd bought at the Edmonton airport, he went downstairs for a breakfast of porridge and tea, sausage and eggs, and Irish bacon. Then he paid his bill at the desk, found his rented car where he'd left it at the curb around the corner, and drove east out of town.

In Malin, far to the north, not far in miles, but seeming far because of the narrow, twisting, cut-back roads, Roy had no trouble finding the Singletons' inn. It was at the east edge of town, what there was of the town, and it was closed.

On the front door of the residence three funeral wreaths hung still, the flowers long since withered and dead, the ribbons discoloured and frayed by the weather. Roy got out,

285

walked around the buildings, and rapped on each of the outside doors. No one answered. At the entrance to the pub, a small card behind glass announced that Abe Singleton was the proprietor in residence. Just at the edge of that sign someone had tucked a printed card that read *Rest in Peace*. On the door beside it a sign said *Closed Till Further Notice*.

Roy went back to his car, walked around it, then leaned against the fender, staring at the building, uncertain about his next move. As he stood there a tiny, very old woman approached, heading toward the village, a bundled-up child holding on to her hand, a mid-sized black dog, burrs in its coat, trailing behind.

Smiling at the woman as she came to a spot opposite his car, Roy said, 'Excuse me. I'm looking for the people who operate this place. Would you be kind enough . . .'

The woman didn't break step, speak, or look in his direction. Neither did the child. They moved on past him, eyes straight ahead. Even the dog, snarling softly and baring his teeth, made no eye contact. He stayed at heel behind the old woman, his tail between his legs, and slunk past.

At a whitewashed cottage two hundred yards down the road, Roy heard voices inside as he came to the front door, and a radio playing softly. As soon as he knocked, however, the voices stopped and the radio switched off. As he stepped back from the door, he saw a lace curtain flutter and fall into place. He knocked again, several times, but the house was dead silent now and no one answered.

In the village he had no more luck. People either didn't answer him at all or they pretended total ignorance of a family named Singleton. At last Roy got into his car and drove back and forth on the narrow roads around Malin. Each time he saw a church with a graveyard alongside, he got out of his car and walked among the burial plots. At last, the third time he stopped, he found what he was looking for. A fresh grave without a marker, and a smaller grave on either side of it.

He found the priest, Father Malachy, in his cottage behind the church. When he came to the door, Roy said, 'I've come to pay my respects to the Singleton family. And I'd like to make a proper donation to your church.'

When they were sitting in Father Malachy's parlour, Roy said, 'I had trouble finding their graves. The people I questioned in the village wouldn't give me any answers at all.'

Father Malachy smiled, broke an oatmeal cookie in two, and dipped it in his tea. 'These aren't sociable people in my parish. They've always kept to themselves. The way they see it, if you're not one of them, heaven knows who you are. Even a man from Sligo or Galway gets short shrift here in the wintertime.'

'And in the summer?'

'Ahh . . . in the summer it's a question of commerce. Only commerce. In America I think they say money talks.'

'That's right. Louder all the time.'

Father Malachy smiled. 'The same here. But only in the summer. In winter we live in the style of our grandfathers.'

When he got up to leave, Roy asked the priest for an envelope. He put some folded bills inside it and sealed it. Standing in the doorway then, still holding the envelope, he said, 'Mrs Singleton's relatives in New Zealand wrote and gave me the address where she's staying. But I'm afraid I've misplaced it.'

Father Malachy sensed that he was being manipulated, didn't like it, but made the only choice that seemed reasonable. 'She's down in Buncrana . . .' When he paused, Roy held out the envelope and the priest took it. 'She's at St Boniface Hospital.'

Little more than an hour later, in the convent building adjoining the hospital, a tall, very thin nun with clear, pink skin came into the room where Roy was waiting. 'I'm Sister Josephine.'

They sat on straight chairs, facing each other across a plain square table. 'You've come all the way from America.'

'From Canada, actually.'

'Are you a close relative, may I ask?'

'I'm not a relative at all. I'm a friend. I lived with the Singletons for several years, up until a year or so ago.'

'I'm sure she'll be delighted to see you. We've been hoping someone would come.'

'No one's been to see her?'

'Of course. I didn't mean to imply . . . Father Malachy's been here. And two of the women from Malin drove down. People *have* tried to see her and comfort her. The problem is that she *refuses* to see anyone.'

'How long has she been here?'

'Since the day after the accident. She refused to attend the funeral mass or to go to the interment. She never saw her husband's body, or either of the children, after the accident.'

'How is she now? I mean is she being treated for some . . .'

'Physically there's nothing wrong with her. Her condition is self-willed, we think. She is not catatonic, but she's behaving as if she were.'

'She won't talk at all?'

'Let me put it this way. She will not have a conversation. She follows instructions, eats proper meals, and keeps herself clean. And she will communicate in any way that's necessary to help us or to make her wishes known. But beyond that she will not talk at all.'

'Does she read or something? What does she do?'

'She does nothing. She sits in her little room in a chair, like the ones we're sitting on now, and looks out the window. Every moment she's awake, she sits there looking out through the glass at the hills across Lough Swilly.'

Chapter 7

*T*he following morning, when Roy went to the hospital again Sister Josephine said, 'I told her you had come all the way from Canada.'

'What did she say?'

'She didn't say anything.'

When they came into Annie's room, she was sitting in a chair by the window, her thick hair pulled back in a loose knot, her face pale and scrubbed.

'Here's Mr Lavidge,' Sister Josephine said. 'I told you last evening he'd be coming to see you today.'

There was no reaction from Annie. Her expression didn't change and her eyes didn't turn toward them. She continued staring out the window. After a long pause, Sister Josephine said, 'Won't you say something to him, Mrs Singleton? He's come such a long way. He wants to help you if he can.' Still no response. When the nun turned back to Roy, a questioning look in her eyes, he said, 'It's all right. I'll just sit with her for a while.'

He sat there in the room for more than an hour, his chair against the wall, out of Annie's line of vision. He was as silent as she was, his legs crossed, his arms folded. Finally, at eleven in the morning, he got up went to the door, and opened it. He turned in the doorway and said, 'I'm leaving now, Annie. I'll be back this afternoon.'

Back at the inn he telephoned Father Malachy and told him what he planned to do. Father Malachy gave him the names of several people he should contact, and Roy spent the next hour on the telephone. That afternoon, from two thirty to four, he sat again in Annie's room. She didn't speak and neither did he.

For the next five days he drove back and fourth twice a day between Buncrana and Malin. For an hour or two each morning and each afternoon he sat in Annie's room. 'Has she said anything to you?' Sister Josephine asked him.

'Not yet. But she will.'

On the sixth day, in the afternoon, a soft steady rain falling outside, Roy said, 'I won't be coming here to see you for a while, Annie. I thought it would be good for you to talk with somebody you know. But I see I was wrong. It looks as if you want to be left alone, so that's what I'm going to do.

'I plan to stay here for a while. I'm going to open the inn. I got the keys from Mr Gogarty, and I've found a woman who'll cook and clean. And a girl to make the beds and help out in the kitchen. Everything else I'll do myself. So I won't have much time to drive down here to Buncrana. I'll keep in touch with Sister Josephine, though. If there's anything you need, tell her and she can get in touch with me.'

For more than a month he didn't see her or talk with her. But every day he called Sister Josephine. When she spoke to Annie, the sister always mentioned that Roy had called. 'He says he'll be down to visit you as soon as he's able, but according to Father Malachy that may not be soon. He said Mr Lavidge is working himself like a machine. He's put a new name to the place, the Malin Post Inn he calls it, and he's had handbills printed up and sent out all over Donegal and over into Tyrone and Derry counties, offering special rates and music two nights a week. And the locals like him, Father Malachy says, so he's starting to pour a lot of Guinness every day.'

Another month went past with only one visit by Roy to Annie's room. It was as silent as the rest. But this time she looked at him, a slow, searching look as he came into the room and took his seat on the straight-backed chair against the wall.

At the close of that month, more than two months now since he'd come to Ireland, he came to see her once again. Again she looked at him as he came into the room, a longer look this time before she turned away. As he talked, she put her hand up to the side of her face, fingertips touching her temple, shielding her eyes from him.

'I'm going back to the States, Annie. The government has pardoned everybody who resisted the draft. So it looks like I can go back to school and try to take up where I left off.'

He paused but she didn't answer. At last he went on. 'This wasn't what I had in mind when I came over here. I thought maybe I'd stay in Ireland. I figured I could be of some help to you running your place over here and that it might not be a bad life.

'A couple months ago I was all excited about bringing the

inn back to life, sprucing it up, making it pay. And I've made some progress. You know you're doing something right when you start to see the same faces every day, when there are two or three regulars waiting outside when you open up in the morning. And when people drive up on a weekend from Gleneely and Carndonagh and from as far as Greencastle. I've even been renting the rooms on weekends, mostly to people from the Six Counties.

'So he possibilities are there. I can see it. I mean some money's coming in and I order twice as much beer as I did six weeks ago. But I can see it's something you don't care about now. So I asked myself the other day, "Why should it mean anything to me?" That's when I decided to pack it in and head back to the States.'

She spoke then, for the first time since he'd first come to see her. She turned from the window, looked at him, and said, 'When are you going?'

'As soon as I can sit down with Gogarty and work things out. He's down in Cork for a few days, but when he's back, when he gets somebody to take over, I'll be off. Ten days maybe. Two weeks at the longest.'

Three days later, as Roy was working in the barroom of the inn preparing for morning opening, a car pulled up in front, a woman in nun's habit behind the wheel. Roy walked to the leaded window and watched as Annie got out of the car carrying a small satchel. She looked after the car as it drove away, then she turned and walked to the outside door of the manager's residence just beside the tavern. Roy heard the door open and close, heard her footstep as she climbed the stairs. He went back to his work behind the bar, then listend to her moving from room to room upstairs, and waited. After a long, silent time, no movement at all on the second floor, he heard her come down the back stairway into the kitchen. The connecting door opened and she stepped into the bar. When she saw him in the dim light, she said, 'All of Abe's things are gone. I looked in the children's room and all their clothes and toys are gone, too.'

'I put everything in boxes. Stored it all away. I thought it might make things easier for you when you first came home.'

'I thought you didn't expect me to leave St. Boniface.'

'I didn't. Not for a long time. But I didn't think you'd stay there forever.'

Chapter 8

*I*n Russell's files of research and notes, I found this short sketch about Annie's family.

Her grandfather, Boris Kazin, was a watchmaker in Vyborg, in the west of Russia. After the October revolution in 1917, he escaped to Finland with his wife, Sonja, and their two sons. By 1920 they had settled in Germany, in Karlsruhe, and the following year, a daughter, Olga, was born. In 1935, sensing what was to come in Germany, hearing the slogans chanted in the street, seeing them painted on walls, the Kazins moved to France, to Dijon, where Sonja Kazin's cousin was a rabbi. When the Germans invaded France and occupied Paris, the Kazin family was sent back to Germany, the two boys and both parents. The daughter, for reasons that no one understood, was ordered to stay behind in Dijon.

When she was seventeen, wild and restless and desperate for some news of her family, Olga went to Paris, tried to find friends who might know something about her parents; but she found no one. She made friends then with people her own age who were fighting with the underground, and a few months later she was in Marseilles, trained in firearms and explosives, living a gypsy life, shifting from one dark, abandoned apartment to the next, and inflicting as much damage as possible on German troops and German shipping.

Jesse Granger was a New Zealand seaman, serving on a freighter that carried the Swedish flag. Operating in conjunction with the International Red Cross, his ship came and went at Marseilles, carrying food and medicine. Jesse was a genial red-haired man, ten years older than Olga. There is no history of their relationship. No diary and no snapshots. Nor is there any record of how, exactly, he contrived to have her travel from Marseilles to Auckland in March 1940. But she did make that trip, arriving in Greymouth, on the South Island of New Zealand, in April. Two months later, on June twelfth, she gave birth to a daughter with auburn hair like her father's. She named her Annie.

Six months later Olga had gone back to the war, this time as a military nurse with the Anzac forces. Annie stayed beyond in Greymouth with her father's sister, Ruth Granger.

'I'm one up on you,' Annie told Roy. 'I never saw either one of my parents. My mother was killed in an air raid in North Africa, and my father's ship was torpedoed between Lisbon and the Azores. As far as I know they never saw each other after I was born.'

'Who raised you?'

'My aunt Ruth and my father's parents. The whole family were publicans and innkeepers. They'd had a place called Granger's, a small hotel in Greymouth, for seventy years. it was on Richmond Quay, just beside the Grey River. I lived there and worked with the family till I was fifteen. Then Grandpa Granger's sister, Thelma, died. So Ruth and I went up to Nelson to take over the little bed-and-breakfast place that Thelma had owned for years. I stayed in Nelson till I met Abe. As soon as we got married, we left Nelson, and I've never been back.'

'Abe said you wanted to go there instead of coming here to Donegal.'

'I did. Ruth's old and sick and she can't handle the place anymore. She wanted us to take it over. But Abe had other ideas. So we came here instead.'

The winter had ended and they were well into the soft, wet spring before Roy learned exactly what had taken place that ugly November night when Abe and the two children died in his burning car at an army roadblock south of Culmore on the highway leading into north Derry.

When she finally told Roy what had happened, it was as though she had managed to remove all the jagged corners from the story, as if she had worked her way past those images of blood and shattered bones and splintered glass that had tortured her through the weeks she spent at St Boniface. Rather than *telling* it, she seemed to recite it, as though it had been painfully memorised, then repeated internally till all the pain was squeezed out.

'You knew Abe,' she said. 'I don't have to tell you what he was like. You saw him drink. You saw him sit up the way he did, sometimes for the whole night, black and silent because of all kinds of things he couldn't explain, even to himself. As I remember, he took you along on a few of his maniac drives through the mountains at three in the morning.'

'He scared hell out of me,' Roy said. 'I never understood what that was all about.'

'Neither did I. And neither did he. Everyone just thought it was part of his general craziness and they looked the other way. That was Abe's talent. he could make people look the other way. They forgave him anything because of all that high energy. He could make people laugh, even people who didn't know what to make of him, and he could always function. Abe never copped out. If he hadn't slept for three nights and had drunk enough for six men, he could always crank it up and get the job done when the time came. Never sick. Never tired or hung over. Never giving anybody a reason to feel sorry for him. So nobody ever did. Me especially. Now I feel different. Now I feel so sorry for him it makes me tremble. But when he was alive everything was so *definite*. He had such conviction and so much authority. He made people feel he must be right no matter what. At least that's how I reacted. After we got married, when I saw that things weren't the way I'd expected them to be, even then I never blamed Abe. Not really. I always figured that I'd fooled *myself,* so I had no one to blame but me. But all that was before, before we left Canada and came here to Ireland. After that things changed. Very fast. Before, he'd been a big loud guy with a good heart and some bad habits. But once we got here, once we settled in, he started to come apart. It was scary to watch him. I don't know yet if he drank like a fool to keep his hands from shaking or if his hands shook because he drank so much. All I know is that he had a glass in his hand from morning to night. And almost every night he was out on the roads, in his car, like a crazy man. Up to Malin Head and back, across to Culdaff Bay, more often than not shooting at trees with his revolver as he raced along.'

'When did that start? The gun stuff?'

'In the cradle, I think. I never knew Abe to be without a gun. Usually he had two stuck away in our closet. A revolver and an automatic. He had them in Canada too. But the police in Banff threatened to take them away from him if he didn't behave himself. So the guns stayed locked away when we were at the St Albert.'

That last night, she said, had not been appreciably different from any other night. 'We were sitting in the snug after closing, the two of us, just as you and I are doing now. Abe had been drinking whiskey and lager all evening, but he switched to brandy after we closed. I remember thinking, as I sat there, across the table from him, what a phenomenal constitution he must have. There was just no measuring the amount he was able to drink and still function. Sometimes when I would expect him to fall down unconscious, he would rattle on half the night about Irish history and Irish literature, quoting from Yeats and Synge and Joyce. Not drunk talk. Beautiful, clear speech flowing out of him, up out of that great ocean of whiskey he was carrying inside himself.

'He talked about generals and military leaders, most of

295

them people I'd never heard of, giving me details of their strategies and campaigns. And the Bible too. He would quote long passages from the Old Testament when the notion hit him.

'But that last night he was strangely quiet. The British had just announced they were taking over direct rule of Ulster. I thought he'd be all fired up by that because he'd been dead set against the cease-fire. But he shrugged it off and said, "They've got the edge on us, Annie. They always did and they always will have. When Victor is my age, the fight will still be going on."

'That's all he would say about it. Mostly he sat there talking about the children, about things they'd said or done when they were little. We sat there till two in the morning, with one yellow bulb burning in the snug, just talking about the kids. It had been a long time since we'd had a talk like that, a long time indeed, and I should have been smart enough to see that it meant something, that there was something churning inside his head. But it all went past me till it was too late. When I went upstairs, I felt good about things.

'As I was getting ready for bed, I heard Abe come up the stairs. Then I heard him open the door to the kids' room down the hall. He often did that, looked in on them before he came to bed. So I thought nothing of it. After I was in bed in my nightgown, when I heard him go downstairs again, that didn't surprise me either. I knew that meant he was off on one of his wild drives. But when I heard his engine start, for some reason I got up and looked out the window. As his car rolled out onto the tarmac it looked to me as if someone was in the front seat with him. I ran down the hall then to the children's bedroom. Both their beds were empty.

'I threw a coat on over my robe, went outside, and started our little truck. I had some notion that I could catch him. But it was futile, of course. By the time I was out on the road he had more than a five-minute lead on me; there are four roads leading out of Malin, and I had no way of knowing which one he'd taken. So I turned north on the road to Lag and drove almost all the way to Malin Head, scared to death and crying like a baby. I turned around then and wound my way back toward Malin on those pitch-black narrow roads. When I finally got home it was past four in the morning and the constable was waiting for me. He told me what had happened. Abe had driven across to Moville on Lough Foyle, then straight down the lake road to the border. Instead of stopping at the frontier post south of Muff, he'd speeded up, crashed through the barrier, fired his pistol towards the sentry station, and kept going toward Derry. But five miles down the road there was a British army roadblock and they were waiting for him. As soon as he fired one shot out the car window, they answered with automatic weapons. The car went through the barrier, slammed into a petrol lorry that was parked on the far side, and caught fire.'

In his written report to headquarters, the British lieutenant in command on the scene concluded with this comment:

THE BURNING CAR IGNITED THE TANKS OF PETROL AND THREE EXPLOSIONS RESULTED, PRODUCING A BALL OF FIRE THAT BURNED THE TREES AND FIELDS FOR FIFTY METRES ROUND AND FORCED US TO WITHDRAW ALL MILITARY VEHICLES AND PERSONNEL TO A SAFE DISTANCE.'

Chapter 9

*B*it by bit, as the months passed, Annie peeled away the layers of her relationship with Abe. Tortured by the loss of her children, finding herself able to deal with that pain only by burying it deeper and deeper inside herself, she reversed the process where Abe was concerned. She forced herself to see him clearly at last, to acknowledge both his qualities and his shortcomings with an honesty she had never allowed herself during their marriage.

'Abe had a fetish about fidelity,' she told Roy. 'He thought love and fidelity were synonymous. He used to stand behind the bar in Wellington or Christchurch and lecture on the subject. Not in a boring way. Abe always managed to get a few laughs no matter what he was talking about. He used to say a *real* man is a man who is content with one woman. "Show me a Casanova," he used to say, "and I'll show you a man who doesn't trust his own peter." I'm sure he said it to you—he said it to everybody else who would listen, that he never looked at another woman from the first day he set eyes on me. Did he ever tell you that?'

'Fifty times at least.'

'Did you believe him?'

'Sure why not? He couldn't buy a pack of cigarettes without telling the counter girl what a terrific wife he had.'

Annie smiled. 'He was really good. He fooled you just like he fooled everybody else.'

'What do you mean?'

'I mean we were married seventeen years, and in all that time I don't think a week went by that he didn't sleep with somebody besides me. But he fooled me just like he fooled you. At least he did for a while. I watched all the women cuddling up to him in whatever bar he was working in, and I thought, "Everybody's sweet on Abe but he's only sweet on me." By the time I realized I'd been kidding myself, we had Victor. And Stephanie was on the way. So I did what a lot of women do. I decided my kids were more important than my pride.'

'Did you ever talk about it?'

Annie shook her head. 'If we had, we'd have split up right then and there. You see, Abe really meant everything he said about monogamy and fidelity. That was the most important fact about him. He never could get *ideas* and *behaviour* straightened out in his head. I think he really believed that if he *thought* the right things and *said* the right things, then it didn't really matter so much if he didn't practise what he preached. That's why we could never talk about it. Because Abe survived on the lies he told himself. Not *lies* maybe. Maybe that's too strong. But his *conception* of himself was the only reality he knew. It was important to him. It was *all-*important. So if I'd shot him down, if I'd said, "You're a two-faced bastard. You tell everybody who'll listen how much you love me, and an hour later you're in bed with some little bird who works at a car-rental desk," that would have ended everything. In the first place it would have killed him to realize that I knew what he was up to, but most of all it would have saddled him with something he couldn't face about himself. Does that make sense?'

'Not very much.'

'Of course it doesn't. But that kind of self-deception was the centre of Abe's life. He was stuck with it. He had to believe he was something he wasn't. And when he couldn't believe it any longer . . . I don't know . . . I've thought about it so much it's all crosses and circles in my head. I guess it was the same way in his.'

'I thought he was a terrific father. That wasn't fake, was it?'

She shook her head. 'Not at all. He didn't have to pretend anything there. All his other values were out of whack, but not where Victor and Stephanie were concerned.'

'Why do you think he took them with him that night?'

'I've never found the answer to that. I know how it looked to everybody else. One big heroic gesture, him against the British army. But I've never believed that. As crazy as he got sometimes, I don't think he would have taken a chance like that with the kids. All I've ever been able to figure was that he wanted to do something big and flashy for them to see. If the rest of the Provisionals thought he was reckless and out of date, at least his kids would see that he was the kind of man he pretended to be.'

'But, Jesus, he must have known—'

'I don't think so. I think he thought the breakthrough at the frontier post would be easy. And it was. What he didn't count

299

on was the army roadblock so close, only five miles past the frontier. I think he planned to swing west again before he got to Derry and go back across the border at Bridgend. It's not far. He could have been back in Donegal in less than half an hour.'

Roy shook his head. 'You don't really believe that's what he was thinking, do you?'

'Part of me believes it,' she said, 'and *all* of me *wants* to believe it. There's no way I can make it easy for myself. At least this makes it a little bit easier.'

Chapter 10

The first time they lay beside each other in bed, over a year after Roy had come to Malin, Annie said, 'Did you know this was going to happen?'

'No. Did you?'

'God, no,' she said. 'It's like incest. It *is*. I mean it. I've always thought of you as ... I don't know ... like a brother maybe. A nice younger brother.'

'Terrific. And I've always thought of you as my mommy.'

'I'm sure there's a way I can make you pay for that, but I'm not sure yet what it is.'

'You brought up incest. I didn't.'

There was indeed a perfume of incest about it. Because they had become easy and familiar with each other in ways that only families know. They slept in separate rooms on opposite sides of the hall, but they shared the same bathroom, the only bathroom in the manager's residence. Annie made

Roy's bed, cleaned his room, and washed his laundry. Mended his socks and ironed his shirts. She had always cut Abe's hair and the children's hair. Now she cut Roy's hair. They ate together as often as their work would permit, did the accounts together, and took walks together.

They also took care of each other when they were sick, a matter of necessity, since apart from their bed-and-breakfast guests of any particular night, Roy and Annie were the only people in residence at the Malin Post Inn.

They were sick infrequently. Annie had occasional sinus headaches, which were relieved when Roy massaged her neck. When she strained her shoulder by lifting something heavy in the kitchen, he rubbed liniment into the sore muscles. They ministered to each other when they had colds or the flu, bandaged each other's cuts and abrasions, and when she had a bad spell of cramps, Roy brought hot-water bottles to her bed.

But neither of them was seriously ill until Roy had been in Malin for more than a year. He got soaked through one day helping a drayman unload his truck in a cold rain. When a chest cold developed, he refused to go to bed. Two days later he had a hard cough and was running a fever. By the time a doctor came up from Buncrana, Roy had pneumonia.

Annie closed the bar and the kitchen and spent her full time nursing him. She gave him injections morning and night, administered his prescribed oral antibiotics, spooned out his turpin-hydrate-and-codeine cough mixture four times daily, and sponged him with cool water and alcohol to keep his fever under control. But four days and nights passed, his temperature going as high as a hundred and five on two occasions, before he began to sweat and cool down. He was in bed for fifteen days before the doctor allowed him to get up and go back to work.

When he was fully recovered, gaining back some of the weight he'd lost, he knocked on Annie's bedroom door one night. After they'd closed the bar, she'd gone upstairs, and he'd stayed below to restock for the next morning's trade.

When she answered his knock, he opened the door. She

was sitting up in bed with a book, her bed lamp glowing beside her.

'You weren't asleep, were you?'

'Not at all. Is everything all right downstairs?'

'Locked up tight.' He walked over and stood beside her bed. 'When I was sick .. I mean did I thank you enough for taking such good care of me? If I didn't, I want you to know how much I appreciate it.'

She smiled. 'I drew up a long list of my fees and expenses this morning. As soon as I total it, I'll turn it over to you. I expect prompt payment. In cash.'

'I was probably a lousy patient. I've never been sick like that before.'

'You were a wreck. Between the medicine and the fever, you didn't know where you were half the time.'

They looked at each other for a long moment without speaking. Then slowly she reached out and her fingers curled around his hand. 'I was worried about you. You were so weak. I was afraid . . .' She ran out of words and looked away from him.

He sank down on the edge of the bed, and put his arms around her. He saw tears in her eyes before she buried her face against his chest. They sat there clinging to each other for a long time. Finally she looked up at him and said, 'You'd better get out of here.'

'I don't want to.'

'You'd better.'

He pulled her to him and kissed her. Looking at her face, then, in the soft light, her dark lashes thick and wet, he kissed her again.

'What are we doing?' she said.

'Don't ask me. I don't know.'

She brought her hand up and cupped his cheek. 'Don't you care?'

'No, I *don't* care. I don't give a damn about anything.'

'Neither do I.'

Chapter 11

On their fourth wedding anniversary, Christine and Fred gave each other a handsome gift. They bought a house on the Pacific Coast just south of Santa Barbara, a sprawling walled estate, more than two hundred years old. It had been built by the Cabrillos and had stayed in their family through succeeding generations until Esteban Cabrillo died, a childless widower, and his surviving niece decided that two million dollars added to her trust fund was more attractive than a house, a pool, stables, and gardens that cost, annually, one hundred and twenty thousand dollars to maintain.

As soon as she and Fred took title, Christine wrote to Russell.

> An army of workers is putting our hacienda in shape for your inspection. I will expect you at the beginning of the second week in March, one month after your birthday. Will you be fifty or fifty-one or what? No matter. Since I am thirty this year, all ages will be frozen from now on.

The day Russell arrived Christine produced, that evening, a dinner party for forty. A string quartet played Schumann and Handel during dinner, and a Mexican orchestra played for dancing till two in the morning. Five hours later Fred had to fly to Sacramento for an emergency meeting on building-code legislation, but Russell and Christine slept late. After an eleven-o'clock swim they had a leisurely breakfast in the garden.

'How did you like your party?' she said.

'Very impressive. All kinds of embroidered people. All strangers.'

She laughed. 'Strangers to me too. They're Fred's friends mostly. People he knew when he was married to the legendary Original Mrs Deets.'

303

'Is she legendary?'

'Only in our house. I just joke about her like that. I'm sure she's a perfectly keen young woman. We ran into her once at a vernissage in Palo Alto, and when Fred introduced me to her she blushed. What do you suppose that means? He said he'd never seen her blush all the time he knew her.'

'Didn't you say she lived here in Santa Barbara?'

'*Did* but *doesn't*. Moved north a couple years ago. Napa Valley. Converted barns and home-baked bread. Lots of schmarmy ladies with annuities wearing dirty jeans and no underwear, pretending they're poor and passing herpes along to the Mexican farm workers.'

After breakfast she showed him the rest of the house and the grounds that he hadn't had time to inspect the day before.

'Now I know where Daisy Buchanan moved when she left Long Island.'

'Is there a hidden meaning in there somewhere?'

'I don't think so,' Russell said. 'I was just looking at the horses and the stables and the lawn sloping down toward the sea, and it jogged my memory.'

'But there's no light twinkling on our dock.'

'Good. I'm glad to hear it.' Then, 'I guess an acquisition like this means you've made a permanent move out here.'

She shook her head. 'Not at all. I still expect to be half and half between here and Lake Forest. But when we *are* here, we'll have this nice place to be in. And when Fred's here by himself, it will be easier for me to check up on him. I've bribed all the servants so they'll call me and snitch on him as soon as he walks into the house with some little cream puff he met on somebody's yacht.'

'Bad casting,' Russell said. 'I don't see Fred in that role.'

She smiled. 'Neither do I. But I'm bribing the servants anyway. Just in case.'

'What about Grace? Will she be spending time out here, too?'

'Not a chance. Nothing's changed in that department. I don't think anything *will* change. As a matter of fact she's lost ground. She used to talk to people on the phone, but last year

304

she had the phone taken out of her room. Only two of the servants are allowed to come into her wing of the house. She sees *them*, she sees Margaret once a week, and she sees me. But that's it.'

'She never leaves her room?'

'Almost never. Except to swim. She had an indoor pool put in, just adjacent to her bedroom. She swims there at night, in the dark, when everyone in the house is asleep. She also goes to the greenhouse at night when the gardener isn't there. We had a tunnel built so she can walk there from her bedroom no matter what the weather is like outside. So she goes and sits in the heat among the orchids. But always by herself.'

'It's hard to believe.'

'Of course. It's heartbreaking. But she does her best when she's with me. She tries to pretend that no matter how much everything else has changed, it hasn't changed things between her and me.'

'But it has?'

'Of course. How could it not? She doesn't use herself anymore, so everything has started to function differently. Her smile, her voice, the expressions on her face. Her brain gives the proper signals, but everything is slow to react. The spontaneity is gone. Some old instinct tells her to make a laughing sound so she does. Her mind says smile and her mouth obeys. But by then the moment is gone. It's a thing you see sometimes in old people, when the neural system isn't plugged in just right. But when you're looking at Grace, at that smooth and tender skin that seems not to have changed since I was six years old, when you look at that brand-new, untouched face and you realize that behind it something is happening, or failing to happen, then it's . . I don't know . . it's a feeling I can't describe. It's the greatest pain I can imagine facing in my life. I can't think of anything that would gouge so deep and tear me up inside the way Grace does. It's not her fault. I don't mean that. It would kill her if she heard me saying what I'm saying to you now. I go out of my way to laugh and gossip and act like a fool when I'm with her. I never let her know if something is disturbing me. I just try to *be there* on a regular basis, all clean and shining, playing the healthy daughter role. But every day when I leave her, not every *single* day but close to it, I go to my room, clear on the other side of the house, lie facedown on my bed, and cry myself to sleep. Brilliant, huh? Maybe I'm in worse shape than she is. But however I feel, whatever kind of fix I'm in, I can't change it. I feel as locked into her future as Grace is.'

'What would she say if you told her you have to be out here with Fred? What would she do if you left Lake Forest?'

'She'd lead the cheers. She'd hate it if she thought I was staying in our house just be be near her.'

'Then you're only tied there because . . .'

'Of course,' Christine said. 'Because I *believe* I'm tied there. But *that* is the strongest belief in my life. Nothing overpowers it or supersedes it. I'm not comparing Grace to a flawed baby, to some kind of imperfect child, but whatever that feeling must be, that agonizing set of frustrations and guilts that can't be resolved, *that* must be the closest thing to how *I* feel. That overpowering need to *help* someone, to make their life better, coupled with the iron knowledge that there is absolutely *nothing* you *can* do, *no* way you can make their life better. It's like a weight around your neck that you're desperate to get rid of but you know if you ever do get rid of it, it will kill you.

'I tell myself I'm reasonably well balanced, but as soon as I start to talk about Grace, as soon as I *think* about her, I can't handle it.' She held her hand up. 'You see . . . right now my hand is shaking. Let's talk about something else. Tell me about your son.'

'Married twice. Divorced once. His new wife expects a baby at the end of the summer.'

'You're the sexiest-looking grandfather I've ever seen.'

'That's because it hasn't happened yet. I have a theory that the moment a man get a telegram telling him he has a grandchild, he goes instantly grey at the temples.'

'Not a chance. You're my hero. No bad things will ever happen to you. How long can you stay with us?'

'Two or three days.'

'Come *on*. Stay at least a week. I thought maybe you'd tag

along with us to Chicago next week. We have a new jet now. A pilot and everything. Fred got demoted to co-pilot. Wrecked his ego.'

'He sure looks great, wrecked ego or not.'

'Yeah, he's a pretty man, isn't he? Some people improve with age. Fred's one of them. He's one of the good guys.'

'Can I ask you a personal question?'

'You'd better. If you don't, I'll ask *you* one.'

'I thought you'd have two or three kids by now. I figured you someplace down the line as an eighty-year-old matriarch with a gang of children and grandchildren.'

Christine laughed. 'Me too. That's what *I* thought. But it just hasn't happened. At least it hasn't happened yet. The doctor says maybe I'm too nervous, but I told him I never felt nervous till he said I was. I don't know. I'm fatalistic. I figure if I'm going to have children, I'll have them. If I'm not, I won't. I'm happy and Fred's happy and we'll take what comes.'

Later that afternoon she drove him into downtown Santa Barbara and they walked up and down the shopping streets. After she showed him the Spanish-style city hall and the art museum, they walked back to El Paseo, sat there in the cool patio bar, and ordered margaritas.

'How'm I doing?' she said then. 'Give me a rating.'

'I think you're doing great.'

'Don't try to make me feel good.'

'I'm not. How do *you* think you're doing?'

'I don't know. Sometimes I think I've done the best I could. Other times I'm not so sure. I used to think that once a person was really grown up, once *I* was grown up, I'd be in control of things, that I'd have some feeling of accomplishment, and I wouldn't be bombarded with surprises every day, things I couldn't handle.'

'So . . .'

'So I don't have many surprises in my life. *That* part worked out. But I don't have much feeling of accomplishment either.'

'I wouldn't lose any sleep over it. The main thing is to stay afloat. The only people I know who are genuinely pleased with themselves are people who have never done a damned thing. If you never risk anything, you don't know what failure tastes like. The harder you struggle, the more you aspire to, the more you realize how little you've been able to do.'

'You don't feel that way.'

'The hell I don't. I've had a couple of marriages that petered out. And I sure as hell never learned the trick of being a father. I've written some passable books and made some money, but I never came close to what I was after when I started.'

'You're crazy. I love your books.'

He smiled. 'A lot of people do. But I don't.'

'That's because you're a grouch. Are you working on something now?'

'Not exactly. I'm *wrestling* with something now. The characters won't sit still. They jump around a lot.'

'Like real people.'

'That's it.'

After they ordered their second drink, she said, 'Did you ever hear from Roy? A letter or anything?

Russell shook his head. 'Why would he get in touch with me?'

'I don't know. He liked you. I just thought . . .'

'Did *you* ever hear from him?'

'Not a word. He vanished.'

The waiter come back with their drinks then. As he carefully lifted each frosty glass off the tray and set it on the table, Christine gave her full attention to folding a cocktail napkin into a small triangle. When the waiter left, she looked up again at Russell. 'I'm going to tell you a secret.'

'Never tell a secret to a novelist.'

'I want to,' she said. Then, 'I went through a very bad period right after Fred and I were married. Not because of him. I don't mean that. He was darling to me. He always has been. The problem was I felt so guilty about Roy, about the way I'd handled that whole thing. I decided I had to get in touch with him somehow, to try to explain why I'd done what I'd done. So I wrote him a letter. But I tore it up. Then, finally, I wrote again. And this time I mailed it. By then I'd decided I couldn't give Roy up. I told him that.'

'Any answer?'

She shook her head. 'I'm sure he never got the letter. Because when we got back to Lake Forest, I called the St Albert in Banff, where I'd sent the letter, and the manager told me they had no forwarding address for him. I was all ready to hire investigators to find out where he was hiding. But Grace shamed me out of it.'

'You dropped the whole idea?'

Christine nodded.

'So how do you feel now?'

She laughed. 'I don't know.' She sipped from her drink. 'Suspended animation, I guess. If I ever had a choice, I don't have one now. Too much time has passed. I'm old and wise now. I can recognize a stacked deck when I see one.'

'Does Fred know any of this?'

'We haven't talked about it, if that's what you mean. But Fred's no fool. He knew how things were between me and Roy. But he also knows I love *him*. I've always loved Fred. Since I was fifteen years old. That's not about to go away.'

'But neither is Roy. Is that what you're saying?'

She smiled. 'Anybody who tells you you can't love two people at the same time is either inexperienced or ugly.'

'What if he showed up at your door some afternoon?'

'You mean Roy?'

'That's right,' Russell said.

'He wouldn't.'

'What if he did?'

'I used to ask myself that a lot. But not so much now. Like I said, too much time has passed. If he *did* come to find me, I know I'd be glad to see him. I'd still want to try to explain why I acted the way I did. But I wouldn't run upstairs, pack a bag, and drag him to the nearest motel. That's the fantasy I *used* to have. But it's not operative anymore. I'm like a reformed alcoholic who's been away from booze so long she's stopped missing it.'

Chapter 12

One night Roy told Annie about his drive north from Duluth with Abe, about their stop for dinner at Eveleth. 'He was acting strange as hell that night. He was making jokes about you having a crush on me. What was that all about?'

'What do you think? That was one of Abe's games. There was always some little teasing hint that I was making eyes at somebody. I don't mean we had fights about it. It wasn't a big jealousy thing with him. It was just something he liked to talk about. When we were first married, I couldn't handle it at all. It made me feel creepy and awful. But if I said that to Abe, he just laughed it off. Later, when I knew him better, when I knew about his other women, I decided it was some kind of trick he played on himself so he wouldn't have a bad conscience.'

'Did he say things to you about me?'

'Of course he did. He started as soon as you and Christine came to work for us. He was never quite sure how to deal with either one of you. He had a thing about *you*, especially. He *liked* you. I don't mean he didn't. He liked you a lot. But there was something else there, too. Envy, I guess it was. You're twenty years younger than he was, for one thing. Abe had a real problem dealing with getting older. And besides, you had a scrumptious girl following you around. That certainly caught his attention. He thought you had a secret, I guess, and he wanted in on it. It sounds childish when I describe it like this, and maybe it was. But in your case I think he thought you'd bring him luck or something. He was convinced he was going to persuade you to come to Ireland with us. At first he thought you and Chrissy would come, and then after you two had your problems he was dead sure you'd come by yourself.'

'Yeah, I know. And in a way I felt guilty about not going. I thought I owed him one. If he hadn't helped me out when I was in Chicago that time, when Chrissy was in the hospital, I could have spent a few years in jail.'

'That's exactly what he wanted you to think,' Annie said.

'What do you mean?'

'I mean he engineered that whole operation down there. There weren't any government people after you. That was all Abe and his friends. He directed that whole thing by telephone from the St Albert.'

'Why would he do that? What's the point?'

'That's what I asked him,' Annie said. 'He said he wanted to scare you away from Chicago and back to Canada before the police down there really *did* get a line on you. At least that's what he told me. But I think his real reasons were a lot more complicated than that.'

'How do you mean?'

'I think he wanted to get an edge on you in some way. He wanted you on his side, indebted to him. Did he ever bring it up, later on, that you owed him something?'

Roy shook his head. 'He never mentioned it.'

'That's what I thought. That wasn't Abe's style. But all the same I'm sure he knew that *you* remembered. He thought he'd set the hook.'

Whenever they talked about Abe, Annie spoke of him with warmth and respect, as someone she had loved and lived with and had children with. But there was no hint of an emotional hangover. As confusing as their relationship had sometimes been, as tragic and heartrending as its conclusion had turned out to be, it seemed that she had come to terms with it. Still . . . when Roy came upon her occasionally, looking at pictures of Victor and Stephanie, sitting alone in the bedroom with tears in her eyes, or when he heard her weeping quietly in the night, he always assumed those tears for her children were also for Abe.

When her aunt Ruth died in New Zealand, when the time came for Annie to go there, because she'd promised she would and because she very much wanted to go, she said to Roy, 'It's something I *have* to do. But you're not part of the bargain unless you want to be.'

311

'Good. I've been wondering how I was going to wiggle out of it.'

'Don't make jokes. I'm serious.'

'So am I,' he said.

'It's not the way it sounds. I'm not trying to get rid of you. Nothing like that. I don't know what would have happened to me if you hadn't come here. I've been so happy I feel guilty about it. But all the same . . . you're only thirty years old. You haven't lived in your own country for almost ten years. You might want to go back there. You might want to finish your education.'

'I'm going with you,' he said.

'You might have all kinds of plans about work and whatever else you want to do with your life.'

'I'm going to New Zealand.'

'I mean I've been in hotel work and bed-and-breakfast places my whole life. It's all I know. But you can do all kinds of things. Anything you want to do—'

'Will you please shut up?'

'New Zealand is my home. I love it. I grew up there. But that doesn't mean *you'll* like it. It's a plain country. Not fancy at all. People work hard and go to bed early.'

'*We* work hard and go to bed early.'

'You may hate it,' she said.

'That's right. Maybe I will. And if you keep trying to get rid of me, I may end up hating *you*. When that happens, I promise you I'll leave you a nice note on the kitchen table, pack my extra shirt in a paper sack, and disappear. Do they have any dusky natives in New Zealand?'

'Maoris.'

'Good. I'll find a sexy Maori lady and disappear in a canoe. How's that?'

Annie smiled. 'Someday I'll get you to talk serious.'

'Never. You wouldn't like it anyway. I'm boring when I'm serious.'

Chapter 13

'*A* lot of people died last year,' Russell said. 'Mister Ed, the talking horse, for one. Sally Rand and Sid Vicious and Tolstoy's daughter. Barbara Hutton and Nelson Rockefeller found out that even all that money couldn't help them live. They spun off, too.'

He and I were sitting in the restaurant at the Guggenheim Museum, deep drifts of snow outside, the temperature low, the wind slamming against the windows. We had seen an exposition of abstract expressionist paintings, by a group who had once been known as the New York School. Action painters.

'Very interesting how the worst consequences we can figure out are all connected with death in one way or another. The Orientals have it all over us there. They don't give a damn about dying. They think it's a reward. But how did Lord Mountbatten feel when his boat blew up? Not Oriental, I'll bet. I doubt if he blessed the IRA with his last breath. And what about Norman Rockwell? Do you think he died with the conviction that he was a great painter? I hope not. Very bad if you're still deceiving yourself on your deathbed. Did Galento still think he was a better man than Joe Louis? Did Jean Seberg realize just before those pills wiped her out that she never should have left that little town in Iowa?

'All mysteries. People think problems get solved when somebody dies. Not true. All kinds of shit hits the fan. Kids leave home, families split up over who gets the forty-dollar fruit bowl, brothers have fist fights in the side yard, and mothers take their daughters to court.'

Since his return to New York from Uruguay I had seen Russell a lot. At least three days a week we met for breakfast at a coffee shop on University Place, and he was a regular guest at our house on Thursday evenings and for lunch on Saturday. He spoke openly and often about his illness. He

313

refused to take it seriously and would not permit us to. 'Anyone who helps me to a chair or serves me gruel automatically loses my friendship and is stricken from my will. My doctor says it's a miracle I wasn't dead a year ago, and all the while my lady friends cry out in the night for mercy. There's a very good chance that my penis will live on, in its own apartment with an unlisted phone, long after I have moved to my one-room box underground.'

His appearance was remarkably unchanged, primarily, he explained, because he had resisted treatment by drugs or chemotherapy. He had instead discovered a young woman doctor from mainland China who tested him for allergies, designed an exotic but nutritious diet for him, and supplemented it with mammoth doses of vitamins and four aspirin tablets a day. 'She also, I suspect, lusts after my body. I have noticed a yen for fellatio sparkling in her slanty eyes. But I explained to her as gently as I could that she is too old for me. She is, after all, almost thirty.'

When he and I were by ourselves, eating breakfast or tramping up and down the streets of the East Village, he was often more candid about his situation. 'I tell myself that I'm doing a whole Dorian Gray sequel, that by sheer bravado and bullshit I'm managing to stay intact while somewhere, in an old photo album, a picture of me is aging and deteriorating, the veins closing up and the flesh pulling away from the bones, the eyes sinking deep into their sockets.'

'You're nuts. Did you ever hear of remission? I think you're going to beat it. It looks to me as if you've already beat it.'

'That's what my doctor says. But I know better. I can feel my bones getting lighter. My blood keeps me awake at night racing back and forth through my veins. My taste and smell and hearing are all sharp and keen as an animal's. I've never felt more electrically alive than I do now. And I love it. But I'm not deceived. And you mustn't be either.'

At the Guggenheim that afternoon, after looking at the paintings by Pollock and de Kooning, Kline, Motherwell, Guston, and Rothko, after we'd found a seat in the near-empty restaurant and ordered a bottle of Médoc, Russell said, 'Well, what do you think?'

'I don't know. I get nervous when museums start to deify painters. I remember most of these guys from the fifties, when they used to hang out at the Oak Tavern on University Place. A lot of these pictures I saw then.'

'So what do you think?'

'I don't know. It just seems like a long way from there to here. Four of those guys are dead now, and a lot of the pictures look dead too.'

Russell nodded. 'They sure as hell do. It's a tricky thing about painting. When it's that new, when it *seems* to be that new, *look out*. All that newness looks like something else now. There's always a tip-off in the early pictures. Kline's work wasn't outstanding till he attracted attention with the black-and-white abstracts. Neither was Pollock's till he started to drip paint out of cans. Some of Motherwell's *Elegies* will knock you over, but finally there's something literary and intellectual about his stuff. And the recent things I've seen are empty. Four black lines on a blue background. As for de Kooning, he still draws like an illustrator and he has a bad colour sense. His work looks as if his heart's in the advertising business. He's like the first of the pop artists. Rothko's another problem. All taste and no balls.'

Later that afternoon, as we rode downtown on the Fifth Avenue bus, Russell told me about his plans to go to Australia. He'd been invited to spend two weeks in Sydney at the national film school, lecturing to young screenwriters. 'They asked me a couple times before. Once I couldn't make it and the other time I wasn't in the mood. But now I figure is a good time.'

'How long do you plan to stay?'

'I haven't given myself a deadline. No return dates. That's the way I used to travel when I was young and crazy. Open-end and one clean shirt under my arm. If I really like it down there, I may stay on and try to get a start on the book.'

'Are you ready to write some pages?'

'Jesus, I hope so. I've got notes and research and background and maps by the bushel. I've been telling myself I need all that crap, but what I really need is a kick in the ass. Some notion, some sentence, to get me off the dime.'

He said he also planned to stop in New Zealand on his way home. 'Somebody told me it's a combination of the American frontier and provincial England fifty years ago. Eighty million sheep and only three million people. Sounds good to me.'

'Didn't Annie Singleton come from New Zealand?'

He nodded. 'That's another reason I'm going there. I want to get a feel of those towns she came from. Greymouth and Westport. And Nelson, where she and Abe Singleton met and got married. Once I've stomped around there for a few days . . .'

'You should be ready to start chapter one.'

'You got it. Unless I'm kidding myself. Do you think I'm kidding myself?'

'About what?'

'About writing this bloody book. Sometimes I think I'm too close to it. Sometimes I think I don't even *want* to write it.'

'Sure you do. You're halfway home.'

'Wouldn't that be nice? Wouldn't it be jolly if I were?'

BOOK 5

Chapter 1

I had a postcard from Russell mailed from the Sydney airport the day he arrived. After that I heard nothing for more than a month. Then . . . a short message written on the back of a menu.

> You poor bastard. Still enslaved by the notion that art is eternal, that writing is a noble calling. I, on the other hand, footloose and cynical, am aware that my best work will never get done.
>
> Am I drunk? Of course. Having finished my bullshit lectures about filmmaking, I am now off for an open-end tour of this odd continent, guided by a young woman named Rose from Mudgee (that's a real town, so help me God) who swears that I am not only sexy but profound.
>
> Since I'm a guest of her country, I am reluctant to disagree with her.

For the next weeks there came a hail of postcards, some blank except for the address, one with a lipstick signature from an unidentified female mouth, but most of them written solid, edge to edge, in Russell's small but legible handwriting. The postmarks made clear his travel route. Melbourne, Hobart, Port Adelaide, Kalgoorlie, and Perth. Alice Springs then, and Darwin, over to Cairns, and down the east coast, driving through Townsville, Rockhampton, Bundaberg, and Brisbane, and back at last to Sydney. From there he wrote a letter.

318

I now know more than I ever expected to know about Australia and Rose knows more than she *wanted* to know about me. But they're sturdy, these Australians, and she is no exception. She feels, I'm sure, that it was a unique experience, something she can draw on in her future years as a filmmaker. Maybe she's right.

Anyway, be that as it may, I am off now, leaving tomorrow, to explore and conquer New Zealand.

One evening as we were having dinner, Amy said, 'I've got bad feelings about Russell.'

'What kind of bad feelings?'

'I don't think we'll ever see him again.'

'Of course we'll see him again. If he's not here by May, I'll be surprised.'

'I thought he said he might stay longer.'

'He did. But in April it starts to get rainy in New Zealand. And cold. He'll be standing out there on the doorstep before you know it.'

In his notes, under the heading *Observations and Conclusions*, he wrote:

New Zealand is not heaven. It is not even the Garden of Eden. But there is still innocence here. And beauty. When I am banished at last for writing unkind truths about America, I hope I will be sent to New Zealand. I hope I'll be welcome here.

He travelled by train from Auckland to Wellington. It was his first sight of the lush New Zealand fields and hills and endless meadows.

Thirty shades of green, all carpeted together. And swift clear rivers cutting through. Odd blends here of Tahiti and Wyoming. Those humpbacked, green-purple South Pacific mountains. And in front of them the rolling, neat-fenced fields of Cornwall. But more exotic than England, this landscape. Something biblical in it. Some bizarre artist's vision.

He wrote cards from Dunedin and Invercargill, from Queenstown, Haast, and Greymouth. And a letter from Westport. And at last a card from Nelson, on the northern coast of the South Island.

This is it, *mes enfants*, the paradise we were promised in Sunday School. I asked if there was any industrial pollution hereabouts, and an old gentleman explained, very seriously, that the scented breezes wafting in from the hop fields and apple orchards sometimes cause people to complain. Tomorrow I'm off to research the Granger clan (Annie Singleton's maiden name was Granger).

Two days later, I had a letter from him, written on Hotel Rutherford stationery.

Is life following art, *defying* art, or is it bent on destroying it? Pay close attention and decide for yourself. I located the address of the Granger House, the small private hotel that Annie's father's family have owned and operated for nearly a hundred years. When I found it yesterday, after a walking tour with my visitor's map, I saw a frame colonial building, white and historic, three storeys tall with wide verandas, surrounded by lawns and trees and situated just on the far bank of the Maitai River, facing southwest, across Queens Gardens toward the town proper and the cathedral.

The river curves beautifully just there, and it was a dry clear afternoon, so I sat for half an hour on the opposite bank of the stream looking across at the hotel and enjoying the sunshine. And wondering what I might learn about Annie Singleton.

You know me. I am absolutely unflappable and unperturbable. Chaos does not shatter or surprise me. I

320

learned long ago that if one is never surprised, then there is no problem about *recovering* from surprise. It's a technique, of course, but one that can be mastered.

But . . . when I rang the call bell at the reception desk of the Granger House yesterday afternoon and a young woman came through a doorway to greet me, I felt as if my face was doing a full range of reactions, like a cartoon mouse being surprised by a cartoon cat.

Standing half turned from the desk, looking toward the main-floor sitting room, my first statement already rehearsed and poised for delivery inside my mouth— 'I'm anxious to get some information about the Granger family who once owned this hotel. I'm especially interested in Annie Singleton'—I turned back as someone said, 'Yes . . . may I help you?' and looked smack-dab into the eyes of Annie Singleton. As I was doing all the cartoon reactions described above, she said, 'My God. I can't believe it.' She turned back to the door she'd come through and called out, 'Roy . . . come out to the desk. You'll never believe who's standing here.'

Are you with me, Ben? The man in the back was Roy Lavidge. Annie Singleton is a widow now. Her husband and children were killed in an automobile accident in Ireland. I don't know the details yet, but I expect that somebody will tell me before I leave here. The operative facts are these: Roy is no longer with Christine and Annie is no longer with Abe, but the two of them, Roy and Annie, are decidedly with each other.

Chapter 2

*R*ussell's letter to Christine came to her in Lake Forest. Fred had left early that day to fly to California, and she was sleeping late. The mail came upstairs at eleven on her breakfast tray. After she drank her juice and ate a poached egg on toast, she poured herself a second cup of coffee. Then she read her mail, saving Russell's letter till last.

She had always assumed that somehow she would hear of Roy again and she was determined to be armed against that moment whenever it came. So she *was* prepared, as much as anyone could have been.

It seemed logical and right also that the news should come from Russell. The mere fact that it came from him gave added impact. When she said to herself, 'Russell found Roy for me,' she felt a surge of feeling for both Roy *and* Russell.

Also, because Russell wrote at the close of his letter, 'I wouldn't be telling you this if I didn't know you could handle it,' because he made that very specific, she realized that she *could* handle it.

As she sat in her bed that morning, neatly folding the letter and slipping it back inside the envelope, she assured herself that the fantasies she had been tortured by in the past few years were over now. The mystery was solved, the last jigsaw piece was locked in place.

There was no indication in Russell's letter that Roy had asked about her. He was living a life that suited him, one would guess, just as she was. Knowing always how he could reach her, he had made no effort to do it. Knowing now where *he* was, how *she* could reach him, she knew that *she* would not do it either.

As she took her shower that morning and washed her hair, she told herself that as soon as she saw Grace, she would tell her about Russell's letter. But when they were together later in Grace's sitting room, Christine didn't mention it. She also planned to tell Fred when he called that evening. But she didn't. She told herself that *her* knowing was enough. The circle was complete. Roy could be put away now, tucked away peacefully into the past.

Still, something nagged at her. When she began to suspect what it was, she wouldn't admit it to herself. But at last she couldn't push it away any longer.

Annie Singleton. That was the surprise she couldn't deal with. She had always told herself that Roy would be with *someone*, wherever he was. If she had been able to spy on him in Rocky Mountain House or Grande Prairie, if she had seen him with Lois or Enid or Patsy or any of the other young women he had passed his evenings with, she would have said to herself, 'Why shouldn't he do what he wants to? God knows he doesn't owe *me* anything. I have no hold on him.'

It was one thing then to envision him with a succession of nameless and faceless women. But the thought of Roy lying beside Annie Singleton was something altogether different. Physical jealousy spread through Christine like an injection of Novocain.

She got out Russell's letter and read it again. It said that when Abe and Annie had gone to Ireland, Roy had not gone with them. On the other hand, according to Russell, Roy had left Canada and had gone to Ireland as soon as he had learned about Abe's death.

Looking for one solid answer, Chrissy found, instead, a thousand answers, all connected in some way but all different. But whatever she concluded, whatever she chose to believe at any particular moment, she could not get Annie and Roy out of her mind. Like a child leafing through a magazine, she saw them on every page.

Through the month of May and on through June, Christine followed her normal back-and-forth pattern between Lake Forest and Santa Barbara. In California she and Fred rode and sailed, went to dinner parties, concerts, and polo matches. When she was in Lake Forest, especially when Fred was away, she lived a quieter life. Reading, playing tennis, occasional visits with Margaret, a few hours every day with

323

Grace. But Roy was constantly in her thoughts. She took out the box of snapshots she normally kept in the back of her closet, pictures she'd taken on Martha's Vineyard, at Foresby, and a great many photographs from the time when they were in Banff. She sat on the chaise longue in her bedroom for hours at a stretch, studying those pictures.

At last, when she felt secure about what she proposed to do, she went, one afternoon, to see Elizabeth Griggs.

After she'd sat with Christine for almost forty minutes, Elizabeth said, 'I think you're about to make a really serious mistake.'

'That's what I was afraid you'd say.'

'I know what you're feeling. Your instinct tells you to *act*. Not a bad instinct normally. But there are also times when the only thing to do is *nothing*; times when almost *anything* you do will get you into trouble.'

Christine sat silent for a long moment. 'I must not have explained it right,' she said then.

'I think you did,' Elizabeth said. 'I see how you feel. You want to satisfy your sense of order. But for that to work, all the other people involved would need to feel the same way *you're* feeling. And *if* they do, it would be a miracle. Most people, once they've dealt with any kind of pain or personal loss, are not anxious to deal with it again. It's why women walk out through the side doors of restaurants to avoid meeting their own sisters, why divorced men abandon their children rather than face a continuing relationship with their ex-wives.'

'Don't you think that's ridiculous?'

'Of course I do. But *surviving* is a strange activity. People work out all kinds of recipes and techniques. All they care about is whether they *work*.'

'I must be very dense this afternoon. It's hard for me to see how what I've said could generate the reaction I'm picking up from you. It's really not that *important*, is it?'

'Of course it is. Otherwise you wouldn't be here talking with me about it. You know you're playing with a loaded gun. That's why you want me to tell you you're not. But I can't do that, Chrissy. What you want and what you *think* you want are two entirely different things.'

'You think I'm lying to you?'

'No. And it wouldn't bother me if you were. I hear lies all the time. I'm only disturbed when people lie to themselves.'

When she left Elizabeth's house that afternoon, Christine was unsure of her next move. Questioning her own desires and decisions, she was eager to do as she was told. But time turned her around. Two weeks later she drove down to Chicago one afternoon and finalized the plans she had been postponing.

Chapter 3

*F*red Deets had a relationship with Margaret Jernegan that Christine accepted but did not understand. He was fond of her in a way that Christine wasn't and Grace wasn't.

It wasn't as though he had illusions about Margaret. He knew she was devious and manipulative, capable of duplicity in a business situation and intent on getting her way in all departments of her life. He also realized that Margaret had almost no control over the two people she was most anxious to influence, Grace and Christine.

Because of past experiences with Margaret, her daughter and granddaughter suspected her motives even when she was blameless. When she telephoned, they answered with caution. When Christine visited her, it was always with trepidation. She had stood too often on those thick Chinese rugs, sat too

325

often in the Louis XV armchairs, and promised herself she would never come there again.

But with Fred, Margaret had always behaved differently. She preferred dealing with men. She particularly liked attractive men. Also Fred was the son of Nelson and Eileen Deets.

The Deetses were younger than Margaret, Nelson by twelve years, his wife by fifteen, but they had been her neighbours and loyal friends for more than thirty years. She had gone out of her way to help Nelson with her investment knowledge and advice, her uncanny instinct for where the bodies were buried. He often said, 'Half my money I earned, the rest of it Margaret helped me to steal.' It was a compliment that she cherished.

So it was inevitable that Margaret would have a special feeling for Fred. As he grew up, she spent as much time with him as she did with Christine. She was delighted when it seemed certain that they would marry. At that time she used to hug Fred and say, 'You'll be my relative one way or the other.'

Fred had seen firsthand how Margaret had suffered when Christine broke their engagement. It was the only time he saw her weep. 'How dare she do that to you? How dare she trot back here with some mongrel she picked up in the East and upset all our lives?'

Fred knew also that he and Christine would never have survived their separation, his first marriage, and all the resultant complications if Margaret hadn't been steady at the tiller. She had written to him when he was in Vietnam, always saw him when he was home on leave, and kept him posted, whether he liked it or not, on Christine's comings and goings. When he got married, she sent a handsome gift, and on the card she wrote, 'I haven't given up on you yet.' When his wife asked what that meant, he said, 'She's an old lady. Friend of my parents. She's got a crush on me.'

Whenever he saw Margaret, during the years that Christine was in Canada, she always said, 'That's not going to work. I promise you.' When he was divorced, she said, 'I'm sorry for you and your wife. But I think things will turn out for the best.

If you and Christine aren't married with a year, I'll be surprised.'

She always let him know when Christine would be coming to visit from Canada. 'Try to be here if you can. Even if she doesn't see you, it's good for her to know that you're still attached to Lake Forest. You're part of her life. Sooner or later she'll realize that.'

When Grace had her accident, as soon as Fred heard the news from Margaret, he flew to Chicago. His being there at that critical time had led at last to his marrying Christine. He was sure of it. and it wouldn't have happened without Margaret.

So Fred was grateful to her. He also felt sorry for her. He knew she had earned the imperfect relationship she had with Grace and Christine, he had no patience with her instincts and her methods, but all the same he sympathized with her.

So Fred saw Margaret often. He visited with her at least once a week. Late afternoon usually. They had cocktails together in her library and discussed currency reforms, the World Bank, and the Federal reserve system. And she predicted, always, what the prime rate would be in the next month.

Occasionally she talked about Grace or Christine. But not often. On the last weekend in June, however, during their second cocktail, she gravely told him about Christine's plans.

Chapter 4

*T*hree days later, when they were getting ready to go back to California, Christine said, 'I've been thinking about taking a trip.'

327

Fred had considered carefully how he would handle the news when it came. he decided at last to play it straight.

'That's what I hear. Margaret says you're going to New Zealand.'

'When did she tell you that?'

'Saturday, I think it was.'

'Why didn't you say something?'

'I didn't want to spoil your fun,' he said. 'I figured you wanted to tell me yourself.'

'I did. But I see Margaret fixed that. She really is a pill.'

'How did she find out?' Fred said.

'Who knows? How does she find out anything? If I write a cheque on Tuesday I think she gets a photocopy of it by messenger on Wednesday. It's really boring.'

'It doesn't matter. Tell me again. I'll be surprised.'

Christine smiled. 'I'm going to New Zealand.'

'No kidding. When?'

'How does next Friday grab you?'

'That's pretty fast.'

'I have to hurry or I'll miss the bad weather.'

'Let me see if I remember,' Fred said. 'It's almost July here. Middle of summer. That means it's winter down there. You sure you want to face that?'

'That doesn't matter. I'm only going because Russell's there.'

'How's he doing?'

'He's holed up in Christchurch trying to get started on a book. But what he's really doing is looking for a reason *not* to start. So I'll give him one. He can show me the sights.'

'Sounds great,' Fred said. 'Maybe I'll come along.'

'I'd love it. Can you leave on such short notice?'

'I guess I could. Tunstall's pretty much up to date on all the projects. And we could talk on the phone every day.'

She smiled at him. 'Or if that doesn't work, I could go down on Friday and scout around for a couple weeks. Then you could fly down and meet me.'

'Would you like that better?'

Something in his manner made her wary suddenly. 'No,'

she said. '*I'd* like it better if you came with me on Friday.'

'I think you're right. Friday's a little quick for me. You go ahead, and if you like it, I'll fly down later.'

'You don't feel funny about my going, do you?'

'I don't feel funny about it at all,' he said.

'Then why do I have this feeling that we're playing cat and mouse? Like you're saying one thing and *thinking* something else.'

'Why would I do that?' he said. '*You're* not doing that, are you?'

She laughed suddenly. 'I give up. I surrender. I feel like the bird in a badminton game.'

When she laughed, he thought that meant the game was over, that she was going to tell him now what Margaret had already told him. They sat there on the veranda looking out across the gardens; they smiled at each other like two sleepy cats. But she said nothing. Finally he said, 'Margaret told me your friend Roy's living in New Zealand now.'

'That's right,' she said. Quick response. Total control.

'How did you find out about it?'

'Russell ran into him down there. He wrote me about it a few weeks ago.'

'Did he tell you to keep it a secret?'

'I'm not on trial all of a sudden, am I?'

He shook his head. 'I just asked a simple question.'

'Nothing wrong with the question. I just see an odd look in your eyes.' Then, 'There's nothing secret about it. To tell you the truth it was not exactly fascinating information for me, and I didn't think it would be for you either. I saw no reason to bring it up or discuss it. I'm no more interested in Roy now than you are in the Original Mrs Deets.'

'That's what I told Margaret. But she thinks if Roy's in New Zealand and you're making a sudden trip there . . .'

'I don't give a damn what Margaret thinks. And you shouldn't either. Do *you* care what she thinks?'

'Not at all. I just wondered why you hadn't told me.'

'Now you know. I just explained it.'

'I understand he's living with Mrs Singleton, the woman you knew in Canada.'

'That's what Russell said.'

'Are they married or what?'

'I have no idea. It doesn't concern me,' she said. 'And I'm not sure why it concerns you.'

'It doesn't. Just curiosity. When somebody tells me a story, I like to know all the facts.'

'Then you'll have to ask Margaret. I don't know any facts except what I've told you.'

'Are you getting annoyed with me?'

'No. why should I?'

'I don't know. But you sure as hell look annoyed.'

'I don't like to be given the third degree, Fred. You wouldn't like it either. The thought of you and Margaret sitting over there *discussing* me really tees me off. You know how I am about her.'

'We didn't say anything that you couldn't have heard.'

'That's beside the point. The point is I don't like to be *discussed*. Certainly not by her.'

'She's not out to get you.'

'Bullshit, Fred. Don't defend her to me. I *know* her. She's always out to get somebody. It's her nature. She's a fox in the chicken house.'

'She just said she'd hate to see you get into a situation that might upset you in some way.'

'What does that mean exactly?'

'Well, I guess she meant . . .'

'Does that mean that the entire country of New Zealand is off limits to me because somebody I used to know lives there now? Does Margaret think I'm going there so I can lay hands on Roy Lavidge? Is that what *you* think?'

'No.'

'Maybe she thinks you should lock up my passport and forbid me to go. Was that her advice?'

'No.'

'Because if it was, that's fine with me. If you don't *want* me to go I *won't* go. It wouldn't be any fun for me anyway if I thought you and Margaret were on the phone with each other every day trying to figure out where I am and what I'm doing.'

330

'All right, Chrissy. Cut the crap.'

'What does that mean?'

'Just what it sounds like. Don't try to twist things around and put me on the defensive, because it won't work. I told you you're not on trial and you're not. But neither am I. I wasn't sucking around Margaret trying to get information. But when she tells me you're going on a trip that I don't know anything about, and when she tells me she thinks you're going because you want to see Roy Lavidge, how do you expect me to react?'

'I expect you to trust me.'

'I *do* trust you. But we're not talking about some guy you went to a football game with and never saw again. This is serious stuff, whether you want to admit it or not. We split up once because of him. You lived with him for a few years and you were all set to marry him . . .'

'Jesus, Fred, where are you *going*? What is this all about? All of a sudden were back at the beginning. Are you saying what I think you're saying? Do you think that all the time you and I have been married, I've had somebody else in my head? Do you think I could have married you if I was still in love with Roy?'

'No, I don't think that.'

'You don't sound very positive. Aren't you sure?'

He paused, started to speak, then seemed to reconsider.

'What is it, for God's sake? We're having a terrific fight,' she said. 'This is no time to hold something back.'

'I'm not fighting.'

'Whatever you call it, let's deal with it. Let's say what we mean.'

'I told myself I was never going to ask you about this.'

'Too late for that,' she said. 'Now you *have* to.'

'When we were in Portugal after we were married, you wrote Roy a long letter.'

Christine looked up, their eyes met, and she didn't look away. So he went on. 'The letter wasn't delivered. It was returned to my office in California, and they sent it along to my office here.'

'Did you read it?'

331

'Does it matter?'

'What kind of question is that? Of course it matters.'

'Why?' he asked. 'Either I read it and I decided to forget about it, or I didn't read it and threw it away.'

'My name was on the envelope. Why didn't you give it back to me?'

'I considered that. But I decided the mere fact of my handing it to you would be like asking for an explanation. I didn't want to put pressure on you.'

'Don't you think you're putting pressure on me now? Aren't you asking me to tell you what was in the letter? Either that or telling me after all this time that you already know what I wrote?'

'No. I'm not asking you tell me anything. You asked me if you'd ever given me a reason to think that you're still hung up on Roy. So I mentioned that letter. It wasn't something I could just forget about. I couldn't stop myself from wondering.'

She sensed they were reaching a critical corner, where everything might depend on whether she spoke or remained silent, on whether she drew a correct conclusion or an incorrect one. Finally she made a choice. 'That means you *didn't* read the letter.'

'Why do you say that?'

'Because you said you couldn't stop wondering.'

She sat watching him, her stomach muscles very tight suddenly. At last he shook his head. 'I didn't read it. It never occurred to me to read it. I put it in the paper shredder at the office.'

She considered the possiblity that he might be lying to her, that he did in fact know what was in the letter. But she rejected that possibility and said, 'I wish you had read it. I wish I had a copy of it now. I can't remember all of it, but in essence it was an apology. I felt guilty about the way I'd treated him and I told him that. I said it was all my fault, that I had been young and crazy and stupid, that I'd tried to get away from all the things I'd grown up with and it hadn't worked. I told him I needed to be myself again, that I needed

332

to be with you, and there was nothing I could do about it except to tell him I was sorry.'

She walked over to where Fred was sitting, knelt on the floor by his chair, and put her arms around him. 'I'd give anything if you'd read that silly letter. I hate it that you've spent all this time wondering about it.'

'It wasn't that serious.' He pulled her head against his chest. 'Let's forget about it.'

She sat for a long time with her arms around him, feeling the steady beat of his heart against her cheek. And slowly, inside her, an unpleasant suspicion took root. She decided he had read the letter after all, that he knew she'd lied, that he knew everything.

Chapter 5

*L*ate that afternoon, before she walked across the compound to see Margaret, Christine went into the sitting room of her bedroom suite on the second floor, opened the bottom drawer of her writing desk, took out a file folder labelled *Correspondence—Personal*, and opened it flat on the desk top. She checked through the pages of stationery there, mostly notes from her women friends, until she came to the letter Russell had written about Roy and Annie. she took it out of the folder and studied it closely. At last she put it back and returned the folder to the desk drawer.

As soon as she walked into Margaret's sitting room, she said, 'How did you know I was planning to go to New Zealand?'

'I honestly can't tell you. Maybe someone from Sattler's mentioned it to me. If you want to keep secrets from your family, you should find a different travel agent for yourself.'

'Don't worry. I *will*. But it has nothing to do with keeping secrets. I've been running my life for quite a few years now and I expect to keep on running it. Without any outside help, Margaret. From you or anybody else.'

'Are you so rude to other people as you are to me?'

'No,' Christine said. 'Other people don't meddle in my life the way you do.'

'I don't see how I've meddled. Are you saying that you planned to go off to New Zealand without telling Fred?'

'No, of course not.'

'Then what damage have I done? He didn't find out anything from me that he wouldn't have learned from you.'

'That's the point. I wanted him to hear it from *me*.'

Margaret carefully repositioned herself in her chair. 'Such a little thing to get excited about. But if you want me to apologize, I apologize. Now, will you sit down? When we see each other so seldom, I think it's wasteful to spend the time bickering about unimportant things.'

'Unimportant to you, Margaret. *Not* unimportant to me.'

'But I told you I'm sorry. Can't we put it aside now?'

'No, we can't,' Christine said. 'I want you to tell me how you knew that Roy Lavidge is living in New Zealand.'

'Were you planning to tell Fred about that too?'

'No, I wasn't.'

'That's what I was afraid of,' Margaret said. 'That's why *I* told him.'

'You still haven't answered my question.'

'That's true. and I don't plan to answer it. You seem to think that because I'm your grandmother and because I love you, that gives you some licence to be as high-handed with me as you like. But it doesn't. You are very protective of your own rights, very anxious that no one should meddle in *your* life. You seem to forget that *I* have the same rights you do. I am allowed to make whatever choices seem sensible to me. No matter how free and independent you are, both you and

Grace, you're still part of my family. The only family I have. I am well aware that you don't have to come to me for money. And I know you'd cut your throat before you'd come to me for advice. All the same, if you expect me to sit back quietly and say nothing when I think you are about to make a mistake that could change your life, then I say you're expecting too much. The three of us have to look out for each other. You can't say that you and Grace haven't had a free hand through the years. You also can't say, if you're honest with yourself, that you've used that freedom very wisely. If you remember, I was opposed to your working at Martha's Vineyard that summer. I was heartbroken when you broke your engagement to Fred, and although I tried not to make matters difficult for you, I thought your going to Canada was a disastrous choice. Was I wrong?'

'Hindsight makes a genius out of anyone.'

'Perhaps it does. On the other hand, some people learn nothing from it. Have you?'

'No, I'm just as crazy and impulsive as I was when I was five years old. And I want to stay that way.'

'That's easy to say. Easy for you,' Margaret said. 'Not so easy for the people who love you. You may not mind if you're hurt, but I mind very much *seeing* your hurt. I can't just sit by—'

'Yes, you can Margaret, and you *must*. I've never pretended to have a perfect record. I have all kinds of faults and I've made all kinds of mistakes. But I don't do it on purpose. I want what I want. So does everybody else. But I don't want to trample on everybody to get it. On the other hand I don't expect to get through my life without hurting *anybody*. And I don't expect that I won't be hurt myself. I can't just crawl into a hole like Grace has done and be *safe*. *Safe* is *dead* as far as I'm concerned. I love my life with Fred. It's like a storybook. But I don't regret for an instant the time I spent with Roy. Just because something ends badly doesn't mean it was bad from the beginning. Other than *your* life, which is guaranteed prosperity, and Grace's life, which is guaranteed solitude, I don't know of any guarantees. Do you think Fred couldn't come home tomorrow night and tell me he's in love with somebody else? I don't think he *will*, but I never forget for a moment that it's a possibility. I'm not trying to build an indestructible shelter for myself where I'll never be cold and never have the rain fall on me. I want to build something *inside* myself if I can, something that won't dissolve every time I fall down and skin my knee. Because when the chips are down, that's all I've got. That's all I'll ever have that I can be sure of keeping, whatever ability I have to run and jump and reach for whatever brass ring I see. And not come to pieces when I miss it.'

Margaret smiled. 'Is that your philosophy of life?'

'No. I don't have one of those and I don't want one. I just want to *have* a life. One that makes sense to me. I'm perfectly willing to live with my own bad choices, but I refuse to have somebody else's mistakes forced on me.'

'Can't I offer you a cocktail?'

'No, thanks. All I want is an answer to my question. I want to know how you knew about Roy Lavidge.'

'I thought we dealt with that.'

'We *dealt* with it but we didn't answer it. You made a speech about your *rights* instead. I just want you to know about one right you *don't* have. No one is allowed to go into my desk and go through my letters.'

'Are you accusing me of that?'

'No. I don't think you did it yourself. I think you had one of the servants do it.'

'I can't believe what I'm hearing,' Margaret said. 'Are you really suggesting that I—'

'Yes, I am. Because it's the only way you could have known. Nobody knew except me and one other person. And that person would never tell anyone.'

'Well, at least you trust someone. I thought you didn't trust anybody.'

'I don't.' Christine got up, walked across the room to the telephone, and dialled a number.

'Not even your mother,' Margaret said.

'I'm not talking about Grace. She didn't know.'

When Elizabeth Griggs answered the telephone, Christine said, 'Hi. This is Chrissy. I'm sorry to bother you, but I have to ask you a question. I'm sure I know the answer but I have to ask you anyway. So please understand and don't be offended. I'm calling from my grandmother's house and she's sitting here listening. Is there any chance that you might have talked with her or my mother about anything you and I have discussed?'

Christine stood by the telephone table looking across the room at Margaret as she listened to Elizabeth's reply. Finally she said, 'Of course I understand that. But there were only two ways the information could have been passed on. I thought I knew which one it was, but I had to be absolutely sure.'

'Who *was* that?' Margaret said as soon as Christine hung up the receiver.

'You don't know her. She's a friend of Grace's and a friend of mine.'

'Then why would you discuss me with her?'

'I told you. I want to know exactly where you got your information. And now I know.'

'Not at all,' Margaret said. 'You don't know a bit more than you knew before.'

'Let me put it this way. There are five women working in my house here. You know all of them. By the day after tomorrow I expect to hear that one of them has been discharged. Only you know which one it is. You work it out with my housekeeper. If *she's* the one to be let go you'll have to do it yourself. I won't have someone in my house who's reporting to you.'

Margaret smiled. 'I have my own staff to worry about. If you're not pleased with some of yours . . .'

'If you do as I say,' Christine went on, 'I'll try to forget that we ever had this conversation. If you refuse to do it, then this is the last conversation we'll ever have.'

Early that evening Christine and Fred flew to California. Late the next day, Christine had a phone call from Mrs Rader, her housekeeper in Lake Forest. 'Mrs Jernegan has asked me to discharge one of the housemaids. I thought I should speak to you before I do it.'

'Which one is it?'

'Luisa. The Mexican woman. She's been with us since the first of the year. Seems to be a good worker.'

'What did Mrs Jernegan say about her?'

'She said she'd had a report from the employment agency that the woman can't be trusted. A family in Winnetka let her go because they suspected her of stealing.'

'Have we missed anything in the time she's been with us?'

'No. Since she was responsible for your room upstairs, I've checked all your things once a week.'

'I think you'll have to let her go,' Christine said. 'If Mrs Jernegan feels she can't be trusted, I would rely on her judgement. She has an instinct about these things.'

'It just seems odd to me. Because Luisa worked six weeks for your grandmother before she came to us.'

'Yes,' Christine said. 'That does seem odd, doesn't it?'

Chapter 6

*F*rom the airport in Auckland, as she waited for her connecting flight to Christchurch, Christine sent a picture postcard to Roy and Annie in Nelson.

Guess who blew in! Fred and I are about to make the grand tour of New Zealand. Delighted to hear about you two from Russell. He gave me your address. I'm not sure if Nelson is on our itinerary, but I hope it is. When we get there, *if* we get there, maybe we can have a fancy dinner together

Love, Chrissy.

Russell met her at the Christchurch airport around the middle of the day. 'Are you wiped out?' he asked.

'I thought I would be but I'm not. That's some flight from Los Angeles to Auckland. Thirteen hours nonstop. And I lost another day besides, didn't I?'

Russell nodded. 'International Date Line. But that's all right. You'll pick it up when you go back.'

When they were in a taxi heading toward the city centre, she said, 'Were you surprised when you got my letter, saying I was coming down?'

'What do you think?'

'I think you were surprised. I was a little surprised myself. But after you wrote me from here, I started reading up on New Zealand, and the more I read, the better it sounded. Fred and I talked it over and decided to have a look.'

'So where is he?'

'He'll meet me here later. He gets bored with sightseeing, so I'll do all that before he shows up.'

'You're going to see a lot of rain and cold weather down here on the South Island.'

'I don't *want* sunshine, for God's sake. The sun beats down so much in California I get sick of it. I love these misty days. I want to take that trip you took. All the way down the coast to Invercargill, Stewart Island maybe, then back up to Queenstown. I'll save Mount Cook till Fred gets here.'

'When do you plan to start on this trip?' Russell asked.

'Depends on you, in a way. I thought I'd stay for two or three days here in Christchurch. If you're not tied up. I hoped we could spend some time together.'

'No problem. I'd like it.'

'You sure I'm not screwing up your work schedule?'

He shook his head. 'Still pawing the dirt like a bull.'

'Can't you just sit down at the typewriter and tap out *Chapter One* at the top of the page and go on from there?'

'Some people can, but not me. I have to know where I'm going.'

He had reserved a suite for her at the Clarendon, where he was staying. After she registered at the desk, she said, 'Let me take a fast shower and then we'll have some lunch. I'm starving.'

He waited for her in the private bar just opposite the hotel desk. By the time he finished a Scotch and soda, she was back downstairs, wearing a tweed skirt and a silk shirt with a cardigan over her shoulders, knee socks, and low-heeled walking shoes. 'Am I quick or am I quick?' she asked.

'No vanity,' Russell said. 'That's your secret.'

'Is that a compliment or should I run and hide?'

'As I used to say to my first wife, "Your problems are not physical".'

'What did she say?'

'She wasn't amused. She was French. The French are hardly ever amused.'

After the waiter brought their wine, a basket of bread, eggs, and mayonnaise, Russell said, 'I need to ask you a question.'

'Nothing withheld.'

'I wasn't sure how you'd react when I wrote you that I'd seen Roy. But as it turned out there was no reaction at all. That surprised me.'

She was sure of her ground here. She'd known the question was coming. 'I was a little surprised myself. Surprised at the news of course. More surprised at my reaction. I can remember, not so many years ago, if somebody had told me I'd never see Roy again, I'd have come apart. But . . . we fool ourselves, don't we? The sun keeps coming up, the rain keeps falling, and all of a sudden the things we thought could never change have changed. Zap. The mouse eats the tiger.'

'Meaning what?'

'Meaning I can think of him now without trembling. I can discuss him with you and no rockets go off in my head. I can see him as someone I loved desperately. But I can also see that the desperation's gone now. I guess everybody loves like that once in their lives. Somebody picks you up and squeezes you so dry you think the whole game is over. But it's not. You struggle along.'

'I take it you don't plan to see him while you're here.'

'I don't know,' she said. 'Maybe I will. Maybe I won't. We'll see after Fred gets here.'

'No curiosity?'

She smiled. 'Of course I'm curious. More curious about Annie in a way than I am about Roy. I really liked her. And I admit it surprised me to hear that they're together now. Living together, I mean. You know how it is. When you know people in one set of circumstances and all of a sudden those circumstances change, whirl around and flip-flop completely, it's hard to know how you feel.'

For three days they walked and drove and bicycled around Christchurch and the surrounding countryside. The hotel manager said, 'You've brought us a false spring. Very unusual to have sunshine and clear skies this time of year.'

After visiting the parks and museums and cathedrals of the city, after strolling beside the River Avon, they drove in a long slow loop down the peninsula, through Motukarara, Little River, and Hill Top, then due south to Akaroa and back north past Diamond Harbour and Governor's Bay to Christchurch again. They ate sumptuous dinners, drank deeply of the wine, danced in discotheques till they closed, and walked slowly back to the hotel through the cool early-morning streets.

When he put her on the southbound train, early in the morning of the fourth day, the fine, seductive weather had stopped suddenly. A slanting rain was pounding down and a fog of coal smoke hovered low over the hollow where Christchurch rests, between the hills and the ocean.

'Thank you,' she said, as they walked through the station toward her train. 'I had a lovely time. But you spent too much money. I must owe you three thousand million dollars.'

'Just about.'

'Did we scandalize the hotel? Do they think we're lovers?'

He shook his head. 'Not at all. I told them you're my niece.'

'Daughter of your sister Grace?'

'Something like that,' he said.

'Wait till Grace hears that one.'

'I don't think I'd tell her that if I were you.'

'I won't. I'll just tell her you treated me with brotherly respect, which is true, and fatherly generosity, which is true, and that I can see why she was so crazy about you.'

As the train rolled through the fog and rain, first stop Miaru, one hundred sixty-four kilometres to the south, Christine let her thoughts wander back and forth through the past three days. It all seemed cocoonlike, parenthetical, a child's visit to the fair. Half dozing in her tilt-back seat, she felt light boned and relaxed. Capable of unusual deeds. Recalling her conversations with Russell about Roy, hearing them replay in her memory, she could feel herself being persuaded as she had persuaded him. She was, indeed, she felt, released now from the bonds that had held her to Roy. Her description of her itinerary through Timaru, Dunedin, and Invercargill to Stewart Island, then north again to Queenstown had been repeated and discussed so thoroughly, she had almost come to believe it.

But when her train pulled into Timaru, she got off with her luggage, took a taxi to the airport, boarded the next plane back to Christchurch, and connected there with a nonstop flight to Nelson. Exactly as she had intended from the time she booked her trip that afternoon in Chicago.

Chapter 7

*W*hen Annie saw the postcard from Christine, she said, 'We're undone, Lavidge. Your lady friend's coming back to claim her property.'

'Is that the way you see it?'

'That's the way it looks to me.'

'I don't think so.'

That night, when they were lying in bed, Annie said, 'I hope she does come. I'd like to see her. I really liked Chrissy a lot.'

'I know you did.'

'I always felt sorry for her, too. Did you know that?'

'No.'

'I couldn't help thinking she was trying for something she couldn't reach. It's like knowing you're special, that you've been raised in a protected way to prepare you for a particular kind of life, but all the time you're saying, "I don't want to be special. I want to be exactly like everybody else." You know what I'm trying to say?'

Roy nodded. 'I'm just not sure it applies to Chrissy. She wanted to explore a little and see what other people were up to. But whenever she skinned her knee she needed to go back home.'

'I didn't think that,' Annie said. 'I thought she *couldn't* be what she wanted to be. But I always thought she was trying.'

'You're probably right,' Roy said. 'You get a better fix on people than I do.'

After a moment, Annie said, 'Does that mean you want to drop the subject?'

'It *could* mean that but it doesn't. I'm not protecting old bruises, if that's what you mean.'

'I didn't mean that. But it wouldn't shock me if you were. I wouldn't be surprised if you said you didn't want to see her.'

'I *don't* want to see her,' Roy said. 'But I'm not going to lock myself in a closet if she shows up here. I used to be crazy about her. You know that. But I'm not crazy about her now. I'm not crazy about her and I don't hate her. The only person I'm crazy about is you.' He pulled her close to him. 'Any question in your mind about that?'

'No questions.'

'I just don't want your sentimental Russian blood to get the best of you. I don't want you to get noble all of a sudden and

343

decide to turn me over to Chrissy. A nice house gift. From one liberated woman to another.'

'Not a chance. If she comes here to capture you, she'd better bring a gun with her. I don't plan to trade you in for a long time yet.'

'What about those talks we used to have in Malin when you told me you were just acting as my companion.'

'Companion? I never said that.'

'Words to that effect. You gave me the impression that you were just keeping me company till Chrissy and I managed to get together again someplace down the road.'

'Maybe I did. But that's not how I felt. I just didn't want to fool myself. I didn't want to sell myself on something I couldn't have. After Abe was dead, when I was in the hospital there in Buncrana, I had all those long days to sit by myself and think, to try to make some sense out of things. Finally I decided I had to be alone, to live by myself, because the kind of order and peace I needed just couldn't be had in any other way.

'The nuns thought I was crazy, not talking, not reacting, all those weeks, but that *silence* was what saved me. Those hard white surroundings without voices or sounds. No conflicts or instructions, no opinions or ideas. Just blank, soft time wrapped around me like eiderdown.

'Even when I left there finally, when you shamed me into coming back to Malin, that solitary future I had chosen was the armature inside me that made it possible to leave the nuns. I knew I would have to work and contribute and speak and listen when I was back at the inn, but I told myself that would in no way disturb my decision for silence.

'Then you changed it. You changed it all. By just being there, by being matter-of-fact and dependable and kind. By refusing to treat me as an invalid or a mental patient. And finally you woke me up physically, something I thought would never happen again. After Abe and the children were killed, I felt as if all the nerve endings had been burned out of my body. I couldn't smell or taste or hear the way I had before. I ate food only to survive. My only passion was sleep.

344

'But then you came into my room that night after you'd been sick for so long and I . . . You know how it was. You know how *I* was. And you seemed to feel the same way I did. I couldn't get over that, for weeks afterward. I couldn't believe it.'

'God, you're really something,' Roy said. 'You're a tower of self-esteem.'

'I can't help it. I've always been that way. I get my confidence from other people. If somebody thinks I'm wonderful, then I can convince myself that I'm tolerable. If someone believes I'm only tolerable, then I think I'm worthless. So when you and I . . . when I found out you cared about me, when I admitted to myself how much I cared about *you*, it scared hell out of me. I knew it was all going to blow up in my face. So I had to tell myself it wasn't important, that it didn't really mean anything to you *or* me. And the easiest way I knew to persuade myself of that was to keep Christine in the picture, to pretend that she would show up finally and the two of you would take up where you left off.'

'But you don't feel that way now?'

'No. I told you that,' she said.

'You're not going to turn me over to Chrissy to keep as a pet?'

'I'm not going to turn you over to anybody.'

'What if I take one look at her and collapse in a fit of passion?'

'Then I'll murder you.'

'Don't blame me,' he said. 'I'm a victim of circumstance. You should murder her.'

'I'll murder you both.'

He laughed softly in the darkness and kissed her. 'You look like a wholesome woman. But inside you're black and dangerous.'

'That's right, chappie.'

'I wonder what Dr Freud would have made of you.'

'He would have served me Chinese tea and dismissed me.'

'As a hopeless case?' Roy asked

'Not at all. As a totally sane and only slightly abnormal woman.'

Chapter 8

From her corner suite on the top floor of the Hotel Rutherford, Christine had an unobstructed view north across Nelson City, to the harbour, and to Tasman Bay. Looking east across Trafalgar Street she could see Queens Gardens, and beyond it the Botanical Reserve with the Maitai River cutting through the town between them. And just opposite her east windows, on the wooded knoll of Trafalgar Square, the high stone tower of the cathedral.

She had decided that the best tactic was to be simple and direct. As soon as she had checked into her hotel and had some lunch, she would stroll through the streets to Granger House, ring the desk bell as Russell had done, and present herself.

From a street map of Nelson City she chose the best walking route. Around Trafalgar Square to Trafalgar Street, then straight north through the heart of the business district, past Hardy Street to Bridge Street. East then, past Collingwood and Harley streets, past the art gallery and along the north edge of Queens Gardens, and across the Maitai River to Avon Terrace. There, according to her map and according to the description Russell had given her, she would find the Granger House.

Once she was inside the Rutherford, however, with her clothes hanging in the closet and her luggage put away on a high shelf, she decided it would be best not to move too quickly. So she ordered lunch and ate in her room. And at two o'clock she went to the hotel beauty parlour on the mezzanine and had her nails manicured and her hair shampooed. That evening she again ate in her room. She watched television, glanced through the local newspaper, and went to bed at ten o'clock.

The following morning she was up early, dressed and ready to leave the hotel by nine. She called the hall porter and reserved a car and driver for ten o'clock. But when he called up to say the car was waiting, she cancelled it.

Her plan had been to drive out through Stoke and Richmond, then follow the coast road to Mapua and on to Motueka. Lunch there, then back to Nelson, where in the middle of the afternoon she would go to call on Roy and Annie.

She decided, however, that it was only fair to them to warn them she was coming. So after breakfast she looked up the phone number of the Granger House and dialled it.

Although she had expected Annie to answer the telephone, she considered the possibility that it could be Roy. So she was prepared for that. But when she heard his voice, when he picked up the receiver after the third ring and said, 'Granger House,' she froze, tried not to breathe, and held the mouth-piece tight against her cheek till he broke the connection. When she replaced the receiver in its cradle, her hand was shaking.

She stayed in her rooms for the rest of the day. At two clock, when she went down to have her hair washed again, she asked the hotel transportation desk for a timetable showing flights to Auckland and flights from there to Los Angeles.

When she ordered up her dinner that evening, she also asked for a bottle of champagne. She drank it with her meal, and gradually felt the knot of panic dissolving in her chest.

At nine o'clock she called down for a car. Twenty minutes later her driver crossed the Maitai River on Bridge Street, turned into Avon Terrace, and stopped. 'It's just there,' he said. 'That's the Granger House.'

'It looks deserted.'

'The private hotels are always quiet at night. Most of them don't do dinner, and they don't serve spirits, so the guests who want a bit of fun have to find it on the outside. If you want me to ring the bell and make an inquiry for you . . .'

'No thanks. That won't be necessary. I just wanted to see the place.'

The following morning, as soon as she finished breakfast, Christine telephoned the Granger House again. This time

Annie answered. 'You *did* make it to Nelson,' she said. 'I'm delighted. When we got your card . . .'

'I've changed plans half a dozen times. Fred's not here yet. So I'm trying to fit in with his schedule. I decided if I didn't come to Nelson now I might not make it at all.'

'I wish I could ask you stay here with us,' Annie said, 'but our guest rooms are all plaster dust and holes in the floor. This is our slow time, the only chance we have to redecorate and make repairs.'

'It's all right. I'm at the Rutherford.'

'You made a good choice. When can we see you?'

'Whenever you want,' Christine said.

'Come over now. I'll make us a fine lunch. Do you know where we are?'

'I have a map. I'll walk down.'

'Don't do that. It's supposed to rain today. I'll have Roy drive over to get you.'

'No. It's fine. I really *want* to walk. I'll see you in an hour or so.'

After having spent hours during the past two days planning what she should wear when the time came, Christine simply took off her robe now, dropped it on the bed, opened the bureau drawers, and took out a sweater, a skirt, and a blue-checked shirt, twin sister to the outfit she'd worn her first day in Christchurch. Walking shoes and a trenchcoat, and a man's cap on her head.

Walking out of the hotel into the crisp, cool morning, clouds moving fast across the ocean edge sky and the sun burning through, bright and warm, Christine felt strong and clearheaded, all her trepidations of the past days worn away. She turned right at the hotel entrance and followed Nile Street west across to Rutherford Street. Turning north then, she walked toward the harbour, passing Theatre Royal, Achilles Avenue, and Anzac Park and turning east on Halifax Street, passing the central post office.

Checking her pocket map, she turned north again on Trafalgar Street, passed the Air New Zealand office, and crossed the river. She turned on Grove Street, then angled southeast by the river on Shakespeare Walk. At the next footbridge she recrossed the river and followed its windings by walking on the thick grass at the edge of the water, past the municipal swimming pool to Bridge Street. Realizing it was past the hour that she had specified, Christine tarried, nonetheless, on the steep river bank opposite the Granger House. She sat in the grass, her back against a tree, looking across the stream as Russell had done, studying the handsome old building, watching the workmen come and go until it was almost midday.

She got up then, climbed steeply to the bridge, and crossed the river. As she walked across the hotel lawn toward the front entrance, Roy came out on the porch to meet her. 'We thought you got lost.'

As she climbed the steps, she said, 'I was exploring. I guess I lost track of time.'

Roy called back through the open door. 'She made it, Annie.' Then he turned back to Christine, put his hands on her shoulders, and said, 'Let's take a look at you.'

'Wild and woolly, I'm afraid.'

Annie came out through the front door then and put her arms around Christine. 'Isn't it nice to see you,' she said. 'And how beautiful you look.'

'Look at her,' Roy said. 'No wear and tear at all. The years went by and she didn't notice.'

'You really do look marvellous,' Annie said.

'You know what they say. Saints and fanatics never age.'

Annie laughed. 'Who said that?'

'And which category do you fit in?' Roy asked.

'Neither one. I just said that because I'm nervous.'

Annie put an arm around her shoulders and led her inside. '*Not* in New Zealand. It's not allowed. When people get nervous here we ship them off to Australia.'

They had a drink in front of the fireplace in their private sitting room at the back of the house. Then they sat at the round table in the big open kitchen, red brick floors and leaded windows on three sides, plants growing in great jars on the floor by the windows, a black border collie watchful in one corner, two cats tangled together asleep on the rug, and ate an elaborate lunch.

They sat at the table for three hours, eating, drinking, laughing, and talking, dancing back across the years somehow and re-creating the atmosphere of their hundreds of meals together in Canada. As though they had been carefully coached, each of them, they spoke only of pleasures and triumphs, tightroping neatly around the agony of Abe's death and the sadness of Grace's accident.

'Compared to the St Albert,' Annie said, 'and compared to the public house we ran in Donegal, this old place in this sweet clean city is a joy. Since we serve no food except breakfast, we have none of the headaches about what food to buy, how *much* to buy, how to recook and disguise the leftovers for tomorrow's menu, how to avoid spoilage. And how to keep a good staff in the kitchen. How to keep them from making love in the pantry during the noontime rush or slashing each other with steak knives. We also serve no beer or wine or spirits to our customers. We save it all for ourselves and our friends, for special occasions like this one. Sounds too good to be true, doesn't it?'

'The logical question is, how can we make any money?' Roy said. 'The answer is, we don't. We have ten rooms here. The average tariff is ten dollars per person per night, bed and breakfast, a hundred dollars gross income per day if were full up, seven hundred a week. In a year that means we take in thirty-five thousand. *If* we're full every night. But were not. We're lucky if we average half capacity year round. That means seventeen thousand gross income. And the food and the laundry and the heat and the electric and the maintenance all have to come out of that. Plus the rates to the government. The government, God bless them, won't let us sustain a loss, but they won't help us turn a profit either. So we eat well and buy our clothes, do most of the work ourselves, and earn a living. But only that. It's a common thing here in New Zealand. It's the way most of us live. Small houses, small salaries, and small profits.'

'It's village life of the best kind,' Annie said. 'A perfect place to be relaxed and indolent.'

'Are you relaxed and indolent?' Christine asked Roy.

He smiled and nodded. 'Even more than the natives. We had a Maori gardener and he gave me a Maori name. It means "the slow man who smiles a lot.".'

Late in the afternoon they walked her back to the Rutherford. 'I hope you'll stay on as long as you can,' Annie said. 'We have a bit of free time now. We can show you some terrific places.'

When they left her at the hotel entrance, Christine said, 'It was sensational lunch. I'd forgotten what a lovely time we all had in Canada. This afternoon made me remember.'

As Roy and Annie walked back down Trafalgar Street toward home, Annie said, 'Did it make *you* remember?'

'A little bit.'

'What did you remember?'

'Mostly I remembered how long ago it was.'

'Not so long,' Annie said.

'Maybe not. But it seems like forever.'

'She looks marvellous.'

'Of course she does,' Roy said. 'When she's dead and buried, Chrissy will still look marvellous. But so what? I don't trust people who look the same at thirty as they did at twenty.

'Look who's talking. You haven't changed much.'

'Sure I have. A few grey hairs here and there. Some character lines where there didn't used to be any. And a very old soul inside. And it's all your fault. Living with you would age anybody.'

'I know you're kidding,' she said, 'but it could be true.'

'Oh, my God, there she goes again. Let's list all the shortcomings of Annie Singleton.' He stopped and turned her to him, on the busy sidewalk at the corner of Bridge and Alma streets, put his arms around her, and kissed her. 'You are a woman without qualities,' he said. 'You're a strange-looking duck, you have questionable intelligence, and you're too old for me. But I love you. How can a perfect man like me love an imperfect person like you? God knows. But I do. Now let's go home and take a nap. I'm not accustomed to these boozy lunches.'

351

From the time they received Christine's postcard, Roy tried to imagine the sensations he would feel if she did, in fact, show up in Nelson. Anger would not have surprised him. Or resentment. He knew it was possible that all that walled-up feeling from the time of their breakup in Canada could come rushing out of him. He didn't expect it to happen, but he accepted the fact that it might.

When he saw her, however, when she crossed the lawn and came up the steps to the porch, and later, when he sat beside her at the table in the kitchen, there were no disturbing tides of any kind running inside him.

He did have, however, a reaction he hadn't expected. A purely sensory one. He could not close his eyes, as they sat at the table, to a flickering montage of the naked time they had spent together. He didn't even try. As he recited his lines during the luncheon conversation, Christine to his left and Annie across the table, he felt no need to dismiss the other Christine who lolled naked about the room, on his lap, or on the table. He felt neither guilt nor confusion. It was a familiar sensation, an opiate they had both responded to from the beginning. It had brought them together and held them together. But it hadn't been enough to keep them together. Not then. Not now.

The luncheon experience was different for Annie. Less intricate. But more disturbing. She came away from those three hours with a clear picture in her mind, one she could not erase. As she carried food to the round table, as she served it, as the three of them ate and talked together, as she looked across the table, she saw, as though in a camera viewfinder, Roy on the left and Christine on the right, not close together, but together all the same, as she had seen them through those months in Canada. A perfectly matched set, easy and attractive together, complementary in every way, a pair, a couple.

All through that evening and later as she lay awake in bed, that picture stayed in Annie's mind. It nestled there, just behind her eyes, until she went to sleep. And even then the image remained. Moving now. In her dreams she saw Roy

352

and Christine living in the Granger House, walking in the garden, eating at her table, lying in her bed.

When Annie woke up in the morning, later than usual, Roy was not in bed. She lay quietly on her back listening to the sound of the hedge clippers downstairs in the side yard. At last she got up and walked to the window. She stood there watching him work, his head bare, wearing jeans and sneakers and a heavy sweater. Suddenly then, as she watched, he stopped working. He stood with his arms at his sides, staring blankly at nothing.

Annie felt a chill suddenly, as though she had opened a door without knocking and seen something she wasn't meant to see. She let the lace curtain fall back into place and stood behind it, still watching, as Roy stared off at some secret landscape. In the silence of the bedroom she felt her heart thump.

As soon as he turned back to the hedge, lifted the clippers, and began to work again, she pulled the curtain aside and tapped on the windowpane with her fingernails. When he heard her and turned his face toward the upstairs window, she saw, or imagined she saw, an unfamiliar expression there.

The expression stayed on his face for no longer than a finger snap. When he smiled up at her then, she smiled back and waved her hand. Then she put on her robe and went downstairs to make breakfast.

Chapter 9

*I*n Russell's notes I found the following scrap of dialogue, a conversation that took place between him and Christine.

Her eyes looked pale and washed and her cheeks were very pink. But the tears were over by the time she got to me. She looked determined. Hacked out of stone.

'I thought for a minute you wanted advice,' I said.

'So did I. But I changed my mind. I've tried to be sensible but sensible doesn't work. Now I have to put my money on the table and spin the wheel.'

'That's the way losers talk.'

'Maybe so. But it doesn't matter.'

'Is he really worth it?'

'What kind of a question is that?'

'Straight question. I've known Roy almost as long as you have. I like him. You know that. When I thought you two were going to stay together I was tickled to death. But things happen. Sometimes you can muscle the world around and make it spin the way you want it to. But most times you have to know when you're licked.'

'I'm *not* licked,' she said. 'I never think I'm licked. What are you smiling at?'

'You sound like Grace. That's the way she used to talk. But she found out that sometimes you can't pull it off.'

'No, she didn't. Grace didn't have the guts to pull it off. Nobody defeated her. She surrendered.'

'That's easy to say when you don't have the same choice to make.'

'It doesn't matter,' she said. 'I know exactly what *I* would have done. I'd have chosen you and given up my baby. I'd have gambled on being able to get the child back later.'

'And what if you couldn't?'

'I'd have felt lousy about it. But I'd still think I made the right choice. And I'll tell you something else. If Grace had it to do over again, she'd do exactly what I'm saying I'd do. She's never had a happy day since the last time she saw you. And she never will.'

'Did she tell you that?'

354

'She didn't have to. I *know* her. I know her better than she knows herself. And I know *me*. Maybe I didn't before, but I do now.'

'You still didn't answer my question. Is he worth it?'

'He's worth it to me. I'd give up anything for a chance to be with him.'

'Even Grace?'

She nodded. 'Even Grace. She gave you up for my sake, I gave up Roy for hers. And we each made a mistake.'

I sat there looking at her, seeing her as Grace and knowing that I loved her, not as I'd loved Grace, but as Grace's daughter. 'You just made me feel very old,' I said.

'Not you. You'll never be old.'

When did that conversation, in fact take place? Was it just after the meeting in Nelson between Christine and Annie and Roy? I think so. I know that Christine left that night in a rented car driving southwest toward Christchurch, and I know she was back at the Hotel Rutherford in Nelson three days later. Whether she made that entire eight-hundred-kilometre round trip is not clear in my mind. Perhaps she telephoned Russell and he met her somewhere between the two cities. But they certainly saw each other, and she undoubtedly made clear to him what she planned to do.

Chapter 10

Christine had not called Fred in California since the morning she'd left Christchurch to go first to Timaru and then to Nelson. Now, three days after she had seen Roy and Annie, had lunch with them in the Grange House, she sent him a telegram.

> PLANS CHANGED. COMING HOME.
> YOU WOULDN'T LIKE IT HERE.
> WILL CALL YOU FROM AUCKLAND
> WHEN I KNOW DEPARTURE TIME.

Later that morning she telephoned Annie at the Grange House. 'Sorry you haven't heard from me. I was gone. Rented a car and wandered off through the countryside by myself.'

'I *did* call you.' Annie said. 'Where did you go?'

'I'll tell you all about it when I see you. Can you have lunch?'

'It'll have to be a girl's lunch. Roy went off to Picton this morning to pick up some stuff from the ferry. He won't be back till tomorrow.'

'Then it will be just the two of us. We'll have a good gossip. How about one o'clock here in the hotel dining room?'

'I'd like it better if you came down here. The Rutherford's too fancy for me.'

'Nothing doing. It's my turn. Put on your earrings and we'll pretend we're two fine ladies.'

After Christine had showered and dressed, it was still almost two hours before she was due to meet Annie. She stood by the window for a long time, looking north across the city toward the ocean, feeling strong and clear in her mind, sure of herself, sure of what she proposed to do. At last she sat down at the writing desk in her sitting room, took out a packet of hotel stationery, and wrote a letter to her husband.

Since I am unsure about my future at the moment, I am also not certain that you will read this letter. If you *do* read it, it will not be a surprise to you. I will have talked to you on the telephone and you will know, firsthand, what's happening with me. So this letter will be, I hope, some kind of explanation, something to make you hate me less.

I don't like myself much right now. That's not true either. I *do* like myself for having the guts to do what I think I have to do. But in relation to you I can't make the pieces fit. It would be so easy if I felt differently about you, if I didn't love you.

I do love you, sweetheart. I always have and I'm sure I always will. I love you in every way a woman can love a man. You've never disappointed me or bored me or mistreated me in any way. You've never made me feel inadequate or foolish. Even when I was.

You remember, I'm sure, how fiercely possessive of you I was when I was fifteen years old, how jealous I was of all those long-legged college girls you used to bring home to Lake Forest. I thought of you as *my* property and it was agonizing that you didn't realize it, that *nobody* realized it except me. Many nights I went to sleep with murder in my heart.

When we got together finally, young as I was, I felt as if all the major pieces of my life had locked into place. I knew, as sure as tomorrow, that no calamity of any kind could shake apart the thing we had.

Do you think I exaggerate? I don't. If two people were ever meant to be together, then *we* were. I have the same convictions about that now as I had when I was fifteen.

I just read over what I've written. I believe every word of it. I stand squarely behind it. All of it. And yet I'm telling you, I will have told you by now, that it can't work anymore. I have to go away again, for the same reason I did it before, because of a stubborn, unpredictable man named Roy Lavidge.

I'm not going to beat this to death. You know the circumstances as well as I do. If I had never met Roy, you and I would have been divinely happy all our lives. But I *did* meet him and it changed me. I didn't realize how much until I tried to change back. By that I don't mean that our marriage, yours and mine, was a compromise. Not in any way. I genuinely felt as if I was back where I belonged. I believed that until I came here to New Zealand and saw Roy again. Now I know for sure what I have to do. Whether it makes sense or not, whether I'll be happy or not, I have to stay with him if he'll have me.

She read the letter over, signed it, put it into an envelope, and addressed it. Then she put the letter into her smallest piece of luggage and locked it up.

At one o'clock she met Annie downstairs in the dining room. Christine began to talk earnestly almost as soon as they sat down across from each other at the table. They ordered a bottle of wine, but neither of them drank more than a few sips. And their plates of food went back to the kitchen almost untouched. When Annie got up and left almost two hours later, Christine stayed at the table. She sat there drinking the wine by herself, not trying to wipe away the tears on her face.

Early that evening she flew to Auckland and checked into the Intercontinental. She left careful instructions at the Hotel Rutherford as to where she was and how she could be reached.

That night, Roy telephoned Annie from Picton. 'Are you all right?' he asked.

'Sure. I'm fine.'

'Your voice sounds funny.'

'I think maybe I'm catching a cold.'

A few minutes after she hung up the phone, Annie went outside carrying a small valise, locked the door behind her, and got into the taxi that was waiting at the kerb. On the way to the airport, as the car moved southwest on Waimea Road, a light rain began to fall. Watching the steady sweep of the windshield wipers, Christine's words kept echoing softly in her memory. 'If you tell me to go away, I'll go. But don't say it unless you're sure you love him more than I do. Unless you're sure he loves you more than he loves me.'

The next afternoon, when Roy came home, he asked the workmen if they'd seen Annie. 'Not today. Haven't seen her at all.'

Feeling empty and sick suddenly, Roy went upstairs to their bedroom. He found a note there in the centre of the bed.

> Don't be mad at me. I need a few days to myself. I'm just being selfish. I need some time to think.
>
> A.

Chapter 11

*F*rom the moment he read the note from Annie, Roy knew there was a connection between that message and Christine's visit to Nelson. Nothing else made sense. Annie had no talent for secrecy or intrigue. She could not have spoken to him on the telephone the night before, knowing she was going off somewhere by herself, unless . . . again he came back to Christine. When he called the Rutherford to ask if she was still registered there, the desk woman said she had checked out the night before. 'But she asked us to say that she can be reached at the Intercontinental in Auckland.'

When he called Christine in Auckland, she said, 'I'm sorry I missed you yesterday. I was just back in Nelson for one day.

I was hoping the three of us could have lunch together.'

'Did you see Annie?'

'Sure. We gossiped and giggled and had a big time. You missed it.'

'Did she mention that she was going away for a few days?'

'No, she didn't,' Christine said. 'Isn't she there?'

Roy had already called two of Annie's women friends in Nelson. He told Christine the same story he'd made up to tell them. 'I know she's in Wellington. There's a three-day conference there for hotel managers. I just don't know where she's staying. She left a note for me, but one of the workmen here spilled paint on it and I can't make out the name of the hotel.'

'She didn't mention Wellington to me,' Christine said. 'I don't have any idea where she's staying.'

When she hung up the phone, Christine felt hopeful for the first time in a very long time. In Nelson, his hand still resting on the telephone receiver, Roy felt powerless to do anything but wait. And not hopeful at all.

For the rest of that day and for the two following days, he worked from early morning till dusk with the men who were remodelling the hotel. He mixed concrete, carried timbers and cinder blocks, the heaviest, muscle-straining jobs he could take on. After the men left for the day he continued to work, scraping, painting, plastering, till he was too tired to go on. He made himself a sandwich then, drank a bottle of beer, stripped off his clothes, and fell into bed. But he couldn't sleep. Though his body longed for it, his mind would not give up, would not run off, would not allow him to go under. He lay on his back in bed, the wind shaking the window frames, the rain pelting against the glass, and tried to piece together some assessment of where he was and where exactly he was going.

For three nights running he lay there, heavy on the mattress, just a sheet over him, but feeling stifled and too warm in the cool bedroom, wrestling with the puzzle of Annie, needing to see her, but angry with her too, baffled by her behaviour, desperate to talk to her. Questions ricocheted back and forth in his mind, but no answer came forward. Except one. And that one he ignored, pushed away, tried to disregard completely.

As long as his eyes stayed open, as long as he had control over his thoughts, he pondered the mystery of Annie, considered all possibilities, weighed every chance and circumstance, examined every possible solution, kept her face just behind his eyes, reminding him, nudging him forward, keeping him awake.

But far into the morning, when his senses surrendered at last, when he slipped into a soft hollow, more unconscious than asleep, he dreamed of Christine. He woke up feeling used and guilty, trying to push the night away by splashing cold water in his face and swallowing cups of scalding coffee.

At last a letter came from Annie, from Australia, post-marked Melbourne.

You must forgive me if this letter seems abrupt. I'm not able to handle involved explanations right now.

I'm not coming back, Roy. I expect to stay here in Australia for some time, maybe permanently.

I'm going to sell the Granger House. I've told Albert Hacker to put it on the market at once. I expect the people who own the Naumaui will buy it. They've been after it for a long time. I also told Hacker that you are to be given half the purchase price, whatever that amounts to. If you get stubborn and hard-nosed and won't take the money, I told him to simply put it in the Nelson and Westport Bank in your name.

I've thought this over carefully. I won't change my mind. I couldn't even if I wanted to. I didn't realize until I saw Chrissy again that she's been living with us all the time. Not in your mind maybe, but in mine. When the three of us were sitting in our kitchen, I felt as if she lived there and I was the guest. I can see your face as you read this. You think I'm crazy. I know that. And maybe you're right. But crazy or not, the feeling is real. I don't think you've ever stopped loving her and I *know* she still loves you. If we hadn't seen her again, I could have lived with it. But we *did* see her, and ever since she walked up on our front porch I've felt like an outsider.

Don't screw it up, Roy. She wants to be with you, that's *all* she wants, and I think you want to be with her. So don't let anything stand in your way. Not her husband. Not me. Not anybody. Most of us don't get second chances. So don't wreck it.

Annie

An hour later, Roy was sitting in Albert Hacker's real estate office on Hardy Street. They had known each other since the first week Roy came to New Zealand.

'What's going on?' Hacker asked.

'I thought maybe you could tell me. All I know is what she said in her letter.'

'Then you know more than I do,' Hacker said. 'She called me from Melbourne and told me to put the place up for sale.'

'And since you're my friend, you told me.'

'It's business, Roy. She told me not to. She said she wanted to tell you.'

'Do you know how to get in touch with her in Melbourne?'

'She's not *in* Melbourne. She said she was leaving there the day we talked.'

'Going where?'

'She didn't know. Said she'd get in touch with me.'

Roy walked slowly back toward the hotel. The turmoil he had felt for the past days was gone. All the choices and alternatives that had bounced around in his head like glass marbles were settled quietly now.

Even in his loneliest moments in Rocky Mountain House or Grande Prairie, he had not asked himself how his life would have been changed if he had never met Christine on Martha's Vineyard, if he hadn't followed her back to Foresby. He knew that the final decisions and vetoes had always been his. He did not blame her. He did not feel sorry for himself.

Nor did he feel sorry for himself now as he sat in his

bedroom rereading Annie's letter, trying to find secrets between the lines.

Since it was clear that she was not simply leaving him but was leaving him to Christine, he could only conclude that they had reached some decision between themselves, had drawn straws perhaps. Or rolled dice. Or cut cards.

Still he did not feel sinned against. But he was quietly determined to make some decisions of his own now, to take some action, to tie down some of the balloons that floated back and forth, just out of reach, above his head.

Chapter 12

*W*hen Christine answered the knock at her door and saw Roy standing there in the hotel corridor, she said, 'I can't believe it.'

'Didn't you expect me?'

'I didn't know what to expect.'

'I hope I didn't wake you up.'

She was wearing her robe and nightgown. 'I was out late last night. I went to a silly play. Then I couldn't sleep when I got back here. So I just woke up half an hour ago.'

He was still standing in the hallway. 'You want me to wait for you downstairs?'

'No, please . . . I'm sorry. I forgot my manners. You surprised me. And I'm still half asleep. Come in. Did you have breakfast yet?'

'Just some coffee at the airport.'

'Good. I'll take a fast shower and make myself presentable and we'll have some breakfast.'

After she ordered the food on her bedroom telephone, she got into the shower. When she came back into the sitting room ten minutes later, her hair was pulled back in a loose knot and she wore a floor-length silk dressing gown buttoned up high at the neck.

'You look like a geisha girl,' Roy said.

'Is that a compliment?'

'I don't know. I've never met a geisha girl.'

The food arrived then, and was set out on a table by the window. Eggs and ham and waffles and coffee. And a bottle of champagne in an ice bucket. She poured some of the wine into their glasses before she sat down. '*You* may not be celebrating,' she said, 'but *I* am. It seems like a lifetime since the last morning we had breakfast together. Am I allowed to make a toast to the old days?'

'Sure. Why not?'

After she set her glass down she said, 'I'm glad you're here.'

He smiled. 'You don't even know why I came.'

'Sure I do. I know you. You're mad as hell at me about something. When you're all calm and laid back with that nine-year-old's grin on your face, I know I'm in for trouble. But you know something . . . I don't give a damn. I don't care *why* you're here. I've been waiting for a long time to sit down in a room alone with you. And now we're doing it. So I'll take my punishment.'

'I'm not a policeman. I'm not mad at you.'

'Yes, you are. And I don't blame you. You know I had lunch with Annie a few days ago and now she's gone. You didn't fool me with that story about losing the name of her hotel in Wellington. Do you know where she is?'

'Someplace in Australia, I guess. I don't know where.'

'You haven't heard from her?'

Roy nodded. 'I had a letter. Mailed from Melbourne. She said she was selling the Granger House and she wasn't coming back to New Zealand.'

'Was that all?'

'No. She thinks you and I should get back together.'

'You mean that's why she left? So there'd be nobody standing in our way?'

'You've talked to her since I have,' Roy said. 'I thought you might know.'

'You *are* mad at me. You're mad as hell.'

'No, I'm not. I don't guarantee I won't *get* mad, but I'm not mad now. Now I'm just curious.'

'You're going too fast for me.'

'I'm in no rush. Take your time.'

Christine sipped champagne and picked at her food. When she put down her fork, she said, 'After Fred and I were married, I wrote you a letter from Europe trying to tell you how sorry I was for the way I'd handled things, for the way I'd messed things up for you and me.'

'I didn't get it.'

'I didn't mail it,' she said. 'I tore it up. But a few weeks later I wrote you another letter, a longer one. I told you I realized I'd made a terrible mistake. I said I wanted us to get together and stay together, on whatever terms you wanted. I said I would go *anywhere*, meet you anywhere you said. I said I would do anything to try to make up for the damage I'd done.'

'Did you tear that letter up too?'

'No. I mailed it to the St Albert, but they returned it. Said they had no forwarding address for you.

'That's right. They didn't.'

'I tried every way I knew to locate you. Talked to your uncle in Maine, tried to call your father in California . . .'

'He doesn't have a phone.'

'I found that out. It drove me crazy for months, for years, wondering where you were. Finally I decided I'd never see you again. I'd never know anything about you. Never find out what kind of life you'd made for yourself. Then, after a long time, I heard from Russell and he told me you were here in New Zealand. Starting then I did a big snow job on myself. I decided that if you and Annie were happy together, the best thing I could do was stay away from you. But on the other hand, I told myself, there was no reason why I shouldn't see New Zealand. If it was as terrific as Russell said, why not? I

365

wouldn't have to see you and Annie, wouldn't have to visit Nelson at all.

'Even when I sent you the postcard from Auckland the morning I arrived, I was still lying to myself. But a few days later I was in Nelson. And as soon as I screwed up my courage, I called you. I was afraid to talk to you, scared to death of seeing you, but I kept pushing myself all the same. Couldn't you tell how petrified I was when we all had lunch that day?'

Roy shook his head. 'You seemed fine to me.'

'Well, I wasn't. I was . . . I hope this doesn't embarrass you; I've been waiting so long to talk to you, I can't do anything but blurt out everything that's in my mind . . . I just . . . I don't know what I expected. I guess maybe I'd swallowed all that stuff you read and the things people tell each other, about how disillusioning it is to see somebody you were once crazy about, how you always say to yourself, 'My God . . . what did I see in *him*?' But let me tell you, those people are crazy. When you walked out on that porch and I saw you, looking the same, smiling at me, *acting* the same, I did a whole flip-flop. The whole wrenching, physical jolt, *that* part of it, I'd forgotten about. And it really knocked me over that afternoon. I went back to my hotel, went upstairs, and lay on the bed staring at the ceiling. I knew I had to get out of there or I would do something really stupid. So I checked out, rented a car, and took off. I wasn't sure where I was going, but I knew I had to leave Nelson and I knew I wasn't coming back. But three days later I was back in the Rutherford, on the phone, making a date with Annie.'

'Why'd you come back?'

'Why do you *think* I came back?' she asked. 'Because I couldn't stay away. I couldn't just say, "Fiddle-dee-dee," get on the next plane, and fly back to Los Angeles. If there was any chance for you and me to be together again, I had to try. If there was *no* chance, I needed to know that.'

'Is that what you told Annie?'

'I can't remember what I told her exactly. I was crying so much I'm not sure I made any sense. But I tried to tell her the *truth*. As simply as I could. I told her what I'm telling you now, how much you mean to me, how much I've regretted these years we've been apart. God knows what all I said. But I remember very clearly saying that all she had to do was to tell me to leave, to leave her alone and leave *you* alone, and I'd do it. And I meant it.'

'What did she say?'

'She didn't say much of anything. I talked my brains out and Annie just sat there and listened. But I remember, just before she left me to go home, I said, "If you tell me to get lost, Annie, I'll do it," and she said, "I can't tell you that Chrissy. I'm *not* telling you that."'

'So she left instead.'

'I didn't know that. I had no idea what she was planning to do. All I knew was that I felt lousy and selfish and guilty. I checked out of the hotel that afternoon and flew up here to Auckland.'

'Leaving clear instructions where you could be found.'

Christine smiled. 'I told myself I was leaving that information for Fred in case he tried to call me. But I wasn't fooled. I felt guilty but still I hadn't given up. I didn't think you'd be trying to reach me, but in case you did, I wanted to be sure you'd know where I was.'

They stayed a long time at the table, finished the coffee and the wine and a second pot of coffee. When the waiter came at last to remove the breakfast things, to wheel the table out into the corridor, they sat by the window in two deep chairs facing each other, a low table between them. Roy listen as she tried to explain the special relationship she had with Grace. And how the two miscarriages had disturbed her. How she had come to blame their being in Canada for all the unfortunate things that were happening.

'I don't know how you put up with me,' she said. 'When I look back at that time and try to reconstruct those crazy days in my mind, when I think about my reactions, I see someone I don't recognise. At every critical corner I made the wrong turn. I really earned whatever unhappiness I got. The fact is I earned a lot *more* than I got.'

As she talked, as he sat there looking at her, young and lovely in the changing light through the curtains, physically untouched by all the emotional chaos she was remembering and describing, he sensed a tender and vulnerable centre inside her, one that had been there always, certainly, but which had moved, through the past years, closer to the surface. As he listened, the anger that had pushed him to come to Auckland slowly subsided.

The vindictive speech he had begun to compose years before in Banff, had added to in Malin, and had finished and revised in the days since he'd received Annie's letter from Melbourne repeated itself softly in his head as a kind of baritone counterpoint to Christine's voice. 'I guess there are lots of people who think the way you do, but you're the only one I've ever met.' That was how his speech began. Then, 'Is it the money? Is that what gives certain people the idea that *wanting* something is enough, that everything else can be explained away if you just prove to yourself that you really *want* something? Don't misunderstand me. I'm not crying about the way I was treated. People break up all the time. But now I wonder, who *was* that girl? She decided to give up the man she was engaged to because she liked me better. Then she gave me up to marry him. Because she liked *him* better? Maybe. But now she's willing to give him up again. To take *me* back? It looks that way.'

He heard the words in his head but he didn't say them. Now he knew he didn't have to. He had turned a critical corner. He was able to sit, low in his chair, watching her and listening to her, able to see her at last with clarity and compassion, able to remember exactly how things had been at the beginning, able to enjoy that memory.

He did, however, ask her about Fred Deets. Late that afternoon, the weather grey and unseasonably warm, as they sat in a rose cloister on the grounds of Auckland University, he said, 'What happens to him now? Does he know everything you've been telling me?'

'He doesn't *know*. But he knows you're in New Zealand and he suspects you're the reason I came down here. He knows how I am. He knows how I feel and what I think. Also, he's a tough guy. Nothing's ever going to sink Fred.'

That was as close as they came, she and Roy, to discussing what would come next. After that first long session at the breakfast table she seemed to want to stay on the high ground, to talk about pleasant things from the past, to enjoy the moments, as they walked through the streets of Auckland, visited a picture gallery, stopped for drinks at the Royal International, and strolled through Albert Park on the way back to her hotel.

They had dinner that night at Pelorus Jack on Rutland Street. Lemon fish and a lovely dry white wine from Australia. Two pieces of a rich black chocolate cake for dessert, and espresso with the Rémy Martin.

Back at her hotel, they made love on her splendid bed with the late lights of Auckland shining through the window, fog drifting in from the harbour and warning horns moaning through the night. They slept as they had always slept together, her head on his shoulder, her arm across his chest. But in the very early morning, she had a bad dream. She whimpered and groaned and turned away from him and slept the rest of the night at the far edge of the bed with her face towards the wall.

He stayed with her for three days and three nights. They hired a car and drove up to Whangarei and back, down to Hamilton and across to Tauranga. They ate and drank, laughed and danced, and stayed fully inside the moment.

'This is like a honeymoon,' she said.

'Good. We owed each other a honeymoon.'

On the fourth morning, when she woke up, he wasn't in the bed. She put on her robe and went into the sitting room. He was standing at the window looking out. When she walked over to him he smiled and put his arm around her shoulders.

'You're going back, aren't you?' she asked.

'I have to.'

She said nothing for a moment. Then she turned her face against his shoulder and said, 'Jesus, Roy . . .'

He turned her to face him and lifted her chin. 'It wouldn't work, Chrissy. You know it wouldn't work.'

'No. I don't know anything like that. I remember everything you ever said to me.'

'So do I. But that guy's not around anymore. When I met you, I had all kinds of big ideas about myself. All phony. Since then I've found out I'm not a pusher. Some guys need only one jacket and two pairs of pants. That's the way I am. I have to struggle. That's all I know. I need to be around things that break down so I can fix them.'

'I'm broken down. Fix me.'

'You've never been broken down and you never will be. You come from a different place. All you have to do is pick up the phone and two hours later you're on your way to Tokyo. Or London. Or wherever. I think that's terrific, but it's not for me. I need a small life. One I can handle. I'm a plain guy, honey. I was plain when I met you. I'll be plain when I die.'

'*I* can be plain.'

'No, you can't. And I don't want you to try. I want you to be what you are.'

She looked up at him. 'Is this how it's going to end, just like this?'

'No. This is just where it stops. The good stuff doesn't end, does it? That's what you always told me.'

'I guess you're going back to Annie,' she said. 'Is that right?'

He nodded. 'If I can find her.'

She stepped away then, pushed her hair back with one hand, and smiled at him. 'I've got a better idea. Let's fly down to Mount Cook and stay in the lodge for a week. Then maybe we'll whip over to Sydney and go to the opera. Or play some roulette down in Tasmania. Loosen up, Lavidge. What do you say?'

When he didn't answer, she said, 'It doesn't matter what I say, does it?'

'It matters, but it doesn't change anything.'

She went with him in a taxi out to the airport. Just before he walked through the boarding gate to his plane, she said. 'I have a question. Promise me a straight answer?'

'I'll do my best.'

370

'Why did you come up here to find me? Why did you come to Auckland?'

He shook his head. 'That's a tough one. I can't answer that.'

'I wish you'd try. It means a lot to me.'

'I don't know, Chris. I guess there's no good way to say good-bye to somebody you care about, but I figured we could do better than we did last time. If you're lucky enough to have it good . . . I mean we had it too good to end it as bad as we did. I thought we deserved something better. Does that make sense?'

She nodded. 'It makes me sad, but it makes sense.'

After his plane took off, she sat at the bar in the airport lounge and ordered a champagne cocktail. When the bargirl hesitated a moment, staring at her, Christine said, 'I'm crying. That's all. Didn't you ever see anybody cry before?'

'Yes, but . . .'

'You'd better get used to it, because I expect to be doing it for quite a while.'

After her third cocktail she tried to telephone Russell in Christchurch. The desk man at the Clarendon said Mr Atha had gone to Rangiora and would not be back until dinnertime.

'That's fine. Leave a message that Christine is flying down to have dinner with him.'

She had another cocktail before her plane left and a split of champagne during the flight. When she arrived at the Clarendon, Russell had not come in yet. So she ordered a bottle of Perrier-Jouët and waited for him in the private bar just across from the hotel desk. Her face was composed and very lovely now, and the tears had stopped.

It was nearly seven o'clock when Russell came back to the Clarendon, checked at the desk, and was directed to where Christine was waiting. When he walked over to her, she stood up, knocked over a glass, and put her arms around him.

'What a nice surprise,' he said. 'But aren't we a little wobbly?'

'Very wobbly. Walking on eggs. You'll have to hurry and catch up.'

371

As they went up in the elevator to his rooms, he said, 'Did you book a room?'

'Couldn't,' she said. 'Travelling light. No luggage.'

'It's all right. I'll call down and get you squared away.'

'That's what I've always wanted. To be squared away. When I was little I thought that meant they buried you in a square coffin. In a square grave.'

When they were inside his sitting room, as he turned away from the door, he saw that she was crying. Standing very straight, her arms straight at her sides, her cheeks shiny with tears. Russell walked over to her and put his hands on her shoulders. 'What's the matter? What *is* it?'

When she didn't answer, he put his arms around her. 'Take it easy. It's all right. Tell me what's wrong.'

Her face was flushed from crying and her body felt warm and soft through the silk of her dress. She buried her face in his neck and held on to him as though she was falling. 'Oh, God, Russell . . . I feel so rotten and helpless. I feel as if I'm not worth anything to anybody.'

Chapter 13

*A*s soon as his plane landed in Nelson, Roy took a taxi to Albert Hacker's office.

'Have you heard anything from Annie?'

'Not yet,' Hacker said, 'but I expect to. We've got an offer on the hotel and I'm going to advise her to accept it.'

Roy shook his head. 'We're not going to sell the place, Albert. It's off the market.'

'Have you talked to Annie?'

'No. This isn't her idea. It's mine.'

'That makes things complicated for me, Roy. Because the only name on the title is Annie Singleton. And my instructions from her were to sell.'

'Suit yourself, Albert. But you know you've got instructions to give me half of the money when the deal goes through. Isn't that right?'

'That's right.'

'And *I've* got a letter to that effect from Annie. I showed the letter to Casper Sutherland in the office of deeds and titles, and he said there's an implication of co-ownership there no matter what the title says. Certainly enough for me to bring a legal action, get a restraining order against a sale. And that's what I expect to do. If I have to I'll tie you up in court till hell freezes over.'

'I don't know why you're after me on this,' Hacker said. 'The simplest thing would be for you and Annie to settle it between yourselves.'

'That's right. Except I don't know where to find her. And I don't expect her to contact me.'

'Then what can I do?'

'When she calls you, tell her what I've said. Tell her the Granger House is all redecorated now and ready for business. That I'll be taking in guests starting this weekend.'

Five days later, Annie came back. She arrived in the late afternoon. The plane from Sydney had landed in Christchurch and she'd taken a connecting flight from there. Roy came out to meet her when he saw the taxi pull up at the kerb.

'I got my hair cut,' she said.

'Yeah, I see you did.'

'You hate it, don't you?'

'No. It looks nice.'

'Men always hate short hair. I felt lousy and blue one day in Adelaide, so I had a manicure and a pedicure and got my hair cut.'

He carried her bag inside and put it in their bedroom. She followed him, took off her coat, dropped it on a chair. Then she sat down on the edge of the bed. He stood looking down at her, his back against the door of the armoire. Finally he said, 'You're really a fool, do you know that? What did you think you were doing?'

'I told you. That's why I wrote you that letter.'

'That letter didn't tell me anything. Except that you'd decided to sell the hotel.'

'I just wanted to get out of the way. I knew that as long as I was sitting here . . .'

'As long as you were sitting here I wouldn't have the guts to leave.'

'It's not that. I thought you wouldn't want to hurt my feelings.'

'Well, you wasted a trip,' he said. 'You went all the way to Australia and all the way back and I'm still here. Nothing's changed except you've got short hair now.'

'What about Christine?'

'What about her? I'm sure she's back in California by now, showing her husband all the snapshots she took in New Zealand.'

'Did you see her?'

'I had to. You practically gave me an order. You *wanted* me to see her, didn't you? Wasn't that the idea?'

Annie nodded her head and looked down at her hands. Roy walked over to her and tilted her face up. 'I went to Auckland to see her and I stayed three days. Now I'm back.'

He sat down on the edge of the bed and put his arms around her. 'You're stuck with me, Annie.'

*W*hen I finished this manuscript at last, when all the separate blocks and pieces had been wedged into position, sanded and varnished, Amy and I flew to Los Angeles, to Honolulu, and from there to New Zealand. We took a bus from Christchurch across the South Island to Greymouth. In an old churchyard at the edge of Victoria Park, looking west across Erua Moana towards the ocean, we found Russell's grave. As we stood there in the frosty afternoon, walled in by elaborate monuments for dead seamen and soldiers and coal miners, the final entry in Russell's notebook, the last words he wrote before he died, echoed softly in my mind.

We all know how much there is to forgive, how often we sin and are sinned against. We all know, too, that the cruellest sins of all are those that are committed in the name of love.

STAR BOOKS BESTSELLERS

FICTION

THE PROTOCOL	*Sarah Allan Borish*	£2.25* ☐
SEASON OF CHANGE	*Lois Battle*	£2.25* ☐
LET'S KEEP IN TOUCH	*Elaine Bissel*	£2.50* ☐
DANCEHALL	*Bernard F. Conners*	£1.95* ☐
DREAMS OF GLORY	*Thomas Fleming*	£2.50* ☐
DEAR STRANGER	*Catherine Kidwell*	£1.95* ☐
PHANTOMS	*Dean R. Koontz*	£2.25* ☐
THE PAINTED LADY	*Françoise Sagan*	£2.25* ☐
LAMIA	*Tristan Travis*	£2.75* ☐

FILM TIE-INS

EDUCATING RITA	*Peter Chepstow*	£1.60 ☐
TERMS OF ENDEARMENT	*Larry McMurtry*	£1.95* ☐
PARTY PARTY	*Jane Coleman*	£1.35 ☐
THE WICKED LADY	*Magdalen King-Hall*	£1.60 ☐
SCRUBBERS	*Alexis Lykiard*	£1.60 ☐
BULL SHOT	*Martin Noble*	£1.80 ☐
BLOODBATH AT THE HOUSE OF DEATH	*Martin Noble*	£1.80 ☐

STAR Books are obtainable from many booksellers and newsagents. If you have any difficulty tick the titles you want and fill in the form below.

Name _____

Address _____

Send to: Star Books Cash Sales, P.O. Box 11, Falmouth, Cornwall. TR10 9EN.

Please send a cheque or postal order to the value of the cover price plus:

UK: 45p for the first book, 20p for the second book and 14p for each additional book ordered to the maximum charge of £1.63.

BFPO and EIRE: 45p for the first book, 20p for the second book, 14p per copy for the next 7 books, thereafter 8p per book.

OVERSEAS: 75p for the first book and 21p per copy for each additional book.

While every effort is made to keep prices low, it is sometimes necessary to increase prices at short notice. Star Books reserve the right to show new retail prices on covers which may differ from those advertised in the text or elsewhere.

*NOT FOR SALE IN CANADA

STAR BOOKS BESTSELLERS

NON-FICTION

BODYGUARD OF LIES	*Antony Cave Brown*	£2.50* ☐
OIL SHEIKHS	*Linda Blandford*	£1.95 ☐
WHY MEN RAPE	*S. Levine & J. Koenig*	£1.95* ☐
THE COMPLETE JACK THE RIPPER	*Donald Rumberlow*	£1.60 ☐
CRIME SCIENTIST	*John Thompson*	£1.60 ☐
THE ELEPHANT MAN	*Sir Frederick Treves*	95p ☐

BIOGRAPHIES

RICHARD BURTON	*Fergus Cashin*	£1.95 ☐
CLINT EASTWOOD: MOVIN' ON	*Peter Douglas*	£1.00* ☐
CHARLES BRONSON	*David Downing*	£1.95 ☐
IT'S A FUNNY GAME	*Brian Johnston*	£1.95 ☐
IT'S BEEN A LOT OF FUN	*Brian Johnston*	£1.80 ☐
ORDEAL	*Linda Lovelace with Mike McGrady*	£1.50* ☐
BETTE DAVIS: MOTHER GODDAM	*Whitney Stine with Bette Davis*	£2.25* ☐

STAR Books are obtainable from many booksellers and newsagents. If you have any difficulty tick the titles you want and fill in the form below.

Name _____

Address _____

_____

Send to: Star Books Cash Sales, P.O. Box 11, Falmouth, Cornwall. TR10 9EN.

Please send a cheque or postal order to the value of the cover price plus: UK: 45p for the first book, 20p for the second book and 14p for each additional book ordered to the maximum charge of £1.63.

BFPO and EIRE: 45p for the first book, 20p for the second book, 14p per copy for the next 7 books, thereafter 8p per book.

OVERSEAS: 75p for the first book and 21p per copy for each additional book.

While every effort is made to keep prices low, it is sometimes necessary to increase prices at short notice. Star Books reserve the right to show new retail prices on covers which may differ from those advertised in the text or elsewhere.

*NOT FOR SALE IN CANADA